James Burnley

West Riding Sketches

Anatiposi

James Burnley

West Riding Sketches

Reprint of the original, first published in 1875.

1st Edition 2024　|　ISBN: 978-3-38282-869-1

Anatiposi Verlag is an imprint of Outlook Verlagsgesellschaft mbH.

Verlag (Publisher): Outlook Verlag GmbH, Zeilweg 44, 60439 Frankfurt, Deutschland
Vertretungsberechtigt (Authorized to represent): E. Roepke, Zeilweg 44, 60439 Frankfurt, Deutschland
Druck (Print): Books on Demand GmbH, In de Tarpen 42, 22848 Norderstedt, Deutschland

WEST RIDING SKETCHES.

WEST RIDING SKETCHES

BY

JAMES BURNLEY.

(SAUNTERER.)

LONDON:

HODDER AND STOUGHTON,

27, PATERNOSTER ROW.

BRADFORD: T. BREAR.

MDCCCLXXV.

THE favourable reception accorded to the author's previous collection of sketches—*Phases of Bradford Life*—has tempted him somewhat further a-field; and he now ventures forth with a volume less strictly local in its aim, hoping that his endeavour to depict sundry lights and shadows of the busy, earnest life of the West Riding will not be unacceptable.

The first seven sketches are re-published from *All the Year Round*, and the author here records his thanks to Mr. Dickens for being permitted to re-issue them in this form.

CONTENTS.

INTRODUCTORY.

T is, no doubt, a proud thing to be able to say, "I am an Englishman," but still prouder is the boast if the Englishman can add, "and a Yorkshireman." Of course, no sooner have I said this than appellants on behalf of all the remaining counties rise up and indignantly protest, but, for all that, being a Yorkshireman myself, I venture (with all due respect to the Lancashire witches, the Lincolnshire fens, the Cumberland lakes, the Derbyshire peak, Bow Bells, Gog and Magog, and all and whatsoever else there may be in other parts of this "merrie England" of ours to give pleasure and delight) to designate the patriotic Yorkshireman, with his stalwart form and beaming face, as the most birth-proud member of the human race. Whether the Yorkshireman is justified in this high self-appraisement or not is another thing. Certainly he has for a long time been credited with the possession of a greater amount of shrewdness and cunning than his fellow-

B

countrymen, but this has been due, I imagine, more to the falsifications of the drama and of fiction than to anything else; for, much as I have seen of Yorkshire wariness and Yorkshire caution, I have not found the denizens of Middlesex or of Lancashire at all behindhand in these matters.

The stage Yorkshireman, with his grins and guffaws, his outlandish dialect and variegated garments, has no counterpart in real life, and, many as have been the actors, from the elder Mathews downwards, who have won a reputation for portraying Yorkshire characters, they have none of them succeeded in giving anything like a truthful impersonation. The dialect most commonly adopted by these character delineators is that of Zummerzet, very much tortured, to which is added a dash of the Irish brogue; but of the real, weighty, Chaucerian English, of the hearty, nervous pronunciation, which form the distinctive features of the language of the Yorkshire rustic, I have found but little trace in the speech of the numerous theatrical representatives of Yorkshiremen whom I have hitherto seen.

It is probable, I think, that the Yorkshireman's pride in his native place indirectly proceeds, in a great measure, from the fact that the county to which he belongs is the largest shire in the three kingdoms. So extensive a province is able to enclose within its inner limits a people who are so far removed from the outer world as to enable them to cherish their ancient characteristics, and preserve them from being thoroughly effaced by the rush and roar, the polish and affectation of modern progress. In the North and East Ridings specially is this the case, for commerce has been chary of carrying her screaming railway whistles, her manufacturers, her speculators, and her armies of workmen amongst the wolds, the hills, and the moors which constitute so great a portion of these ridings, and consequently they still retain much of their primitive beauty and peacefulness. The tall, broad-shouldered, Saxon-faced farmer; the happy-eyed-housewife; the ruddy-cheeked farm lass; and the honest, simple-minded serving-man (all as fresh and as real as if they had stepped out of the pages of Henry Fielding), live their lives out in these remote Yorkshire regions much as they did in the middle of the last century. Their surroundings have been but little altered, their characters, therefore, have not suffered any great change either.

In the West Riding, however, the old and the new clash together so indiscriminately, the prose and the poetry intermingle so curiously, that it requires one to be "native and to the manner born" to distinguish the lines of demarcation. Taking the town populations of the West Riding as a

whole, we meet with a strange mixture of ancient
simplicity and modern veneer, original characteristics and distinct innovations, both in manner and
speech; but in the midst of these hybrid components
there stand out in bold relief a number of primitive-
minded souls who are as unalterable in their natures
as the un-Darwinised tiger of the Indian jungle.
They were Yorkshire to begin with, and Yorkshire
they will remain to the close. Wave after wave of
change may pass over them; but they will stand
firm and immovable in their adherence to the
traditions and customs of their forefathers. The
vernacularisms of their parents are retained in
their daily conversation, and words common enough
in the Canterbury Tales and the Fairy Queen, but
totally obsolete in the English literature of to-day,
are "familiar in their mouths as household words,"
varied here and there only in the breadth of the
vowel sounds. Le Follet may come forth month
after month, changing the fashion of a lady's outward adornments, if it likes, but Mrs. Dorothy May-
dew will keep faithful to her print gown for week-
days, her stuff gown for Sundays, and her white
frilled cap for all days, through every mutation.
The tailors may, if it please them so to do, exhibit
their wonderful pictures of uncomfortably dressed
gentry staring idiotically into vacancy, as induce-
ments to their customers to adopt another cut of

costume, but old Mr. Cosyface will still insist upon wearing his knee-breeches and his ancient Prince-Regent swallow-tail. He will not, you may be sure, think of coming within half a century of the present style. His children may approach the latest style within a quarter of a century, perhaps, if they strongly desire to do so, but he will never consent to their donning the new-fangled whimsicalities of attire which fashion so rigorously prescribes to her truest votaries.

But this West Riding life is invigorating, though so varied, and the dash and spirit of the new order receive such substantial support—ballast, so to speak—from the steady, plodding spirit of the old, that there is little wonder that prosperity so largely prevails. The whole of the civilised world is represented in miniature in the West Riding. As an industrial centre, it is almost unparalleled in the variety and extent of its operations. Leeds is the head-quarters of the woollen trade, and Bradford the head-quarters of the worsted trade, and the large villages which cluster round both boroughs are all busily employed in one trade or the other. Then, there is the immense coal district; there are the two famous ironworks of Low Moor and Bowling; and there are the towns of Halifax, Huddersfield, and Dewsbury, famed respectively for carpets, tweeds, and shoddy. In the West Riding there are

towns with forests of factory chimneys vomiting
forth smoke, and thousands of looms and spindles,
revolving, panting, and humming; there are towns
swarming with colliers and foundrymen, black and
grimy; there are towns nestling in quiet valleys,
looking as quaint and picturesque as if the wonders
of steam were unknown there; and there are miles
and miles of splendid scenery, where mountain,
glen, wood, and river charmingly alternate. These,
and much more, are amongst the present characteristics of West Riding life. The towns are thronged
with bustling traders from all parts of the world,
and not a few of the regular residents are people
who have migrated thither from continental countries. Here and there are quiet nooks where
fertility and beauty of landscape combine with the
antiquated habits of the people to produce a picture
which it is both pleasant and instructive to contrast
with pictures of more populous places. From the
lonely life of the shepherd amongst the remote
Craven hills to the monotonous, confining toil of
the factory worker is a great step, but both
extremes, with all their intermediate gradations and
fillings-in, are to be found in the West Riding.

It is fitting, I think, on this brief showing, that
an attempt should be made to paint some of the
different phases of existence, some of the various
scenes, which this important district presents to

our study. I, therefore, propose to officiate as limner of a few scenes of Yorkshire life,—scenes which may perhaps serve as a contrast to the numerous pictures of London life which have been so plentifully (and, indeed, so welcomely) scattered over our literature during the last two or three decades.

BINGTON.

THE town of Bington lies "deep in the shady sadness of a vale," but in what precise wapentake, division, or liberty need not be further particularised. Suffice it to say that Bington comprises within its parish boundaries all the chief characteristics of West Riding life, ancient and modern. Some portions of the town, and some portions of its people, retain the quaint picturesqueness of the drowsy, jog-trot past; while other portions (of town and people) are fully abreast of the age and participate to the utmost in its advantages and its follies, its intense earnestness and its insane frivolities. In describing Bington, therefore, I am enabled to group together in antithetical array most of the different features of existence which the West Riding can present.

Bington was a thriving town hundreds of years ago, when many of the mushroom cities, which have sprung up and expanded into greatness within the last half-century, were but obscure hamlets.

Its situation is one of peculiar beauty. The main
street is the high road on which the High-flyer and
Rockingham coaches were accustomed to travel in
the days when Mr. Squeers used to escort his
newly-caught pupils to the attractions of Dothe-
boys Hall. This street is a narrow, undulating
thoroughfare, and is bordered on each side by a
most incongruous assembly of buildings. Entering
the town from the Woolborough side — Woolborough is a large, smoke-hued, densely-populated
town a few miles away to the east—we first come
upon a row or two of rude, stone cottages, tenanted
chiefly by families of factory workers; then we
drop down to a bit of level road, on one side of
which there stands a batch of large, plate-glass
windowed shops of the latest pattern, while on the
other side of the road the houses stand with their
gables all awry, looking discontented and miserable
beside the great staring shop-fronts of the upstart
buildings opposite. Two or three ancient hostelries
certainly attempt to shine down the shops by dress-
ing up their crumbling walls with plenty of clean
paint and plaster, and exhibiting at their doors and
windows their typical landlords and landladies,
rotund, jovial, and rubicund; but some of the old
houses, erst inhabited by the gentry of the district,
lie about in a most straggling fashion, with fronts
looking into backs, and backs into fronts, and with

outbuildings, corners and jagged arms of wall jerking out in the most zig-zag and provoking manner. Further down is an old mansion converted into a bank; opposite that is the new Mechanics' Institute; and further down still is the railway station, approached by a lane, at the top of which stands, with an inviting stone front and four rows of scrupulously clean windows, the principal hotel in the town. The proprietor of this great addition to the hotel accommodation of Bington is none of your antique, long-pipe-sucking, bluff landlords, such as are found higher up the town; he is a keen man of business, who knows the value of pretty barmaids, and gives the cold shoulder to the lolling, lounging topers who get drunk cheaply and sleep and get drunk again without ever leaving the premises. He believes in serving his liquors over the counter, where imbibition is rapid and change of visitors frequent, and, despite the new Licensing Act and the sneers of his slow-going rivals, he will probably make his fortune in a very few years. A short distance beyond this new hotel we find the old parish church, with its ivy-mantled tower, its hoary walls, and its crowded graveyard, where the monuments and mounds rise up in thick confusion, like the half-remembered memories which they were erected to keep green. In this church repose the remains of mediæval knights and squires, whose ancestral

mansions are still retained by their latest succes-
sors. A vicar, of very quiet-going religious views,
who lives out by the river in a handsome house
generously presented to him by his flock when the
old vicarage fell to decay, directs the spiritual con-
cerns of the parish in a most comfortable and good-
natured way. True, there has appeared a ritualistic
firebrand at the new church of St. Betty's, who
froths and fumes and endeavours to frighten the
people into penitential exercises, but the old vicar's
serenity is undisturbed; he still (either by virtue of
his comfortable doctrines, or by the mere attraction
of the ancient church itself) contrives to keep
nearly all the best families of the neighbourhood
within his fold. Then, there are numerous conven-
ticles at which the Dissenters worship—devoutly
and honestly enough in the main, I have no doubt,
but without gathering to themselves that amount
of display of costume and magnificence which
throngs to the parish church. These dissenting
chapels are mostly hidden away in back streets or
thrust into spaces of waste ground, but when the
fine summer weather makes its appearance their
congregations turn out into the streets, with their
hymn-books, their ministers, and their deacons, and
chant a rousing strain, and pray with all the vehe-
mence of their lungs on behalf of the ungodly
multitude which lingers in idleness in the highways

and byways, gossiping at gable ends, or leaning over walls, staring with bovine tenderness at the cows in the pastures.

After the main street has got to the old church, it gives a somewhat rude turn, as if determined to avoid making the entire circuit of the churchyard, and shoots off in a straight line through clusters of suburban villas and past nice rows of houses erected for the special preservation of the town's gentility, when that gentility could no longer breathe freely, or comport itself with its accustomed dignity, as it became hemmed in by encroaching regiments of factory workers, smelling of oil, bedaubed with oil, and wearing a black and seared aspect.

Having traversed the principal—indeed, the only —street of the town from end to end, the sketcher lets his eye follow the configuration of the surrounding country. Four parallel lines intersect the valley. One of these is the main street, which we have already travelled over; a second is the river, which is spanned by a triple-arched bridge, at one end whereof rises a flour-dredged corn-mill; the third is the railway; and the fourth is the great Leviathan canal. The canal and the river belong essentially to the past; the main street has an eye to past, present, and future; but the railway seems to point to the future alone. From the side of the valley *which is bordered* by the river, there rises a

succession of fertile woods, "like cloud on cloud,"
and, in a green expanse beyond, there stands the
ancestral mansion of the squire of the parish. On
the opposite hillside, that slopes up to a purple
ridge of moorland which boldly defines the western
horizon for a great number of miles, the green of
the pastures and meadows is dotted with palatial
residences of merchant princes and manufacturers.
Thus, the representatives of the old and the new
confront each other, and try to stare each other out
of countenance; the one backed up by a sense of
prestige which is the outcome of high birth, the
other emboldened by a feeling of superiority
engendered by the knowledge that wealth can even
outbuy the advantages of birth and station. There
is no love lost between the two orders of men. The
squire manages to enlist under his banner all the
remnants of ancient gentility which have survived
in the neighbourhood, while the money-made
seigniors command the sympathies of the migratory
hordes who have found 'their way to the town to
assist the steam-god in his great work of filling the
world with new garments. Now and again, the
squire and the merchant meet on the magisterial
bench, when a poacher has to be tried; but their
sympathies are at variance even there, often, it
must be admitted, to the decided advantage of the
poacher.

Circling round the main street, in the spaces
between the parallel lines before-mentioned, are to
be found those huge, oblong, gaunt factories which
have wrought such a transformation in Bington
during the last half century; and jammed in on
every available ledge and corner of land that could
be found in their immediate vicinity, are the
dwelling-houses of the poor, standing in alarming
disorder, rising tier upon tier, overlooking each
other's roofs, and defying sanitary and architectural
laws with a freedom and an audacity which local
boards and medical officers have evidently been
powerless to control.

Turning from the physical nature of things
Bingtonian to the characteristics of the people, we
find that they consist of about as many different
types as are to be met with in any other community
of Englishmen, only that some of the types are
more pronounced and distinct than elsewhere. The
great distinctive feature of Yorkshire character—
thorough heartiness and good fellowship—is present
in a marked degree in Bington. The original
Bingtonian is a guileless, unsuspecting creature,
who works hard, sleeps well, and does not require
exciting amusements. His dialect is broad—full of
oh's and ah's—his figure is broad, his wit is broad,
and his patience is broad. He is a very Rip van
Winkle in his easy-going nature; but outwardly,

perhaps, he is the most perfect representative of Punch's John Bull that is now extant. Go where you will in Bington—into the factories, the public‐ houses, the shops, the cottages, or the mansions— you will see some of these fine-limbed, broad‐ featured men, recognisable everywhere as the most substantial examples of the Saxon type of humanity. In too many instances, however, you note that these distinguishing features are gra‐ dually fading into feebleness before the pressure of unhealthy toil, and you see forms at the loom and at the spinning-frame which tell you that they started in life with a good prospect of reaching the full Saxon standard, had not the exigencies of their position brought them under enervating influences. The Bingtonians who get their living away from the factory are a stalwart and a sturdy race; but the foreigners from the agricultural districts and from Hibernian shores possess less magnitude of proportion, although it is only fair to add that the wiriness of the foreigner's nature makes him physically able to endure almost as much as the more bulky Yorkshireman, and so long as he can avoid being struck or sat upon by the native, his chances of existence are not much smaller than those of his rival.

The language to be heard in Bington, and, to a much greater extent, in the more populous towns of the Riding, would puzzle a Max Müller or a George Borrow. The factories and workshops have proved veritable Babels. They have produced the Cockney-Yorkshireman, the Irish Yorkshireman, the Welsh Yorkshireman, the Scotch Yorkshireman, and the South and West county Yorkshireman. Unless a factory immigrant is old, and has become confirmed in his own local speech, he is sure to imbibe something of the accent and peculiarity of language of the great body of his fellow-workers; but, on the other hand, the native catches up a little of the foreigner's lingo, and thus, amongst them, is produced such a medley of sounds and expressions as sets the stranger's teeth on edge. The most wonderful product of this association of peoples and races, however, is the Continental-Yorkshireman ; the Frenchman, Swiss, or German, who so far forsakes his nationality as to confuse his foreign accent by interlarding his speech with the most outlandish of Yorkshireisms. This is doubt-less done at first as a mere whim, but by-and-bye the whim grows into a habit, and the result is a lingual absurdity which is much more curious than it is entertaining.

Tennyson's Northern Farmer so nearly approaches in speech the ordinary Yorkshire dialect, that no Yorkshireman can fail to understand it; and Mrs. Gaskell, in her Sylvia's Lovers, has given something of the dialect of North Yorkshire; but exceedingly little has been done to reproduce with anything like truthfulness the language of the native of West Yorkshire. Of late years, however, there have been issued from the local press a large number of almanacs and comic pamphlets written wholly in the dialect, but the real dialect-speaking West Yorkshireman has yet to be introduced into English literature. Dialect almanacs, witty and racy though they often are, are not adapted for the uninitiated reader; they can only be appreciated by the people who belong to the soil where they have been produced, and, therefore, can never be accepted into the literature of the country. Of course, there are many obstacles in the way of the novelist who desires to introduce a Yorkshire character into a work of fiction, for to be faithful in the one matter of speech would probably prove fatal to the acceptability of the novel by the non-Yorkshire public. What is to be condemned is the repeated introduction of Yorkshire characters in fiction and upon the stage, and the palming them off as the genuine article. Let writers and actors acknowledge that they are unable or unwilling to reproduce the true Yorkshireman, and no fault can be found, but do not let them in their representations say, "Here is the picture of the real, living man," when Yorkshiremen themselves are unable to recognise him.

c

Charlotte Brontë was successful in local portraiture
to a certain extent, but she was evidently afraid,
courageous as she was, of thoroughly filling-in her
outlines.

After turning back and reading over the last few
sentences, I begin to think that, to use a homely
phrase, I have "put my foot into it." For have
I not undertaken the task of depicting the real Si-
mon Pure?   Have not I written at the head of these
pages the title "West Riding Sketches?"   "True,
true," myself answers myself.   "But then," interposes a third self, "you have already said that a
faithful reproduction would not be understood by
the general public, so you had better give us as
much description and as little dialogue as possible."
Acknowledging the justice of this conclusion, I
leave the question of dialect, and proceed to tell
my readers something of the way in which the
Bingtonians amuse themselves, for people are never
more natural than when giving themselves up to
enjoyment.

THE BLETHERHEADS.

T is the middle of Summer; a period when darkness is almost unknown to those who go to bed betimes, as the Bingtonians do. Indeed, the bridge of darkness is so short that the twilight and the dawn are almost able to shake hands across it. During this delightful season the Bingtonians, when the day's work is over, lounge on the river bridge, go haymaking into the fields, row on the river, watch the canal boats through the locks, loiter about the railway station, or ramble through the woods. But, above all, they are fond of indulging in practical jokes. If they can induce a greenhorn to fetch a "pennorth o' strap oil" from the grocer's, or the second edition of Cock Robin from the bookseller's, their delight is unbounded. Occasionally they will get up a spelling tourney on the town bridge, when a wiseacre, in solemn tones, will perhaps demand to be informed what is the longest word in the English language, and great will be his joy if no one can answer him, thus

affording him the opportunity of displaying his
own orthographic powers by drawling out, in his
tortuous, backward and forward style, the following
[little army of letters :—magnificanbandanjuality ;
and his hearers will probably be so overawed by the
loud-sounding word as to forget to ask whether
it has any meaning.   The Bingtonians are also
addicted to cutting clothes-lines, tapping water
tubs, tying ropes across the lanes, and making
ghosts ; but when Bletherhead time comes round,
they eschew all minor amusements and unite in a
grand Bletherhead Carnival.

The word Bletherhead (to speak learnedly) is
derived from the Yorkshire, and signifies empty-
head or noodle.   Blether is Yorkshire for bladder,
hence the word Bletherhead and its significance.

I have already said that it is Summer and that
the weather is beautiful ; I now beg to add that
it is Saturday afternoon ; that the factories are all
closed, and that there is nothing to prevent an out-
door celebration being carried out with the most perfect success.   The main street is crowded with people,
all of whom appear in exuberant spirits.   It is a
thoroughly Yorkshire crowd, in which boisterous
laughter bubbles up at every point, and in which
all the seven ages of man (and woman) are represented.   The throng thickens into a positive crowd,
in front of the Dog and Dragoon, whose windows,

up-stairs and down, are thrown wide open, reveal-
ing an excited gathering of mysterious figures—
Chinese, Hottentot, Patagonian, Red Indian, Black
Indian, male and female—partaking of the flowing
bowl, while a band of music, with Brobdingnagian
instruments, composed mostly of tin, is stationed in
front of the house.

A startling placard, plastered upon the ancient
butter-cross, and on sundry stable and barn-doors,
has already told me that the Bington Bletherheads
will hold their Grand Annual Festival in the Royal
Albert Park that same afternoon. It has further
announced that the Loyal Bletherheads will be
attired in full costume, and will proceed in procession from the Dog and Dragoon to the Park at three
o'clock, there to partake of a stupendous banquet.

At five minutes to three, the head of a South
American Planter stretches out of the Dog and
Dragoon window, and commands "the musicianers"
to "play up, or give us wer (our) brass back." At
this, the big drum wakes up with a few thundering
bangs, and the trombones give a long wailing yawn
of discontent. The conductor—who, as to his hat,
is a brigand, as to his jacket, a hussar, and as to his
terminations, a trooper—tosses off a foaming tan-
kard, gives one or two of his men a poke with his
hand-brush bâton, and then there rises upon the
Summer breeze such a combination of sounds as

never mortal listened to before. When, Orpheus took his lyre to the nether regions, he could never have known anything about a Bletherhead band, or he would assuredly have proceeded differently. The tootle-tootle of the fife finds its antithesis in the blatant roar of the serpentine tin instrument which coils four times round the body of the stoutest performer; the clear, ringing tones of the cornets are well contrasted by the angelic squeaking of a dozen penny trumpets, and, clinching all, in emphatic fervour, can be heard such a beating of drums, tin cans, pots, and frying-pans, as could not be surpassed even by the regimental bands of the wild tribes of Central Africa. What the tune is I cannot make out. Now it sounds like a donkey Miserere, now like an Ethiopian breakdown, now like the Old Hundredth, and now like Dinorah's Shadow Song, played in half a dozen different keys.

The band is still playing in front of the Dog and Dragoon, the crowd surging and shouting around it, when the before-mentioned South American Planter stalks out, and commands the band to form. Obedient to the order, the band staggers a dozen yards forward into the street, and then there come out of the front entrance of the public-house all the distinguished foreigners before observed in the up-stairs room. They come out in couples, as if they were stepping out of Noah's Ark.

Two gaily caparisoned steeds, probably more accustomed to coal-carts than gorgeous processions, await the foremost pair—the King and Queen of the Bletherheads. The King is brilliantly accoutred; brass rings, garlands of straw, can-lid medals, and other royal insignia, adorning his stalwart figure. His Consort is a gushing, six-foot bride of nearly as many stones weight as Summers. This Amazonian fair is attired in robes of innocent white, and wears across her swarthy brow a wreath of dandelions. Her voice sounds singularly masculine as she beseeches the admiring crowd to " get aht o' t'gate " (get out of the way), while she leaps on; and her leaping on is a feat which would put to shame many a professional equestrian. It may be also mentioned, as a further token of her masculineness, that there is a decided evidence of moustache on her upper lip.

When the royal pair have got fairly seated on their steeds, an escort of Banditti, Allemanni, and Zingari gathers round them, the band strikes up a triumphal roar, and the procession marches off, amidst the tempestuous salutations of the crowd. On they go, down the main street, past the old church, and out over the bridge, and on to the rural lane leading up to the Park.

What an impressive procession it is! All the gipsy tribes of the world, and even of the heathen mythology, must be represented. There are Brah-

mins, Fakirs, Ancient Druids, Turkish Giaours,
Knights (not Good) Templars, Corsairs, Pirates from
the Archipelago, Maories, Grand Bashaws, Mussul-
mans, Cossacks, Irish Peasants, Scotch Highlanders,
Harem Queens, Ashantees, Hottentots, and Heathen
Chinees. There are Apollos, Jupiters, Junos, Pans,
Gorgons, and Hydras. Young Endymion is there;
so is grey-haired Saturn. Meg Merrilies is there,
with her staff and her mysterious eyes; the inevitable Claimant is there, supported by his Counsel
and the Captain of the Bella; Brian de Bois Guil-
bert is there; Ivanhoe and Rebecca are there; and
Old Parr and Henry Jenkins are there, apparently
on the look-out for Mr. Thoms. For head-gear,
sugar-loaf papers and saucepans are patronised;
indeed, there seems to be every possible style of hat
worn, except the regulation chimney-pot. The faces
of the processionists are painted red, blue, and green;
and their garments vary in colour and texture, from
the saucy Dolly Varden gown and hat to the tat-
tered and torn habiliments of the Donnybrook Fair
rioter.

On the procession goes, in gorgeous array, up the
steep hill, arriving in due course at the Park—a
barren tract of enclosed moorland. On a level
plateau, the Bletherheads pitch their tents, light
their camp fires, and set their soup-pans on to boil.
Here Old Par, attired in a woolsorter's pinafore,

dismounts from his chariot; here the potato locomotive brings up the rear of the procession; here
gingerbread and hot pie-stalls are speedily erected;
and here the Bletherhead troupe of musicians prepare to discourse sweet sounds; for, when the banquet is ended, certain light fantastic performances
are promised.

Presently the soup boils, and the Bletherheads
feed in a very primitive style. Then the band
takes up its position in the orchestra and begins to
play a waltz. The leading instruments are two
immense guitars, the bodies of which instruments
bear such mysterious inscriptions as "Thorne's
Trinidad Cocoa," Colman's Mustard," "prime
quality," and the like. The leading guitarists see-
saw in such delicate style as to bring out the half and
quarter tones with remarkable effect. It would be
ungenerous not, at the same time, to acknowledge
the efficient playing of the tin whistles, the crumpled
horns, the penny trumpets, the pots and the pans.
A frying-pan solo by a South Sea Islander, and a
penny-trumpet duet between an Egyptian Mummy
and a Pale-green Indian, are also really exquisite
performances.

But the dancing eclipses everything else. Sir
Roger dances with Azucena, Ivanhoe with Meg
Merrilies, the Scotch Highlander with an Ancient
Druid, Old Parr with an Indian Squaw, Endymion

with the Heathen Chinee, &c. The King and Queen, however, frisk it by themselves, refusing to be separated.

And so the revels proceed, and Bington gathers there her beauty and her chivalry as spectators—people come even from the neighbouring towns—and the Bletherhead festivities are acknowledged to be an immense success. So they go on, dancing, capering, eating and drinking, until sundown, when the procession re-forms, and wends its way back to the Dog and Dragoon, where the Bletherheads see the night out, and the Bington Carnival is at an end.

WOOLBOROUGH.

GRAND surprise is Woolborough. Everybody who visits it feels it his bounden duty to express profound astonishment at its sudden leap from humble obscurity to the dignity of a trade metropolis; and it is worthy of note that the native Woolboroughite is quite as much surprised at the rapid transformation as the stranger is. Three-quarters of a century ago, Woolborough did not own more than ten thousand inhabitants, and had not a public building larger than a third-rate hotel; in the present year of grace it has a population of about sixteen times ten thousand, and an array of public buildings which, to quote the familiar language of the Woolboroughite, " would do honour to any city in the world." Woolborough is treated much in the same way as a great overgrown boy, with whose growth the tailors are unable to keep pace. Year by year its old streets are found too small to admit of a proper display of its strength and vigour; consequently the said streets are constantly being let out, patched up, and renovated. The Corporation is perpetually rushing up to Parliament to obtain extended powers, and coming back and cutting and slicing the town in all directions, rooting out of existence every remnant of antiquity that can possibly be found,—and a very few decades constitute antiquity in Woolborough. Now and then, a miserable ratepayer, with a deeper respect for his pocket than for the reputation of his native town, will give vent to a protesting groan, but he will be quickly silenced by citizens who possess a juster idea of the town's importance.

There is hardly any distinction to which Woolborough, in its present flush of prosperity, does not lay claim. First and foremost, it claims to be one of the chief industrial centres of the world. The visitor will be told that its manufactures are dispersed over all the ends of the earth. From Nova Zembla to Ceylon, from Canton to San Francisco, it matters not what point of the compass you may explore, the products of the Woolborough looms will be found hanging in graceful folds on supple female forms, heightening beauty and toning down ugliness. The belle of Patagonia, no less than the senora of Madrid; the light of the Eastern harem, as well as the squaw of the Indian savage, rejoice to wear the many-coloured robes which the Woolborough factory-girls are employed in weaving. All this, and more, the Woolboroughite will dwell on with pride, when commerce is spoken of. And if you try to humiliate him by suggesting that although the town may be great in a manufacturing sense, it still has no fine historical associations, he will point to the ancient Parish Church, and ask you to remember that it dates from Tudor times, and that it was hung round with woolpacks when the town was besieged during the Civil War.

There are three historical events which the youth of Woolborough are taught to bear in mind, above all that the school-books may tell them of the glories of classic Greece or Rome, and these are:— That in the time of the Normans a desperate wild boar was killed in a neighbouring wood, which is now renowned for stone; that a ghost appeared to the Earl of Newcastle, in an old suburban hall, and got him to " pity poor Woolborough," instead of putting the inhabitants to the sword, for the honour and glory of King Charles, as he had intended; and that the first factory in Woolborough was erected in 1798. To be unaware of these three events is to be altogether dead to local knowledge; and to be dead to local knowledge, in the eyes of a true Woolboroughite, argues nothing short of imbecility.

Having been made aware of all these circum- stances of greatness, the envious stranger will next bethink him, probably, that he may depreciate the town by saying that it has not produced any of those great men who, as Longfellow tells us, leave their "footprints on the sands of time." But even to this the proud Woolboroughite will have a ready answer. He will remind you that Woolborough is the birthplace of an archbishop, of a celebrated mathematician, of a famous botanist, and of Parkgate, the local Whittington, who has been thrice mayor of, and once M.P. for, the borough. Greater men than these Woolborough does not wish for.

At this point, the stranger may haply suggest that, admitting all these elements of greatness to be existing in Woolborough, there are still one or two other places on the globe which can vie with it in point of size; indeed, not to go far away, that there is the town of Allwool, only ten miles distant, with a population larger by a hundred thousand than Woolborough. But this reminder will be scorned more vigorously than any of the others. Census tables are a delusion and a snare, you will be told; and Allwool gets its vast population only by incorporating within its borough boundaries half a dozen distant suburban villages, while modest Woolborough is content with a radius of about a mile. And thus the Woolboroughite will run on.

I made the acquaintance of Woolborough "many and many a year ago," when "I was a child and it was a child;" we grew together, but, although I

long since attained the fulness of my stature, Woolborough has continued to expand, and now seems to
possess greater growing power than ever. The
town is situated in the heart of the manufacturing
district of West Yorkshire, and is more full of tall
chimney-towers than an Eastern city is of minarets.
These commercial beacons stud the landscape as
closely as masts in a harbour, and give the town
quite a monumental aspect; and an air of funereal
gloom is imparted to the place by the smoke-clouds
which are emitted from these chimneys, and which
hang sullenly over the factory tops. " Sweetness
and light " are not consistent with commercial greatness, hence Woolborough sees but very little of those
elements of extreme civilisation. White is an unknown colour in Woolborough, having long since
ceased to be used by local painters and decorators.
The atmosphere, considered as an element of food,
is excellent. It has been asserted that on some days
in the year it can be cut with a knife, but this is
probably an exaggeration. Most newspaper correspondents who visit Woolborough declare that the
town is built of brick. Whether or not this is due to
the fact that the smoke gives the buildings that
dingy appearance which is only associated in the
popular mind with the appearance of brick tene-
ments, it is difficult to say ; but I am in a position
positively to affirm that Woolborough is built

wholly of stone. Its giant mills are stone, its hundreds of chimneys are stone, its mansions are stone,
its warehouses and public buildings are stone, its
cottages are stone, and (let it be spoken in a
whisper) the hearts of many of its inhabitants are
stone. In Woolborough, it is the rule that if you
are not going up you are going down. You may
wish as you like to be able to say with the celebrated
commander that when you are up you are up, and
when you are down you are down, but you are
generally compelled to rest content with being
"neither up nor down." There are certainly three
or four level streets in the town, but they are
altogether of modern invention. Local historians
unite in saying that Woolborough lies in a basin,
and whosoever walks along the streets of Woolborough, be it on pleasure or on business, never gets
far without climbing up or sliding down some portions of this basin. The horses have a worse time
of it in Woolborough than pedestrians, woolpacks
being heavy articles to drag up steep hills; but the
town does not fret very much at these drawbacks,
believing in the wisdom of the old proverb, that
"money makes the mare to go whether she's
got a will or no." In truth, the genuine Woolboroughite believes that money is the root of all
good, whether it has any connection with evil or
not.

Though exceedingly grimy, the town has a sturdy and defiant look about it. It would take nothing less than an earthquake to upset the foundations of some of the many-storeyed, substantial stone mills and warehouses which form so prominent a feature of the town. During the last twenty years Woolborough has been a fine field for the exercise of architectural ingenuity. Merchants and manufacturers have been continually requiring new warehouses and new factories, and village Christopher Wrens and mute, inglorious Inigo Joneses have had no occasion to "waste their sweetness on the desert air." Perhaps it would have been better if some of them had; for, although several of the public buildings and warehouses are really fine specimens of architecture, in many instances the passion for novelty of design, and the love of meaningless ornamentation, have produced such mongrel structures as were never before seen. Thus it happens that amongst the Woolborough warehouses we find now an Italian Prison-house, now a Doge's Palace, now a Norman Keep, now a Grecian Temple, now a Gothic Chapel, and now—and this "now" comes the most often of all—an edifice which combines each of these styles. In point of size, however, these warehouses are matchless; tall as an Edinburgh house, and often covering as much ground as a royal palace. After dark, on winter nights, when all the

D

factories and warehouses are lit up, the town looks
exceedingly picturesque—prettier, perhaps, than if
the streets had been more regularly built. The
factories, except a few of very modern date, have all
been erected from a design which probably dates
from a period long before the Tower of Babel was
projected. They stand "four square to all the winds
that blow," and that is about as much as can be said
of them.

Apart from the architectural features I have mentioned, Woolborough shows a good proportion of
villa residences, churches, and chapels, and a vast
expanse of narrow streets where nothing but two-
storeyed stone cottages are to be met with.

It is time, however, that I should say something
of the people of Woolborough, for a hundred and
sixty thousand persons take some little photograph-
ing. In the first place, then, there is no aristocracy
in Woolborough. True, there is a baronet connected
with the town, but he has too much regard for his
health to live there. This baronet won distinction
in three ways—by discovering a new fibre, by
founding the finest industrious colony in the
world, and by his bounteous charity. It must not
be imagined, though, that because Woolborough
does not know much about the "upper ten," or of
great county families, that it does not uphold dis-
tinctions of grades; for, although the highest and

the lowest are alike dependent upon trade, in few places is there to be found a stricter worship of caste. A man's social altitude is generally settled by the length of his purse. In a town like Woolborough, therefore, which abounds with self-made men, the highest society is very variously composed, and is, of course, broken up into political and religious coteries, and is swayed by jealousies and animosities, like most other societies. The clergyman, the minister, the lawyer, and the doctor will be admitted into these charmed circles, but a cash reputation is the only "Open Sesame" for any one else. On the next level, we make the acquaintance of what is generally termed "respectability," as distinct from wealth. This class is exceedingly numerous in Woolborough, and comprises small tradesmen, managers, salesmen, travellers, shopkeepers, and clerks. Then comes what it used to be the fashion to call "the million," which, in Woolborough, includes an immense army of weavers, spinners, twisters, doffers, overlookers, woolsorters, combers, and what not. But even these are capable of being variously subdivided. The woolsorter will think it an act of condescension to associate with the comber, and the overlooker would scorn to rank himself with the spinner. On Sundays, however, when Jemima, the weaver, and Harry, the twister, are dressed in their best garments, the stranger would have a difficulty (if he did not hear them speak) of distinguishing them from members of some of the richer families. It is often hard, under such circumstances, to tell Jack from his master.

Between the rough exterior of the ancient but still living race of manufacturers, and the veneer of the new race, the difference is exceedingly great, and sometimes the former is put to humiliations in consequence. The following story may serve as an illustration. A rich Woolborough manufacturer bought a large landed estate, and with it a fine baronial hall. Time was when the manufacturer had gone ragged and shoeless ; but a singular capacity for looking after his own interests had helped him up to the position of a millionaire, ere yet he had grown wrinkled and grey. He had the old hall fitted up more gorgeously than it had ever been before, even in its palmiest days, and he engaged as many retainers as if it had been necessary for him to hold the hall on

> "The good old rule, the simple plan,
> That they should take who have the power,
> And they should keep who can."

He had not been many days in his new home, however, before he began to feel restless, and to long for the old busy life and homely associations which he had exchanged for this " gilded ease." Under the influence of this feeling he walked down to the village inn, and was on the point of entering the bar, when the landlord stepped forward and stopped him, saying, "You mustn't go in there, there's some *gentlemen* in." Without in the least resenting the affront, the rich man betook himself to a humbler apartment and called for a pint of ale. Seeing that the visitor, though evidently poor, was a stranger to the village, the landlord was prompted to put a few questions when he brought the ale in. " Are you thinkin' o' settlin' in the village, then ? " he asked. " Ay, I think I am," was the response. " Who're you goin' to work for ? " inquired the landlord. "Myself," replied the manufacturer. " Indeed ! " said the landlord, with an air of surprise, " have you been takin' a bit o' land, then ? " "Why," answered the landowner, " I've been buying a field or two, and a bit of a house up yonder," pointing to the hall. A sudden light dawned upon the landlord. " Surely, it isn't Mr. Bagwick, is it ? " asked Boniface, betraying great confusion. "That's my name," replied the visitor, calmly. "My dear Mr. Bagwick, you really must excuse me; I humbly apologise. Pray step into the bar." Mr. Bagwick merely smiled and said, "This room is good enough for me, thank you," and the dumbfoundered landlord was obliged to retire, to meditate on the weakness of human judgment.

Generally speaking, the Woolboroughite, whatever his station may be, is industrious. There is
little room for idlers in so busy a place. From six
o'clock in the morning to the same hour at night,
the mills are buzzing and humming, the looms
clattering, the spindles whirling, the steam engines
panting and groaning, and the bulk of the population is assisting and guiding the machinery in its
great work of furnishing the world with clothes.
At half-past five in the morning, the steam-engines
wake up with a scream, and for the next half-hour
the streets echo with the tramp of hurrying feet;
children in clogs, men-weavers in "smocks" and
caps, women-weavers in shawls and harden skirts,
woolsorters in "chequer brats" (long pinafores),
spinners in whity-brown pinafores, foremen in
broadcloth, and masters on foot, on horseback, and
in vehicles, haste to the factories. At eight o'clock
they rest half an hour for breakfast, and at noon have
three-quarters of an hour more for dinner. Then
there is no halt until the day's work is concluded,
when the workers hurry home, with the dirt and
odour of the looms, spindles, warps, weft, oil, and
steam clinging to them and scenting the air.

The workpeople are, as a rule, cheerful and
healthy. The dialect is pretty generally spoken
amongst them, and perhaps they do not care so
much as they ought to do for the arts of politeness.

They will, however, compare favourably, in point of education and vigour of mind, with any other class of workpeople in the country. Unhealthful work and unhealthful habitations often combine to produce sickliness and deformity amongst the workers, but recent restrictions upon the hours of labour, and still more recent sanitary enactments, have done much to improve such matters.

A good deal of the " foreign " element exists in the Woolborough trade. A large proportion of the labouring population are from Ireland, the " bould pisantry " attaching themselves very kindly to factory work and factory wages. There is also a considerable sprinkling of German nationality amongst the Woolborough merchants. The Germans betake themselves to the villas and mansions; the Irish " flock together " in cottages and cellars in the lower quarters of the town. These lower quarters, however, are not wholly given up to the Irish, but are likewise inhabited by a number of English people, who are intimately acquainted with the ale-house and the police cell. In these districts the policemen are seldom far apart—often, indeed, they do their perambulations in couples—for " rows " are frequent and violent amongst these turbulent islanders. The Germans seem to make themselves content in the town of their adoption, often becoming legally naturalised. There is one instance of a

German having been mayor of Woolborough. The
Irish, however, well as they thrive under factory
rule, never forget that patriotism demands from
them that they shall denounce the Saxon tyrant
whose yoke they bear. Home rule meetings are
frequent, therefore, in Woolborough, and a good
deal of Celtic eloquence finds vent on these
occasions.

Woolborough amuses itself variously and fitfully.
The entertainment which is successful to-day may
prove a dead failure to-morrow. There are times
when Nillson and Patti combined would hardly
"draw," and there are times when mediocrity will
carry all before it. The "society" of Woolborough
has never yet been able to make up its mind whether
it is "proper" to go to the theatre or not, hence the
local temple of Thespis generally shows a beggarly
array of empty front seats. Now and then a popular
London tragedian or comedian will come down to
Woolborough, "starring it," and perhaps a few of
the worshippers of propriety will pay a stealthy
visit, but as a rule, the playhouse is regarded with
pious horror, and its frequenters are classed amongst
the irretrievably lost. Let the play, the opera, or
the comedy, however, be represented in a temple
less profane—in the great St. Gorgon's Hall, for
instance—and no such timidity, hesitancy, or horror
are manifested. The performance, which at the

theatre is vitiating and wicked, at St. Gorgon's Hall is exhilarating and improving. Thus it happens that stock companies are never seen in Woolborough, except in the pantomime season, the rest of the year being given up to six nights' engagements of stars and sticks. But if the play is not the thing in Woolborough, the concert is. The concert provides ground upon which propriety and its presumed antithesis can cordially unite. Woolborough has the reputation of being an extremely musical town. It possesses a choral society whose lung-power is not exceeded by any choral organisation in the country. Some of its members are to be met with at all the great musical festivals, and it is on record that they once had the honour of singing " by royal command." In times gone by, these lusty choristers used to give more distinctiveness to their singing than now, by strictly following out the rules of local pronunciation. On one remarkable occasion, indeed, at the Crystal Palace, the chorus singers of Yorkshire and Lancashire introduced some striking features into their vocalism, by adhering to their respective local accents. The chorus, " We Fly by Night," was finely rendered by the alternations of Yorkshire bass voices and Lancashire altos. " We floy by noight!" volleyed the former, while the latter broke in with their soft, melodious " We flee by neet ! " the effect being, as the musical critics

say, marvellous. In the winter season the Woolborough merchants and manufacturers got up a
series of half a dozen subscription concerts, and
these are always successful. There is no hesitation
about going to them. Fashion decrees that
everybody who claims to be anybody must go
to the subscription concerts, and to the subscription concerts, accordingly, everybody goes.
They are worth going to, however, and are the
means of providing the town with the highest
musical talent available. Mr. Warpman, the town
councillor, may occasionally nod over Beethoven's
Sonatas or Bach's Fugues, as he will nod on a Sunday over the vicar's sermon, and Mr. Noils may
privately consider Mendelssohn a nonentity in comparison with the composer of the Rollicking Rams,
but they will not on these accounts neglect to attend
the subscription concerts. On Saturday nights,
during the winter, St. Gorgon's Hall and the
Mechanics' Institute are also the scene of " popular " concerts, in which the Great Prance, the Little
Alloyed, Herr Presto, the Mumbo Jumbo Minstrels,
and the Belle Blanche alternate with song, jugglery,
serenade, and dance; almost invariably attracting
large audiences. Then there are the Dulluns and
Cassandra music halls, and sundry alehouse concert
rooms, all of which absorb their proportion of
amusement-seekers.

In summer, Woolborough excursionises, plays cricket, promenades in its parks, and lives very much *al fresco*. Every summer Saturday sees the panting Woolboroughite hie away on the wings of the railway train to some remote corner of the island, for he always believes in having the longest possible ride which time and money will permit. And as for cricket, there are hardly a dozen yards of green upon which there is not a hotly-contested match on a Saturday afternoon. In winter, football takes the place of cricket to a slight extent, and the mystic game of " knurr and spell " is played nearly the year round. Every autumn, too, there is a two days' race meeting on Woolborough Moor, when a few of the cab-horses of the town are set to run for the Pig and Whistle Stakes.

The great thing in Woolborough, however, is its trade. In the making of a lady's stuff gown it is marvellous how many interests are involved. It would take a political economist to trace the article through its various stages of production, from the time when, as wool, it leaves the back of the sheep, to the time of its being donned as a robe. Shepherds, sorters, combers, spinners, weavers, dressers, overlookers, twisters, scourers, bleachers, dyers, finishers, and a hundred others are all concerned in the matter. Then there are the gigantic industries connected with the providing of tools for the making of the gown. Iron-founders, smelters, boiler makers, engineers, machine makers, shuttle makers, bobbin makers, picking strap makers, and so on. The mere act of buying and selling the finished goods also engages an immense number of people—manufacturers, commission agents, merchants, book-keepers, carriers, carters, &c.

Perhaps then, after all, the Woolboroughite is justified in his boasts as to the importance and extent of the interests and resources of the town. A trade which allows its merchants to do business to an aggregate value of about fifty million pounds a year, which has a yearly banking account of more than one hundred million pounds, and which can use above twenty million pounds' worth of raw material in a twelvemonth, is at all events worthy of mention.

TRESSY.

A LONG run of prosperity has permitted en-croachments of selfishness in many Bing-ton households, where otherwise the most perfect disinterestedness would have prevailed. For several years back the clash and whirl of the loom and the spinning-frame have known no cessation, except during the period prescribed by law, or on occasional feast-days. Wages have also been higher than at any previous period, so that many families, who once had the greatest difficulty in making ends meet, have been elevated into a sphere of plenty such as, in the old days, they would have imagined unattainable. But, with the increase of money, with the extension of the power of being generous, in many instances there has been a corresponding increase of selfishness. Thrift is a fine old York-shire virtue, but when it expands into mere selfish-ness and greed it becomes a very objectionable vice indeed. It must not be imagined, however, that I would represent West Riding working life as being generally permeated with selfishness; I only wish to point out that the vice is strongly manifest—more strongly than it was in less prosperous times—amongst our factory operatives, though we have still sufficient large-heartedness, honesty, goodwill, and charity amongst us to entitle us to name those qualities as amongst the chief characteristics of West Riding life.

When the factory operative, who has all his life been struggling for a bare existence, suddenly finds himself and family earning " money enough and to spare," he is somewhat at a loss what to do with his surplus cash. If he be a man of an equable mind he will apportion that surplus variously. He will save a portion against that terrible rainy day with which the working man is constantly being overawed; he will devote something to the better provisioning of his table, and he will set apart other portions for improving the mind and adorning the body. Often, however, the recipient of good wages is too narrow in his ideas for this, so he seizes on one of these things only. He will, perhaps, keep on in his old way of scant living, and carry every spare farthing to the savings bank, or to the building society; he will, perhaps, avenge the hunger of the past by keeping a perpetual feast upon his table; or he may try to hide the remembrance of the rags of his youth by decking himself and family in costly garments and jewellery.

A parent who has really permitted himself to give way to any of the follies alluded to, looks upon his children as mere machines, whose working value is as much a matter of calculation as if they were so many looms or spindles. The law permits Johnny or Polly to be sent to the mill at eight years of age as a half-timer, and at thirteen as a full-timer, at such and such wages. Unless sickness intervenes, the calculation of their pecuniary value can be made with precision, and the parent whom I have in my mind's eye will be as exacting on the point as Shylock with his bond. On the other hand, children of such parents do not get far into their teens before they begin to calculate also. Polly says to herself, "I am earning twelve or fifteen shillings a week, and paying every fraction over to my father, and seven or eight shillings a week will be as much as ever I shall cost him. I'll insist on paying for my board and lodging only, like Jenny Farsight and Ruth Blundell, and then I can get more clothes to go out in on Sunday." Then comes the tug of selfishness with selfishness—the most bitter of all conflicts—and perhaps in the upshot Polly leaves her home, and prematurely sets up on her own account in lodgings.

At the head of this sketch is written the name of Tressy, which will at once be assumed to belong to some more refined creature than a common factory girl. Betty, Sarah, Jenny, Molly, or Dorothy might be all very well for such a girl, but Tressy, the diminutive for Theresa, applied to a girl who works in a mill, whose garments smell of oil, and whose language is broad and vulgar, would be a piece of presumption. So the " fine lady " would argue, but, fortunately for this world, " fine-lady-ism " is not allowed to rule, and the West Riding parent would very soon tell any one who interfered with his liberty on such a.point, that his child had as much right to a high-sounding name as anybody else. Of late years the Bettys, Graces, Phœbes, and Nancys, the Jonathans, Josephs, and Abrahams have been getting less numerous, while there has been a rapid increase of Lavinias, Lauras, Ethels, and Florences, Claudes, Algernons, and Augustuses, so that, after all, Tressy is not so surprising as at first sight it might appear.

Tressy, then, was a factory girl, the eldest of a family of four children. Thomas Drubford, her father, was originally an agricultural labourer in the North Riding, and early learnt the art of living on the smallest possible amount of food, but tiring, in course of time, of his hard life and scanty fare, migrated, in search of better fortune, to the manufacturing districts. There Thomas presently got employment, and began to feel what it was to live. Both he and his wife learned to mind a pair of looms, and were soon able to earn from twenty-five

to thirty shillings per week between them. At first
Thomas could hardly believe in his good fortune.
On a Saturday, when he and his wife had got their
wages safe home, he would be so overjoyed and surprised at being the possessor of such an amount of
wealth, that he would even fetch the neighbours in
to feast their eyes upon it. As time wore on, however, Thomas got more accustomed to the sight, and
began to have an ambition. Now ambition is a very
fine steed to ride if you are a good equestrian, but
it is calculated to upset the mental equilibrium of a
rider who is not aided by a good ballast of intelligence and patience, and it must be confessed that
Thomas was very poorly ballasted indeed. He
started for a certain goal, it is true, but he only
knew the hedge and ditch road to it. For awhile
the enriched agricultural labourer let his money go
from him loosely, in the luxuries of eating, drinking,
and wearing, but the moment his ambition seized
him, he settled into a parsimonious dolt. And what
was this ambition? Was it to become a manufacturer, a member of a local board, or a magistrate?
No, indeed; all that Thomas desired was to become
a cottage owner, a small landed proprietor.

Poor little Tressy early felt the effects of her
father's ambition. While her mother.was away at
the mill, Tressy, who was put out "to mind" during
working hours, was being alternately shouted at,

3

shaken, and slapped by her nurse, who, besides minding Tressy and three others, washed the exceedingly dirty clothes of several mill-going families. At night she would be fetched home to be continually in the way of her mother, who had to scramble through her domestic duties as best she could, in the small space of time allotted to her. Once in a while, when it occurred to the father that Tressy would have to be taken care of if it were intended that she should live to earn any money towards buying his cottages, he would take her upon his knee, and, in doleful tones, " sing a song of sixpence " to her, or tell her the story of the little pig going to market, but, generally speaking, Tressy's happiest moments were those which she spent in sleep. Every morning, Sunday excepted, she would be dragged out of bed between five and six o'clock, summer or winter, hot or cold, and borne away to the soap-suds and the ill-temper, finishing her slumber, perhaps, on a heap of dirty clothes, or tied in a chair. Thus the time went on, year succeeded year, until Tressy had reached her sixth summer, and three other Drubfords had been born to the soap-suds and the ill-temper. About this time Tressy discovered that there were such things as green fields, and woods, and rivers, and that there were such beautiful objects as buttercups and daisies. How happy was little Tressy when she first fell in

with the buttercups and daisies ! How eagerly she
plucked them ! How tenderly she carried them!
And how ruthlessly the she-dragon flung them into
the street when Tressy, her little heart overflowing
with joy, and her face radiant with smiles, held up
her beautiful wild bouquet to the washerwoman's
gaze ! But, after that, Tressy seldom failed to make
her escape from the side of the washing-tub, when
the weather was fine, and in this way she had a short
experience of that fairy life which all children live
at some time or other, whether born to the gutter or
the palace. At seven years of age, Tressy was sent
to school, where, for twopence a week, she received
the valuable teachings of a girl some three or four
years her senior.

When Tressy was nearly eight her father and
mother made her the subject of constant conversation, and, although the mother pleaded for something better than the mill for her daughter, Thomas
would hear of nothing but Tressy being made a
half-timer, in order that his store might be increased.
At eight years of age, accordingly, Tressy "passed
the doctor," and was introduced to the spindles.
Corporeal punishment was at that time much more in
vogue than at present, and poor Tressy, who could not,
try as she would, get through her half-days at the mill
without an occasional yawn or sleepy nod, would
frequently drop in for a smart " strapping " at the

hands of the overlooker. Now and then her mother
would see that she had been crying, and threaten to
go and expostulate with the overlooker; but the
father, who was in constant dread lest some unfortunate circumstance should happen to deprive him of
Tressy's earnings, would generally put in his veto,
by observing that he supposed she deserved all she
got. As a half-timer, however, Tressy learned to read
at last, and thereby discovered another new world.
She also made companions, and, between reading
and friendship, contrived to forget the discomforts
of home. Thus matters went on until she reached
the mature age of twelve, when the father and
mother again laid their heads together. The father
would have it that Tressy looked "fourteen, if a
day;" the mother would plead that Tressy was
"nobbut wake," and "couldn't eight hardly nowt,"
but Drubford, who had by this time (with his eleven
years' struggling and pinching, and the sending to
work of two more of his children) saved about half
the value of a cottage, insisted that his wife's plead-
ings were "all gammon;" so Tressy, by a not uncommon misrepresentation, was palmed off to the
factory doctor as thirteen years old, and advanced to
the dignity of a full-timer. From spinning she was
subsequently elevated to weaving, and in time could
earn as much money as either of her parents.
Thomas Drubford's income was thus largely aug-

mented. Tressy worked hard at the loom all day, and at night worked quite as hard in washing, scrubbing, cleaning, or sewing, being permitted an hour or two now and then to walk in the fields with her companions, or to read the cheap periodicals. Before long, however, Thomas Drubford began to object to these companions. One of them "paid for her meat," and had a nice sum of money every week to call her own; and another had begun courting. These were examples which he must not permit Tressy to follow, if he meant to have his cottages, and that he meant that was more and more manifest every day, as the discomforts of his home amply testified.

But by-and-bye Tressy grew dissatisfied with her plain attire; she longed for brighter dresses, and neater bonnets, and it soon became evident that a certain young man named Bob Dobson, who had hopes some day of being an overlooker, was the person whose eye she desired should see her in these better garments. Her father pooh-poohed her timidly-preferred requests. For Bob he expressed his unmitigated contempt, and would not allow him to enter the house. The combined influence of Bob and her female companions, however, made Tressy resent her father's selfishness, and, as many other girls had done before, she left home and went to live in lodgings. Her father first entreated and then

commanded her to return home, but, backed up by
Bob and Co., she resisted.   This was a sad blow to
Drubford, but he tried to get compensation by ex-
torting more work from the children who remained.

Drubford's wife, worn out by pinching and hard-
work, died soon afterwards, and Tressy went back
to live with her father.   Before another year was
over he married again, taking to wife a woman who
could perhaps earn a shilling a week more than his
first wife.   Tressy refused to live with her stepmother, and went back to lodgings and indepen-
dence, but not for long, unfortunately.   One
day she was obliged to leave her work and go
home.   Her health seemed failing.   Her cheeks had
always been pale, but now they grew paler and
hollower, and her eyes grew less bright.   For a few
months she lingered on at the mill, being off only a
day now and then ; but eventually she was obliged
to hand the shuttle over to some one who had not
undergone as much wear and tear as she had, and
stay at home altogether.   Month succeeded month,
and still she grew no better.   Her savings went in
doctoring, Bob's savings went also, and then her
father, for whom she had in times gone by earned
so much money towards the cottage he was now on
the point of purchasing, was appealed to.   "I shan't
do a farthing !" was Thomas's reply ; " she left my
house of her own accord, and has no claim upon

me." Christian charity was invoked on behalf of
the poor, dying girl, but that did not hold out for
long; then the law was appealed to by the sorrowing Bob, and that failed. The father was then
hauled up before the guardians. His answer was,
" She can come home when she likes, but I'll not do
anything else for her." In this state of affairs the
poor penniless girl went "home," but the peevish-
ness of her stepmother and the groans of her father
almost drove her mad. It was then that Bob came
to her rescue again and took her back to lodgings,
where she died of consumption a few weeks afterwards. Bob did his duty manfully. He had her
buried in the quiet cemetery on the hill-side, cut
a rude headstone for her grave with his own hands,
and never afterwards opened his lips to Thomas
Drubford, who has now got his cottage and his un-
pitied remorse as the reward of his selfishness.

This picture, with little variation, has been seen
by most people who have been brought up in the
West Riding factory district, and, I take it, that the
wrong of the man who neglects his family in the
way I have shown is almost as great as the wrong of
the man who squanders the earnings of his family in
drink. The latter has occasional intervals of kindness and affection, the former hardly ever.

KNOTS.

TO the genuine West-Yorkshireman, marriage is either a desperately serious or an immensely comic affair—a drama of deep pathos or a screaming farce. The denizen of the large town often learns to address his ladye-love in language polite, if not poetic, and is as desperately earnest a lover as can be instanced. But, then, the type Lothario musters strongly in the town, whereas in the country it is comparatively unknown. To the country, therefore, we must go for distinctive features.

The farmer's man and the farmer's maid have a very limited lovers' vocabulary, consisting mainly of chuckles, grins, sheeps' eyes, and pontings. The foundryman and the blacksmith are also lovers who use few words; but those few are, as a rule, dreadfully emphatic. The factory lad and lass do their courting in a very systematic fashion. Once or twice a week, with the regularity of clockwork, William Henry will present himself at or near the

door of his sweetheart's abode, calling her out, perhaps, with a sharp whistle, and then the two will go
for their evening's walk, in as methodical a manner
as if they were performing some penitential duty.
Very few words will be exchanged between them,
and least of all will they talk of love, for it is the
frequent boast of the women of the factory class
that they would never, on any provocation, tell a
man that they loved him. A girl who can be
so imprudent as to tell a lover to his face that
she is fond of him, is regarded as a bold-faced
hussy who ought to be shunned, and of whom
no good is possible. With such views prevail-
ing, it is, perhaps, not astonishing that these
country lovers should be such a tongue-tied race as
they are.

There exists a time-honoured anecdote in the
West Riding, illustrative of this silent style of court-
ship, which is worth while repeating. A young man
and young woman walked out together for the first
time as lovers, by some mysterious understanding,
felt but unexpressed. Only once during their walk
was the silence between them interrupted, when the
youth touchingly observed, "Treacle's risen, Mary."
"Has it?" said Mary, affectionately. On they
walked, through fields and country lanes, and
nothing more was said until the time came for parting. Then the ardent lover mustered up courage to

ask, "When mun I come agean?" "When treacle settles," was the calm response, and they went their several ways.

These silent courtships proceed more by divination than arrangement. After the pair have done the walking out penance for a length of time, the real intention of marriage will crop out by some such announcement as, "I've bowt a rocking-chair for thee, lass." This is sufficient; it is as effective as any fervent love avowal; and is followed by a general preparation on the part of the girl as well. She will buy such things as looking-glasses, pots, pans, and ornaments out of her own money, and will perhaps also knit a hearth-rug or work a bed-quilt as her contribution to the furnishing of a home. But if any post-nuptial disagreement should take place she will bid her lord to "gi' me my awn an' I'll go," so that she never really sinks her proprietary rights in the effects got together by herself. Often this matter of furnishing will be indefinitely postponed, and the young people will get married, and live with "the old folks" of one side or the other. It rarely happens, however, that this style of living conduces to comfort. When a son takes a young wife home to his mother and sisters, it is generally to make his bride's life unhappy. Any token of affection on her part will be ridiculed as "fond," while the slightest show of reserve will be regarded either as pride or coldness. The up-shot invariably is, that the son quarrels with his kindred, and, rating himself for a fool that he ever married without first having "a home of his own," he is glad to settle in any poor cot that he can get, and furnish it by degrees.

In the matter of wedding, the villagers of West Yorkshire proceed variously, while in the large towns of the Riding the customs attending the nuptial ceremony differ little from those of other populous towns. Marriage by banns is almost universal, and the act of entering the banns is styled "puttin' t'spurrins in." When once the "spurrins" have been put in, the friends of the parties concerned evince the keenest interest in the coming event. The wedding almost always takes place at the parish church, an opinion seeming to prevail that the knot connubial cannot be so securely tied at any other place. Each Sunday upon which the banns of marriage are published, friends of the contracting parties will go in numbers to hear "t'spurrins read over," and, as the clergy-man reads out the two names, glances of delight will be exchanged, and the friends will go back to the bride or bridegroom elect with the joyful news that they have heard "t'names read aht." When the happy day arrives, the bride and bridegroom, and one or two other couples, set out on foot to the

church, in the gayest of gay attire, the lads of the
village crying after them :—

> "A wedding a-wool, a clog and a shoe,
> A pot full o' porridge, an' away they go."

The ladies of the party will be dressed in raiment
of very decided hues—blue, yellow, and green being
favourite colours—and will wear bonnets exceedingly gorgeous as to trimming. The gentlemen will
be sure to have white waistcoats and "flaming"
neckties, and, wet or dry, will carry umbrellas, their
hands grasping the stick half way up. All kinds of
fun will be poked at them as they proceed in awkward procession; but they will go on their way,
unconscious of any feeling but that they are cutting
a tremendous dash. On reaching the church the
bride will probably be chaffed on the "I will" subject. She will be told to clear her voice for the
promise to obey, and she will threaten to say nothing of the kind. Perhaps, after the ceremony,
she will pretend to have evaded the promise by sub-
stituting the word "bay" for "obey," or something
of that kind. Sniggering is the rule, during the
performance of the ceremony, with this class of
people, and the parson is frequently called upon to
admonish them for their levity. When the knot has
been tied, the wedding-party will parade the town,
do a large amount of staring in at shop-windows,
and then get away home for merriment.

Now and again a locality is put into a state of excitement by the marriage of the son or daughter of some rich manufacturer or merchant, when the wedding usages of society will be observed as closely as at St. George's, Hanover Square. Large numbers of spectators will be attracted to the church; bride, bridesmaids, and bridegroom will be almost stared out of countenance; the bells will be set a ringing; and, while the "happy pair" are speeding away to some distant honeymooning land, the parents will be giving a ball to their friends and a dinner to their workpeople.

Occasionally certain spots in the West Riding will be made lively for a day by a wedding of another description. Rusticity is, above everything else, fond of fun, and if a real rollicking wedding-party can be got up, it is delighted. Such an occasion presented itself not long ago in one of the villages of the Northern Division of the Riding, when Sammy Trotters, the old besom-hawker, took to wife the greengrocer's widow, Betty Blobs—two ancient personages, whose persons and donkeys were as familiar to the inhabitants as was the old church-tower itself. When it became known that Sammy and Betty had "made a match of it," the people roared with glee. A deputation, representing the inhabitants, and consisting of a coal-dealer, a railway porter, a blacksmith, and a landlord

—a landlord is always essential to the success of an affair of this description—waited upon Sammy and Betty, congratulated them upon the conclusion of such a distinguished alliance, and assured them that their besoms and potatoes had left such an impression upon the hearts of the townspeople that they could not think of letting so important an event pass without an attempt being made to do honour to it; they begged, therefore, to be permitted to get up a triumphal marriage procession for the happy day. Sammy replied feelingly on behalf of the besoms and potatoes, and assured the deputation that he was overwhelmed, that he had never expected such a proof of their affection, that he could never forget their kindness, and that they might thenceforward command him, in respect of besoms and potatoes, to be lower than any other house in the trade. Betty wept until there was hardly a dry spot upon her apron, and then told the deputation to " get aght ! " after which the deputation courteously retired, and did not burst into laughter for more than three minutes. At the end of the three minutes, however, the blacksmith sat himself down on a doorstep, and held his sides, while his three companions gathered round him, shouted, roared, and doubled up.

When the wedding-day arrived, the promised procession was organised. The pot and pan band (twelve in number) headed the procession; a halberdier followed on horseback, and then came the representatives of various trades:—a salt hawker with his wheelbarrow; a milkman carrying a pump handle; a hot-pie merchant holding one of his own pies on a toasting-fork; a vendor of "long strong leather bootlaces" wearing a collar of unlaced boots; a toffee-hawker with a dripping tin in one hand and a pot of treacle in the other; and many others. On the heels of the trades representatives came six variously-minded donkeys, pulling the old besom cart, which had been suitably decorated with pieces of broom, besom-handles, potatoes, cabbages, and turnips, emblematical of the union of the two houses of Trotters and Blobs. On this cart sat the bride and bridegroom, smiling and bowing. The rear was brought up by a number of male bridesmaids, decked out in the bonnets and cloaks belonging to their grandmothers. The whole of the village turned out to see the procession start off, and half the village accompanied the revellers to the town where the nuptial rites were actually performed. The clergyman not improbably scolded them for their unseemly conduct, but he did not, at all events, decline to perform the ceremony.

It is a wedding custom in the West Riding for the bridegroom to provide what is termed a "hen-drinking,"—a tea in honour of the bride. The bridegroom will perhaps contribute a sovereign or a half-sovereign towards this hen-drinking, and the friends who constitute the party will each subscribe a small sum in addition. Rum and tea, and possibly that indigestible compound of lard and flour known as "fatty cake," will be amongst the things which will go to form the success of the "drinking."

The standard of matrimonial morality is much higher in West Yorkshire—especially in the rural districts—than in many other parts of the country. This is due in a great measure to the fact that, in a village, everybody minds everybody else's business as well as his own. If a case of conjugal infidelity be discovered—and it is almost sure to be discovered if it exist in such places—the "lads of the village" will not neglect to avenge it. The offender's effigy will perhaps be paraded through the village and burnt at the culprit's door, amidst shouts of contempt and derision, two or three nights in succession; and in very flagrant cases the antiquated practice known as "riding the steng ' is resorted to. I have myself witnessed this practice within the last five years. The "steng" is a long pole, upon which the offender is set astride, and marched shoulder-high through the village, anybody being at liberty to salute the victim with a missile as he is borne along. A man rarely remains in a place after having been subjected to this humiliating punishment, preferring to take his "diminished head" to some remote region where he can live unknown. The feeling from which such practices as these were engendered has not yet departed from the races who inhabit West Yorkshire, and so long as it survives the morality of the people must necessarily remain high.

A RUN THROUGH CRAVEN.

THERE is almost as great a contrast between Woolborough, with its hundreds of factories, and the quiet Craven villages and dales through which I must now ask the reader to accompany me, as between the stillness of the backwoods of America and the hurry and excitement of New York—as great a contrast as we are accustomed to imagine between mediæval England and Victorian England, and yet both Woolborough and Craven are in the West Riding of Yorkshire. It is doubtful whether any district in this country has undergone so little change during the last two or three centuries, or has felt in so small a degree the influences of that progess which we are so wont to boast about, as the higher dales of Craven. Indeed, spending a day or two in these limestone regions is like shutting oneself out from "the world" altogether, or being spirited back into the feudal period. If you want to forget that there is such a thing as a steam engine; if you want to elude any everyday presence that may have grown hateful to you; if you want to know what solitude really is, and to feel that there is still peace to be had, slip quietly away to Kettlewell, or Conistone, or Arncliffe, without leaving your address behind you. Then, if you like, you will find rest and repose. You will find yourself face to face with the quaint humdrum life of two hundred years ago; in a country where the May-pole and the stocks still administer to the pleasures and pains of the people; where the village pump and the village "pound" are existing institutions, almost as much as they were in the days of Tom Jones and Squire Allworthy; where the genuine English squire still holds a sort of baronial sway and has the squire-al title always given to him; and where the parson has the full and comfortable spiritual control of the villagers in a far more complete sense than the dweller in a large town would ever suppose. Few persons who hurry on through the border-land of this place of retirement—through Keighley, Skipton, and Settle—to seek the better-known pleasure haunts of Cumberland and Westmoreland, have any idea of the beautiful scenery and rural delights that are to be met with only a few miles away. They see the towering heights of Whernside, Pennygent, and Ingleborough, and say something complimentary as to the appearance and altitude of

those Yorkshire mountains; but they seldom halt
in their journey northward to explore the tract of
country of which those hills are, as it were, the
guardians.

The poet, the artist, the angler, the naturalist, and
the geologist have, however, long been familiar with
the district, and the pleasure-seekers who follow in
their wake are a yearly-increasing race, though, as
yet, they have not been sufficiently numerous to
cause the innkeepers to charge holiday prices for
lodging and entertainment. Wordsworth, in his·
White Doe of Rylstone, and The Boy of Egremond,
has sung the beauties of Craven, and embalmed some
of its romantic history in the enduring music of his
verse. Turner painted some of his grandest pictures
from studies in the valley of the Wharfe; Landseer, too, loved to linger in the romantic loneliness
of Craven; and Creswick's many scenes in the
"North countree" are chiefly reminiscences of days
spent by him amidst the streams, the winding roads,
and rustic villages of this out-of-the-way corner of
England. In the Aire, the Ribble, the Nidd,
and especially the Wharfe and its tributary streams,
the angler is generally assured of abundant sport;
amongst the Craven caves, hollows, woods, and
mountain sides, the naturalist can always meet with
specimens that will fill him with delight; the
geologist can there roam through pre-historic seas

and gulfs, and chip limestone scar and millstone grit to his heart's content; and, for the antiquary, there are ruined castles, ancient halls, and haunted glens —in fact, there is not much change in the aspect of the district since the days when Dr. Whitaker wrote so quaintly and learnedly concerning it.

The favourite way of entering Craven is, perhaps, by Ilkley, a romantic village lying adjacent to Otley, on the hill-side between the Wharfe and Rombalds Moor. Here there are some extensive hydropathic establishments—notably the one called Ben Rhydding—and in the summer and autumn months a large number of visitors make Ilkley their rallying point for excursions to Bolton Woods, Malham Cove, the Clapham and Settle caves, and the Yorkshire moors and mountains. Farnley Hall, near Otley, too, has almost come to be a shrine, for the sake of the grand Turner gallery that is to be found there, and because of the fact that it was at this old hall that the great artist often sojourned during his visits to the valley of the Wharfe. It is not by this picturesque route, however, that I propose to penetrate into the interior of Craven at present; I prefer, rather, to leave the beaten track, and, instead of lingering amongst the more frequented and more accessible haunts, to dive into the remoter dales, and wander at will—

"Amid the rocks and winding scars."

We will, therefore, enter this Craven solitude
from the Airedale side, turning away from the railway at Skipton. Here we are fortunate enough
to catch the conveyance which, by a stretch of
politeness, is dignified with the name of a coach,
although known to the inhabitants mostly as the
"posst," by reason of its conveying Her Majesty's
mails. Our driver is entrusted with numerous com-
missions before we start. A servant lass wants a
parcel to be left at a farm-house for a certain Jacky,
who, we may presume, is her lover. A stalwart
Saxon-faced yeoman sends a brace of birds to his
mother, who lives at Kilnsey. Then there is a ham
to be left at "Owd Billy's," a bonnet-box to be left
at some hall, and hampers and baskets innumerable
to be dropped at wayside inns. We proceed
through the town at an extremely slow pace, calling
at one or two hostelries to take up stray passengers,
most of which stray passengers, as they walk from
the inns to the coach, are smoking long clay pipes.
On we go, past the ancient Norman Castle of the
Cliffords, to which race Fair Rosamond belonged;
past the old church where repose the remains of the
first and third Earls of Cumberland; and out upon
the high road, which grows more and more lonely
at every turn.

Although our driver does not appear inspired
with much reverence for ancient associations, or with

much admiration for natural scenery, he is, withal,
an observant man, with a well-stored memory and
a practical mind. The biography of every person
in the Craven dales seems at his fingers' ends. He
knows where every resident originally "cam' frae,"
and has something to say as to the position and
prospects in life of the occupants of each of the
different halls, farm-houses, and cottages that we
pass. But human habitations grow few and far
between as we proceed. Half-a-dozen houses form
a village up in these dales, and it does not take
much more than twice that number to make a town.
And as for population, there seems to be none. So
few were the persons that we met on the road, that
the driver had time to tell the complete history of
each one before we came up with another. The
advent of a new resident in these regions causes a
tremor of astonishment to run through the entire
district; the new-comer is a summer's wonder.
Unfortunately, the departures of residents are more
numerous than the arrivals, the higher towns and
villages being thinner in population now than they
were a century ago. We came across empty houses
in most of the villages, and rents are merely
nominal—ninepence a week for a roomy cottage
being considered rather high. One landlord, whose
acquaintance we made, owned a block of three sub-
stantially-built stone houses (all empty), situated

in a lovely spot, near the foot of one of the great
hills, and on the banks of a romantic stream, and
these three dwellings he offered to throw into one
—to make a mansion of them, in fact—in consideration of a yearly rent of five pounds! As a
further instance of the sparsity of population here-
abouts, it may be mentioned that a short time ago,
a tradesman, with more spirit than foresight, be-
thought himself to build a small cotton-mill in one
of the Craven towns; but when he opened it he
found it impossible to get "hands" to work it. He
might almost as well have tried to introduce the
manufacture into the Desert of Sahara, for in the
end he had to pull the mill down, and leave the
people to their ancient ways. Indeed, it is only a
very few years since the district reached the stage-
coach period of civilisation, and the same interest
appears to attach to the passage of the coach
through these places now as, forty years ago, in
more populous localities, was caused by the appearance of a railway train. As we passed through each
village, a crowd of about six persons would assemble
to watch our arrival at and departure from the
village inn, the coming and going of the "posst"
being clearly the chief event of the day. ·

The scenery increases in beauty as we get further
away from railway land; the fells and scars grow
more numerous, the dales and gills spread out

before us with greater clearness, and the outlines of
the mountain tops become more distinctly defined.
Soon after leaving Skipton, we come upon a house
known as the None-go-by, and are told that it
derives its name from a custom which existed down
to a period within living memory, that every newly-
married couple passing that way had either to leave
a shoe there or fourteenpence, which sum would
hardly be deemed a fair equivalent, perhaps, at the
present day. An ancient hall, called Scale House,
not long since restored, next comes under our
notice; and then—

> " High on a point of rugged ground,
> Among the wastes of Rylstone Fell,"—

we discern the ruins of Norton Tower, whence
Richard Norton " and his eight good sons " went
forth to join " The Rising of the North," in 1569,
and the spot round which Wordsworth has thrown
the halo of poetic romance in his White Doe of
Rylstone. The village of Rylstone, or Rilston, as it
is now called, is a picturesque little place, a very
Auburn, eminently fitted for the scene of a pretty
poetic legend. Cracoe comes next, then Linton
(where there is a hospital, and where the high road
passes through a stream which is, at times, impossible to ford), and then Grassington—contracted by
the natives into Gerston. Grassington is, as towns
go in these Northern fastnesses, a place of some

size and importance. It has a population of about a thousand, and owns a Mechanics' Hall and four inns. There is also a fine old mansion here, which dates from a far-back age, and it is on record that Edmund Kean, ere fame had got hold of him, once had the honour of acting in a barn at Grassington. From Grassington we push on to Kilnsey, but the sun has sunk to rest before we leave the comfortable fireside of the inn at the former place, so that our passage through Grass Wood, which many people account superior in beauty to the historic woods of Bolton, is performed in the dark. But it is a clear night, the sky is one mass of stars, and the dusky firs and pines of the wood stand out in mysterious relief on each side of us. The scene, grandly beautiful as it is by day, looks wild and weird in the darkness, and the stories that are told of a horrible murder committed there during the last century, and of the murderer being hung on a gibbet from one of these same tree branches that we are looking at, do not conduce to rid us of the fears and forebodings that the wood seems to inspire. The wood has also been the scene of one or two romantic suicides, of which the dalesmen tell over their fires of a winter's night, with as much interest as if they were speaking of events of yesterday. Indeed, if we give ear to tradition, which is almost as many-tongued as rumour, we cannot help pictur-

ing Craven as a district as specially given up to
ghosts, goblins, witches, and other superstitious
horrors as a Christmas number. It was in these
dales that Eugene Aram—the real Aram, not Lord
Lytton's—was born and passed his youth, and
where he doubtless acquired that air of misanthropy
and mystery which clung to him throughout his
career.

Kilnsey is our next halting ground, and here we
take our ease for a brief space at the only inn in
the village, the rendezvous of one of the chief
angling clubs in the North of England. The bar-
parlour contains a couple of walking tourists, deep
in the study of their guide books, and a gentleman
waiting for a post horse to carry him a stage further; the tap-room is tenanted with the unusually-
large company of seven persons—shepherds, miners,
and farm labourers—who are nearly all drinking
gin, which is as common an article of consumption
in these dales as in the London palaces devoted
particularly to its sale. They have at command, in
Craven, some of the finest ale in the country, but,
presumably because it is produced amongst them,
they leave it for strangers to appreciate, and will
have nothing to do with it themselves. At this inn
we hear the Craven dialect in all its purity, but as a
certain anonymous writer has said in that speech,
"What a fearful girt gauvison mun he be at frames

to larn th' talk of another country afore he parfitly
knaws his awn," I will not attempt to transfer this
peculiar language to print. The Craven inns are
exceedingly clean and homely, partaking partly of
the character of farm-houses. The business of
public-house keeping in itself would be insufficient
in these dales to yield a livelihood, so the landlord always unites the two occupations of innkeeper
and farmer. Such large fires are kept in the inns,
that we are led to inquire if there has been some
recent discovery of immense coal seams in the
neighbourhood. "It's half Threshfield and half
Skipton," says the landlady, pointing to the fire ;
and then ensues a long explanation as to the relative
value of each. Skipton coal is coal that is fetched
from the railway, and may have come from any of
the great coal districts ; Threshfield coal is obtained
from a place of that name near Grassington, but in
quality it is not equal to the other, as the. following
anecdote will suffice to show :—" I remember," said
one of the farmers—speaking in the dialect which I
have already said I would not attempt to reproduce
—" I remember once being at my sister Mary's, at
Skipton, and she said to me, ' Well, our Sam and
me, we've been wed seventeen year come next
Nidderdale Rant, but never while now have we had
anything in the house that we could keep.' ' Whatever can it be that you've gotten ?' I said, for I knew

only too well that they were none of a saving turn.
'Well,' she went on, 'we've now got two things
that we can keep, and those are Threshfield coals
and Irish bacon; the one we can't burn, and the
other we can't eat.'"

My friend Grantios and myself walk on a few
minutes in advance of the "posst," telling the driver
we will await him at the Scar. Such villagers as
are abroad carry lanterns in their hands; we, however, have to be content with the starlight. We
soon arrive at the well-known Kilnsey Scar, a great
frowning limestone crag, a hundred and seventy feet
in height, and with an overhanging projection of forty
feet. According to the late Professor Phillips, this
crag, in the pre-historic period, was a promontory
against which a pre-historic sea lashed and foamed.
At present it is the principal feature in a landscape
of unusual beauty, and, though there is no sea to
wash against it as of old, there is the pleasant river
running almost at its foot. The Scar is so close to
the high road that it almost seems, in the darkness,
to hang over us as we stand looking up at its grim
face! But that same distance which lends enchant-
ment also perpetuates deception, for although it
seems the easiest thing in the world to throw a
stone to the top of the Scar, it is not one in a
hundred persons who can throw one to its base.
Of course we tried, and equally, of course, we

failed. The foot of the crag is strewn with thousands of stony evidences of similar failures. Before
the "posst" overtakes us there is another peculiarity about the Scar that we do not neglect to bring
out, and that is its wonderful echo. I should not
like to assert that it will match with Paddy Blake's
famous echo, which, when asked, "How d'ye do?"
replied, "Very well, thank you;" but the Kilnsey
echo will fling you back a song, a threat, a jest, or
a laugh so readily and loudly as to set your
thoughts running towards the world of spirits, or,
at all events, towards the world of mythology. My
companion called the goddess forth with an operatic
stave or two, while I, and a number of minor
echoes, kept up a running chorus. I hardly know
how people do to "make the welkin ring," but I
half imagine that we accomplished that feat beneath
Kilnsey Crag that night.

Presently our coach overtook us and we were taken
on to Kettlewell, a quaint old town which nestles
at the foot of Great Whernside. Here, at a comfortable inn, yclept The Race Horses, we stayed for
the night, and next morning went through "the
Slit," and over "the Top" to Arncliffe, where we
halted for another day, enjoying a seclusion which
perhaps would be unattainable elsewhere in England. What a pleasure it was to feel that we were
sixteen miles beyond the reach of a railway! Here

we were in the midst of wild, picturesque mountain scenery, amongst a hardy, cheerful people, who live in contentment in regions remote from steam engines and machinery, from newspapers and popular amusements.

The night that we stayed at Kettlewell was perhaps the most memorable of the year. A grand christening party was being held at one of the principal farm-houses in the neighbourhood, and nearly all the town had been invited. A Penny Reading had also been announced, unfortunately, for the same night at the Mechanics' Institute. It was impossible that Kettlewell should find a sufficient number of people to make both entertainments a success the same night, although an audience of fifty would have sufficed to crowd the Mechanics' Institute, so it was at last decided to postpone the reading until another week. So much for the amusements of the dalespeople. Their work is as unvaried. All the land in the higher dales is grazing land, and a large portion of the population is employed in shepherding. The fields are altogether unploughable, the white limestone rock cropping out above the surface in every direction. Every hill-side has its immense sheep pasture, and standing on some of the hills and looking down upon the long stretch of undulating scenery that lies below, the same craggy, wild aspect presents itself far and wide. There is hardly a tree to be seen for miles in some of the dales ; the tall limestone walls, built in the rudest fashion, run zig-zagging up and down the hill-sides, but there is nothing else to break the continuity of the landscape. One or two gentlemen proprietors have taken to planting trees —especially has this been done by Sir John Ramsden, at Buckden—and the effect has been in such cases to convert bare tracts of land into sylvan paradises.

The working population are farm labourers, shepherds, or lead miners, but of late years the lead mines have been less productive than formerly, and consequently many miners have migrated to other parts of the country. I must not omit to mention, however, that there is still another portion of the working community that deserves mention, and this portion is made up of sheep dogs, who evince an amount of intelligence which almost puts them on a level with their masters.

Our advance upon Arncliffe was made during a stiff gale, which at times threatened to blow us back upon Kettlewell. Once we had begun our ascent of the hill which divides Arncliffe from Kettlewell there was no shelter to be had from the elements, whatever their humour might be. There are many stories told of people being lost in crossing from one dale to the other. A summer or two ago,

a party of gipsies attempted to cross from Arncliffe
in the night time. It was about eleven o'clock when
the gipsies passed through the village, and not a
person in the place was out of bed. The party,
consisting of men, women, and children, passed
through the quiet village and up the hill-side, but
in the dark they were unable to find "the Slit," a
sort of mountain pass through which the road goes.
Groping about helplessly on the mountain-side,
running the risk of being precipitated from some
rocky cliff every moment, they were seized with
terror and began to call loudly for help. "Lost!
Lost!" was the cry that rang through the sleeping
village, and over the wide dale. Soon all the inhabitants were astir, and the male population, with
lanterns in their hands, turned out and rescued the
affrighted gipsies from danger.

Arncliffe is about the most picturesque little
village in England, and I and Grantios sojourned
there for the best part of a day, happy in having
found perfect seclusion and perfect natural loveli-
ness. The village-green at Arncliffe is a cheerful
patch of grass, on which a flock or two of geese
are constantly nibbling and cackling. In the
middle of the green stands the ancient pump which
constitutes the entire system of waterworks for the
village. On the four sides of the green runs a single
line of dwellings, ranging in quality from the one

or two new houses with slated roofs, occupied by the moneyed yeoman, to the tumble-down cottages with thatched roofs, tenanted by the village cobbler or the village tailor,—and these make the entire village. But high or low, big or little, slate or thatch, all the dwellings are scrupulously clean and tidy. The squire's house stands a little distance back from the green, in the midst of its own grounds; and not far away is the residence of the vicar, almost vieing with it in point of respectability. It does not take one long to get thoroughly acquainted with the social and commercial life of Arncliffe. The spirit of competition finds no harbourage in the village. There is but one butcher, one tailor, one shoemaker, and one blacksmith. When one of them dies a successor will doubtless be found, but the existence of two of a trade contemporaneously is an impossibility. The shoemaker is one distinct individuality, into which the idea of plurality never for a moment enters. If I wanted to write a philosophical treatise or to become a recluse, Arncliffe is the place to which I should retire. With its bonny river, its surroundings of woods and hills, and its sturdy race of villagers, it offers attractions that one may look for in vain in more frequented places. There is a charming novel of country life ready to any writer's hand in this out-of-the-way Craven village.

From Arncliffe we turned reluctantly away towards the Malham Moors, and made our exit from Craven by way of Bolton Woods, Addingham, and Ilkley, going on foot the whole of the distance, halting now at a road-side inn, now at a lonely farm-house, for refreshment. The " posst " is well enough in its way, but, for the thorough enjoyment of rural life and scenery, commend me above all to the marrow-bone stage.

SENT TO WAKEFIELD.

PEOPLE living outside the limits of the West Riding have no idea of the dreadful import of the three words which I have placed at the head of this sketch. In common parlance Wakefield is the synonym for the House of Correction that exists there, and to be "sent to Wakefield" means nothing more nor less than to be sent to prison.

How I came to be sent to Wakefield is neither here nor there. Let it suffice that I have been there, and that I am not too proud to tell the secrets of the prison-house. I am willing to confess, too, that I had a strong desire to suffer temporary incarceration, and long pondered upon what I should do to have my desire gratified. One friend suggested that the simplest mode of gaining admission to the gaol would be for me to break a window in the Woolborough Town Hall; another recommended me to drink an extra bottle of wine at Mrs. Jones's evening party, and enrol myself at the police-station amongst the "drunk and right-eous;" and a third counselled me to apply to a magistrate to order me to prison as an example worthy of imitation. What it was that prompted me to seek to entomb myself with common robbers and felons I might find it difficult to explain. Perhaps conscience had been telling me that I had trodden too fiercely upon Alderman Gobble's corns in that article of mine on "Corporate Rotundity;" perhaps I had stolen more than I could ever return from the heart of the gentle Amarinta; and perhaps—a thousand other things. However, "where there's a will there's a way," says an old proverb for which I have much respect, so, in the end, I succeeded in getting "one of Her Majesty's Justices of the Peace for the West Riding of the county of York" to sign an order for my admission within the walls of the Wakefield House of Correction. I have resolved that further than this the how and the wherefore of my confinement in prison shall never be divulged. You might as well seek to discover who was the Man in the Iron Mask, or who Junius was, as to get me to make any fuller confession than that which I have recorded above.

Time was when there was a good deal of romance hanging halo-like round the walls of a prison; but that was in days when Justice had yet an eye left—

an eye to her own interests. It was in days when a man could be imprisoned for frowning at a palace door, for singing an "owre true" political song, for having a pretty wife, for being successful in love or war, for nothing and for everything. With a Shallow at one end of the judgment-seat and a Jeffreys at the other, prison-romance was manufactured at a very rapid rate. Then, indeed, there was something fascinating in the solitude of captivity; then Alathea could be told and could believe that—

> "Stone walls do not a prison make,
>   Nor iron bars a cage;
>   Minds innocent and quiet take
>   That for a hermitage—"

then the heart of a whole nation could be stirred to sympathy for an unfortunate prisoner. But since Justice lost her second eye there has been a dearth of interesting prisoners, and we are now compelled to build our prison-romance solely upon the career of those criminals who have performed some deed of extraordinary atrocity. Our grandfathers and great-grandfathers were much better off in this respect than we are. They had their Baron Trenck —that glorious old captive whom no prison was strong enough to hold; their prisoners of the Bastile, and English political offenders galore. More recently they had the imprisonments of Leigh Hunt, William Hone, and others to excite them;

but since the time of the Chartist agitation, when
Thomas Cooper penned his "Purgatory of Suicides"
in Stafford Gaol, we have had exceedingly few
attractive prisoners.

Of course I was taken to Wakefield by a policeman. How could it be otherwise? And Robert
was a gentleman; he did not put the handcuffs
upon my wrists, as he did upon the wrists of two
other persons committed to his charge. True, we
had no van to carry us between the stations, police
and railway, either at the Woolborough or Wakefield end, but vans and the millennium are still
confidently looked forward to. Robert and I beguiled the time with stories of police and court
experience, but my fellow-prisoners were sullen and
morose, and had no taste for conversation. I will
not further reveal their appearance, or attempt to
describe their offences. I have been reserved on
my own account, and I will be so on theirs. The
only thing I will say is, that they—and all other
prisoners that I ever met with—were (on their own
showing) entirely innocent.

The sight of Wakefield that warm June morning
naturally set one's thoughts running upon the associations that are indissolubly connected with the
town. I thought of it as the "Merry Wakefield"
of Robin Hood's days, when the famed freebooter,
and his comrades, Will Scarlet and Little John,

were not unfrequent nor altogether unwelcome
visitors ; and I thought of the old ballad which tells
us that—

> "In Wakefield there was a jolly Pinder,
>   In Wakefield all on a green."

This "jolly" personage was the hero of "The
Conceyted Comedie of George-a-Greene, the Pinder
of Wakefield," published in 1599 ; the play wherein
the Earl of Kendall, who has halted at Bradford
with his followers, shows his affection for the town
by saying—

> "I will lye at Bradford all this night;
>   And all the next."

The muse of history descends at this point with
such a numerous collection of pictures of ancient
Wakekeld that I am compelled to bid her avaunt.
She offers several stirring battle-pieces, a ruined
castle, a May-day scene, and a score of others, but,
even though Shakespeare is the artist in one
instance, I will not let my imagination run riot
amidst them.   I am for the prison, and, for the
present, have nothing to do with any other place.

The lane which leads to the prison entrance is
straight, as a lane ought to be upon which so many
people are brought whose ways have previously
been very crooked.   It is bounded on one side by a
low stone fence, beyond which is a field and the
atmosphere of liberty; on the other side it is

bounded by an oppressive length of high, solid
stone walling, without a chink or a loophole, and
this is the wall of the prison, beyond which there
reigns the completest thraldom. A more decided
contrast it is difficult to conceive. Only a very
short distance from the liberty side of the road
there is the railway also, and there is generally a
locomotive puffing its steam there in a way that
must be exceedingly tantalising to the prisoners as
they disappear into the house of detention. The
engine's sportive whistle must pierce the very soul
of the Wakefield captive.

Having arrived at the gaol gateway, on one side
of which stands the Governor's house and on the
other the residence of the Chaplain, I and my
fellows are taken into a small office where the
Reception Warder sits ready to receive us. Each
prisoner's name is compared with the warrant of
commitment, and, on their being ascertained to
correspond, the warder gives the policeman a receipt
for the bodies he has brought, and Robert takes
his leave. Another warder, a sort of gaol Charon,
now appears and leads the prisoners, by what seems
to be a subterranean passage, to the reception cells,
where they are treated first to a bath, and then to a
fresh suit of clothes, an inventory of the clothes and
anything that they may contain being taken down,
read over, and signed by the prisoners. Very often

the garments inventoried are not worth the paper upon which the inventory is made out; indeed, the habilimeuts of the two men with whom I entered would have humiliated a scarecrow. Each prisoner is submitted to the closest scrutiny, every mark and distinctive feature of his body being duly chronicled. It is rather strange that these people, whose identity often depends upon the recognition of marks, should be the persons most addicted to the practice of tattooing and marking. As an evidence of the exteut to which this sort of thing is done I cannot do better than give a couple of specimens, taken at random from the prison chronicles—a well-executed photograph (one inch long in the face) of each person who is a felon accompanying his description. Oue is described thus :—" 5 ft. 5½ in., slender; two boys and bird on breast; two men, two women, flags and bracelet on right arm; five women, one man, and bracelet on left arm ; lion on right hand; E anchor and W on left hand." This man might have been bred amongst the Pacific Islanders, judging from the profusion of his skin decoration. A ring through the nose was all that he required to make him look complete. The next description is evidently that of an adventurous thief, for he is said to have a " gun-shot wound on the left arm, a letter under the left breast, and sabre cuts."

The reception cell is occupied by the prisoner during the first night of his incarceration. It is here that, unless he be merely sent to await his trial at the sessions or assizes, he receives a visit from the hairdresser, who gives him what is facetiously called "the Wakefield crop," and also relieves him of his beard and moustache, if he have any. In the morning the doctor calls to see him, and writes a report upon the state of his health, specifying his working capability, and directing what class of diet he is to have. All prisoners are thus disposed of by the doctor on the morning after entering the prison, after which they fall into the ranks, and are, as far as possible, divested of their individuality.

For some reason or other I am permitted to make a survey of the prison before being asked to conform to the regulations of the establishment, and thus it happens that I soon find myself discussing the capabilities and advantages of the House with a gentleman whose knowledge of the place is full and accurate, and whose courtesy is worth remembering. He is my Virgil, showing me the wonders and terrors of the West Riding Inferno; for Inferno it must be and ought to be, despite its clever management, its cleanliness, and its completeness. He conducts me, in the first place, to what is known as the new part of the prison, which was

built in 1846, and affords accommodation for over
800 inmates.   In shape it is like the half of a cart-
wheel, with long, broad flagged corridors, like
spokes, branching across.   There are four storeys
of cells, stretching every way, with staircases and
iron bridges crossing here and there.   Standing at
the centre point, from whence these lines of cells
proceed, one is greatly impressed with the vastness
of the place.   It is clean, cold, silent, and stony;
it looks merciless and impregnable; and as a prisoner is passed now and then to his cell, one has no
difficulty in realising what Wordsworth called "the
solitude of blank desertion."   A warder sits at a
desk at the centre of the block, his eye taking in
the whole range of cells ; not a movement anywhere
outside the cells but can be noted by him.   The
total number of prisoners in the House that June
morning was 1291, made up as follows:—1010
males, 235 females, and 46 military prisoners.
The average number of prisoners admitted daily is
28, but on the day previous to my admission the
number had reached 60.   Virgilius supplies me
with some suggestive statistics with regard to the
admissions during the previous year.   For the year
ending the 30th of September, 1873, there had been
committed, 6554 males, and 1825 females, making a
total of 8379 prisoners, and showing an excess of
954 over the previous year, exclusive of 125 mili-

tary prisoners received under contract with the
War Department. Taking England and Wales
through, however, the West Riding shows some
favourable criminal statistics, for while in the country generally there is an average of one committal
to every 151 of the population, the proportion in
the West Riding is one to every 209. But the fact
remains that of late years the number of prisoners
committed to the Wakefield House of Correction
has gone on increasing at a rapid rate. The number
of committals in 1867 was 5762; in 1868 it was
6638; in 1869 it was 6899; in 1870 it was 7114;
it 1871 it was 6792; in 1872 it was 7425; and in
1873, as we have seen, it was 8379. In the seven
years thus accounted for, Bradford does not
stand well, but Halifax shows up so badly,
that I am at once reminded of the ancient
saying which asks the Lord to deliver us from that
and sundry other places. In 1867, the committals
from Bradford and the surrounding district were
882; in 1873, they had increased to 1411. The
year 1867 gave the Halifax committals at 361 (a
very modest number), but 1873 advances the
number to 1202. From 1872 to 1873 the increase
in Bradford had been 206; in Halifax it had been
524. In Sheffield, Doncaster, Rotherham, and
Keighley, a decrease of crime was shown. Sir
Wilfrid Lawson and his followers will be able to

make good capital out of the statistics yielded by
the West Riding Prison, for, during the last seven
years, the committals for drunkenness have been
more than doubled.   In 1867, there were 1186 persons imprisoned for this vice; in 1873, the number
had swelled to 2596.   Serious offences have not
increased, happily, but beeriness and prosperity
have augmented together.   This state of things
fully explains the fact that year by year the average
length of sentences becomes shorter.   In 1866, the
average number of days of each sentence was sixty-
three ; in 1874, it was forty-seven.   If we are able
to go on long enough in this way, the result will
not be unsatisfactory, for a decrease of sixteen days
in the average length of each sentence every seven
years would, in the course of time, taper off at last
into the innocent, expressive cipher; after which .
the lion and the lamb might with safety lie down
together.

   The long lines of whitewashed cells, tier above
tier, look as lonely and forsaken as it is possible for
habitations to look.   They give me a complete idea
of a peopled solitude.   The seclusion of the hermit,
the loneliness of the wilderness, the isolation of the
convent can surely not be so oppressive and weari-
some as this.   Within these walls, this fine June
morning, while the sun is shining and the birds are
singing outside, upwards of twelve hundred persons

are passing the day in jading confinement. An awful stillness hangs over the place. No prisoner is permitted, under severe penalty, to exchange a single word with any of his fellows during the whole term of his captivity ; indeed, it is seldom that he has the opportunity of coming within speaking distance of any one but his keepers, and, unless he be in his cell, he is always under their watchful eye. Virgilius and I promenade the stony spaces between the rows of cells for a brief period, until I have been able to get the full aspect of the house impressed upon my mind. We pass hundreds of massive wooden doors, on the inner side of which " cabined, cribbed, confined," there are as many prisoners ; constituting collectively such an army of desperadoes, such a concentration of brutality and viciousness, of depravity and worthlessness, as, if let loose, would be sufficient speedily to overpower all the hundred and sixty officials who are engaged keeping watch and ward over them. What stories these walls could tell ! Words of remorse and repentance will surely often be spoken to them, as well as curses and threats. Behind those doors are to be found criminals of every hue, from the drunkard up to the murderer. A man who had killed his mother under circumstances of the most savage atrocity had been brought into the house that very morning.

Wife-beaters, shop-lifters, embezzlers, deserters, stabbers, fraudulent bankrupts and thieves, rogues and vagabonds in general, are all represented here. How many more there would be if everybody got their deserts, we will not stay to conjecture. "Thereby hangs a tale." Some of the delinquents have got seasoned both to crime and its punishment, and are callous; others are still smarting under their first disgrace, and may possibly be saved from a further social descent. Each cell door contains a small glass eye, and the warders can, at their pleasure, lift the iron lid and take a peep at the inmate without his being able to discover who is looking, Peepholes are to be found in other parts of the prison also, permitting a whole workroom to be surveyed in the same secret way. Besides each door there is a ticket denoting the number of the inmate, and if he be a Roman Catholic, as a very considerable proportion of the prisoners are, a label lettered "R.C." appears above the door, as a guide to the priest. There is another contrivance near each door which likewise merits mention, and that is a ticket which enables the prisoner to communicate with the warder at his will. The prisoner pulls a string on the inside, and straightway a bell rings, and the ticket before-mentioned, upon which the number of the cell is painted, is propelled outward from the wall, so that the warder at once sees from whence the summons comes; and the little machine is so arranged that when the bell has once been rung the ticket cannot be withdrawn, otherwise tricks would often be played upon the custodians. But we have not done with the door even yet, for in the middle of it there is a trap, secure enough from inside control, through which the prisoner's meals are put. The lock is the work of a genius, for it only permits of being opened from the outside. The prisoner might devote the entire term of his confinement to discovering the way to it, and be foiled when he had done. Escapes are now altogether impossible. Even if a prisoner worked his way through the door in any way, his passage would be intercepted at every turn, both by stone walls and human hands.

After lingering on the threshold of the cells for a while in this way, I am then privileged to inspect the interior of some of them, and to converse with one or two of the prisoners. Each cell is 13 ft. long, 7 ft. 6 in. wide, and 10 ft. 6 in. high. On the side opposite the door is a small window, guarded outside by a strong iron grating. The floor of the cell is of stone, and the occupant is compelled to wash it twice a week. The central portion of the apartment is occupied with a loom for weaving mats, and a stool and a table of primitive pattern are provided for the use of the inmate. In one corner is a shelf,

H

on which repose a Bible and a Prayer-book, as well
as any volume that the prisoner may have been
furnished with from the prison library. Above the
bookshelf, there hangs a card giving every detail as
to the prisoner's name, trade, offence, term of
confinement, and date of discharge. Of course I
take care to consult these tell-tale cards as soon as
I enter the cell. In some cases the offender bears
the examination unflinchingly; in some cases protests of guiltlessness follow; and once a decided
blush, and a declaration that this is "the first and
last time" was provoked. "What are you in for?"
is our first salute. "Well, you see, sir, there was
me an' another man, and the other man——"
"Oh, yes, exactly; how do you like your work?"
"I likes it moderate, sir; perhaps I shall like it
better when I gets better used to it." "Do you sleep
well?" "Sometimes, sir." Sleep! what a horrid
thought it was to fancy oneself sleeping there,
alone, in the dead of night, in the darkness! I shud-
der, and feel a passing wave of pity touch my heart
as I look upon the victims of this desolation. I remember how the "black air" represented all things with
double terror to the evil conscience of Milton's
fallen man; I conjure up visions of the chilling and
crushing darkness in which one of Poe's prison
heroes groaned and suffered; and I feel that
imprisonment by night, when there is no light,

when distant doors can be heard shutting with deadening thud, and when the very silence seems to give a tormenting hiss in one's ear, must be a terrible and fearful experience. Then, if at any time, "flashes of purity" will follow and tell the poor victim what he "might have been." In this way I was conversing now with a burglar, now with a vagrant, now with a pickpocket, now with a thimblerigger, now with a cut-throat. Their looks did not, as a rule, belie them, for crime is a careful limner, and bestows the full force of its art upon the physiognomy of its subject.

From an inspection of the cells, I accompany Virgilius into the open air for a few minutes, and see a batch of prisoners taking walking exercise. The sight is certainly an odd one. I see four cause-ways, each in the form of a circle, beginning with a small one and expanding into one of considerable circumference, with grass covering the intervening spaces. The outer circle is occupied with a number of the most able-bodied prisoners, in variegated suits and skull caps, walking briskly round and round. A distance of several yards separates one from another, a regulation that is enforced in order to prevent the men from speaking to each other. Several warders occupy the next inner circle and make the pace for the exercisers. The smaller circles are promenaded by the more aged and less active, and in remote parts of the ground there are one or two cripples going about on sticks and crutches. In this way an hour's exercise is given to each prisoner every day. The felons are clad in suits of yellow and black, while the others are attired in more sombre garments. As they pursue their hour's dull round, I cannot help thinking that they have the appearance of culprits just rescued from the hangman's rope, undergoing a final process of resuscitation.

I was now led across the yard to the portion of the prison erected about 1820, where what used to be the Governor's house stands, a circular brick erection with a balcony running round an upper storey, from which his governorship could overlook the rest of the prison buildings, watch the comings and goings of his satellites below, and take an airing and smoke a pipe at the same time, if he chose. The oldest portion of all stands close by, and is built in the form of the letter H, and it is here chiefly that the female prisoners are confined. This building dates from 1770, and is, I believe, the site of the building referred to by Dr. Whitaker as "one Mr. Kay's house, a gaile then lately built up in Wakefield," to which place "Calverley of Calverley" was committed by Sir John Savile, in 1605. We were attended through this part of the prison by a female warder, and there made the acquaintance of the Matron of the establishment, and visited a prisoner or two in their cells. The women are dressed in coarse, loose-fitting garments, and are employed largely in washing, sewing, and other feminine occupations.

The next move was to the workrooms, where the manufacture of matting is carried on on a more extensive scale than in any other place in the world. About a thousand people were actively at work that day in this business, either in their cells or in the workrooms. And what ponderous machines the matting looms are! Warp and weft as thick as one's finger, and shuttles like little coffins. There is no light clickity-clackaty movement here, as in worsted weaving; the belts and pulleys may whirl, the engines may pant and groan; it is no use, the only sound the looms utter is, " ksh—sh—lish ! ksh—sh—lash !" There is almost time to take a walk between the passing and re-passing of a shuttle; and as for " traps," they are impossible; it would take all the power of a locomotive to snap the fibrous threads that fill these gigantic looms. These workrooms are all on the ground floor, and the same silent system is pursued here as in the other parts of the prison. In each room three or four warders are kept perched up aloft, like Dibden's " sweet little cherub," and the strictest supervision is exercised throughout. In

one place the prisoners are spinning the fibrous
material; in another they are weaving it; in a
third they are clipping it and smoothing it; and so
"on, and on, and on," as the fairy tales used to say.
Wherever machinery can be of assistance it is
brought into requisition.   Of course the mat
weavers who do their work in their cells have no
help from Giant Steam.

Having seen the whole process of mat-making, I
next visit the packing-room, where thousands of
yards of matting of all descriptions are warehoused.
Large bales lie ready to be despatched to New
York, San Francisco, and other remote corners of
the earth, showing that the commercial connection
of the prison is a very extensive one.   Mat-making, I
learn from a paper read by Captain Armytage, the
Governor of the Prison, before the Social Science
Congress, in 1873, was introduced into the West
Riding Prison so far back as 1841, and since 1848
the large sum of £147,652, after paying all expenses,
has been earned by the prisoners in this establishment, chiefly by mat-making.   The amount of the
prisoners' earnings last year was £7405 10s. 4d.; in
addition to which it was estimated that work had
been done for the prison by miscellaneous industries
to the value of £2672 8s. 2d., making the total
earnings for the year £10,077 18s. 6d.   Formerly
there was little else than penal labour, entirely

unproductive, engaged in in prisons, and even now
the law only tolerates, and does not fully recognise,
industrial labour in gaols. Wakefield Prison, however, has been a pioneer establishment, and to it
the mat-making trade owes its entire development.
After success had attended the introduction of the
trade into the West Riding Prison, people outside
took up the business, and they have now the
audacity to denounce the prison competition as
unfair to them, forgetting that the prisoners were
the first in the field. Mat-making is peculiarly
adapted to prison labour ; it is readily learned, and
the material is so cheap that the worker, however
wilful or stupid, cannot commit serious waste or
damage. Prisoners with distinct trades in their
fingers — such as shoemakers, tailors, joiners,
coopers, smiths, painters, dyers, &c.—are, after
serving the preliminary term prescribed by the
Prisons' Act, put to their own occupations; but all
prisoners, in the early part of their confinement,
are set to the mat-making, and the great majority
of them never do anything else during the whole
term of their incarceration. I inspected the black-
smiths' shop, the dyehouse, and other detached
workplaces, where the prisoners seemed to apply
themselves as closely as if a glass of ale and a
pipe of tobacco awaited them. What would the
majority of them not give for just one pipe of

the delicious weed! No privation comes so hard
to many of them as the enforced abstention from
tobacco.

The prisoners are not permitted to lapse into
idleness. At half-past five in the morning, a bell
rings for them to leave their hammocks, and at six
they commence their day's labour. From half-past
seven to eight they breakfast; from one to two
they have dinner; and at seven p.m. their day's
work ends, and they have supper served. In two
hours more, at nine o'clock, they turn into their
hammocks to sleep—perhaps to dream of the day
of deliverance, of the time when language will be of
use to them again, of the time when they will be
free to begin a new career or to lengthen out the old
one, as inclination or circumstances may permit.
This is the prisoner's daily round, or rather week-
day-ly round, except that he passes a portion of
every twenty-four hours in school, chapel, or parade
ground, as the regulations of the House may
prescribe.

The Treadmill was a place which I regarded with
considerable curiosity. Wakefield and the treadmill had always been inseparably associated in my
mind; indeed, I am not sure that before I entered
the house I did not expect to see half the inmates
of the prison climbing the interminable and historic staircase. I remember, anent the treadmill, a

story which presented some amusing features to me until the day of my visit, when I immediately saw its utter impossibility. A certain doctor (so the story went) was passing near the House of Correction one day when a just-liberated prisoner stepped up to him and implored him in the most piteous terms to treat him to a glass ef beer, frankly acknowledging that he had but a few minutes before terminated a three months' sentence, that he had no money, and that he was dying to drink. "If you'll only do this, sir, I'll tell you something that'll be of great service to you," the man said. The doctor yielded, and had the satisfaction of seeing a fellow-creature enjoy a draught of beer as much as if it had been the nectar of the gods, whatever that might have been. When he had finished, the man said, "I thank you, sir, from the bottom of my heart, and what I don't mind telling you is this, that when you go on the treadmill always take the side next to the wall, it's a sight the best, and helps you wonderfully." Now, when I got to the treadmill I found first that there was no wall to get hold of anywhere, and that, instead of seeing half the prisoners tramping up the hill to nowhere, I only saw about a dozen. But that dozen was enough to remember for a lifetime. The mill has accommodation for fifty-six climbers, twenty-eight on each side. A small engine is kept running with the wheels, as a sort of steadying power, but round and round the wheels go with a terribly persistent monotony. This work is only given as a punishment for some breach of the prison regulations, and it is so hard that only those men whom the doctor certifies as of first-class physical capabilities can be put to it. A grim warder stands over them watching every step they take. The front of the wheel is boxed off into compartments, each admitting of one treader only at a time, so that not only is a man unable to speak to, but he is unable to see any of his fellows. Complete isolation and thorough punishment are thus gained. A man who has to serve a day on the treadmill does six hours' getting upstairs without ever reaching the top. First, he goes on from a quarter past eight in the morning to a quarter to one, and in the afternoon he climbs from half-past two to four o'clock. The men are almost denuded of garments, for it is broiling work, even in the middle of winter. A rest of ten minutes is allowed for every half hour; half an hour on, ten minutes off. The ten minutes' rest is only about sufficient to permit of the half hour's floods of perspiration being mopped up. Virgilius directed me to mount the dreadful stairs and I obeyed. Appeal against his order I had none. I have in my time ascended mountains, mill chimneys, monuments, and other high places, but never did I make so tiresome an ascent as that of Mont Treadmill. My knees gave way in the first three minutes; in the next hundred seconds my ankles went; and then— and then—I made a rapid leap to *terra firma* and feinted. After that I went off with Virgilius, leaving the poor rascals apparently to "go on for ever," like Tennyson's brook.

The cooking establishment was the next department that I was introduced to, and, as dinner was just ready for serving, Virgilius commanded a plate of soup to be brought to me. It came, I saw, I conquered! I won't say that the table of my friend Smithkins does not offer greater culinary delicacies than the correctional soup, but I can vouch that the latter is at least wholesome and eatable, which, I can fancy I hear some prosecutor saying, is more than the fellows deserve. If any of my readers desire to know how to make this cheap and nutritious dish, here is a list of the ingredients. For each pint of soup:—Meat and liquor from 6 oz. beef, weighed with bone, 1 oz. onions, 1 oz. Scotch barley, 3 oz. peas, and 16 oz. potatoes, all weighed previous to cooking. The other articles of diet used in the Wakefield Prison are chiefly suet pudding, gruel, and bread. A 1 lb. suet pudding contains $1\frac{1}{2}$ oz. of suet, $6\frac{1}{2}$ oz. of flour, 8 oz. of water. It used to be generally understood that the gruel or "skilly" was manufactured thus:—One quart of water boiled down to a pint; sufficient for one meal. The fact is, however, that 2 oz. of oatmeal are used per pint. There are four classes of diet, varying with the length of a prisoner's stay. The first week he is limited to the Drab diet; 6 oz. bread for breakfast; 6 oz. bread, 6 oz. flour made into pudding, 1 oz. treacle, for dinner; and 6 oz. bread for supper. Then comes the Blue diet, after the first week, when gruel, cheese, and potatoes enter into the bill of fare. After a month, and up to the third month, the Red diet, introducing suet pudding, comes in; and after three months it is always the Yellow diet, when the prisoner can regale upon 8 oz. bread, a pint of gruel, and an ounce of treacle for breakfast, and so on. Prisoners who come for ten days and under are rather indifferently treated, their diet consisting of a pint of gruel for breakfast and supper, and 16 oz. of bread for dinner daily. I was privileged to watch the cooks making dinner for their 1200 guests. They seemed to be steaming potatoes by the ton, and while I was there half a dozen men were engaged stirring several reservoirs full of soup. There were prisoner-cooks, as well as professionals. Everything was scrupulously clean, however; the copper and tin lids "shone as any glasse," as did the head of Chaucer's hero. From the soup kitchen we naturally went to the bake-house, where fine white loaves were piled up in waggon loads. A sack of flour is baked in each oven at one fell swoop, and a sack averages 175 loaves, each 2 lb. 2 oz. in weight. The day previous to my visit, the bakehouse had turned out 1036 loaves, from six sacks (120 stones) of flour. The bread is made on the aërated principle, and is considered quite equal to any that is baked.

I now tried to realise what a prisoner's Sunday would be like. I visited the Church, and also the Catholic Chapel and the Confessional. In the Church 700 persons can be accommodated at once. Three services take place every Sunday, and it will be readily believed the Chaplains have plenty of hard work to do in ministering to their sinful flocks both week days and Sundays. It is during the time of worship, if at any time, that a prisoner finds an opportunity of speaking to a comrade. If instead of "Good Lord deliver us" he chooses to say, "How long have you got to stay?" and if instead of "We beseech Thee to hear us, good Lord," the reply of "I go out to-morrow week, my boy," is substituted, there seems little chance of detection. I also visited the dark cells, the baths, the spacious garden, the consultation rooms, &c., &c., and saw the outside of the hospital, where some sixty prisoners were confined. The number of deaths and births in the prison are about equal, averaging twenty-five per annum.

And now, by certain arts and wiles known only to myself, I get Virgilius to grant me leave of absence, and I at once make arrangements for regaining my freedom.   Ordinary prisoners have to see both the doctor and the chaplain before being released, and those gentlemen report upon the physical and moral health of their patients. After that the prisoners are put in their own clothes, and at eight o'clock in the morning are permitted to depart. Virgilius relieved me of these formalities and I left him, very favourably impressed with the able and efficient control exercised over this monster prison-house, covering over twenty acres of ground, by the Governor and his staff.   The cost of keeping up so extensive a concern is very great, and it would be much greater but for the admirable arrangements that are in force for making the most that can be made of the labour power of the prisoners.   For the year ending September 30th, 1873, the total expenditure was £27,734 5s. 0d., the average cost per prisoner being £23 16s. 11¼d., or, deducting the average earnings of the prisoners, £17 9s. 7¼d.   From a record of the year 1821, I find that in that year the total expenditure was only £4918 10s. 9¾d.

Two excellent Industrial Homes, one for males and one for females, exist in Wakefield.   They are indirectly connected with the House of Correction, and every discharged prisoner has the privilege of entering. The Home for Males is self-supporting; the Female Home relies largely on voluntary support. Both institutions are wisely conducted, and reflect great honour upon the charity and philanthropy of the ladies and gentlemen by whom they have been promoted,

And now I am in the streets of Wakefield once more, free as William Tell when he showed the crags and peaks the hands they first beheld. Leland, who visited Wakefield in the 16th century, describes it as "a very quick market toune, and meately large : well served of flesch and fische, both from the se and by rivers, whereof divers be thereaboute at hande. So that all vitail is very good chepe there. A right honest man shal fare well for 2 pens a meale." Leland would find matters very different now. I was well enough served both "of flesche and fische," and sundry other dainties, for the correctional soup, or something else, had whet my appetite, but I did not dine for anything like "2 pens."

I now summon the shades of John Howard and Mrs. Fry, and lay down my pen for a brief space.

A NIGHT WITH THE KING OF EGYPT.

IT is not every day in the week that one has the chance of making the acquaintance of a King or a Prince, such representatives of hereditary virtues keeping rather too much within their own divinity to let the hem of their garments flutter in the atmosphere of common life. I ought to consider myself as particularly fortunate, therefore, in that I actually met with and spoke to a sovereign potentate on a certain morning one winter, when old Father Christmas was only about four days off. The eminent personage with whom I met on that eventful morning was none other than His Majesty the King of Egypt.

The morning was peculiarly miserable. The "low-lying mists" and choking fogs which we had almost come to regard as immovable weather-incumbrances, as bad to get rid of as a rheumatic leg or a railing wife, had taken unto themselves wings and flown, leaving the streets they had vacated in the power of as relentless a snow-storm as Woolborough had been visited with for some time. Now, that inexorable fate in which most of us have some belief, ordained that I should be out in a certain suburban lane at three o'clock that very morning, and ordained also that the King of Egypt should be taking an airing there at the same time. It was, to say the least of it, an odd coincidence. In my own case, the performance of certain business duties had caused me to be there at that unearthly hour; but, with His Majesty, I fear it had been different. He had evidently been indulging in the " flowing bowl," and had in consequence been bowled over.

The snow, with an admixture of sleet, was driving very hard in my face at the time that I came up with His Majesty. The ground had a white coating several inches in thickness, and there being no track, no welcome preceding footsteps into which to place one's feet, my homeward progress was somewhat slow. I persevered, however, and, as each successive chime sounded from the ancient clock in the Parish Church tower, I found myself slightly in advance of the position I had held at the chiming of the previous quarter. So I struggled on until I neared the respectable region of Belle Vue, when, to my alarm, I saw a strange figure, attired in the most fantastic robes, standing up to the thighs in a snowdrift. A lamp close by enabled

I

me to see the figure more clearly, and anything
more grotesque, or less in keeping with the scene,
it would have been impossible to imagine. The hat
worn by this mysterious figure was, in appearance,
something between an academical cap and the head-
covering of a commander-in-chief. Over its shoulders was thrown a sort of mantle, and below that it
wore a spangled doublet and gabardine, and—
heaven save the mark !—corduroy trousers and
clogs !

In language something like that used by Thomas
Ingoldsby on first seeing " the vulgar little boy "
on Margate Jetty, I asked the figure what it did
there ?

Judge of my surprise when the mantled personage
immediately brandished a cutlass in the air, and
exclaimed,—

" I am the King of Egypt, as plainly doth
appear."

" Whether you're the King of Egypt or of Tim-
bucto," I said, " I'd advise you to get out of that
drift, unless you wish to be taken home on a
stretcher."

" I'm come to seek my son," he went on, " my
son and only heer."

" Then I don't think you're likely to find him
hereabout," I said, " so come along with me and I'll
put you into the right track."

" Well," he cried, putting up his cutlass and looking more amiable, " have you seen owt o' St. George ? "

" No."

" Or Slasher ? "

" No."

" Or Little Devil Doubt ? "

" Not one of them."

By this time I had begun to suspect that my new acquaintance was an escaped lunatic, though I could not imagine how he had come by his very strange garments. However, in common humanity, I was bound to preserve him from falling a victim to the inclemency of the morning, so I invited him to accompany me to my lodgings. In a while I succeeded in getting him to take hold of my arm, and I led him on to Grogram Terrace, where I reside. Long before we arrived there (and it was desperately dilatory work in the deep snow) I discovered that the King of Egypt—who could not be more than thirteen years of age—was in a very bad state of intoxication, the fumes of beer and smoke escaping from his lips in a particularly unpleasant way. Arrived at my lodgings, I conducted him to my sitting-room, placed him in one of Mrs. Blossom's hardest chairs, and turned up the gas, shutting the door carefully, so that the quiet, sleeping household should not be disturbed.

"Now, my friend," I said, calmly eyeing his pink calico mantle and his spangles, "I want to know positively who you are?"

"I am the King of Egypt, as plainly doth appear," he answered again.

"Indeed," I rejoined, drawing him a bottle of soda water and handing it to him, "and what about the Khedive and his suzerain the Sultan?"

"They don't belong to our lot," answered the King, drinking greedily.

Bit by bit his kingliness thawed, however, and at last I learned who and what he really was. His name was Georgy Martin, and his dwelling place White Abbey, one of the poorer quarters of the town. On the previous night, it appeared, he and a number of companions, who formed a mumming party, had gone to the further end of the town on a performing expedition, and one of their patrons had treated them with more malt liquor than was good for them. Georgy had got drunk and lost his mates, and was wandering helplessly in the direction of White Abbey when I fortunately came upon him, and saved him either from falling a victim to the snow or the policeman. Georgy was a " bobbin lad" at some factory, and remembered, as soon as he became sober, that he would have to be at his work at six o'clock that morning, and that his mother would probably " wollop" him when he reached home. Feeling really very much interested in the lad, I gave him another bottle of soda water, and volunteered to see him home. His tone and manner changed entirely, as he recovered his consciousness, and instead of the kingly imperiousness with which he assailed me at first, he addressed me with a much greater obsequiousness than ever I was able to command from any individual before. I saw him home, where his widowed mother, as might have been expected, was waiting up for him, weeping and lamenting. She did not "wollop" him, as he had prophesied, but thanked me most fervently for bringing her son home, and promised him he might stop from his work until breakfast time. I did not part from Georgy without getting him to arrange for me to go with their mumming party another night, being anxious to make the acquaintance of such eminent personages as St. George, Slasher, &c.

So it came about that on the Thursday night following I met Georgy again, and he took me to a cottage house in White Abbey, which served as the rendezvous of the mumming party. The house was that of a cobbler, who seemed to look upon the mummers as his pupils. "Now, my lads," he said, "this gentleman's goin' round wi' ye a bit, to-night, so ye must be careful what houses ye go to. Don't go anywhere where ye're likely to get kicked out;

take a public-house or two, they're the best. Are ye all here?" "All but Lord Bateman," said a feeble voice at the cobbler's elbow. "An' he's here an' all," said a little rosy-cheeked fellow who came bounding into the room at the moment. The *dramatis personæ* were now fully assembled and numbered some ten or a dozen lads, from ten to fourteen years of age. They were everyone factory lads and were decked, from the waist upwards, in gorgeous calicos and ribbons, which had been cut and trimmed by their sisters or mothers; but, strange to say, none of them had deemed it necessary to do anything on behalf of his nether . limbs, which were encased in the ordinary greasy garments of real life, contrasting grotesquely with the mantles, bucklers, sashes, and hats above them.

Well, we sallied forth, and were soon surrounded by enthusiastic hordes of urchins bent on "seein' t'mummers." There was a good deal of shouting and bustle, and a stranger might almost have fancied, had he been at a far enough distance, that the party was really going forth to sack some foeman's castle. I walked with the King of Egypt, and succeeded in worming from him some of the secrets of his bosom. Amongst other things, he assured me that St. George was the part which he ought to have taken, had full justice been done to his dramatic abilities; in fact, he begged to tell me that their present St. George was "nowt bud a duffer." He'd no conception of the character, and was "nowt o'clock wi' t'swerrd" (with the sword). We presently turned up into a back street, and there began an almost house-to-house call, much after the lively style adopted by the sweeps. " D' ye want t'mummers?" said the personage denominated the Fool, putting his head in at each door. The greetings with which he was met were various. "I'll mummers ye if ye arn't off!" cries one gruff voice, coming towards the door, and away they all scamper. " I'll thraw a bowl full o' watter on ye if ye don't cut," shrieks another voice. A third sets a dog at them; a fourth speaks not, but seizes the poker and rushes into the street after them, like an infuriated bull; a fifth says " Come at Kirsmas, an' ye'll be sooin eniff." But the mummers are a persevering race, not easily daunted by non-success, "so on, and on, and on " they go, like the good little boys and girls in the fairy tales, and are duly crowned with success in the end. " Let's try t'beershops," suggested Slasher, who remembered the parting words of the cobbler. We accordingly relinquished our house-to-house call amongst the cottages, and turned into the White Abbey Road and tried the houses of public resort, into one of which we at last gained admittance. "Come on, lads," shouted the Fool, "it's all reight," and in we crushed, with an immense number of boys at our heels.

"Mak as little muck as ye can, lads," said the landlady—a stout, brawny widow, with a bold face and a powerful arm.

" Come on, wi' ye !" cried a voice in the company.

" Can onny on ye sing ' Wild Shepherds ' ?" asked another voice.

"Let 'em begin wi' their actin'," said the landlady, as she brought in two foaming pints of liquor.

The drinking company was not of what we term the "respectable" type, most of the drinkers being addicted to very hard swearing and the expression of rather questionable sentiments. I had purposely come dressed in the most ordinary attire at my command—and my tailor would tell you that that is very ordinary attire indeed—but that it drew down on me the general contempt of the drinkers was obvious from their looks, and from the evident application to me of one or two obnoxious words from the slang vocabulary. But in the end they seemed to become oblivious of my presence, and went on with their confidential drunken chatter. I heard one ruffian swaggeringly assert to another— of course, he was terribly drunk—that he'd " smash her" when he got home. " She's actually had the impudence to meet me at t'miln gates an' ax me for some brass, d—— her."

The Fool now advances into the middle of the sanded floor, but before he begins, one of the drinkers asks, "Who's that, then?"

"That's t'Fooil," answers St. George.

"An' begow, he lewks it," added the questioner.

"Room, room, brave gallants, give us room to sport," cries the Fool—

> "For to this room we wish for to resort,
> Resort, and to repeat to you our merry rhyme,
> For remember, good sirs, this is Christmas his time."

He concludes by calling upon St. George to step in and clear the way; and that celebrated champion, bedight in calico and spangles, and see-sawing the air with a broad-sword, takes the place vacated by the Fool.

"I yam Sint Jarge," he says, "who from ould Ingland sprung."

"Nivver i' this world," rudely interrupted a drinker, "it's ould *Ireland* thah means; but go on."

St. George repeats in the most emphatic style that he "from ould Ingland sprung," and modestly adds that—

> "My famous name throughout the world hath rung.
> Many bloody dades and wonders have I made known,
> And made false ty-a-rants tremble on their thrawn."

Thus he goes on until, in justice to his own merits,

he is compelled to sum up his character by declaring that—

> "A man to hayqual me I've never found."

Then enters the renowned Slasher, whose voice is feeble in the extreme, and always sounds to be " in the distance." Slasher's sisters have been better needlewomen than the sisters of his sainted opponent, consequently his spangles and finery appear far more brilliant. Slasher begins by a few tall statements about his valour and his fame, and has the effrontery to tell the dragon-slayer that—

> "For to fight with me I see thou art not able,
>   So with my trusty sword I soon will thee disable."

St. George resents such language as this, and exclaims—

> "Dishable ! dishable ! It lies not in thy power,
> For with my glittering sword and spare I soon will thee devour."

He then threatens to break Slasher's head ; after which he suddenly runs and asks a friend in the background to tie him his " finger-poke," a cotton finger-bag which seems to cover a recently-acquired wound. While St. George is thus getting his wounds bound up, Slasher makes the following astounding statement :—

> "My head is made of iron,
>   And my body's made of steel ;
>   My hands and feet of knuckle-bone,
>   An' that'll let 'em feel !"

Then ensues a fierce hand-to-hand sword encounter between St. George, with his "finger-poke" adjusted, and Slasher. "Two up an' two dahn," whispers the latter to the former as they begin, and they dash at each other's swords with a fury which draws forth the appreciative applause of the audience. By-and-bye, however, Slasher looks, for a moment, at the sanded floor in a business-like way and lies down upon it, St. George slinking off as if he had some misgivings as to the exact state of the law with regard to homicide. The Fool re-appears . at this critical juncture and, alluding to the dead Slasher as his "chiefest son," offers ten pounds for a doctor, and immediately a sort of mountebank Esculapius pops in and undertakes the job of restoring the deceased Slasher, with his iron head and steel body, to life. The Doctor's speech is intensely amusing, and he speaks it, "not tripplingly upon the tongue," but in a steady, spasmodic fashion, placing a very strong emphasis upon, or almost giving two distinct pronunciations to, every third or fourth syllable, and gliding almost imperceptibly over the rest. The Fool asks him what's his fee?

"TEN pounds is my FEE, but Jack if THOU be an honest MAN I'll only TAKE five of THEE."

The Fool says, "You'll be wondrous cunning if you get any aside;" mistaking, as I suppose, the stage direction "aside" for a part of his speech.

At this point the dead Slasher shows signs of returning animation, lifts his head up and whispers to a boy standing near, "Lend us thy cap, Bill; it's blessed hard ligging a' t'top o' this here sand." Bill grants the request and the play proceeds.

The Doctor then informs the audience that he has travelled in Italy, Titaly, High Germany, France, and Spain, and declares that he can cure all sorts of diseases.

"What's all sorts?" asks the Fool.

"The itch, the pitch, the palsy, and the gout," cries the Doctor, "If a man gets nineteen devils in his skull I'll cast twenty of them out." He then talks of having crutches for lame ducks, spectacles for blind humble-bees, &c., &c., and finishes by offering a bottle for Slasher to drink from. Of course Slasher is resuscitated, and seems ready to meet St. George again, who enters at that moment. Slasher, at this juncture, says something about hearing a silver trumpet, and instead of rushing upon his ancient foe, he sneaks away, in company of the Doctor and the Fool, leaving St. George to do a little more of his own biography.

"I yam Sint Jarge!" begins the champion.

" So thah's tell'd us afore, ye clahtheead," cries a voice near the fire, "be sharp, an' get on wi' thy feightin'."

Nothing daunted, England's patron saint resumes,

"I yam Sint Jarge, that nowble champion bowld,
An' with my trusty sword I won tin thousand pounds in
    gowld;
'Twas I that fought the fiery dragon, an' brought him to the
    slaughter,
An' by those means I won the King of Egypt's daughter."

No sooner has he said this than he is confronted with another foe, who evidently ought to be a black man, but isn't. This personage tells us that he is the "Black Prince of Paradine, born of high renown," and he swears to "fetch St. George's lofty courage down;" in fact, he asserts that not only will he kill him, but he'll make him "die to all eternitee." St. George calls him a "black Morocco dog," at which the drunken wife-beater before alluded to sings out, "That's it, lad, intul him; say it agean an' give it him wi' t'bit o' t'top." St. George and the "black Morocco dog" then have a "set to," and the latter is defeated and lays himself down upon another borrowed cap. "Thah lewks weel nah, Johnny," cries a bold-faced girl, who was peeping over the heads of the boys in the passage, "I'll go an' fetch yar Sarah to lewk at thee. Keep deead whol ah come back."

St. George now commands the people at large to take the Prince of Paradine "and give him to the flies."

"That he may nevermore come near my yighs."

There is no immediate response to this command,
but my old acquaintance, the King of Egypt,
Georgy Martin, comes upon the scene and repeats
the statement that he had so much astonished me
with on our first meeting in the snow-drift. He
says :—

> "I yam the King of Egypt, as plainly doth appear,
> I come to seek my son, my son an' only heer."

St. George coolly informs His Majesty that his
only son and heir is slain, and the King asks,
"Whom did him slay, whom did him kill?" The
champion then boldly asserts that he was the
perpetrator of the crime, and adds,

"Had you been there you might have fared the
same."

"See thee!" the voice of the bold-faced girl was
heard to say just then, for she had returned with
the Prince of Paradine's sister, "he's thear, laid o'
t'floor."

"Eh, Johnny," said the sister, "I'd noan ha'
been at all t'pains 'at I wor to mak thee them cloas,
if I'd known they were nobbut to lig dahn in."

"Shut up wi' tha," groaned the Prince, "it's i'
t'piece; isn't it?"

To return to the King of Egypt and St. George.
The King tells St. George that he is a "cursed
Christian," and that he has ruined him and slain
his only son, and concludes by calling upon Hector

to "fight and kill at his command." Now, Hector, as soon as he came on, convinced me that he was too weak a person to cope successfully with a man of such valour and prowess as St. George. He spoke in the most perfect sing-song and the broadest Yorkshire dialect. He told St. George that he'd make his blood "run like Noah's flood," but everybody felt that he was making a very rash assertion. St. George told him not to be so bold, and threatened to send him to Black Sam before he was "three days old," probably meaning "three days older," though as to the whereabouts of "Black Sam" I am profoundly ignorant. Hector hereupon asserts that *his* head, like Slasher's, is made of iron, his body made of steel, and his "hands and feet of knuckle-bone." Then the two fight, long and desperately, St. George again proving victorious.

"How much longer are ye goin' to be?" says the landlady, who looks in at this point, and is evidently beginning to think that her beer is not going off so rapidly as it ought to do.

"We'se have done in a minute or two," says Slasher, who is standing near.

Hector is not slain like the others; but being wounded, thinks he has had enough of it, and pretends to hear a silver trumpet in the distance, and sneaks off. Mr. Fool now re-appears, and

makes an appointment to meet St. George, "across
the water at the hour of five;" after which he
is left alone, the dead Prince of Paradine and
the King of Egypt having taken themselves
away.　The Fool calls upon Little Devil Doubt
to "enter and clear the way;" whereupon a
four-year-old boy, carrying a small besom over
his shoulder, comes into the centre of the room,
and says, "Here tome I, ikkle Divvle Doubt; if
roo don't divv me money, I'll sweep roo all out.
Money I want, an' mo-ney I trave, if roo don't
divv me money, I'll sweep roo all to de drave!"
The mummers showed their knowledge of the
public taste to a nicety by this attempt to introduce an infant prodigy into their ranks.　The
applause bestowed upon the child was immense,
and the cap he carried round for coppers was
very extensively patronised.　Many of the drinkers
offered ale to the mummers to drink, but I
prevailed upon the King of Egypt to resist any
such temptation.

After leaving the beerhouse, the mummers proceeded to other houses of a similar description, but
while I remained with them, they did not gain a
second permission to perform.　They were generally
run out of the houses as if they had been stray
dogs, and treated ignominiously.　But they bore
their ill-treatment very meekly, and the King of

Egypt told me, in confidence, that they expected, before Christmas was over, to make three or, perhaps, four shillings a-piece!

Such was my experience of mumming in the present year of grace.

In the olden times, when the wassail-bowl formed so prominent a part in our Christmas revels, the mummers were welcome guests both in palace and hall. Wither quaintly sings :—

> " Some youths will now a-mumming go,
> Some others play at Rowland-hoe,
> And twenty other gambols moe,
>   Because they will be merry."

There are several versions of the rude drama acted by the mummers at Christmas-tide, but they are all based on the same model, one outline has served for every one. Such variations as exist are probably due to a desire to give local or political colour to the piece. For instance, in the North of Ireland, St. Patrick and Oliver Cromwell are added to the *dramatis personæ*, and we find the Lord Protector vaunting himself thus :—

> " Here come I, Oliver Cromwell, as you may suppose,
> I conquered many nations with my copper nose,
> I made my foes for to tremble and my enemies for to quake,
> And beat my opposers till I made their hearts to ache."

Who the author of the original Peace Egg was history has not recorded, the immortality of his work, however, is ensured.

K

THE NIGHT TRIP TO LONDON.

HE void that there would be in English conversation were the weather to become a forbidden topic, is terrible to contemplate. What a great calamity it would be to all of us were we not able to use it as a justification of many of our actions. At least, such was my opinion as I sat in my quiet room one night in July, trying to invent some means of escape from the intolerable heat that had settled around me. With the thermometer at eighty odd in the shade, a man might be excused for doing almost any ridiculous thing short of highway robbery, or slandering a Town Councillor. To rest indoors with the "sweat of your brow" trickling down your sun-burnt cheeks was a matter of impossibility. You felt oppressed by tropical laziness, as well as by tropical heat, and did nothing to-day which could be left undone while to-morrow. The shopkeepers even seemed to flag in their exertions to be courteous to their customers, and sat in the coolest shade their premises

afforded, allowing such business as might come
their way to follow them thither. But the spectacle
of the town by night during these melting times
was something still more oppressive to the senses.
Door-steps, yard-walls, tops of alleys, scraps of
greensward, and edges of mill-dams were eagerly
seized upon as lounging ground ; and the consumption of ginger-beer, cider, lemon-kali, and (last,
though not least) beer, was such as to yield to the
dealers in those liquids a collective fortune. Every
one succumbed, more or less, to the influences of
"old Sol," except the cricketing race, which suc-
cumbs to nothing except frost and snow and
unseemly disputes. My deliberations on the heat
question, however, finally brought me to the determination to go under cover of the night to the great
metropolis. So it came about that at midnight on
the very next Sunday I and my fellow-wanderer
and accomplice, Barnacles, stood on the Midland
Station platform at Woolborough fully equipped for
a night journey to town. I had induced Barnacles
to accompany me on my dark expedition by picturing it to him as a new travelling sensation, as well
as an easy means of escape from the burning heat.
Sceptic on most points but actual £ s. d., Barnacles
could not be expected to believe that amusement
and enjoyment could be found in a midnight excursion, so I cannot help regarding myself somewhat

in the light of a conqueror at having subdued such a mass of matter-of-fact humanity into joining me.

The station front did not present a very lively appearance. The cabmen had long since departed without catching any double fares, the shoeblacks had vanished, and even the refreshment-room could not show a sufficient number of customers to keep the two chatty waitresses in full employment. A locomotive or two panted, groaned, and lazily whistled from time to time within the station, and a few passengers and a porter or two moved mysteriously about, but beyond that there was little noise or commotion of any kind. The passengers looked more like a party of smugglers or spies than anything else, displaying capacious throat-wrappings and suspicious-looking head gear. There was no crowding at the ticket-window, and no ear-splitting invitations by porters that we would betake ourselves to a certain platform in preference to any other. We wandered at our own sweet will, treading softly, speaking in whispers, and looking things unutterable. The station-master was on duty, flitting about, exhibiting a suave authority, and allowing us the benefit of his careful surveillance. The train was some dozen carriages in length, but the number of occupants was by no means large at starting. My friend and I (our motives being to gain experience even at the

sacrifice of pleasure) got into a third-class compartment, and there made the acquaintance of a bevy of
female Cockneys, whose ingratitude to the county
of their adoption, which had in all probability fed
and clothed them when their native metropolis had
declined to do so any longer, was shown by the
attempts they made to deprecate the Yorkshire
people by laughing at their industry. "On'y
fency," said one shrewish female, speaking to a
young mother beside her, "what the Yorkshire
husbands 'll do! They'll go work from six in the
morning till six at night, and then set to and help
to wash up the pots and polish the stoves. Oh!
they're fine old mollycoddles, ain't they?" Then
there was a good hearty laugh all round. They
continued their slanderous jocularities until Barnacles said he could stand them no longer. I tried
to get him entangled in their conversation, but it
was no use; they had incurred his disgust by their
empty twaddle, and therefore he persistently
ignored their voluble attempts to gain over his
sympathy. At Jipley Station we took up a
large number of jovial passengers, let loose from
the Tide, but, unfortunately for us, none of them
found their way into our carriage. The ladies
did not prohibit smoking, so cigars were brought ·
into use by way of consolation, and thus we went
on, amidst the hubbub of female voices and the

rumbling of wheels, to Allwool, without stoppage.
Our engine led us grumblingly through Shackley
Tunnel, and then on past Capperley and its sleeping villas, Halverley and its still woods, Mirkstall
and its glaring forge and grand old Abbey ruin,
until at last the brick wilderness of Allwool enclosed our living freight. Here we escaped from our
female persecutors and entered another third-class
carriage, which contained a number of Allwool
people and a single couple from Jhipley. A wonderful picture was revealed here. Health and sickness, jollity and sorrow, pecuniary ease and extreme
poverty, maiden modesty and married familiarity,
age and youth were all represented in this one carriage. A haggard, care-worn woman, with a baby
at her breast, sat in one corner, and three other
little ones, ranging from eight to four years of age,
clustered round her, unconscious of the trouble by
which they were beset, and totally unable to realise
their unhappy situations. Children, happily, live
only in the present, and these three half-clad
young ones could think of nothing but the railway
train, and the long ride they were going to have.
Their eyes beamed with pleasure as soon as the
train started, and they danced and clapped their
hands in appreciation of the new sensation, for, as
their mother told us, they had never ridden on a
railway before. Before we reached Normanton,

however, all but the eldest boy had tumbled off to
sleep, lying upon the bare seats without covering or
pillow of any kind.   The mother was, at this point,
induced to tell us her pitiful story.   It appeared
that she had just been left a widow, and that she
and her children were quite unprovided for.   Being
a Jewess, she imagined that by going to London
and laying her case before her brethren there, she
might be able to get three of her children admitted
into some Jewish charity school, and then she could
return to Allwool and earn sufficient to support herself and the baby by sewing.   I asked her if she
belonged to London.   "No, sir," she replied; "I
don't like the big city.   I could not bear to live
there myself."   Everyone in the carriage showed a
disposition to be compassionate and charitable to
the poor woman, not forgetting a certain young
man who had escaped from Jhipley Tide in a rather
befuddled condition, and whom I will take the
liberty of calling Smasher.   Smasher enjoyed the
very free run of three separate glass bottles, containing alcoholic liquids of different colours, the
two largest of which he nourished near his bosom
in two capacious pockets, and the other was kept in
charge by a bright-eyed country damsel, who was
going sweethearting with him to the great city.
Smasher drank the health of the widow and her
children with a warmth and a frequency which

spoke better for his heart than his head, and, to
prove his undoubted good fellowship, he persisted
in each one that he toasted drinking with him.
There were four other passengers in our division
of the train. One was a tall, melancholy-looking
personage, with a face that would have done honour
to Sir Walter Scott's Edgar of Ravenswood,
Maturin's Bertram, or that most melancholy of all
melancholy people, Kotzebue's Stranger. His
gloomy expression was only a freak of nature, however, for he turned out to be a jolly companion,
and sang us one or two comic songs in a style
immeasurably superior to that of the ordinary
music-hall singer. The others were—an ancient
individual, whose thoughts seemed to run mainly
upon mangel-wurzels and corn; a youth who
chuckled immensely at every bit of a joke that was
perpetrated; and a lawyer's clerk, who was going
to London in search of that tide which Shakspeare
advises us to take at the flood. But Morpheus
turned out to be master of the ceremonies in our
carriage, and one by one the passengers went off to
sleep, with the exception of Barnacles, myself, the
widow, and her eldest boy. The widow was in
great agony during the best part of the journey,
being a severe sufferer from sickness, and the boy
was obliged, as long as he could keep his eyes open,
occasionally to relieve his mother from the care of

the baby. Thus we went on to Sheffield, dividing
our attention between the life that was within and
the apparent deadness that was without, relieved
now and then by the sudden leaping up of
immense tongues of flame from furnace mouths and
cinder ovens, giving views of weird grandeur
which the pencil of a Doré only could pourtray.
At Sheffield we took up another supplement of
passengers, and, leaving our companions, who were
now waking from their slumbers and stretching
out their arms in search of their bottles, we betook
ourselves to another third-class carriage, in search
of further experience. Having made our choice,
and deposited our scanty stock of luggage in our
new lodgment, Barnacles and I, and almost all the
other male passengers, ran off to the refreshment
bar, where three or four young ladies, attired with
as much neatness and with as due a regard to
fashionable hair-dressing as if they had been pre-
siding at a wedding party, dispensed tea, coffee,
buns, and sandwiches at exorbitant prices. There
was no time for chaff or banter. The waitresses
meant money, and the customers meant food
and drink, and nothing else. The head-gear of
the passengers was of the most various description, from the fez to the turban, from the old
"billycock" to the cricketing cap, the rolled
up pocket handkerchief to the white night-

cap. Long before the wants of the passengers
had been supplied, the bell was rung, and
those who were going on were asked to take their
places. There was then such a running to and fro,
such shoutings for Bills, Jacks and 'Toms, such
jumping into wrong carriages, such shrieking of
affectionate wives for missing husbands as I never
heard before. " Hear them," said Barnacles, " I'll
be bound the same women were calling their spouses
the cruelest wretches living but a short time back,
and wishing them at the furthest end of the earth."

Gaining our last-selected carriage, the number of
which Barnacles had carefully noted, we found that
we had dropped upon a musical party. There was
a middle-aged barrister, who was running up to
London to advocate somebody's cause before a
metropolitan judge the next morning. There was
a young couple going up to win fresh laurels in a
London Music-hall, and there was also a young man
with a concertina. These, together with Barnacles,
combined a choir of no small importance for a night
train. The barrister sang in German and Italian,
and displayed a musical capacity much beyond the
ordinary drawing-room quality; the concertina
player sang " Dubalin Bayah," and accompanied
himself in a jerky fashion, except when he came to
the affecting passage where " the ship went daywn,"
and there the pathos was so deep that he stopped

his instrument, closed his eyes, and looked as
sublime as an expiring duck.   The company, however, roused him up with singing a chorus, and he
jerked a polka out of his instrument by way of
compliment.   Barnacles now sang the " Pilgrim of
Love," and I wish Sims Reeves had been there to
hear him, that is all.   More in the way of criticism
of my friend's singing, I decline to say at present.
After an interval employed in telling humorous
stories, asking conundrums, chaffing an old woman
who seemed to regard all the singing and merriment
as a personal affront to herself, and eating and
drinking and helping our companions to eat and
drink, a tall young man with a Hibernian accent
offered to recite a poem by O'Donovan Rossa.   One
or two objected to any display of Irish patriotism,
and we were in danger of drifting into a discussion
on Home Rule, had not the barrister interceded for
the Irishman and got him a hearing.   The reciter
was in dreadful earnest when he did begin, and spat
and threw his clenched fists about with much vigour.
The poem was full of allusions to the poor oppressed
Irish people and their Saxon tyrants, but I fear the
company did not thoroughly appreciate it.

At Leicester we sought hurriedly for another
resting-place, but we were so long in making a
choice that in the end we were obliged to take
refuge in the carriage we had quitted at Sheffield.

The widow's children were still fast asleep, but the other tenants of the carriage were in a more wakeful condition than we had left them. Smasher was fully roused, and had evidently determined to be the central figure of the group. He had a short stick in his hand, with which he belaboured the seat and the carriage sides, by way of giving emphasis to his language. "Hay, lass," he said, addressing his ladye-love with a look of coarse, though probably sincere, endearment, "I'll mak' a man o' thee this time. I've wanted ho'd o' thee this long while, an' by t'megs I've gotten tha nah. Ther's nowt so shewer as that; nowt i' this world. If ivver thah goes back fro' London o' twelve months I'll eyt my booits, ther's nowt so shewer as that." Then he knocked his stick, stamped his feet, and laughed so heartily that he set the compartment laughing with him. Smasher's young lady was a little bewildered by this kind of talk, and it was plain to see she thought there *might* be something more than a joke in it. The mangel-wurzel man began to talk of the country we were going through (the morning having dawned), and pointed in admiring earnestness at the fields of corn and beans we passed. "What's them?" he asked of Smasher as we hurried through a field of mangel-wurzels. "Aw, 1 knaw what them is, they're mangel-wurzels, nowt so shewer as that," replied Smasher; then, pointing to a small, out-lying village, he continued, " but ye don't knaw what yond is." The mangel-wurzel individual acknow-ledged that he did not. Smasher then mentioned the name of the village, and gave a brief description of all the chief towns in England which he had honoured with his presence at different times. After this he drained the contents of his largest bottle, and pitched it out of the window, saying, with a sly look at his sweetheart, "Nowt 'at comes wi' me ivver hez to go back agean; nowt so shewer as that." Then he of the rueful visage sang another comic song about Barney M'Something, and Smasher joined in the chorus, and danced and capered about with much agility. Smasher then felt called upon to pay some attention to his lady, and he apostrophised her in this wise :—"Dash tha, lass, thart a grand 'un. It 'ud nivver dew to let a fine young woman like thee go back agean." This concluded, with all due accompaniments of hand-pattings and cheek-strokings, he turned to the serio-comic individual and said, " I'll tell ye what, maister, ye'd nivver dew for this lass, ye're noan hauf handsome eniff for her, ther's nowt so shewer as that. Yer nose is too long, for one thing; look at me, this is the sort, ther's nowt so shewer as that." The poor widow in the corner, even, was forced into an occasional laugh, and the two children who had been longest asleep woke up, and appeared to enjoy the noise. All this time we were passing through a tract of beautiful country, which has been described over and over again. Away we scampered, as if fleeing from some deadly enemy, over fields yellow with the ripening corn, fields dotted with sheep nibbling the dew-moistened grass and cows carelessly browsing, many hours before the work-a-day world began. But by half-past four o'clock we saw farm labourers in the field, gathering in the hay, and the appearance of one or two women in a potato-field at that hour caused some little surprise amongst us, until Smasher told us that he had often seen women at work " an hahr sooiner nor that; nowt so shewer as that." The time from half-past four to half-past six hung heavily, and I should be ashamed to confess the number of times that I referred to my watch during that period. Barnacles was not himself at all. He could neither go properly to sleep, nor yet keep himself awake. So we went wearily onward, until the suburbs of the metropolis began to show themselves, when we took heart, and talked of our plans for the day. We began to arrange our toilettes, as far as we possibly could, and in due time we found ourselves ready to face the eyes of the vast metropolis. I am glad to be able to state that Smasher showed the goodness of his heart by being handsomely charitable to the poor widow, and that others in the carriage also assisted her, and when we left her she gave us many earnest thanks in return for our sympathies. St. Pancras Station received us at twenty minutes past seven—ten minutes before the advertised time of arrival—and, although our ride had been in many respects more enjoyable than we had anticipated, we were fain to leap upon the platform and feel ourselves free to walk.

What hotel Barnacles and I patronised for breakfast and ablutions, what places of amusement we visited, and what we ate, drank, and avoided that day, are matters with which I do not propose to deal in this sketch, my sole object being to describe the journey to London and back by night.

At half-past eleven, then, that same Monday night, we again stood upon the St. Pancras platform, ready to depart from busy London and hurry back to our "native heath," loving it none the less for our brief sojourn amongst the splendour and vastness of the capital. We had the satisfaction of seeing Smasher and his lady, looking much more subdued than they had been in the morning. The former declared that he had been everywhere, that nobody could lose him in London, that he wanted to go to sleep, and that there was "nowt so shewer as that." We did not join Smasher and Co. in the down journey, much as they had excited our

admiration in the morning, but we got into a carriage occupied by a very miscellaneous company.
In our compartment were:—an old Yorkshirewoman,
who "reckoned nowt" of the Crystal Palace; her
niece, a robust young woman, with an engaged ring
upon her finger, and a disconsolate look in her eyes;
another niece, married, with one of her offspring
nestling at her side; and a meek and mild young
man, also a family connection, who always coincided
with all that was said, and smiled with an amiability
which might be hereditary, but was not pleasant.
At the carriage window, before we started, stood an
elderly female relative and two younger feminine
offshoots of the family, who had evidently come
with the intention of making an elaborate display of
affection.   The elderly female put her head into
the window and whimpered, "Kiss me, Angelina."
Angelina did not obey with as much promptitude
as might have been expected, nor, I am sorry to
say, did the others, who were similarly importuned.
The elderly relative then screwed up her face and
gasped, "I cannot help it," although it was not very
easy to understand what it was that she couldn't
help. At last, however, Barnacles discovered that
she had screwed half a tear into her left eye, and
he whispered, "She weepeth, by Jehosophat!"
"Yes," she went on, addressing her cheerful rela-
tives, "I know it's foolish, but I can't help crying

at a time like this." At all events, the woman was possessed of a strong sense of the requirements of the situation, and zealously strove to fulfil them. "There is a grief that's too deep for tears," I murmured across to Barnacles. He answered, "And it is plain there are tears which are too deep to be turned on without applying to the proper agent—the heart." In spite of all these outside whimperings, we got off with some near approach to punctuality, and then came the grand sleeping tournament. The amusement I enjoyed in watching my nodding fellow-passengers between St. Pancras and Wellingborough I shall not easily forget. The old lady disposed herself in one corner, with her shoeless feet resting lightly against my side; the meek young man sat opposite, and displayed a decided tendency to knock his head through the glass window. The unmarried niece threw her bonnet at her feet, divested herself of her boots, took down her chignon, folded her arms, and went to sleep in a truly business-like fashion. The married niece was weary unto death; her child fell from her knees once or twice, but she could not be wakened up sufficiently for her to realise the situation, so, in the end, the child had to be nursed by Barnacles. In the next compartment a little bushy-bearded man rested in one corner, and, as he slept, his head every now and then suddenly drooped

upon his breast; but the mischief of this sudden
drooping was that, having his hands in his
trousers pockets, he had forced a large, brown paper
parcel, which he carried in an inner coat pocket, so
far out that it stood in close proximity to his nose,
and, every time he drooped, that organ came into
collision with the parcel. But that was nothing; I
don't think the bite of a boa constrictor would have
roused him. Opposite to him sat a young married
woman and a young unmarried man. They both
tried to sleep in an erect position, i.e., without leaning their heads against anything; but, alas, all their
efforts were of no avail. Each of their heads slowly
drooped, and, as luck would have it, one towards
the other, and as often as they came into direct
contact so often did they lift them back to the
starting point and perform the same process. After
a while, however, the young woman's husband, who
up to that time had been resolutely trying to prop
a white pocket handkerchief between his head and
the carriage side, and had failed, came to her
rescue, and, with true self-denial, laid his head in
her neck, taking her shoulder for his pillow, and
thus effectually kept her head from drooping in
the direction of the head of the unmarried young
man, and also made a passable resting-place for his
own head. After reaching Wellingborough we
looked in at one or two other carriages, but the

experience was very nearly the same. Sleep, sleep, sleep. Barnacles and I then betook ourselves to a first-class compartment, and there slept in blissful unconsciousness until we arrived at Sheffield. Nothing else transpired worthy of record, and we arrived back in Woolborough shortly after seven o'clock on the Tuesday morning. To all those in search of a new experience, I would strongly recommend a long night trip. There are several lessons to be learned by it. It teaches you to love your neighbour; it tests your powers of physical endurance; it denudes you, for the time being, of false pride; and it gives you an insight into life which is not as easily obtainable under other circumstances.

ROUND THE MAY-POLE.

OT only does the old order change, "giving place to new," as the poet sings, but the new order changeth, giving place to old, and thus our tastes and habits are continually altering, fading and re-appearing, until we are at last forced to fall back upon the time-worn adage which tells us there is nothing new under the sun. At all events, in respect of May-day festivities we are at present making zealous endeavours to "advance backward," and to revive the customs of our progenitors of the seventeenth and eighteenth centuries. A few years ago, and the poets seemed in a fair way for getting the first of May entirely into their own hands; they sang as lustily as ever of May-queens, May-buds, May-blossoms, May's "jocund train," and the like; and almost the only attempts on the part of the general public to "hail the merry month of May" were evidenced by cart-drivers, who decked their animals and vehicles with gay ribbons, flowers, and rosettes in honour of the occasion. But latterly the citizens of Otley have shown a disposition to renew the ancient May-pole festivities, or the West Riding might soon have ceased to pay any respect whatever to what Tennyson terms "the happiest time of all the glad New Year."

Now, at Otley there has been a May-pole for about two hundred years, but the present generation has known little in connection with it, except that it has stood in the middle of the square, which once was a "green," looking like a forgotten mast, or like a greasy climbing pole for rustics to win legs of mutton upon. A few years ago the lightning struck the ancient pole, as if determined to destroy so useless a thing. It was then that the consciences of the Otley people seemed touched, and they began to repent of their neglect of the poor old May-pole. They then began to feel that some glory had appertained to the old pole, that it represented something in the past that it was a pity to let die, and that there was no reason in the world that they should not, if they chose, resuscitate the ancient May-day custom of which the pole had been the emblem. It was then remembered, probably, that these ancient rejoicings at the appearance of spring had existed amongst the Romans of old—even dating so far back as the half-mythical period of Romulus—that Cæsar's legions had introduced similar customs into

England, and that under the Tudors and the
Stuarts the crowning of the May-queen had been one
of the chief festivities of the year. Shakspeare, and
many contemporary writers, tell us of the pleasures
of May-day, and we read that in 1515 King Henry
VIII. and his court rode "a-Maying from Greenwich
to the top of Shooter's Hill." One of the most
beautiful and most familiar of ancient madrigals,
and one which our local choirs often render with
delicious fervour, is devoted to describing the
delights of "the month of Maying, when merry lads
are playing, Fa, la, la, la," &c. And as for the poets,
they not only seem to claim May as their special
source of inspiration in these latter days, but they
seem to have done so from the first. One of our
very few royal poets—James I. of Scotland—says:—

> "Worshippe, ye that lovers be, this May,
> For of your bliss the calends are begun;"

and Bishop Gawain Douglas, of the Eighth Henry's
time, describes Phœbus ushering May in with

> "Fiery sparkis brasting from his een,
> To purge the air and gilt the tender green."

And, coming down to more recent times, we find
Beattie even recommending the village swain and
"light of heart, the village maiden gay," to repair to
his minstrel's grave, where the maiden is besought—

> "To deck with flowers her half dishevel'd hair,
> And celebrate the merry morn of May."

May-day observances, indeed, seem to have been so thoroughly in accordance with English sentiment and feeling, that when the Otleyites came to reflect upon the business, they probably began to wonder that they had ever allowed the custom of crowning the May-queen to fall into desuetude. Subscriptions were asked for and readily obtained, and in due course a new May-pole rose in the old one's place, and Otley resumed its ancient May-day festivities.

Last year May-day fell on a Friday, but the Otleyites, in order to oblige their neighbours, thought well to defer their May-day rejoicing until Saturday; and in this they were wise. Cheap trips had been announced to run from various towns and villages in the Riding to Otley on Saturday afternoon, and it was really amazing to see what an immense number of people were seized with a desire to assist at the crowning of the Queen of the May. Several thousand persons went from Woolborough, and a very large number from Allwool and other places. It may be questioned whether a greater crowd was ever assembled in the quaint old town, famous for its butter and its "statutes." As usual, the railway officials at Woolborough were unprepared to cope with anything more than an ordinary afternoon's traffic, consequently there was a terrible scene of crowding, pushing, and confusion at the ticket windows. However, the

passengers by the trips were a good-humoured sort,
and put up with these inconveniences and annoyances with commendable quietude.   They were so
full of joyful expectation that they readily forgave
their persecutors, and when they passed out of the
station at Otley and joined the merry May-day
throng they looked as blithe and happy as if they
had had everything their own way.   Every public-
house was crammed with guests, every street was
thronged with waiting spectators, and every window
showed its group of faces looking down at the
crowd.   All—

> " Give themselves up to jollity,
> And with the heart of May
> Doth every breast keep holiday."

But there were plenty of evidences of May in
inanimate as well as animate nature.   The woods
and hedge-rows were bright with new foliage ; the
apple-trees and thorns " were in bridal white ; " and
the hyacinths and primroses in full, resplendent
bloom.   No wonder that the poets should bestow so
much praise upon the month of May when it brings
with it such a lavish dower of beauty and perfume.
Phœbus, too, as in Bishop Douglas's time, did
honour to the day by shining clearly and brightly,
but the " fiery sparkis brasting from his cen " were
very much subdued every now and again by the
insinuating breath of a cold east wind.   However,

in due time the expectant people were rewarded by
a sight of the May-day procession, which came on,
headed by the Brighouse Excelsior Band. Following the band were several "decorated teams and
waggons," and a number of mounted knights,
attended by "foot yeomen," in the garb of beef-
eaters. The members of the Otley Fire Brigade
came next, mounted on their engine. Then appeared a coal cart or two containing prominent
citizens, followed by two or three lorries full of
children, radiant in white dresses, and blue, pink
and green sashes, and looking very innocent and
very happy. At the heels of these came a "group
of ten Amazonian warriors" in tawdry dresses,
looking cold and wan. These ballet-girl warriors
would both have looked better and have felt more
comfortable in front of the Allwool footlights, where
their "charms" were accustomed to be displayed.
Next came the May-queen herself, her majesty and
the members of her court being drawn on a waggon.
The queen condescendingly sat on a kitchen chair,
and over her fair head was a rustic canopy, the
upholstery whereof was well suited to the royal
seat. The queen had been chosen to reign by the
popular voice; she was no mere claimant of hereditary honours. As she proceeded on her way she
was loudly cheered, but her extreme modesty
evidently prevented her bowing the usual acknow-

ledgments to right and left. She was attired in white robes, of course, and held in her hand a royal wand. Her maids of honour were of the rustic type, and formed an excellent sample of the rising beauty of Otley. Behind the queen's car there followed a waggonette containing a number of May-pole dancers, and in the rear of these came the court clown, the court pantaloon, Robert 999 (a mediæval "Bobby"), and a band of Bletherheads. The extreme tail of the procession was made up of "ten full privates of the awkard squad, mounted on ten splendid Jerusalem ponies." Many of the spectators seemed to recognise some familiar pantomime characters in these attendants upon the queen, and greeted them accordingly. There were people who imagined that the mixture of mockery and reality was uncalled for, and that the crowning of the queen ought to be made a more sincere business: but then there is no satisfying everybody, whatever one does. The procession moved merrily on through the principal streets of the town, round the new old May-pole and on to a field over the bridge where the coronation ceremony was to be performed. The people crowded in at the heels of the procession, everybody appearing anxious to do homage to her majesty. The waggons were brought to a halt on a high plateau, where a temporary May-pole had been erected; and there, after allowing sufficient time for the spectators to assemble (and pay their money), the signal was given for the ceremony to commence. A gentleman then advanced to the waggon where the royal lady reclined, and after making a brief speech, in which he adverted in the most complimentary terms to the grace, beauty, and goodness of the queen, he handed her a coronation cake, which had been presented by a neighbouring lady, and expressed his hope that her digestion would be good enough to allow her to enjoy it when she got home. A "village swain" then stepped forward, and, on bended knee, addressed the queen in the following doggerel :—

> "My gracious queen! here at thy feet
> Let me my new-made sovereign greet;
> Thousands here to-day have seen
> Our little, happy May-day queen,
> And every lass within the town
> Bids me give you the May-queen's crown ;
> Long may you wear it, too, with grace,
> An ornament to your bright face."

This done, the swain took the wreath from the fair brow of the queen and in its place put on "the May-queen's crown." Then the queen looked smilingly around and "the welkin" rang with the approving shouts of the assembled crowd. The queen bore the homely name of Sarah Jane ; she was a "maiden of youthful fifteen;" and the father of the royal damsel was a mechanic. She had been chosen by a committee specially appointed for that purpose, and, as far as I was able to judge, their choice was justified by public approval. When the crowning had been accomplished, the village swains and village lasses assembled round the May-pole, and to the strains of the band, began a brisk dance, which was doomed to some interruption, however, because of the ribbons getting "feltered." Then there were rustic sports, such as wrestling, jumping, racing, greasy pole climbing, and what not, resulting in much amusement; and at night the festivities were continued by a grand ball at the Mechanics' Institute. The proceedings throughout were characterised by the utmost good humour, and Queen Sarah Jane was congratulated upon having been honoured by a larger crowd of worshippers than any of her predecessors in the Otley title ever were honoured with before.

CRICKET OFF THE HEARTH.

T is related that when Mr. Disraeli and Lord John Manners visited Bington, in the interests of the Young England party in 1847, the noble poet, whose inmost desire was that "laws and learning, trade and commerce" should die, so long as we had left our "old nobility," astonished the natives of Airedale by bowling round arm in a cricket match in which he condescended to take part. Up to that time the rustic cricketer had been content with "slow bobbers," and such other varieties of underhand bowling as were then known, but when this scion of the house of Rutland took off his coat and attacked the wickets with balls thrown from the shoulder, he was regarded with wondering admiration, albeit there were some few old stagers who resented the innovation as being not bowling but deliberate throwing. Since then, however, the science of cricket has grown and flourished, and now the smallest village club can boast its adept in the kind

of bowling which, a quarter of a century ago, was
only indulged in by a comparative few. And if
bowlers have multiplied, so have batsmen. Cricket
is played everywhere in England, and even everywhere out of England, where a sufficient number of
Britons to make up an eleven can be got together.
Indeed, the one peculiarity of the game is that it is
truly English, no other race of people being able, it
would seem, to endure the exertion which it exacts
from its votaries. This fact alone ought to be
enough to clear the English character from the
charge (which in these days is often too lightly
made by unthinking people) of effeminacy. So
restricted are the participators in the game, that it
is not even taken up with spirit by either Scotch or
Irish. The former stick to their golf, the latter to
the pastime of breaking heads. But here, in England, so long as a passable wicket can be got, so
long as the sun will vouchsafe us sufficient daylight,
we steadily persist in batting and bowling, going in
and being put out. We have one-armed and one-
legged players, clown cricketers, gipsy cricketers and
actor cricketers—nay, I believe, there are even instances on record of matches having been played between married and single females. Foreigners have
tried to master the game now and again; but have
failed miserably. The French have a profound disgust for it, being averse to encounter the hardships

and dangers of the field. A party of Englishmen once tried to amuse the Duchess de Berri by playing a match in her presence at Dieppe; but after several hours' batting and bowling, under a broiling sun, she asked, " When is the game going to begin ? "— mistaking their playing for mere preparatory work. The foreign mind, generally, understands and enters into the game in much the same way. In America, they try to a certain extent to acclimatise the game; but with no very great success. It is related, amongst other Yankee drolleries, that on one occasion our New World cousins got up a match with an English team, on the principle since carried out in their monster musical festivals at Boston, and their visitors, contending against their not over-scientific bowling and fielding, made such a show of batting as, to use their own words, " licked creation." The long-field was stationed on the Allegany mountains, and the balls were caught by players in balloons, or fetched in by the aid of locomotives. To see the game played in perfection, however, it is necessary to visit an English cricket ground, where such an amount of enthusiasm is displayed as is scarcely to be met with elsewhere.

For oneness of purpose and assiduity in the pursuit of a single object, commend me above all to the *genus* cricketer. He equals the lover in devotion, the poet in ardour, the philosopher in enthusiasm,

the warrior in courage, and the man of commerce in
his desire to win greater success than his compeers.
The first object of his life is to attain personal distinction in the game ; the second, to see the club to
which he belongs in the front rank of cricketing
clubs ; and the third, to promote the cricketing renown of his county. During "the season" nearly
all his leisure moments are spent in the field, and
out of the season, during the period of hybernation,
he passes his time in dreaming of cricketing to
come. The alchemists of mediæval days did not
work more diligently in the attempt to realise their
chimerical ideas than the modern cricketer labours
in making a reality of the pursuit to which he has
attached himself. Writers who dilate on the present
degeneracy of the Anglo-Saxon race would probably
refuse to see any evidence of national strength or
vigour in this great English pastime, while others
would point to it not only as the chief outcome of
the muscularity of the English character, but as the
best possible testimony of British hardihood. Such
universality of feeling about a mere matter of pastime is wonderful to contemplate. Every bit of
vacant land in our large towns, all our public parks,
all our village greens, are constantly occupied during the summer with contending cricketers, from
the ragged urchins of the back slums to the most
aristocratic of gentlemen amateurs. In Wool-

borough alone the clubs may be numbered by hundreds; there is hardly a firm or school of any importance in the town but has its club, and on a Saturday afternoon in the season the number of matches played in the district is countless.

Whether cricket was cradled in Surrey or in Kent is a matter upon which I do not propose to give any opinion; nor do I care to bestow any particular attention upon the derivation of the word "cricket," which may come from the Saxon *creag* or *cricce* (meaning a stick bent at the end) or it may not. My present purpose is to describe the game as it is played in and about Woolborough, and to give a picture of some of our local fields as they appear during the progress of a match. My main difficulty will be one of selection—whether to take my readers to witness a match between the South-South-West of England Eleven *v.* Eighteen of Woolborough and anywhere else, or between the Silsbridge Lane Blooming Duffers and the Wapping Road Kangaroos. Perhaps, however, I am in fairness bound to give precedence to the oldest club in the district, and record some of my summer impressions of the field in Torton Road.

Suppose, then, that it is Monday—a very cloudy, April-like Monday—and that one of the great elevens has been announced to play a dozen and a half picked men on the Woolborough ground. Towards

noon, all cricket-loving Woolboroughites who can
elude other engagements wend their steps in the
direction of Great Torton Road, and a brass band
which has scoured the town brings in its train a
large number of waverers, who have been honestly
endeavouring up to that moment to prefer business
to pleasure.   There is much speculation rife as
to whether or not the match will be honoured
with the presence of the three Graces, but more
especially of the one who rejoices in the initials
"W. G.," and who, in cricketing circles, is dignified
with the name of the Leviathan.   On every hand
it is asked, in tones of breathless interest, "Have
you heard whether W. G. has come or not?" but
before I reach the entrance to the field it is whispered
disappointedly about that "W. G." has *not* come,
but that "G. F." will be present. Gaining the ground,
I find the cricketers hard at work, fighting with the
ball.   The Eleven are in the field, and two representatives of Woolborough, gloved and padded, are
endeavouring to frustrate the efforts of the opposite
bowlers and fielders to get them out.   Dr. Johnson
described cricket as "a sport, at which the con-
tenders drive a ball with sticks in opposition to
each other," but the great lexicographer's definition
is dreadfully meagre and misleading.   Had he been
accustomed to see cricket as we now play it, and to
read the newspaper reports of matches with which

our later generation is favoured, he would have written something very different. Since then the game has been advanced from the position of being a boy's pastime to the dignity of a science, to which men of talent are willing to devote a good portion of their lives. The "first gentleman of Europe," in some of his better moments, did not disdain to let his royal hand grasp a bat; and Lord Byron was at one time an ardent adherent of cricket. And now, as a glance at any of our good fields while a match is being played will prove, the game has become still more fashionable.

But, to return to the field in Great Torton Road. It is thronged with visitors, the upper portion of the ground being occupied by an array of fashionable people, who look as well-dressed, as easy, and as animated as any promiscuous out-door assembly could well expect to look, unless it were at a floral fête or a park gala. Thriving woolstaplers hob-a-nob with prosperous manufacturers, shopkeepers with their customers, young ladies with male protectors of every variety,—the parental, the spoony, and the fraternal—and altogether this upper assemblage may be taken as representative of Woolborough's higher socialities. Mingling with these, are a number of cricketers arrayed in many-coloured flannels, who wander hither and thither like champions waiting for their turn at the tournament, and who come in for a rare amount of hero-worship. The spectators turn to them as they pass, and recount their most wondrous exploits one to another, telling of " tremendous hits," scores of two and three figures, uninterrupted series of maiden overs, and killing paces. But, although the majority of the visitors display an intimate knowledge of cricketing slang and cricketing chronology, there is a leaven of ignorance present which imparts more comicality to the proceedings than would otherwise prevail. For instance, I hear one gentleman point to another and remark, " That's young X; he has just left the University, and once played with the Eton Eleven." " What by that ? " exclaims a bluff Woolboroughite, whose notions of public school life are only obscure, " Heaton's nowt to Manning-ham !" The people are wonderfully still though, as a rule, being too intent upon the game to do more than watch the movements of the players. Occasionally a true British thirst comes over them, and they betake themselves to the refreshment-box, and indulge in sundry hasty libations. The non-playing members of the W.C.C. show their connection with the match by hanging about the shed set apart as a dressing-room and repository of stumps, bails, bats, &c., some of them distinguishing themselves by a certain hauteur of aspect which seems to speak of past victories. These players are so dreadfully

familiar with the "crack" cricketers that they
allude to them as "Tom," "Bill," or "Ted," and
criticise each act in the game with a knowingness
which has the effect of overawing the uninitiated to
a painful extent. Now and then they will forget
themselves for a moment, and applaud a "spanking
hit" or a "stumper," if it be by one of their own
men. But these idiosyncracies do not extend to
the general spectator, who shouts with all the power
of his lungs, "Well done, lad!" "Reight ower!"
"Run agean!" or "Well thrown in!" as the occasion may prompt him. Some visitors lie on the
grass "taking it easy;" some stand up and gaze
upon the players as if the battle they are waging is
one of life and death; and some sit upon the
wooden benches and smoke their cigars with assumed indifference; but there is a common bond of
fellowship existing between them all, and men who
are strangers to each other in daily life—men who
ordinarily occupy distinctive social positions—converse together with a freedom which, for the time,
smooths down all inequalities of rank. Even the
man who rushes excitedly about with "correct
cards" seems on a footing of perfect familiarity
with high and low. Every now and then the
scoring board—the cricketing chronometer—has its
figures altered, and then, for a moment, every eye is
turned to see what the new figures reveal. At the

lower end of the ground there is another crowd of
anxious sight-seers, whose enthusiasm is perhaps
greater even than that of the " upper " visitors. If
a ball is sent into the far corner of the field, they
are the persons to shout in exultation ; if there be a
" miss," they are the persons to bite their lips and
grunt an ejaculatory "Ee!" or "Hay!" If a
man is bowled, they are the people to groan
and lament as if the anguish of the moment were
too much to be borne. Their demonstrativeness
occasionally assumes rather odd forms, too, for
the exuberance of their feelings will sometimes
make them go so far as to dance a horn-
pipe step, dig their friends in the ribs, throw up
their hats and caps, or even give a triumphant
" cock-a-doodle-do !" At this end of the ground
there is always present at the great matches an
individual who on the downfall of every wicket
performs a jubilant punch-and-judy fantasia with
his voice, and excites the laughter of the spectators.
Many of the visitors are members of one or other
of the numerous cricketing clubs in the district,
and their comments upon the game would do
honour to a sporting correspondent. If you want
to hear what Casson's average has been this season;
if you desire to learn how many runs Ned Dawson
got in the match against the Sheffield Wheelers ; if
you care to know how excellent Smith's last

season's batting was; if you want to be told of the glories of Woolborough cricket in the old days, when Jack Barker was the wicket-keeper, Ike Hodgson and swift Ned Lawson the bowlers, and Colonel Hirst, " Waddy," " Little Hall," and others were prominent players, it is to this end of the field that you must go. Having thus referred to the appearance of the portions of the ground occupied by the spectators, I will now turn to the smooth, level green, whereon the thirteen human chessmen and their two umpires are stationed. The two batsmen seem men of the Guy Livingstone build; fearless, invincible heroes, who strike the ball over the field with a fierceness which appears successfully to defy the united efforts of the eleven dashing, sprightly fellows who surround them. G. F. Grace may have his balls "on" as much as he likes, Southerton may send up his most awkward twists, and the other nine may display the most extraordinary feats of fielding; it is all of no use, the red ball flies hither and thither, high and low, far and near, and the gallant defenders of the wickets remain at their posts, cheered on at every fresh display of their batting ability by the applause of the spectators. But the longest innings, as well as the longest lane, has a turning, and even a Grace has at one time or other to succumb to the inevitable law which attends all human effort. Wickets fall at irregular intervals, some for honourable scores, others for mere nothings, cyphers, ducks' eggs. To ladies and other strangers to the game, the most perplexing part of cricketing is the "over," the why and wherefore of which it is useless attempting to make them understand, except that it occurs "over " and "over" again. The technical term "maiden " they may in course of time come to understand, but beyond this it is impossible for their minds to carry them. The match proceeds through all its varying operations, now looking promising for the Eighteen, now giving that hope which Pope described as springing eternal in the human breast, to the Eleven, but the prophets have from the first been in favour of what the knowing ones term the Woolborough team—team, forsooth! as if they were horses or oxen—and their predictions are fully verified at the end of the third day's play, when the vanquished Southerners depart to "handle the willow" and "trundle the leather" in other fields.

It will not be expected that I should describe matches at each of the Woolborough grounds, seeing that they are so numerous. Having referred at length to a match engaged in by the parent club, it only remains for me to say that I have seen matches on the Manningham ground which have been as exciting and as well contested as the best; on the Albion ground, both when there has been an umpire's dispute and when all has been as pleasant, as enthusiastic, and as clever as any reasonable cricketer could wish; on the Bowling Old Lane ground, adjacent to the Red Ginn, when the Second Eleven has played better than the First; on those rugged Barkerend fields where Garnett's United and the Clarencers have waged many a severe battle; and on innumerable other fields, urban and suburban, where fingers have been broken, legs bruised, and garments torn to shreds.

One afternoon I had the good fortune to witness a local match between the Conservative Roaring Lambs and the Liberal Blighted Dandelions, in which such prowess was displayed on both sides that they resolved to amalgamate, and go in for the discomfiture of the Moderate Go-Betweens or Two-Stoolmen, of which match the particulars may hereafter be fully announced. On another occasion I was present at a match in which the Six-of-Ones played against the Half-a-dozen-of-the-Others, the latter losing by ten wickets. In this celebrated encounter the umpire gave a player out because he had been fairly spread-eagled, for which unrighteous decision he was chased for a distance of two miles, and then beaten within an inch of his life. It is necessary, however, in the interests of the art, that umpires should be taught by the players how and when to exercise their sovereign power.

But one of the most lively matches of the season
recently closed was one played in Manningham
Park between the Little Bethel Moaners (with Barnacles) and the St. Judas's Backsliders (with the
Poole Alley professional). Wickets were pitched at
two p.m., and the players were fully assembled by
the early hour of half-past four. Umpires were dispensed with as being unnecessary incumbrances,
and each batsman was allowed three "tries" before
he was pronounced "fair on." The ball was a
"cruelled" one, the heart of which was composed
of india-rubber. The Moaners won the toss, and sent
Barnacles (with a white hat and knickerbockers)
and young Scopperill (with a white smock and
clogs) to the wickets, where, in the space of five
minutes, they ran up the excellent score of one,
which was obtained by a shoe-toe hit off himself by
Barnacles. This brought on a change of bowling,
Sam Fizzer going on with his thundering slows.
The first ball in the seventeenth over knocked a
pipe out of the wicket-keeper's mouth, and left him
in the possession of the tooth-ache; the second ball,
by some strange mischance, came into contact with
Barnacles' bat, and rebounded into the hands of the
man at mid-on, who was so alarmed that he allowed
it to fall gently upon the grass, where it lay until
another run had been obtained, the four spectators
—a nursemaid, a policeman, and two children of

tender years—who watched the match with an interest equal to its importance, cheering to the echo. The astonishing play exhibited by Barnacles on this occasion was entirely due to his own unaided exertions, for, although he had taken the precaution to plant a boy in the vicinity of the wicket-keeper to whisper to him when a ball was coming straight, so that he might know when to "let out" and when to put his bat solemnly and steadily down in front of the timbers, it is but fair to say that he only availed himself of this assistance to a very slight extent—a fact in some measure attributable to the disagreement which existed between the wicket-keeper and the boy, with regard to the exact position each ought to occupy. Scopperill succumbed at last to Fizzer, and Barnacles was partnered by Spankem, the great hitter. As soon as Spankem made his appearance the captain of the St. Judas's team motioned his own men further out, one of whom went so far that he found himself in the Turf Tavern bar, when he took the advantage of his position and swallowed a hasty glass ' of British beverage. Spankem speedily showed that he was in good form by spreadeagleing the wicket-keeper with a back stroke of great power; he then got one into a tree for sixteen, and sent the concluding ball in the same over into the bowler's diaphragm, which

effectually stopped its course. Matters now assumed
a serious aspect for the St. Judasers, and it was
resolved to put on Smithkins to bowl in place of
Fizzer, Smithkins having the reputation of being
able to trundle the leather with the true electrical
twist. Smithkins' first ball twisted off three yards
to the leg, and Barnacles twisted after it, but
was unable to overtake it in time to strike an effective blow. The ball then got into the hands of the
slip, and from thence into the hands of the wicket-
keeper, who took advantage of the absence of
Barnacles from his post to throw the ball at the
wickets—and missed them! In his anxiety to reach
the wickets before the wandering ball, Barnacles
laid himself down and stretched out his bat as far
as possible, and it is difficult to say whether if the
wicket-keeper had been fortunate enough to hit the
stumps Barnacles would have been been out or not.
After this remarkably fine display of cricket, run-
getting became a rather slow affair, the Smithkins's
electrical twisters being too many for the bats.
Spankem, at this point, divested himself of his
cap, and struck the next few balls to the square leg
for nothing. At 5.46 Barnacles put his bat in the
wrong place, and Smithkins found his way to his
timbers, thus closing a fine innings of 15, consisting
of a two, thirteen singles, and cyphers. The remaining wickets were disposed of at a rapid rate, none

of the Little Bethelites being able to make a stand
against the destructive bowling of Smithkins. The
last man was caught in a rather smart style by the
mid-on. The ball was skied to a great height, and
fell upon and into the mid-on's hat, damaging the
beaver and awakening the serious reflections of its
owner, but remaining true to the position it had
taken up. A dispute then arose as to this being a
fair catch. One pulled Lillywhite out of his pocket
in support of his assertions, another stigmatised his
opponents as insatiate monsters and sons of iniquity,
and said he didn't care a straw for either Lillywhite
or Lillyblack. In this dilemma the policeman was
called in as referee, and he settled the matter by
running the disputants out of the park.

I might go on and spin you a description of other
matches—the Policemen v. the Military, the Allwool
Lamplighters v. the Woolborough ditto, the Shoeblacks v. the Bootblacks, &c., &c., &c.—but I have
probably said enough to prove that my sympathies
are with the cricketers, and that I am entitled to
have my say upon cricketing matters as well as
other people.

HAIRS AND GRACES.

HAIROLOGY is a science which has more votaries than all the other ologies put together. I must confess, however, that it was not until a recent night that this view was fully and adequately impressed upon me, and had it not happened that, on the night in question, the Woolborough hairdressers had taken it into their heads to give " a public exposition " of their art, in the saloon of St. Gorgon's Hall, I should probably have continued in the uneven tenor of my way, neglecting both my own and other people's tresses in a manner that I am now convinced would have been utterly unjustifiable. But when one comes to regard the delicate filament which nature has provided for the adornment of our heads from anything like a professional standpoint, its importance, beauty, variety, and vastness suddenly reveal themselves, and we feel (by which I mean that I personally feel) that hair-land is a region well worth exploring. Historically, poetically, socially, com-

mercially—as a matter of business or as a matter of
pleasure—in life and in death—regard it as we will,
the human hair is entitled to respectful treatment
and handling. "Only a woman's hair!" were the
words which Dean Swift wrote upon a small packet
containing a lock of Stella's or Vanessa's hair, which
was found amongst his papers after his death.
Only! There's a hollowness, and, at the same time,
a certain pathos in this word. As regarded that
particular lock of hair, the Dean was haply justified
in so using the word, but what short of social an-
nihilation could we expect for a man who at the
present day would dare to affix such a label of
detraction to a lock of feminine hair? But Swift
was not sufficient of a poet to attach the proper
amount of sentiment to a stray tress. Pope, however, did not disdain to make a lock of hair the
subject of one of his best poems, the " Rape of the
Lock" being almost as sure of immortality as the
" Essay on Man." The poets altogether have always
shown the utmost readiness to seize upon a lady's
hair—of course I am speaking figuratively—and it
is surprising what visions of radiant hair arise as
soon as one lets one's thoughts wander, with hairy
bent, into the charmed land of poesy. Literature
generally behaves exceedingly well to the owners
(or wearers) of beautiful hair. A novelist would
have small chance of favour at the circulating

libraries who omitted to describe every hue,
ripple, and every aspect of his heroine's
Indeed, the hair is so important a dramatic
in the hands of the purveyors of fiction that it
be quite easy for the professional builder of *co*
to provide a stock of wigs that should be ad
to every mood and every exigency of em
Madness, for instance, would be impossible wi
unkempt, dishevelled tresses; despair also den
that the hair should be dishevelled, but it
likewise be artistically disposed so as to
additional tragedy to the eyes; and pastoral s
ness requires that the hair should be arrang
simple waves and smooth-lying plaits.   So I
run on and show that there is a particular sty
hair adapted to every human emotion, but the
would be much better performed by a profess
adept.   There is no reason why the idea shoulc
be carried out though, for it would be an ob
convenience to many a lady whose life is one
alternation of storm and sunshine to be pro
with a set of emotional wigs.   Such a wise
vision would enable her to preserve her own tr
in fuller pristine vigour than would all the mac
or balm that ever was made.   Under such
cumstances all that the lady would have t
when she felt a fit of despair, fury, sweetnes
merriment coming over her would be to d

Jemima Ann to bring her her wig of despair, her wig of sweetness, or her wig of madness, as the case might be.

The Woolborough hairdressers, in giving their soirée, evidently meant to take time by the forelock, for, although London and Paris—the sixth and seventh hairdressers' heavens—had had "public expositions" in plenty, the provinces had not been very quick to follow the example set them by those two capitals. Considerable enthusiasm was manifested by the Woolborough shavers and perfumers in the matter, as most people who had to submit their heads and chins to them during the previous fortnight would have been able to testify. My own particular operator had pictured the coming soirée to me in such glowing language that I felt bound to put in an appearance on the memorable night, and I at once admit that the exhibition did not in the least disappoint me. I had endeavoured to persuade Barnacles to accompany me, but that cynical individual said that he did not feel in the mood for barber-ous entertainment. Not choosing to remain hair-splitting with him, I gave vent to my wrath by saying, "Then, dust my wig, if I don't go alone!"

The saloon of St. Gorgon's Hall was about as suitable a place as could have been found for the soirée, and the attendance proved just sufficient to

N

fill it. The middle of the room was occupied with a long table, on which reposed half a dozen oval mirrors, and beside each mirror was placed a chair, the outer boundary of the sanctum being marked by cushioned forms for visitors to loll upon. The walls were adorned with other mirrors; in fact, the members of the society seem to be firm believers in the wisdom of holding up the mirror to nature, whenever it is possible to do so. Down one side of the room a series of stalls were arranged, presided over by professional gentlemen. One of these stall artists reminded me of Ingoldsby's Little Boy Saint, whose

> "Cold lips breath'd an odour quite *Eau-de-Cologne-y;*
> In fact, from his christening, according to rumour, he
> Beat Mr. Brummel to sticks in perfumery."

He looked as if the business agreed with him, too, which is more than can be said of *some* tradesmen. But they were all unexceptionally bland, without being obtrusive. They did not attempt to cram their bear's grease and their tar balls down the visitors' throats, but simply acted as so many guides, philosophers and friends,—which was the proper thing to do. To describe the various articles exhibited fittingly is a task which I will not attempt to perform; I cannot do more than give the impressions of an unprofessional inspection. Beginning at the top of the room, then, we got a peep at the

Claimant's hair. It was of such high value that it had to be protected in a strong black frame, which was perhaps suggestive of mourning, although we hardly dared to conjecture what the mourning might be meant to imply. Every visitor deemed it incumbent upon him or her to examine this very ordinary-looking lock, and the criticisms generally accorded with the critics' favourable or unfavourable opinion of the Claimant's case. Specimens of the shell of the ungainly tortoise next came under notice, both in its original state and in that refined and highly-polished condition in which we are accustomed to see it when it is used as a head adornment. Then there came a delicate assortment of valentines, over which the young ladies lingered fondly and lovingly. "See, Edith; *that's* like the one that Charley sent me !" one sweet-voiced damsel would whisper in her companion's ear, and Edith would smile as tenderly as if she had had the good fortune to receive one herself. From valentines (which it is perháps hardly fair to consider as coming properly within the scope of hairdressing) it was only one remove to a stall resplendent with perfumed soaps, cosmetics, and a host of other aids to artificial beautifying. There were so many inducements to ablution on this stall that I should not have been surprised to have heard some one imploring to be shampooed, and all the rest, on the spot.

The "young swells"—curled dandies whose hair
but for the dresser's irons would have no more
ripple in it than a tallow candle—affected this
stall very much, and showed an acquaintance
with the use of the different articles which was
almost equal to the knowledge of the professionals.
Next I came upon an extensive array of hair, the
whence and whither of which were alike problema-
tical. The vendor of it regarded it with something
like the affection that one bestows upon a favourite
dog. He asked people to stroke it, to feel its
weight, to smell at it, and seemed to expect all
kinds of endearments to be expended upon it.
There were bundles of it from Germany and from
Russia; and some of it was built up into ponderous
chignons, fashionable and artistic, but, to an un-
trained eye, excessively ugly. "Do you know
whose heads all this hair comes from?" asked
one innocent old lady, whose knowledge of adsci-
titious locks was evidently not equal to that of
the two daughters, who uttered an expostulatory
"Oh, ma!" "Why, we don't exactly know whose
heads it comes from, ma'am," replied the artist,
"but it's as sweet and pure as that of a new-born
babe." The speech of a rather mischievous youth
who was standing by unfortunately took the old
lady's attention at this juncture, as he meant it
should do. He pretended to be speaking with

revealed knowledge to a second mischievous youth. "That black hair there," he said, "belonged to a nun who committed suicide in Spain; that brown hair belonged to a young girl who died of measles, or something of that kind, in Holland; and that light brown lot comes from some of the London prisons." The old lady's hair was rather too long to stand on end and "like the quills of the fretful porcupine," or I verily believe it would have done. But there was horror in her eyes if not in her hair, and her daughters got her to sit down until her fright had subsided. The young fellows laughed mightily, and made atonement for the wrong they had done by now praising the hair with all the superlative phrases they could invent, which were not a few. Adjoining the hair exhibition was a display of mechanical contrivances used in hairdressing, including two or three novelties. One of the novelties was a hair-*cutting* machine, which, with all due respect to the inventor, I should scarcely like to hear click-clacking in the vicinity of my scalp. I would almost as soon have my "hair raised" by a wild Indian, accompanied by a flourish of the insinuating "Thomashawk" and an unearthly war-whoop, as have it done by the accidental disrepair of a machine deliberately devised by a Christian. A second novelty was what is playfully termed a "disentangler," which, although it suggests ideas of

Vikings and Robin Roughheads in general having
their clotted *chevelures* clawed straight, is really only
meant for the arranging of false hair, enabling all
the roots of the filament to be placed in the same
position. At this point I heard a gentleman exclaim, "O, here's a knitting machine!" Wondering what they could want with a knitting machine
at a hairdressers' soirée, I went to look at the machine, and I was soon made to wonder no longer.
I thought the gentleman meant knitting which
begins with a "k," but he didn't. At the extreme
end of the table was a collection of theatrical wigs.

"The wig's the thing! the wig! the wig!"

says the old song, but nobody seemed inclined to
sing it. Amongst these wigs I had no difficulty in
singling out those of Mr. Pantaloon, Serjeant Buz-
fuz, Joseph Surface, the Grand Duchess of Gerol-
stein, and a number of piquant soubrettes, domestic
angels, and tragic furies. Having exhausted the
stalls, I turned to the table where microscopic
objects were shown, and, amongst a number of
ordinary examples, found a few that bore some relation to the hair. The section of the hair of a cow,
for instance, was something noticeable. Then there
were a number of books of engravings—old copper-
plates—showing different styles of *coiffures* in vogue
during the last century, as well as some modern
engravings. To people interested in hairdressing,

indeed, there was abundance of gratification to be derived from that soirée. Everybody seemed to be in the best of humours, and all rounds of the Woolborough social ladder (except the lowest) was represented. Of course, the hairdressing fraternity mustered in all their force, and amongst the lay visitors I came upon portly aldermen, merchants, manufacturers, artists, and what not, although in most instances, the male portion of the company had come to protect their wives, sweethearts, and daughters. That the young ladies had nearly all come with the idea of getting "a wrinkle" was evident enough from the earnest way in which they examined everything. During the evening "there was biano blaying," as was the case at Hans Breitmann's celebrated party, and I heard one or two visitors observe, in honour of the occasion, that the pianiste played some "very lively hairs."

It was not until a quarter past eight, however, that the great attraction of the evening was put forward, and then, if you like, both the male and female portion of the company had their interest aroused to the utmost pitch of excitement. At that hour six young ladies, with "long, dishevelled hair," were led forth from an ante-room, and they immediately occupied the six chairs in front of the six looking-glasses. They were all more of the brunette type than of the blonde, which I somewhat

regretted, for I had meant to have seen some of the
real golden hair that the poets are always singing
about, some "manelike mass of rolling gold,"
twisted and braided into glittering magnificence by
the hands of the skilful operator.   The six operators
plied their combs and brushes with exceeding deft-
ness for more than half an hour upon the heads
of the six damsels who had thus relinquished their
tresses to their tender mercies.   How eagerly
every movement of the artists was watched!
And how silently and calmly sat the owners
of the six heads of hair!   The process of building up the two powdered *coiffures* which represented the two styles designated the Louis XV.
and the Pompadour styles attracted the greatest
amount of attention.   As each fresh roll of hair
was twisted into its place, as each fresh dab of powder was applied, the young lady spectators rolled
out their "eh's" and their "ah's" with a fervour
that must have been very flattering to the operators.
At last, however, the final top-knot was satisfactorily
adjusted, and the *chevelures* of Madame du Barry
and Madame Pompadour, of the modern Parisian
ball-room belle and the London concert-room queen,
were fully displayed, to the extreme approval of the
company.   Both the operators and the operated
upon were warmly applauded.   At this point "a
gentleman from London" stepped into the magic

circle and offered a few remarks upon the hair-dressing, and then the company were permitted to walk in slow procession round the six young ladies —permitted, in fact, to make a tour of inspection— after which the performance was over and the guests began to depart. I heard several young ladies declare that they would be able, after what they had seen, to do their toilettes in a similar fashion to one or other of the modern examples ; and for some days afterwards those young ladies would doubtless spend the main portion of their days and nights in binding their hair, even though their mother should *not* bid them.

With the disappearance of the six young ladies and their six hairdressers I imagined I had done with hair-hunting for that night ; but it was not so, or rather the hunting was reversed, and instead of me hunting hair the hair hunted (or haunted) me. I went home to sleep, but a hairy Frankenstein pursued and interposed between me and Morpheus, and I saw nothing but heads of hair and beautiful faces, and all the voices of the night were changed to low whisperings, whose eternal theme was hair, hair, hair. Tennyson had his vision of fair women ; I had my vision of fair hair. The poets, dead and living, flew to my bedside in noisy throngs and dinned their music-words into my ear until I was fairly bewildered. Nearly all of them had got something to say on behalf of yellow or golden hair. Spenser's Belphebe—

> "Her yellow looks, crisped like golden wire,
> About her shoulders were loosely shed;"

and the bride that the same poet glorifies in his "Epithalamium," with

> "Her long, loose yellow looks, like golden wire
> Sprinkled with pearl, and perling flowers atween,"

arose before me. Then came Drummond of Hawthornden, with his "curlèd waves of gold, with gentle tides that on your temple flows;" and after him came Shakspeare's Lucrece, whose hair, "like golden threads, play'd with her breath." Then there was Tennyson's Guinivere, whose "golden head" had been King Arthur's pride "in happier summers;" there was Poe's "yellow-haired young Eulalie;" and Keats's Apollo, whose

> "Very hair—his golden tresses famed—
> Kept undulation round his eager neck."

Milton's invocation to "Sabrina fair," in "Comus," was also chanted to me. The "mighty-mouth'd inventor of harmonies" sang of her thus :—

> "Under the glassy, cool, translucent wave,
> In twisted braids of lilies, knitting
> The loose train of thy amber-dropping hair."

Then there was

> "Fair Yoland, with the yellow hair,"

and Robert Browning's heroine, with her hair

> "Unfilleted,
> Made alive, and spread
> Through the void, with a rich outburst,
> Chestnut, gold interspersed."

The same poet also haunted me with the line which speaks of

> "That fawn skin dappled hair of hers."

Tennyson might almost claim to be the laureate of the hairdressers, in addition to his other laureatship, as was made sufficiently manifest to me in this hair-haunting. Not only does he go in for singing the praise and glory of hair of all shades (although he principally patronises the golden), but he often condescends to describe the very operation of hair-dressing. He describes his mermen as playing

> "With the mermaids in and out of the rocks,
> Dressing their hair with the white sea-flower;"

and his mermaid sings—

> "With a comb of pearl I would comb my hair;
> And still as I comb'd I would sing and say,
> 'Who is it loves me? Who loves not me?'
> I would comb my hair till my ringlets would fall,
> Low adown, low adown."

In the poem of "The Sisters," the sister who has stabbed the Earl makes an unconscious pun as she says:—

> "I curl'd and comb'd his comely head,
> He looked so grand when he was dead."

Keats, however, goes into perfumery, as we
hairdressing. While Endymiou is sleeping, a C
takes

> "A willow bough, distilling odorous dew,
> And shakes it on his hair."

A bit of very ghastly hairdressing is also desc
in Keats's "Pot of Basil."   On finding the he
her murdered lover in the Basil Pot, Isabe
thus pictured :—

> "She calm'd its wild hair with a golden comb,
> And all around each eye's sepulchral cell
> Pointed each fringèd lash."

There is something much more beautiful ir
same poet's description of Madeleine in the '
of St. Agnes," when

> "Of all its wreathed pearls her hair she frees."

As a contrast to this picture may be quoted tl
Andromache, in the "Iliad," on seeing He
glossy hair trailing in the dust behind his
queror's chariot :—

> "Far off were flung th' adornments of her head,
> The net, the fillet, and the woven bands."

Lady Godiva is described by Tennyson, befor
sets out upon her ride through the street
Coventry, in the following words :—

> "She shook her head
> And shower'd the rippled ringlets to her knee."

Tennyson has devoted an entire poem to "The
Ringlet," which, in one place, he calls "a golden lie."
He thus apostrophises the ringlet in question:—

> " O Ringlet, O Ringlet,
> She blush'd a rosy red,
> When Ringlet, O Ringlet,
> She clipt you from her head."

All these past utterances came back to me in my
hairy vision, and a hundred others followed in their
train, the repetition of which would spin out the
present paper to almost an unmanageable length.
The stories of Samson and Absalom repeated themselves, and some of the apparitions struck awe into
my soul. I thought of hair growing white in a
single night "from sudden fears;" I thought of St.
Simeon Stylites with all his beard "tagg'd with icy
fringes in the moon;" I thought of Thersites, "the
ugliest man "—

> " His narrow head with scanty growth of hair;"

I thought of Jupiter, who

> " Waved on th' immortal head th' ambrosial locks,
> And all Olympus trembled at his nod;"

I thought of Swinburne's Faustines and their
"amorous hair;" I thought of the Gardener's
Daughter, with hair

> "More black than ashbuds in the front of March;"

of Spenser's Una, when "her fillet she undight;"
of Moore's heroine whose "tresses' curly flow

darkled o'er the brow of snow;" of Hood's hero
who, because his head was turned, "chewed his
pigtail till he died;" of Jerry Jarvis's wig; of
Dean Swift's wig, "with hanging grown quite
grey;" and so on, and on, and on, until I almost
felt as terrified as Pope Gregory did on seeing the
barefooted friar:—

> " 'Now thunder and turf!' Pope Gregory said,
> And his hair rais'd his triple crown right off his head."

But I was not able to shut the ghosts out even yet.
They came to me with their beards next, and even
with their bald pates.   Geoffrey Chaucer presented
a goodly array.   There was his monk, whose

> "Hed was balled, and shone as any glas;"

there was the Franklein—

> "White was his berd as is the dayesie;"

there was the Miller—

> " His berd as any sowe or foxe was rede,
> And thereto brode, as though it were a spade.
> Upon the cop right of his nose he hade
> A wert, and thereon stode a tufte of heres,
> Red as the bristles of a sowe's eres;"

and there was the Reve—

> "His berd was shave as neighe as ever he can.
> His here was by his eres round yshorne."

But the beard that troubled me most was that of
St. Gengulphus.   Thomas Ingoldsby, describing the

murder of that saint by Mrs. G. and " The Learned
Clerke," says :—

> "But first the long beard from the chin they shear'd,
>   And managed to stuff that sanctified hair,
> With a good deal of pushing, all into the cushion
>   That filled up the seat of a large arm-chair."

And when I had got rid of the flowing locks, the
long beards, the bald heads, and what not, I fell
a-thinking of powders, pomatums, perfumes, and
ointments, until I seemed to be lost in a vast per-
fumer's bazaar. Rowland's Balm of Columbia,
Oldridge's Macassar, Rimmel's Tar Soap, Piesse and
Lubin's Valentines, &c., &c., &c., appeared before
me, and at last I was compelled to get up and read,
in order that the ghosts might be exorcised. I took
up a volume of "Notes and Queries," but I had not
been reading long ere the following brought me to
a dead stop, and made me cast the book aside and
rush off to bed again :—

> "W. Bulleyn says, in his "Booke of Simples," published in
> 1562, 'The Beare is a beaste whose flesh is good for mankynd;
> his fat is good, with Laudanum, to make an oyntment to heale
> balde headed men to receive the hayre agayne. The grease
> of the Beare, the fatte of a Lambe, and the oyntment of the Fox
> maketh a good oyntment to anoynt the feet against the payne of
> travell or labour of footmen.' "

This time Morpheus asserted himself with greater
success, and I at length fell asleep, and went through
a succession of hairy dreams. It is only the last of

these dreams that I still remember, and therein I
imagined I saw two country yokels calling each
other " carroty nops" and " turnip heads," and after
the dispute had been settled by calling in William
Rufus as arbitrator, on Genevan principles, I dreamt
no more.

WOOLGATHERING AT SALTAIRE.

THOUGH the wind was in that quarter which the old proverb describes as "neither good for man nor beast," there was sun enough to temper the eastern blast and make the weather not only bearable, but positively inviting. Woolborough could not hold me. It was not exactly that I had had my nerves shaken by the ghastly sight of the Town Hall statues frowning at each other in stony horror; it was not that the town's unconsumed smoke was stifling me; nor was it that I was greviously overwrought in body or brain, that Worstedopolis was so excessively unpleasant to me that day. But, whatever were my promptings and longings, there could be no doubt that one of those "mysterious somethings" so dear to the heart of the sensational novelist was working its will upon me, and driving me out into the country air. Suffice it that I yielded myself up to its influence, and made my way to the Manningham Railway Station, with ardent yearnings for spring

o

woods, rugged hills, and breezy expanses of mo◄
land. Each and all of these invigorating enjoymex
were within my reach by just allowing myself to
carried to the favourite starting point of Saltai:
At Saltaire you at once stand on the verge of riv
and wood, and the hills and the moorland are wa
ing for you immediately beyond. When I reach
Manningham Station I was startled to find th
Greenwich and my waistcoat pocket were n
agreed as to the time of day, and that the trair
had meant to go by was panting and steaming so:
quarter of a mile at the wrong side of the station
going to Saltaire without me, in fact. After loc
ing for a moment at the receding train, I resolve
with characteristic intrepidity, to hold myself I
holden neither to steam-propelled nor horse-p
pelled conveyance for my Saltaire trip, but
patronise the most ancient of all steeds, "Shan]
his mare." Josh Billings, or some other philos
pher of the phonetic-spelling school, has told
that every disadvantage is accompanied by its co:
pensatory advantage; and so it proved in t]
instance. Although I missed the rapid railw
ride, and had my arrival at Saltaire somewh
retarded, I fell in with little experiences on my w
which soon put to flight any feelings of regret
disappointment that might have held possession
me. The high road from Woolborough to Salta]

is probably the brightest and most picturesque thoroughfare to be found anywhere in such close proximity to a large manufacturing town—where factory chimneys stand almost as thick as trees in a forest—and on this sunny May day it looked really charming. Passing the noble clusters of villa residences which lie planted out in groves on the slopes between the lane and the railway; passing the long wall of Manningham Park, with its overhanging sycamore boughs, I left the town and its immediate suburban belongings behind me, and looked out upon a great stretch of Airedale landscape lying in the distance. I let my eyes wander from Baildon, stuck on the hill top at the extreme right; over the moorland ridges; over the ugly scar of quarry which defaces the rocky height above Baildon Green; and slowly down to Saltaire Mill chimney and Shipley Church, the two chief structural protests against vacuity to be seen directly before me. But my contemplation of the distance was frequently interrupted by what was going on in the foreground. The limestone road was as white as if it had been strewn with the ashes of last year's spring blossoms, and (seeing that I affect to be something of a pre-Raffaelite in my sketching) it is necessary I should add that there was more dust in the air than was either beneficial or agreeable to the eyes or the mouth, and that the people in the lane

had that dredged appearance we usually notice in
the persons of master corn-millers. The walls were
dredged also, and the houses, the trees, and the
hedges; and every now and then a great white
cloud would gather at the furthest bend of the road,
and come sweeping on like a waft of destruction,
leaving nothing untouched in its progress. But
between the gusts there was no lack of pleasure
for both eye and ear. The cuckoo could be heard
echoing itself in Heaton Wood, and the gayest
caroller of all, the lark, sang its gladdest song in
the blue above. Brisk-faced manufacturers sped
along the road in the smartest of smart vehicles—
probably bound for Ilkley—and these were well
contrasted with the heavy " piece " laden waggons,
whose stalwart horses and stalwart drivers plodded
sturdily on to town,—slowly perhaps, but with an
unflinching determination that seemed superior to
any obstacle, human or elemental, that could be
interposed. Now "a solitary horseman," who
might have walked bodily out of one of G. P. R.
James's romances, passed me; now I passed a
clergyman, taking walking exercise with his wife;
now a gipsy-pedlar of the old type, with his little
corkscrew ringlets dangling at each eye corner, and
his make-believe box of tools swung across his
back; now, a couple of mill-girls, with clattering
clogs and merry laugh; and now a student, with

book in hand, sensibly drinking in ozone and theology simultaneously, instead of waiting to burn " the midnight oil." So the time passed pleasantly enough, and it did not seem long before I had passed Shipley Church and Victoria Park, and stood looking down, as I had looked hundreds of times before, at Saltaire. No ; not as I *had*, but as I *ought to have* looked hundreds of times before ; for " the place and all around it " did not appear as Locksley Hall did to the jilted hero of the Laureate's poem, " as of old," but presented beauties and wonders to me which I had before-time neglected to notice.

Factory, streets, towers, cupolas, roofs, chimneys, gardens, railway, the river, and the massive iron bridge which stretches over it, were all spread out before me, and I marvelled at their extent, harmony, and beauty, almost as much as if they had been unfamiliar objects. How was it, I asked myself, that I had so often passed through this place and had not taken the trouble to understand it ? It had been hallowed in poetry, and celebrated in prose ; native rhymesters had sung its glories in every possible metre, and the great master of modern English fiction himself had told us, in his inimitable way, the story of its rise ; it had been visited by celebrities from all quarters of the world (including His Excellency Jusammi T. Kido, from Yeddo ; Ambas-

sador Jakop-y-diddle Foo, from Burmah; Hospodar
Grimgauntoff, from the Danubian Principalities;
and His Highness Sing Smawl, from Canton); and
newspaper correspondents had been buzzing about
the place with as much frequency as if, instead of
being a "palace of industry," it had been a palace
that hedged in the divinity of a queen. Perhaps it
was all this sounding of trumpets and beating of
drums that Sir Titus Salt had been the victim of;
this constant pulling of the Saltaire musical stop;
this incessant exhibition of the Saltaire stereoscopic
slide (much against the will of the founder, I am
sure), that had caused me to neglect it. But, after all,
the public do not always admire where admiration is
not due, and as I looked down at Saltaire that May
afternoon, I acknowledged that I had scarcely done
my duty by the place, and that (much as had been
said and sung and written about it) I, too, would
have my say on the subject. I resolved, therefore,
to forego my visit to the woods and hills for that
one afternoon, and content myself with quietly
viewing Saltaire on one of its ordinary working
days.

The first thing about Saltaire that strikes the
observer is the beauty of its situation. Never were
the prose and poetry of life more exquisitely
blended. The immense factory, with its strong
stone frontage, 545 feet in length, and its six storeys

of windows "all-a-row," has a fine background of
canal, river, pasture, wood, and hill on the north;
while Milner Field, the residence of Mr. Titus Salt,
crowns the eminence on the west, towards far-famed
Shipley Glen, and the castellated mansion of another
member of the Saltaire firm rises up on the wooded
hillside on the east, towards Baildon. These two
architectural adornments stand like giants' castles
keeping guard over the industrial settlement, and
certainly add to the dignity of the scene. The
Leeds and Liverpool Canal washes the northern
frontage of the works, and not many yards from
the canal embankment is the river Aire, the two
waters running parallel from west to east. The
southern and main front of the mill is close to the
Midland Railway, from which lines of rails branch
off into the works, allowing goods to be shunted
into the warehouses on the very trucks that have
brought them from distant places. Saltaire Station
hides itself from notice in the cutting just adjacent,
being on a level with the ground floor of the works,
but approached from the town by a long descent of
steps.

The principal street in Saltaire is loyally named
Victoria Road, and stretches from the Bingley Road,
on the south, to the northern bank of the river Aire,
crossing the railway, the canal, and the river by massive iron bridges. The one bridge which spans both

canal and river is a tubular structure of stupendous
strength, and so perfect in its formation as to keep
up the illusion that it is a continuation of the street,
and not a bridge at all. At first this bridge was
somewhat askew, and not in a line with the street,
but, costly as the operation must have been, it was
afterwards put right, and now Victoria Road is one
of the straightest, cleanest, and best architectured
thoroughfares in the West Riding. A walk from
top to bottom, with a glance here and there to right
and left, will suffice to give the spectator a good
idea of the architectural aspect and completeness of
Saltaire. At the top of the street there are a number
of superior cottages, with bright strips of garden in
front. Then come those chaste and elegant ranges
of Almshouses (numbering forty-five separate dwellings), which stand opposite to each other, and form
frontages of great external beauty. The ranges of
Almshouses on the west side of the street stands
back considerably. Each door has the name of its
occupant or occupants painted upon it, which is an
advantage that visitors will be grateful for. Con-
sulting Mr. Abraham Holroyd's excellent little
" Guide to Saltaire " for my statistics, I find that in
these Almshouses provision is made for sixty residents, and that " each *single* inmate has a pension
of 7s. 6d. a week, and the married pairs, who reside
together, have each 5s. a week allowed " by Sir

;us Salt.   Passing the Almshouses, two noble
ildings devoted to educational purposes are seen
ing each other—the Elementary Schools and the
ib and Institute—both being put back some forty
t from the street line.   These two structures
uld do honour to any town in the world.   The
:b and Institute building is the chief architectural
umph of the town.   Its fine Corinthian columns
l projecting tower are effective ornaments to a
acious and stately building, into the interior of
ich I propose presently to carry my readers.
ə Elementary Schools are grouped together in a
lding in the Italian style.   The three pediments
front of the building are tastefully ornamented,
l, with the Venetian windows and central bell-
ret, give a handsome effect to the whole.   At
ə point I have the pleasure of inspecting four
lptured lions which were originally meant for
ɔ Nelson Monument in London, though I am not
ormed how it was that they got to Saltaire in-
ad.   I only know that the Cockneys would have
ɔn rejoiced to have had such a noble quartet of
mals in Trafalgar Square, during all the years
ɨ Sir Edwin Landseer kept them waiting.   Two
these lions front the Schools, and the remaining
ɔ front the Institute, resting grimly grand
  pedestals at the gateway of each building.
ə animals are named Vigilance, Determina-

tion, War, and Peace, the first two guarding the portals of Elementary Education, the latter staring in antithetical superiority at the entrance to the Institute. Leaving the lions to snarl through all weathers and teach such lessons as they may to the thousands who will look on them, I come upon a few more ordinary dwellings, and then, on the west side, I see a line of spacious shops in which nearly all the domestic buying and selling in Salt-aire is transacted. I now arrive at the railway bridge, and have a full view of the front of the factory. A brief inspection of this gigantic, many-windowed mill-front enlarges one's ideas of magni-tude and vastness to a wondrous extent. What a number of ordinary-sized mills could be merged in the ten acres of ground covered by the factory, sheds, and warehouses here grouped in one stupenduous concern! Within these massive walls are collected four thousand men, women, and children working harmoniously together, sorting, washing, combing, spinning, or weaving the many-coloured fleeces of the sheep, the goat, the llama, or the alpaca which erst were dotting with life the scorching valleys of Chili, the earthquake-embosoming pastures of Peru, the grassy plains of Australia, or the peaceful meadows of our own native England. Are not these facts which it is invigorating to contemplate? How they help one

ɔ realise the power and extent of man's dominion
vɐr nature! All the four elemental forces are
ressed into his service here. Look at the long
ne of underground boilers which lie smouldering,
ɜ it were, at the foot of this huge commercial
ımple, making the incense for these thousands
: worshippers, and creating a power which keeps
hole miles of machinery in steady, undeviating
otion. The bright, shining steam-engines seen
ınting, snorting, swaying and revolving in the
ɑıtral portion of the building present a picture,
ʳen at this distance, which is calculated to set
.e mind marvelling still further upon the great
ıanges wrought in the world by the inventive
mius of James Watt. However, I must not
ıgɐr here meditating upon the greatness of
odern discoveries. There is much more to be
en and wondered at yet, ere I have done; and
ısides, these [marvellings are so familiar and so
.eap, that one is almost compelled to assume that
pose of demeanour which preserves a surface of
lmness over the most depressing as well as the
ɒst inspiriting emotions. Turning my eyes from
.e factory, I notice a square tract of allotment
ırdens, let out to such Saltairites as are desirous
: growing their own vegetables. The gardens are
esh and bright; flowers blending sweetly with the
ıore useful plants and roots which form so neces-

sary a part of the British workman's dinner. There
is a profusion of peas, cabbages, rhubarb, goose-
berries, and other vegetables and fruits familiar in
the mouth of the perambulating greengrocer, and
the walks and beds are kept with scrupulous care
and neatness.   I now pass over the railway bridge,
glancing, as I go, at the pretty little Station down
in the cutting and the long flight of steps which
leads to the platform, taking due notice also of the
large Dining Hall which stands at the foot of the
railway bridge, and affords dining accommodation
for such of the factory people as come from a distance.   Below that I come within view of the
Saltaire Congregational Chapel, a noble edifice,
standing in a large enclosed space between the
railway and the canal, surrounded by beautiful
lawns and trees and shrubs, and looking as peaceful
and as stately as it is possible for a modern temple
to look.   The entrance portico, according to a
technical description of the building which now lies
before me, "consists of a peripteral temple o
Corinthian columns, raised above the ground by a
continual circle of six steps.   The cellar forms th
vestibule to the church; above this is a pedesta
broken by eight boldly-carved trusses, and crowne
by a circular monopteral storey, decorated wit
eight columns, and terminating in a cupola
There is no doubt, whatever its peripteral an

pteral perfections may be (as to which I regret
I am unable to give particular testimony), that
a very chaste and refined bit of architecture,
should not be at all disposed to contradict Mr.
yd when he assures me that it is "the most
site example of Italian architecture in the
lom." The side of the factory buildings which
s opposite to this elegant chapel is devoted to
purposes, and constitutes a fine suite of rooms,
hich the "powers that be" are accustomed to
ate the operations of their four thousand work-
le. It is in these offices that those astounding
uins are made with buyers from Cathay, or
ructoo, or the land of the great Mogul, for it is
y believed that all the distinguished potentates
he world send their emissaries to purchase
tiful raiment for them at Saltaire. Pushing
ard still further down this main street, I come
the canal where the great iron bridge begins.
I have a view, to the right, of the north end
e factory buildings, and to the left of another
s of allotment gardens; while beyond there
is pretty an English pastoral landscape as is to
iet with in the West Riding, with the quiet
and the still quieter canal running side by side
through it. Saltaire Park, with its fourteen
of beautifully-laid-out lawns, its asphalted
its pavilion and terraces, its trees and

greenery, its cricket and croquet. grounds, and its
man-of-war guns, forms a really picturesque com
mencement to this landscape, and looks especially
delightful this afternoon, with a few of the non
working residents promenading and enjoying them
selves in it; some walking by the river's edge
watching the boats slowly gliding up and down th
placid waters, others disporting themselves in th
spaces devoted to the inspiriting amusements o
cricket and croquet. The stretch of river which i
visible to the west of the bridge has its effect con
siderably enhanced by two weirs,—a broad, foam
ing one, which froths and roars in the distance, an
seems to speak of an illimitable force of wate
beyond; and a quiet series of dam-stones, which
slope down underneath the bridge, and allow the
river to leap and tumble over them in a manne
calculated to fill a poet's mind with no end o
similes and pretty thoughts fit for versicles.

And now, having taken my readers from the to
to the bottom of Victoria Road, and glanced at th
external aspect of the chief buildings which go t
form the greatness of Saltaire, I will say a word o
two about the mass of streets and houses which li
to the west of this principal road, and then plung
boldly into some of the interiors and perform th
Asmodean operation of uncovering the roofs fc
you. The streets, which are well-paved and e

tremely clean, are all laid out on the simple system of straight lines; there is no angularity, no corners lopped off, no zig-zags, but you are carried from one cardinal point of the compass to another, whichever street you may traverse. All the houses are of that good, substantial, sturdy-looking stone which seems to be typical of the hardihood and firmness of character of the commercial Briton. They are two storeys in height, and, from the most respectable down to the most ordinary domicile, possess architectural merits which are rarely found in dwellings with such easy rentals. Many of them have small garden plots in front, and turn which way you will, there is nothing but perfect orderliness, cleanliness and neatness to be observed. The cottage windows are a study in themselves, for the endless variety of adornment they exhibit. Ferneries, aquaria, simple bouquets of flowers, statuettes, miniature men-of-war, and rich displays of indoor flowers meet the eye at these windows, and (what is still more remarkable to any one who is acquainted with the aspect of doors and windows in large towns, where there is a multiplicity of landlords whose chief delight in the houses they own is the rent they receive from their occupiers) the paint is bright and fresh. There are not many people in the streets, but this is accounted for by the fact that most of the inhabitants are workers—drones do not exist at

Saltaire—the housewife and the young children only remain at home. It is after the steam-god has gone to sleep that the streets become busy, after the machinery has been hushed for the day; then the workpeople can lounge about and gossip, and smoke and chat at their ease. Those who prefer some other way of whiling away the idle hours have an *embarras de choix* in the way of amusements. Boating, cricket, croquet, amateur soldiering, and what not, for out of doors; and news-room lounging, gymnastic exercises, billiard playing, &c., for within doors. There is every amusement and recreation, every time-killer known to English life, ready for the workpeople to fly to of an evening, except that distinctive and " elevating " resort, the alehouse or gin-shop. This is going a step beyond even the Permissive Bill, but the experiment appears to be amply justified by the result. One or two beerhouses stand temptingly on the borders of this sober region, and are to a slight extent resorted to by Saltairites, but, for all that, drunkards are excessively scarce, and the real old village toper, renowned for his garrulity and rubicundity, has no abiding place within the precincts of the little manufacturing town. Including the Almshouses, there are 820 dwellings in Saltaire, inhabited at the last census by 4389 persons. In the nomenclature of the streets, Sir Titus has, in the first place, shown his loyalty by naming the chief road after his Sovereign, and another road after the late Prince Consort; and, in the second place, he has shown his affection for his family by giving the names of each of his children to other streets.

Having now completed my outside tour, I dive into the inmost recesses of the works, first providing myself with an introduction to a certain directing power in the official sanctum, and then procuring the said directing power for my guide through the endless ways and intricacies of the establishment. Closed is the fine entrance gateway, worthy of triumphal cars and gorgeous Eastern processions, though reserved for what is probably deemed a far nobler purpose, the procession of the troops of incoming and outgoing workpeople. Stragglers and private individuals are obliged to enter through an inquiry office at the side, tenanted by a half-liveried ancient, who looks as serious as if he kept the secrets of the whole concern locked up in his own broad bosom. He is my usher, the link which connects my outside ignorance with the inner mysteries of the place. From this warder I learn nothing, except that Mr. So-and-so is in and Mr. Such-and-such is out; other than such scraps of information as these, he has nothing to impart, although he certainly gives one the impression that he is the guardian of much more important matters than these

P

ins and outs. As soon as he has condescended to hand me over to the directing power before mentioned, I pass out of his sight, but his warning look haunts me during the rest of the day, and, worse than all, he has appeared to me in my dreams in the garb of Bluebeard, with an ominous string of huge keys at his girdle. But, to resume, as it is customary to observe when one has lost his way in rhapsody or digression. We (the directing power and your humble Saunterer) passed through the large courtyard, from which branched off a multitude of ways, leading to cavernous depths and giddy heights, north, south, east and west, and on through some unaccountable inlet, until we reached the main front of the factory, and there we stood for a breathing space looking up at the wondrous pile, like pigmies surveying a Brobdignagian Palace. We then entered the centre portion of the building, in which the engines were sweating and panting (but by no means groaning) in the successful endeavour to keep revolving the two miles of shafting and the thousands of looms, spindles, pulleys, drums and belts contained in the works. The first impression caused by the sight of the two chief engines, which can be seen from the front, is one of simple wonder, but that feeling gradually ripens into one of awe as you become conscious of the power exerted by these beams and wheels and pistons.

The four engines now at work represent 1700 or 1800 horse power; fourteen boilers have to be fed, to provide steam for them; and 2400 tons weight of stone has been used in building the engine beds. The steam-god may pull and tear to his utmost strength, he may try as he will to free himself from his stone chain of 2400 tons, it is all to no purpose, he might as well try to pull down a mountain. No wonder that there should be so little vibration to be felt in the engine-house, for the massive beams, rods and wheels go through their evolutions as comfortably and as easily as if there were no responsibility attached to what they are doing. How dazzlingly bright is every inch of the great engines! If they would only stop for a moment I might adjust my necktie by the endless mirrors which they afford. I am informed that the two jerking arms of machinery which make mocking movements at each other in front of the engines are an application of the Corliss principle. After an inspection of the bottom part of the engines, we ascend a flight of steps and seem to stand in the very midst of the flying wheels and rods, and, look up or look down, we see nothing but great threatening arms moving about, ponderous wheels rushing round with Titanic energy, and huge beams swaying up and down in mighty alternation. Each single part of the engines appears to be trying its best to outdo the other parts. No sooner does one mighty beam come thundering down than the rival beam follows suit, and no sooner does one piston give a mischievous snort than other pistons snort in an equally aggravating way. But there is yet another flight of stairs to ascend ere we are on a level with the upper parts of the great machines, and when we reach this elevation and look down we see a gulf of terrible appearance. What with the heat that arises from the engines and the flush that is engendered by a brief attempt to carry my imagination forward to the results of a suicidal leap into the steaming abyss, I am at this point of my tour of inspection put into a general (very general) state of perspiration.

But, Corliss principle or no, I must not linger further in this warm place, so I am conducted out into the open air again, and have a look at the eleven boilers embedded in the earth between the railway and the mill. Two or three grimy men are the genii who preside over and feed these eleven fiery-mouthed monsters, although the amount of coal consumed by them is comparatively small. Two out of the eleven boilers are twelve feet in diameter, and are arranged with a double allowance of fires, which permits of one fire being kept in a thoroughly heated condition until the other overtakes it, and *vice versa*. From this spot, after givin

a rapid glance at the array of railway trucks, laden
and unladen, which lie about on the Saltaire works'
sidings, I pass into the new wool-shed at the east
side of the factory, where thousands of bales of
wool (embryo dresses) of all qualities, are piled up,
and a number of check-pinafored men move in and
out amongst them as if trying to assure these variegated foreign fleeces that they will receive the
most considerate treatment. Leaving the woolpacks—alpaca, mohair and botany—to themselves,
we once more cross the front, passing the mill
chimney in our transit, and gazing up at its stony
immensity, its height being 250 feet and its base
twenty-four feet square.

We now betake ourselves into the far interior of
the works, threading in and out, hither and thither,
and ascending flight after flight of stairs, until I
find myself landed upon a sort of permanent draw-
bridge, which overlooks a great inner expanse of
the establishment. Here I have no difficulty in
understanding the general disposition of the works.
The connected blocks of buildings are arranged in
the form of the letter T. The upper part of the
letter is typified by the 545 feet of mill frontage,
six storeys in height, which looks towards the
north and abuts upon the railway. The body of
the letter consists chiefly of warehousing, and the
tails of the letter (for you will please imagine it is

a member of the Roman alphabet that I am speaking of) is represented by another stretch of warehousing that looks upon the canal, and is 330 feet long.   Continuing my illustration, or filling up, of the letter T, I now notice that each side of the letter is occupied by enormous sheds, the one on the western side being devoted to the combing processes, and the other to weaving, each shed " measuring 112 feet in width by 210 feet in length."   In the weaving shed there are no fewer than 1200 looms, and there is also a room of the mill which is given up to weaving.   There are ten rooms devoted to spinning, the chief of these being the gigantic room, 550 feet long, at the top of the mill.

By some means or other I presently found myself transported into this topmost room.   I entered it in the centre, and was certainly taken aback by the view.   Looking down upon long rows of spinning frames, seeing figures but dimly discernable moving about in the extreme distance, observing a clock hanging on the wall at the end, and not being able to tell the time in ever so faint a way, I could not but allow myself to drop into another fit of marvelling.   The view on the other side was the same.

From this place we took flight by means of a hoist, the conductor of which stopped us at one of the middle rooms.   In our descent we caught glimpses of the different spinning rooms, but as they were similar (except in point of size) to the great upper room, we did not think it necessary to examine them further. I now got conducted into the warehouse, which stretches from south to north, in which I saw thousands upon thousands more packs of wool, with here and there a dark bit of fleece peeping out, as if unable to endure imprisonment a moment longer. It was here that I saw long rows of windows divided into compartments, at each of which stood a woolsorter, attired in a long pinafore, like an overgrown schoolboy, tumbling and shaking the raw fleeces between his fingers, and sorting the good from the bad, and the indifferent from the very bad. A hundred and fifty men are employed in this not very arduous labour, and, whether the occupation be healthy or not, the men have, at all events, a healthy, cheerful look about them. In a small room adjoining, the alpaca wool is spread out upon immense wire sieves, on its first leaving the sheets in which it has been imported, and here it is submitted to a process of fan-blowing from beneath, which serves to rid the fleeces of much of the dust which had adhered to them while on the backs of living animals.

And now I visited the immense weaving shed, containing 1200 looms, and I know not how many hundred weavers. They formed a variegated picture, altogether, what with the many-coloured garments of the workers and the many-more-coloured hues of the "pieces" they were weaving. Every tint of the rainbow was represented. Rattle, rattle went the looms, the shuttles flying right and left with the speed of so many arrcws, and the weavers seeming to work with a will that foreshadowed good wages at the end of the week. But the staring a poor visitor is subjected to! Oh, dear! let no bashful young bachelor present himself to the microscopic gaze of that multitude of eyes, unless he has made up his mind to endure the sublime torture of the most scarlet of blushes. What effect the eye-shots had upon me I am not bound to say; suffice it that I survived to relate my afternoon's experience. From the weaving shed we crossed over to the combing shed. Here I saw the grim machines clicking, pulling, coaxing, and combing into beautiful silky slivers the wool which I had before seen in the hands of the sorters and in the packs. This process is even more interesting to watch than the weaving. I afterwards had a peep into the place where the wool is washed, and I.had then seen the wool in all its manifold stages—in the sheet, on the dust-sieve, in course of being sorted, in washing, preparing, combing, spinning, and, finally, weaving. I now followed the woven "pieces" into the room of that mysterious individual designated the "Taker-in." The "Taker-in" is not a sharper, however, nor is he a man who makes it his business to deceive; as a rule, he is an undeceiver, for if a weaver imagines that she has a flaw in her work that he will fail to notice she will probably find herself grievously mistaken. A number of weavers were waiting anxiously to have their work inspected as we went in, and we saw the "Taker-in" pulling the "pieces" over rollers in front of windows, and eyeing every inch keenly, in order to see if there were any imperfect work.

I now bid adieu to the directing power and to the "Works" for that one day, and make up my mind to spend an hour or two in learning how the people of Saltaire pass their non-working time. I pursue this quest, in the first instance, by visiting the Club and Institute, which is both social and educational in its objects. The entrance-hall, which is approached by a broad flight of steps, is altogether palatial in its appearance, the walls being delicately-decorated and the ceiling boldly-moulded and very lofty. A remarkably fine clock, presented by Mr. George Salt, hangs in this vestibule and tells the hour to the passing visitor, and one of Admiral Fitzroy's barometers is suspended from the opposite wall. On the right of the hall there is a goodly-sized library of some three thousand volumes of well-selected literature. The

half-denuded aspect of the shelves furnishes sufficient evidence of the books being extensively read,
and the information I elicit from the librarian fully
bears this view out. Crossing to the left side of
the vestibule, I enter the reading-room, which is
a capacious, well-lighted and admirably-arranged
apartment.   The reading-desks and tables are
conveniently placed, and the comfort and seclusion
of visitors appear to have been carefully provided
for in every way. Nearly all the local papers, the
London dailies, and the leading magazines and re-
views lie ready for perusal, and are, I believe, very
generally taken advantage of. Over the massive
marble mantelpiece hangs the life-size portrait of
Sir Titus Salt, which is a good example of the
artistic genius of Mr. J. P. Knight, R.A., and was
presented to the Founder of Saltaire by his workpeople, on the 26th of August, 1871. In one corner
of the room there stands a handsome globe, which, if
mere dimension goes for anything, ought to contain
much more geography than the ordinary globes
are accustomed to hold. Near this there are a few
shelves on which rest a number of cyclopædias and
other important works of reference; and round the
walls are placed a series of Stanford's largest maps.
Returning to the vestibule, I pass on to the large
lecture-hall and concert-room, not staying to notice
the cloak-rooms, lavatories, &c., which fall away to

the right and left. The lecture-hall is a great archi-tectural success, and for simple elegance and beauty is probably unsurpassed by any room of similar dimensions in the kingdom. It is ninety feet in length, sixty feet wide, and forty feet high, and affords sitting accommodation for 800 persons. There are five large windows on each side of the hall, and columns rise in semi-relief between them, and expand and run off into the most charming mouldings, exquisitely pencilled and coloured, and forming a *tout ensemble* which would, I think, satisfy the most hypercritical of art critics. The roof is as delightfully-moulded as the walls. It is chopped up into compartments and panels which are very orna-mental in their character. Round the walls are emblazoned the names of the most celebrated musical composers, and at the upper end of the hall there is a stage thirty-five feet wide, and capa-cious enough to accommodate the largest concert party, unless it be a Crystal Palace Chorus. Leaving this "hall of dazzling light," I make the tour of the rest of the building, passing in rapid succession through the science and art class-rooms, in which I see boys imbibing the principles of chemistry, and girls drawing amidst a wealth of models and statuary; through the large billiard-room, where four huge tables are being trundled over in the most expert fashion by workmen adepts; through another, but

smaller, lecture-hall; through the chess-room, where
pawns, bishops, knights, kings and queens stand
setting problems to each other, the players not
having arrived yet; through the middle-class boys'
and girls' school-rooms, where I hear the sound of
joyous voices and look upon a merry array of faces;
and through the cellular regions, where a splendid
gymnasium is fitted up, and where there is an
armoury, in which repose the bright breech-loaders
of the hundred volunteers who comprise the Saltaire
Rifle Corps.

From the Institute, in which I would fain have
spent considerably more time, I cross over to the
Elementary Schools, and am just in time to see the
children before they break up for the day. Mr.
Morell, the master, kindly officiates as my guide,
and I wander through the various class-rooms and
see the little scholars going through their tasks,
under the guidance of efficient monitors, with a
cheerfulness and a vivacity which are not always to
be found in schools where half-timers are educated.
Every educational aid that experience could suggest
seems to have been called in here, and I am
informed that the children show a wonderful apti-
tude for availing themselves of the advantages thus
afforded to them. The children, both boys and
girls, are mostly attired in working garb, but they
are neat and clean, and look as if both the work

and the instruction agreed with them. There are about a thousand scholars under tuition at present, and they are arranged according to sexes, ages, and degrees of knowledge attained, in four spacious class-rooms, the boys occupying one wing of the building and the girls the other. Three large asphalted playgrounds open out at the back of the building, in which there seems to be room enough to exercise an army of soldiers. One of the playgrounds is under cover, allowing it to be used when the weather is wet, and there is the most ample provision made for gymnastic training.

I next visit the Congregational Chapel, and am as deeply impressed with the grand solemnity of its interior aspect as with the peacefulness and beauty of the landscape around. There is accommodation for about six hundred people in the chapel, and it is very well attended. The tall, Corinthian columns which rise on each side of the building are simple in design, and the general ornamentation of the edifice is in perfect harmony therewith. The seats are elegantly carved, and, railed off by a massive balustrade, stand the pulpit and precentor's seat. On the pulpit side of the building there is erected the Salt Family Mausoleum, in which there already repose the remains of three of the children of Sir Titus, and the wife of one of his sons.

The Saltaire Baths and Wash-houses, in Carolin Street, contribute greatly to the comfort and cleanliness of the people, affording, as they do, accommodation for the washing, wringing, and drying of clothes, and the bathing of the entire population. There are six washing machines in the place, and the arrangements are the best which modern ingenuity has been able to devise.

A peep into the Infirmary, which is situated adjoining the Almshouses, and another peep into the little Chapel, in which the infirm people who inhabit the Almshouses are ministered to at their very doors, complete my afternoon's inspection, and I turn reluctantly away from the picturesque little town, with a firmer belief in man's *humanity* to man than I had held when I left Woolborough.

THE HAUNTS OF AN OLD YORKSHIRE SQUIRE.

"IF you love me, Barnacles," I said, solemnly, yet earnestly, "do not let us go back to Woolborough to-day; let us seek some quiet haunt where the cool breath of heaven can fan our cheeks, and where——"

"Bosh!" murmured my friend, bringing his stick down upon the Wakefield Station platform with an impatient bang. "It's all very well for you to talk like this, after being confined in the House of Correction, but for my own part I prefer returning home. I can quite understand the feeling that makes you hesitate to show the light of your visage to your fellow-townsmen, after what has occurred, but you must remember——"

"I do not desire to remember anything about it," I interrupted.

"You must remember," he went on, giving his stick another bang upon the platform, much to the consternation of a porter whose foot had narrowly escaped being crushed, " that I have my business to attend to, and that if I had known you would have had any objection to return to your native town with me I should probably not have come all the way to Wakefield to meet you."

At that moment a train came rushing into the station, letting-off steam violently from both sides, as it drew up, deafening and confusing everybody.

" Take-sea's-san-wafn-bafn-wafn," or some equally intelligible gibberish, was shouted by the porters, and there was a general precipitation towards the carriage doors, the impression seeming to prevail that the train was "all right" for anywhere.

" Come on !" cried Barnacles.

" Let me entreat——"

" Come on, " persisted my friend, making physi— cal appeal to my coat-collar.

" Take-sea's-san-wafn-bafn-wafn !" kept on the porters, trying to make themselves heard above the hissing engine.

The next minute I and Barnacles were sitting in a comfortable carriage. We were quickly borne from the station and out into the open country. I tried to look disconsolate. Barnacles twirled his stick between his two hands with an air of triumph. How I longed to pitch that stick out of the window. We did not exchange a single word until the train drew up at a station.

"Sandal and Walton! Sandal and Walton!" was the sound that then saluted our ears.

"Sandal and Walton!" exclaimed Barnacles, with a look of intense surprise. 'That's not on our line.' Here, I say, porter, what's this engine-driver of your's been doing?"

"Sandal and Walton! Sandal and Walton!" was the only response.

"Where do you want to go, sir?" asked a fellow-passenger.

"To Woolborough, to be sure," replied Barnacles, as if it were absurd to think there was any other spot on the face of the earth that it was worth his while to go to.

"You've got into the wrong train, then, sir."

Out we jumped, and the treacherous locomotive was soon out of the reach of my friend's anger.

A porter then explained that we had got into a Midland instead of a Great Northern train, but, nevertheless, that if we had kept our seats we should have been conveyed to Allwool, and from thence might have proceeded to Woolborough.

"Why didn't you tell us this before we got out?" cried Barnacles.

"Because you didn't ask me, sir."

It was thus that my friend and I found ourselves stranded at the Sandal and Walton Railway Station. Having gazed at each other with a look of mutual reproach for the space of two full minutes, our eyes saying more than anything that could have been done in the shape of mere words, we thought it well to inquire when we could be forwarded to Woolborough.

"In an hour and forty minutes," said the porter.

"I am glad of this, after all," I said to Barnacles, consolingly, "for we shall now have the opportunity that I so longed for, of bathing in the soft summer breezes, and of feeling that pure air and freedom are still to be found in this Yorkshire of ours."

"Rubbish!" exclaimed Barnacles, as he stalked off after the disappearing porter, whom he overtook and addressed as follows :—"Here, I say, what is there for people to do when they are benighted at this insignificant hamlet? What sort of lions have you at 'San-wafn-bafn-wafn ?'"

"Lions!" cried the man, as his mind reverted to the neighbouring lunatic asylum, and he thought he had better humour his questioner. "We're out o' lions, I believe, sir, at present, though old Splinter, up i' the village, has an uncommonly fine jackass, an' there's a few dogs an' other animals worth notice, but——"

"You mistake my friend," I said to the bewildered railway servant, "he uses the word lion in its metaphorical sense; what he means to ask is, have you any sights worth seeing ?"

"There's Walton Hall, and there's——"

"Just the thing!" I cried. "Walton Hall is the place of all others that I desire to visit. It is the birds' paradise, the place where old Squire Waterton lived in happy retirement after his famous 'Wanderings' were over, the place which is now occupied by an old Woolboroughite whose antiquarian tastes and proclivities will doubtless have led him to keep the squire's ancient haunts in their original beauty, and the place where I am sure we shall receive a true Yorkshire welcome."

Barnacles was hardly less taken with the idea than myself, and we were soon on our way to Walton Hall.

The village of Walton is a quaint old spot, where coats and hats seem to be regarded as unnecessary articles of attire, and where straw-thatched houses still remain to evidence the simple life of the last century. From the village to the hall is a distance of more than a mile, the approach being along a pleasant country road, bordered on each side, for a long way, by lofty trees, making, with the leafy carriage road in the park, an avenue of nearly a mile in length, many of the trees having been planted by the late squire himself. This walk to Walton Hall was just what I wanted; it furnished me with a pleasant, bracing exercise, and called up a flood of memories which speedily drowned—

temporarily, at least—any unpleasant recollections that I might have brought away with me from prison.

I was glad to find that Barnacles was as well acquainted with the writings, habits, and eccentricities of "the Wanderer" as myself. Neither of us had ever made the pilgrimage to Walton before, but, thanks to the squire's personal narrations (which always formed the most entertaining portion of his writings), and thanks, also, to Dr. Hobson's pedantic, interesting, good-hearted, and clumsy biography of the old naturalist, we were able to associate the scene, as we passed along, with well-known events in Mr. Waterton's life. When we reached the lodge, at the entrance to the park, we boldly summoned the keeper, and, after having had certain inquiries satisfactorily answered, proceeded towards the hall. The Leeds and Barnsley Canal skirts the outside of the park walls for a considerable distance, and accords well with the old-fashioned manorial residence, the boatmen and their rude vessels seeming to belong as essentially to the past as did Squire Waterton himself. Once inside the park we were entirely shut out from the busy world. The walls of the park are high and substantial, and represent a circumference of some two and a half miles. From the park walls the ground falls gradually on all sides, until the lake, the island, and, the mansion are reached, when a picturesque bit of level comes upon us, disclosing an attractive sheet of water, rich patches of greenery, and a sturdy, substantial stone hall. We were delighted with the view thus presented to us, and felt as far removed from the dull routine of business pursuits as if we had been suddenly transported to the banks of Lake Como.

What was perhaps the most interesting sight of all, however, was that of the birds flitting to and fro in happy security on every side. The lake was prettily dotted with wild fowl, and from every hedge and tree a bevy of feathered beauties peered and chattered at us as we passed. In Mr. Waterton's time animated nature was supposed to have found its paradise at Walton Hall, and there is every evidence that the squire did all that he could to cultivate the closest terms of friendship with everything that lived, his only abomination being, perhaps, the "Hanoverian" rat, which animal he charmed from the precincts of Walton Hall by a spell almost as potent as that practised by Browning's famous Pied Piper. The sun was shining pleasantly when we made our descent upon this "moated grange" without its Mariana, and everything looked so radiant and joyous that we almost forgot that we were standing in the midst of a gentleman's private grounds.

"Nature and the old squire were capital friends,"
I remarked, just as we came to a stand by a magnificent yew edge that grows at the entrance to what is
termed "The Grotto."

"Yes, and there also seems to be a strong
disposition to form an alliance between the
ancient dame and the new squire," said Barnacles.

At that instant we heard a dog making manifestations somewhere in the vicinity of the house. The
animal was evidently not baying "deep-mouthed
welcome," judging by the manner in which it woke
the echoes.

"But," continued Barnacles, in acknowledgment
of this canine interruption, "there can be too much
even of Nature, especially when it presents itself in
the form of hydrophobia."

He had hardly concluded his sentence when there
came bounding over the lawn in front of the house
an immense animal that partook partly of the
panther and partly of the English mastiff, its colour
being a sort of leaden grey.

"If he takes it into his head to swim over the
lake, or to jump the gate and cross the bridge, our
lives will not be worth five minutes' purchase," said
Barnacles, eyeing the animal suspiciously as it
seemed to be meditating which of us would be pre-
ferable for his first course.

What might have been the upshot had we been
left to ourselves it is difficult to conjecture, but,
happily, there came to our rescue a stalwart gentleman, between whom and the animal there appeared
to be the most perfect understanding. With a
warm English greeting, he advanced over the
bridge and invited us forward, the magic words
" Saunterer " and " Barnacles " for the time
operating as effectively as did Ali Baba's " Open,
Sesame ! " Thenceforward we were free to go
where we listed, to linger beside the lake, to dive
into the grotto, to pass the portals of the mansion
and inspect its inner attractiveness. When we
had crossed the bridge, our enemy, the mysterious
animal, was waiting to receive us. Our host
tried to appease our suspicions by assuring us
that it would not molest us, but Barnacles
pretended to be watching a water-fowl very
intently until I had gone through the form of
introduction with the dog. It was an African
boar-hound, I was told, and I succeeded in gaining
his good opinion by meekly submitting myself and
every portion of my garments to the sniff of his
intelligent nose. Barnacles pretended to be
indifferent to the movements of the animal after
these preliminaries, but it was easy to see by
his generally noticing attractive objects on the
side contrary to that on which the the dog walked,

and seeing none in any close proximity to the boar-hound, that he did not feel altogether safe or happy.

We had now a good opportunity of examining the exterior of the hall, the extent of the lake, and the general appearance of the surroundings. The hall itself does not exhibit any striking architectural beauty, being a plain, commodious, substantial mansion, such perhaps as Mrs. Hemans had in her mind pretty generally when she wrote those lines of hers on "the stately homes of England." The mansion stands on an island, having at one time been surrounded by a moat, which in later times was broadened and converted into a lake. A trim lawn occupies the space between the front of the house and the water, and the cast-iron bridge erected by the old squire crosses opposite the front door. The mansion is three storeys in height, and is entered by a portico supported by four plain pillars. Above the portico appears the coat of arms of the Waterton family, showing an otter with a fish in its mouth, and bearing the somewhat puzzling motto of "Better kinde fremd than fremd kinde," which our host translates as "Better kind friend than inimical relation." Dr. Hobson tried hard to unravel the mystery of this motto, and his free interpretation was, "Better friendly strangers than deceitful friends." The house is entered by strong folding doors, each of which bears a very characteristic impress of the old Squire's ingenuity and originality, in the shape of an iron knocker. The door to the left, which is kept closed, has a knocker representing a human face laughing with mischievous delight. This knocker is a sham, however, for it cannot be got to give forth a single summoning rap; hence the laughing face. The knocker on the other door can be rapped, however, with ease, and the face there represented seems to writhe under the infliction of the visitor's blows, thus being in perfect contrast to its companion.

Having completed our survey of the front of the mansion, we now turned round and took a mental photograph of the spot; the African boar-hound sauntered off in the direction of the kitchen, where a cold collation of bones was probably awaiting him. Barnacles' spirits rose wonderfully, as soon as his dogship was shut out of the immediate land-scape. How briskly he led the conversation now! What a multitude of beautiful objects he suddenly discovered, and what a number of " local notes and queries " he ventured to unburden himself of! Ah, there was the thirty or forty acres of lake encircling the grand old edifice. What particular finny tribe was it that lived and moved there? Pike and perch? (Then came a wondrous story of a pike that devoured all his ancestors and posterity, and then, to show the unselfishness of his character, swallowed himself.) Were those Canada geese that were moving in a flock across to the smaller island; and was that a wild duck that was just flying over our heads? He thought so. And it was across that sheet of water, was it, that Blondin wanted to show his rope-walking abilities? He was glad that the mountebank wasn't permitted to desecrate so lovely a spot. And it was over in that hut at the edge of the lake that the old Squire used to sit for hours, watching the herons? What a pity it was that that noble bird no longer made its haunt in the park! The trees where it had taken up its abode had been taken from it, in the interval that elapsed between Mr. Waterton's death and the occupancy of Mr. Hailstone. How beautiful the yew fence looked from this distance, with the dark foliage of the spruce firs showing beyond. And there was the nesting place of the starling, the jack-daw, and the white owl. Those holly hedges, too, were exceedingly fine. And there at the edge of the lake, near the bridge, was the ivy-covered ruin which, in ancient times, formed the entrance to the island and hall. That bit of ruin was just as it existed centuries ago, was it? Would we go down and look at it more particularly? Certainly.

We went, and there listened to the story how a party of besiegers under Oliver Cromwell had been repulsed at that very gateway by the Mrs. Waterton of the period, in the absence from home of her husband, the lady and her household acting with such heroism as to cause the people of the neighbourhood to give a fête in her honour, at which fête ——Cromwell's party having carried away the horses belonging to the establishment—she had her carriage drawn by six oxen.   Cromwell also destroyed the ancient draw-bridge that crossed here, and in the door there still remains a bullet fired by the attacking party, a brass inscription, on which the fact is recorded, having been put round the bullet by the old squire.   This ruin is surmounted by a stone cross, and altogether forms a most interesting feature of the residence.   Having seen all that there was to be seen in this ivy-mantled ruin, we ascended to the island again, Barnacles going first. The boar-hound met him, and, without going into too minute particulars, I may just remark that my friend went back and read the bullet-inscription again.

We next visited, in company with the boar-hound, the southern side of the house, and saw Boulby's celebrated sun-dial (the handiwork of a working mason who lived at Crofton in 1813), the peculiarity of which is that it contains twenty separate dials,

indicating the exact solar time at as many different
parts of the globe simultaneously. The dial consists of twenty equilateral triangles hewn out of
one block. Near this, too, were the subterranean
boat-houses, affording very convenient access to the
boats. We did not charter one, for I had not for
gotten Barnacles' rowing experiences at Morecambe
when he ran us into the *Myrtle*. At this side of
the house there has been an attempt made to build
a chapel, but the project was not proceeded with
The body of an infant, the child of the old squire's
son, was buried at the spot, however, so that three
generations of Watertons are really buried within
the grounds. The great grandfather of the squir
is said to have his grave within a clump of trees
some fifty or sixty yards from the lake ; and the
Squire himself, as is well known, reposes at the foot
of two favourite oak trees, near the head of the
lake. But, as the poet says, " the old order
changeth, giving place to new ;" and although
Walton Hall has been the home of the Waterton
lords of the manor of Walton, from a very ancient
date, the old name has now disappeared. It is
be hoped that those who have to come hereafter will
be as anxious to preserve the associations of the
place as the present owner is, in which case the old
hall may long be a place of the deepest interest to
naturalists as well as to antiquaries.

Our host now led the way across the "cast-iron bridge," with the intention of showing us the beauties of the grotto. Our friend the boar-hound happened to yawn just as we reached the foot of the bridge, however, and so strange was the noise made by the animal, and so strange was his look, that I verily believed Barnacles imagined that his last hour had come, for he jumped about a yard into the air and, uttering a piteous cry, seemed to totter against the side of the bridge.

"What is the matter?" I asked alarmedly.

"This confounded tooth again, that's all," he replied, and walked rapidly to the other side of the bridge. The boar-hound was not permitted to follow, and my friend's toothache speedily left him.

We had not gone many yards, however, before we came upon a kennel of genuine English mastiffs, clamouring and barking at us through their iron bars, but of these Barnacles evinced no fear; they were too well guarded.

The grotto is a most beautiful retreat, suitable alike for the recluse, the naturalist, and the pleasure seeker. A grove of spruce firs, whose dark foliage contrasts finely with the brighter green of the trees that encircle the spot, affords ample scope for the study of the habits of birds. The mimic ivy-grown temple that forms the chief evidence of man's interference with this umbrageous solitude is a most picturesque object; and I can well understand how popular this resort must have been in the old Squire's lifetime, when it was thrown open to visitors, who were allowed the most kindly accommodation in the way of sheltering and refreshment places. Brass bands were even permitted to invade this sylvan retreat occasionally, and terpsichorean exercise was indulged in either at the base of the grotto or in the large temple. A stream meanders through the grotto, and the considerate Squire had provided steps for visitors to get to the water and wash their hands. Barnacles and I thoroughly enjoyed ourselves threading in and out amongst the trees in the grotto, the birds chirping gleefully on almost every bough as we passed, and the wild flowers gleaming in their myriad colours in every glade. The Squire, however, did not approve of his visitors indulging in mischief, as is shown by a certain "S.A." having his initials branded upon one of the trees as a caution against anyone repeating the act of mischief that he was caught in in 1862. The present tenant of the hall has in some respects heightened the beauty of this place by converting one of the temples into a rosary, and introducing a great many other beautiful flowers, which grow as profusely as the wild ones.

Even now we had exceeded our train time considerably, so we settled down contentedly to make as much of our Walton experience as possible. We visited the flower and kitchen gardens, the nut orchard, the stables, and fowl-houses. We could hear the rooks wrangling with each other in the distant trees; we could hear that unearthly-voiced but magnificent bird, the peacock, screeching forth its monotonous note; we could hear the mastiffs yelling and barking in their play, and still there was a peace and a repose about the scene that were exceedingly impressive. Getting further out into the park, we came upon many curious contrivances devised by the squire for the protection of his feathered friends. He provided the owl with roosting places in the hollows of trees, and had holes made in the garden walls for the special accommodation of the swifts. He studied, in every possible way, the comfort of the birds and animals that were companions to him, and they evidently reciprocated the attachment, and tried to make themselves as much at home, and tried to yield him as much pleasure as it was in their power to do. Mr. Waterton kept a list of the names of all birds that were in the habit of visiting him, or that he ever saw in the park, the list including such birds as the osprey, the kestrel, the carrion crow, the raven, the nightingale, and an astonishing collection of wild fowl. Circumstances have not favoured the perpetuation of many of these breeds at Walton since

the death of the Squire, but since Mr. Hailstone
has been there praiseworthy efforts have been made
to make the place as enticing for feathered visitants
as even in "the Wanderer's" days. The situation
is eminently suitable for a birds' paradise, being in
the midst, as it were, of a continuous line of gentlemen's seats, extending for several miles. The only
sign of commercial life to be seen from the park—
and that only from the higher ground—is shown in
a view of quaint, old Wakefield, some four miles
distant.

Walking round the park that afternoon was a
very enjoyable pastime, especially when the African
boar-hound was not near. By-and-bye we tramped
round the upper portion of the lake and sat down
by the "Wanderer's" grave—a little mound at
the foot of two decayed oaks, rudely walled round
with stone, and containing at the foot a cross
bearing the following inscription engraved in
marble :—

Orate

pro animâ Caroli Waterton

cujus fessa

juxta hanc crucem

sepeliunter

ossa

"Pray for the soul of Charles Waterton, whose
wearied bones are buried near this cross." Barnacle
and I were left alone at this sacred spot, and as the

shades of evening closed in upon us we talked in
affectionate strain of "The Wanderer," picturing
him in those South American travels of his upwards of sixty years ago.   Now we saw him doing
battle with a snake, now riding on the back of a
cayman, now sleeping in a primeval forest with
panthers glaring at him through the dense under-
growth, now stricken down with fever in the jungle,
now standing on the golden angel at the top of the
Castle of St. Angelo, and now bringing home his
mysterious "nondescript;" but wherever we pictured him, and under whatsoever circumstances,
there we always saw a true English gentleman,
kind of speech and simple of manner, genial,
brave, affectionate.   After doing homage at this
shrine in our humble way, we betook ourselves
to our feet once more, making further acquaintance with flocks of wild fowl, and overtaking fresh delights almost at every step.   We passed
the little bridge over the creek where Mr. Waterton
met with the accident which was the immediate
cause of his death; we sat for a moment upon the
half of an old sedan chair just beyond the creek;
we stood and admired the small island in the
middle of the lake; and then passed on to the
hall, our host having kindly promised to act as
our cicerone.   The boar-hound was nowhere about,
so we entered.

R

Gone were the cases of preserved birds and
mals so highly treasured by the old squire; g
was the famous *lusus naturæ* that used to stan
the foot of the staircase; gone was the still r
famous "nondescript," the grand joke of the squ
life; but their places had been filled with co
curiosities and gems of art-workmanship, with b
and manuscripts, with precious lace and nee
work, and I know not what rare relics and ade
ments.   I might as well try to describe a win
the British Museum in a newspaper column
attempt to catalogue the valuable examples of
and learning that Mr. Hailstone has collected in
ancestral hall of the Watertons; besides, there r
be a certain circumspection observed in telling v
you see in a house where you are received as a v
tor.   What poor Artemus denominated "article
virtue" abounded on every hand.   In the hall tl
were old German and brass dishes, elaborate sp
mens of antique metal work; there was a Nur
berg chandelier of the 15th century, representing
Virgin and Child at the top and Satan in an apj
priate position at the bottom.   The veritable s
used by Lord Fairfax (Black Tom) was amongst
curiosities.   Specimens of Italian mosaic of the l
century were also to be seen, and the grouping
arrangement of the various articles were v
effective.   In the dining-room we observed m

beautiful specimens of metal work, framed and hung as pictures; a very rare and curious Persian dish, four feet in diameter, dated 1380, with an elaborate inscription which, we were informed, had been translated by M. Arminius Vambéry; and some choice pottery—Palissy and Wedgwood ware. The drawing-room is a spacious and elegant apartment, brilliant with treasures, and containing a portion of Mrs. Hailstone's famous collection of lace. We had previously seen selections from Mrs. Hailstone's valuable and interesting collection at Leeds, South Kensington, and other places; we had been privileged to see the books which that lady has published on the subject of lace, books evincing a thorough acquaintance with lace and embroidery in its minutest details, but the surroundings of this one cabinet in the Walton Hall drawing-room seemed to give a prominence to its contents that made us delight more in these embroidered intricacies than had ever been the case with any other collection that we had inspected. Venetian, Maltese, Point, Italian, and other various and scarce specimens, suitably labelled and arranged, were there to be seen and admired; the collection certainly deserves to be ranked as one of the chief attractions at the hall. Barnacles said he knew a lady who would literally revel in that cabinet, and I believed him. The music-

sheet bore the name of the purchaser printed upon it—Nicholas Hailstone,—as well as a poem by Gent, from which the following is an extract :—

> "Come sprightly youth, fair virgins, husbands, wives,
> Behold an act that seems to give new lives;
> Divert your thoughts with ravishing content,
> And be immortal made by Thomas Gent."

In one of the rooms now devoted to library purposes the old squire used to sleep, his bed hard boards, his pillow a wooden block, slightly hollowed. For more than thirty years he never slept on any other bed. Another room on this floor was used as a chapel by the squire, who often had a priest located in the hall.

To particularise further as to the contents of the hall would hardly be fair, but I may say that we were surprised and pleased with what we saw, and only regretted that we had not time to make a fuller examination. A banquet fittingly closed our afternoon at Walton Hall, and we then sallied forth homeward. Intoxicated with the beauties we had seen we forgot all about the faithful boar-hound, but just as we reached the bridge the animal came bounding up to us. Barnacles sought protection by suddenly sitting down on the grass. What the result would have been had not our host appeared I cannot pretend to say, but when we were assured that the dog never did more than seize people by

the arm or leg, and lead them safely outside th＿＿＿
precincts of the hall, we were satisfied, although w＿＿＿
respectfully declined to have even such escort ＿＿＿
that.

It was in the darkness of the summer night th＿＿＿
we sought the Sandal railway station, but we to＿＿＿
the precaution not to get into the wrong train ＿＿＿a
second time, and in due course we were safe＿＿＿y
landed at Woolborough.

SINGING CHRISTMAS IN.

"HAIR rather long, sir."

"Yes, rather."

"Won't you have it cut for Christmas, sir?"

"No, thank you; weather too cold."

Thus far the barber and myself. He was the shaver, I the shaved. There was another victim present, however, upon whom the barber's eldest son was operating. I looked straight at him over my towel, and he looked straight at me over his. And, in sooth, he was a man to remember. Nature, in his case, had been a sculptor. To some people she acts as painter, giving them delicate tints as beauty marks; to some she acts as simple mechanist, putting together the parts of the human machine without a care for the harmony of the exterior; to some she stands in the capacity of the rudest clay-worker, leaving them with no feature perfectly formed; but to this man, as I have said, Nature had been a sculptor. She had chiselled and chiselled at his features until they stood out one from another with a sharp distinctness that made his face look hard and fierce and biting. But from beneath his overhanging eyebrows there gleamed a pair of eyes sharp as steel and penetrative as the proverbial gimlet. Even when I was not looking at him I could feel his orbits coursing over my face like a lancet, and I quailed under his gaze almost as much as if he had been a vampire thirsting for my blood. The man of lather had got the right half of my chin cleared of its soapy coating, and his son had got about to the same stage with the other one's chin when the conversation above recorded passed between the barber and myself.

"Weather too cold, you think, sir?" added the barber to my last reply, when a voice—full, rich, deep and sonorous—rose from above the opposite towel, and said in the cheeriest possible way, "Never mind the weather if the wind blows fair; that's my motto."

The music of the voice that said this was like an organ to me, and from that moment I changed my feelings towards the man, and in the facial angles and cuttings, where before I had only read ferocity and wildness, I now saw the index nothing but good-humour and kindliness.

"Yes, sir," said the barber, elevating his voice and increasing the speed of his razor, "that's the proper sort of motto, that is, sir. It reminds me chin a little higher, sir, please—of my brother

William, who died two years ago come next Shipley tide—this razor rather coarse, sir?—he used to say that a fair wind and a blue sky bid fortune come and sickness fly—give the gentleman a clean towel, John—and I always think there's a good deal of truth in—a little powder, sir?—those old sayings—there's the towel, sir."

"Yes," returned the other shaved one, as he transferred a coin from his purse to the barber, "old sayings are like old times, the more we think of them the better we appreciate them."

In another minute he was gone.

"Who is that gentleman?" I asked.

"Oh, it's Mr. What-d'ye-call-him—bother it, it's just at my tongue's end— what is it they call him, John? Mr. What?"

"Mr. Flipper," answered John, "he's a bit of a musicianer, an' lives somewhere up by t' Cock and Bottle. He lodges wi' Mr. Dobkins."

"The very man," added the barber. "Thank you, sir; there's the change.".

I took up my hat—— No, it couldn't be! Surely my head had not grown bulkier with staring at this Mr. Flipper. The beaver which I held in my hand was certainly like my hat, and bore inside the name of the maker whom I always patronised, but, for all that, it was a size too small, and would not allow my cranium to settle easily into it.

"He's taken my hat!" I exclaimed. "I must run after him;" and away I went, on Market Street, along Well Street, and up Church Bank.

It was Christmas eve. The streets were alive with cheerful voices and happy faces; Care had slunk back into its darksome cave, now that it had been confronted with the mistletoe and holly, and it seemed as if the whole population had nothing to do but to follow the behest, to "eat, drink, and make merry." St. George, Slasher, the Black Prince, and Little Devil Doubt were abroad in their glazed calico and spangles; little girlish bands of carollers with their wassail-bobs, popped up here and there; boys with concertinas roamed about the streets, as if they were striving to charm (or frighten) away some evil-spirit; and laughing, bright-eyed girls with escorts of joyous youths, made their way hither and thither to Christmas parties. But I had no time to observe these things closely; my lost hat had to be found. In my trepidation, I almost knocked a goose out of the hands of a young woman, who shouted after me, "Look where you're going to, can't you?" and I tore the skirt of a young man dressed in female attire, who rated me for a "clumsy duffer!" But with all my running and all my anxiety I did not succeed in overtaking the man with the wrong hat. At last I found myself opposite Mr. Dobkins's shop. Had I missed this

Mr. Flipper? Certainly, he might have been walking leisurely through the churchyard while I had been puffing and panting up the hill. And then, again, he might not have been coming home at all; probably he, like a vast number of other people, was going to a Christmas party. I waited a minute or two, but no Mr. Flipper made his appearance, so then I took the liberty of giving a gentle knock at Mr. Dobkins's door.

"Mr. Dobkins in?" I asked of a red-faced young man, who answered my summons.

"Mr. Dobkins in!" he cried. "I should rather think he was. Where else would you expect to find him on Christmas Eve, I wonder?"

"Is Mr. Flipper in, then?" I said.

"Is Mr. Flipper in! I should rather think—

"He was, and that he had got your hat," cried the voice of Mr. Flipper himself, who at that moment came to the door. "Come in, sir."

I stepped inside and was ushered into a parlour, where some ten or a dozen people were assembled round a bright fire, upon which a great yule log crackled and blazed.

"I haven't the privilege of knowing your name, sir," said Mr. Flipper.

"Mr. Saunterer," I replied.

"Well, Mr. Saunterer," he continued, looking round at the company, "I'm very sorry that I made

such a stupid mistake as to run away with your hat.
I have only just discovered it, as my friend Dobkins
here can testify.   But I always say that everything
happens for the best, and if to this little accident
we are to owe the pleasure of making you one of
our party to-night, I can only say I shall be very
much obliged to the little accident.   This, sir, is a
family circle of the good old Yorkshire type, got
together to enjoy a good old Yorkshire Christmas.
Here's Mr. Dobkins," and he pointed to a jovial-
faced little man of about fifty, who sat in a corner
chair with a dark-eyed ringleted girl of five or six
upon his knee, "everybody knows Dobkins."

"Everybody knows Dobkins!" cried the red-
faced youth, "I should rather think they did."

"You're right, Jimmy," said Mr. Flipper, heartily,
"and Dobkins is a man whom it's an honour to
know, too."

"An honour to know!" exclaimed Jimmy, "I
should rather think it was."

"Yes," Mr. Dobkins said, putting his little girl
gently into his chair and standing up with a glass
of mulled ale in his hand, "and I allus say, mysen,
'at if there's a man i' this here world 'at desarves
the right hand o' fellowship, that man is called
Sampson Flipper."

"I should rather think it was," shouted Jimmy
of the red face.

After this bit of mutual back-scratching on the part of Flipper and Dobkins, I was formally introduced to the rest of the company. Of course, I vowed that I was delighted that Mr. Flipper had, by running away with my hat, given me the inestimable privilege of making the acquaintance of such a happy Christmas company, and, having nothing better to do, I allowed myself to be persuaded to make one of the party. It was such a jolly thing to be able to have a new experience; such a jolly thing to be able to escape from the old, humdrum— but no more, I will not betray the Christmas weaknesses of my friend Barnacles to any living soul.

Well, in addition to Flipper and Dobkins, and the rosy-cheeked youth yclept Jimmy, there was Mrs. Dobkins, a round, dimply, smiling matron, who bustled about like a true Yorkshire housewife, trying to tempt all the stomachs that came into her way into the Hades of Dyspepsia; there was Mr. O'Moggarty, a naturalised Hibernian, whose soul for ever turned in eloquent worship towards his native bogs and his native whisky; there was Miss Sabina Dobkins, who was nineteen and had a lisp and a lover; there were half-a-dozen very juvenile Dobkinses, young tendrils that still clung to the maternal apron-string and inherited the family taste for all things nice; there was a certain William Henry, a draper's shopman—

and this was the young man to whom Sabina
Dobkins had vowed to be "ever true;" there
was a Miss Bessemer, a friend of Sabina's; and
there were three Sunday-school teachers named
respectively Streamy, Grimtop, and Badger. The
last-named three were singers. Streamy, who
was very fat and very chubby, had an exceedingly
small tenor voice; Grimtop, who was so lanky
that he might have been undergoing a long course
of training for ascending gas pipes, was a basso
profundo; and Badger, who had the neck of a crane
and a face of many tortuous windings, sang alto.

It appeared that they all belonged to the Mount
Moriah Chapel, and their ultimate intention was to
go out Christmas singing. Mr. Flipper had been
constituted leader and conductor by virtue of his
being the oldest member of the party (except the
paternal Dobkinses, and they, of course, were not
going to stir from the family roof), and by virtue
also of his being a clarionet player. All this was
extremely enjoyable to me, and I very soon volunteered to go with them and assist Streamy to sing
tenor. I will not dwell upon the festive proceedings with which the time that intervened between
my joining the party and its setting out on its
singing expedition was beguiled. Suffice it to say
that we sang once through our entire repertoire;
that we played at all kinds of Christmas games (to

each one of which forfeits were appended); that we were very jolly and very happy; that at twenty minutes to twelve Mr. Dobkins got up with another glass of mulled ale in his hand and made a pretty, complimentary speech, concluding with assuring us all that if there was a man in this world that he admired and loved, that man was Sampson Flipper; that Mr. Flipper returned the compliment in the aptest possible terms; that Jimmy declared he should rather think something or other *was;* and that, in fact, we got thoroughly primed for our Christmas singing, and sallied forth in capital Christmas humour.

We were ten, including O'Moggarty and Jimmy, and I sincerely believe that we were unsurpassed in the way of musical talent by any set of singers that ventured abroad that Christmas. There was not a quarter of the town into which we did not penetrate. At all events, you may be assured of this; that if, as you lay in bed listening to the thousand-and-one Christmas sounds that floated in the air that morning, you heard a particularly clear and sweet treble voice, that was the voice of Sabina Dobkins; if you heard a rich and full tenor voice ringing out its upper G with easy, unstrained power, that was the voice of——well, somebody else; if you chanced to be charmed with the dulcet notes of a more than ordinary sweet clarionet, that was the instrument manipulated so deftly by Mr. Flipper; if you happened to hear a concertina which struck home to your inmost heart, that concertina was Jimmy's; and if you heard a deep voice of such baseness as to make you tremble with awe, that voice issued from the mouth of the tall, lanky, cadaverous Grimtop. Yes; we were a splendid party. I really felt highly honoured to be associated with such a set of distinguished musicians.

"Now, in the first place," said Mr. Flipper, when we had got fairly out into High Street, "we will go to our superintendent's and at the first midnight boom of the Town Hall Clock we will strike up with 'Angels from the Realms of Glory.'"

"Strike up!" cried Jimmy, as he struck a chord at a passing cat with his concertina, I should rather think we will."

"Shtrike up or shtrike down, its all the same to me," exclaimed O'Moggarty, "myself's the boy to do ud."

"Heigh up, lads," shouted one of a gang of young ruffians who were just going to let somebody Christmas in with bludgeons and knob-sticks, "here's the man that struck Barney."

A chorus of boyish laughter greeted this exclamation, and we laughed ourselves when O'Moggarty added, "Faith an' you'll be the man that Barney struck, if ye come within rache o' this shtick."

We had all kinds of encounters between rival singers. The chaff that was floating about was enough to take the wind out of the stoutest amongst us. Flipper was several times charged with being the Waits' clarionet; Streamy was greeted sometimes as Sir Roger, by reason of his stoutness, and sometimes as "that delicate young man;" and our two ladies were alluded to as "the dear screechers," "the High Street nightingales," &c. However, we soon learned the truth of the proverb that silence is golden, so we suffered little and said nothing, instead of saying much and suffering more.

A few minutes before twelve we stood in a circle round the door of Mr. Blacktoe, the Mount Moriah superintendent. We spoke in whispers, Flipper knocking first one and then another on the head with his clarionet as a call to song. "There's a light in the window for thee," whispered the draper youth to the sweet Sabina, who was on a simmer with laughter all the time. "Whisht, ye tykes!" hissed Flipper. "It's just on the stroke." "Bedad, I wish it would be sharp an' shtroke, thin," said O'Moggarty. Then, from all points of the compass, in ones and twos and threes, came eager listeners, but on the whole this midnight audience was orderly and not over noisy. At last the quarters were chimed by the

8

Town Hall clock, and Flipper put his clarionet to his mouth, looked ferociously all round, his well-cut features showing up finely by the light of a neighbouring lamp, and then, as the first stroke of midnight sounded we all burst forth with "Angels from the Realms of Glory." Talk about strength and fervour; where would you find greater strength or greater fervour than we displayed in singing this grand old hymn? We seemed to wake a thousand echoes. Every street resounded with the joyous strains of carollers. Such a mingling of tunes and voices, it would be impossible to hear at any other time. Two-thirds of the carollers were singing " Christians Awake." Here they were giving forth " Hail, Smiling Morn " (though not very appropriately perhaps); there they sang " While Shepherds Watched their Flocks by Night;" there it was " Awake up my Glory;" there it was " Hark, the Herald Angels Sing;" and there it was " As the Moments Roll." The music ebbed and flowed, rose and fell, with cadences sweet and cadences rough, and instruments of every kind (save the primeval bagpipes) blended their notes with the " vocal strains;" and, in spite of much that was absurd and laughable, there was an inspiriting devotional fervour about the music that was thus suddenly chanted to the midnight sky that was exceedingly impressive. Now and then a half-drunken brawler disturbed the effect of this carolling, and wild bursts of laughter (born of Christmas cheer) would sometimes break in upon us. Everybody was up. Those who were not out in the streets were enjoying their Christmas festivities indoors, waiting for the carollers to come, perhaps, or "takin' a cup of kindness" with their neighbours.

As soon as we had finished our hymn the bolts were undone and Mr. Blacktoe, a white-haired, spruce old gentleman, bid us "Come in, my lads and lasses." But there was a slight form to be observed before we were permitted to pass the threshold. "Nah lasses, an' all ye chaps wi' red hair, keep back a bit," cried Mrs. Blacktoe, coming forward to the door. "We're noan bahn to hev Kersmas let in wi' sich as ye. Let's look at ye." She then sharply surveyed us, and Flipper and myself being somewhat darker-visaged than some of the others, were allowed to enter first. As soon as we two had effected an entrance, the door was closed upon our companions and they were not admitted until Flipper and I had uttered the usual Christmas greeting. This ceremony at an end, the whole party burst in, and in another minute we were all eating and drinking as heartily as if we had not broken our fast for a week. How they did press the good

cheer upon us, to be sure! We sang two more
hymns inside, and then we scrambled away to
another house where we were expected.

Vain would it be for me to attempt to recount
our experiences at every place where we halted.
For the first hour our success was uninterrupted.
At every house we were received with the heartiest
manifestations of welcome, and at every house
we were compelled to "eat, drink, and make
merry." The capacity of devouring is never so
fully developed as at a time like this. "Spice
cake and cheese," "good ale enow," "drops o'
summat warm," and "just the least bit o' mince
pie" did their work upon us in time, and whether
any of us began to *see* double or not I am very well
sure that we were not long before we *felt* double.
Oh, that I had had Barnacles with me; that I
could have seen his expansion under the influence
of good cheer; that I could have witnessed the
gradual blossoming of his countenance from the
whiteness of the lily to the richness of the red,
red rose! But it was not to be, and I must
confess that my nine companions furnished me
with plenty of matter for my mental note-book.
The first signs of obfuscation were perceivable in
the way in which the letter S was pronounced.
"Just so" became "jusht sho," and "Christians
awake" became "Krishtians awake." I must,

however, absolve our two *prime donne* from any
charge of this kind, for let it be known in the
exalted region of the Cock and Bottle that the
young ladies were professed teetotallers at every
place that we visited. As our tongues—I mean
their tongues, for if there be one thing that I
pride myself upon more than another it is, &c.—
yielded still more to the festive influences the
letter L was also mercilessly slaughtered. One
of our number, in telling us that all the people
were following us, assured us that "awng ye
peepang fongowed us." But his intention was
there if not the execution, and we forgave him
and smiled.

At one house we came upon a couple of old jokers,
who were full of Christmas anecdotes ; at another
we found a poor young girl dying of consumption,
and were the means of giving joy to her heart by
chanting such music as was in unison with her holy
feelings ; at another we shared applause with a band
of mummers ; at another we were the unwilling
witnesses of family bickerings, which we were
powerless to avert; and at another we found nothing
but drunken revel and riot, and were glad to escape.
Flipper harangued us after leaving each house, now
expressing approval of our efforts, and now admon-
ishing us for having erred and strayed from the
paths of strict harmony. Of course we had not the

effrontery to criticise such a mentor as himself, but my ear did now and then in its helpless uncertainty tell me that the clarionet's squeals and wailings were more discordant than all our vocal slips combined. The general public, however,—represented by unruly urchins and turbulent wassaillers—had no foolish compunction. They even criticised Flipper, the audacious vagabonds! When a youth called out, "Hear thee, Bill, they're killing another pig!" I knew that his remark had reference to Flipper's clarionet playing. When another impudent young villain cried, "That owd woman screams dreadfully!" I was confident that Flipper's instrumentation had produced the observation. O'Moggarty got much excited as the morning wore on, and I had fears that his imagination would run riot to the extent of creating one. While in Wakefield Road, some boys came up and asked if we knew where Johnny's grandmother lived, and O'Moggarty—he alluded to himself as *the* O'Moggarty from two o'clock onwards —answered, with a naïveté worthy of Sir Boyle Roche, "I knows nothin' and cares less." Flipper, who was prone to "melting charity," endeavoured to be more civil to the lads, but it was no use, we could neither make out the personality of Johnny nor his grandmother, so we gave them some coppers and advised them to return home. A fellow-country-man of O'Moggarty's came up directly afterwards.

"Which is the Star of Erin?" he asked, meaning a beershop of that name evidently. "The Star of Erin, ma bouchal," O'Moggarty replied, impressively, "is Home Rule." We moved off, leaving the two to make matters straight as best they could; and, somehow or other, O'Moggarty must have lost his own way in finding the other man's way, for he did not overtake us. We went back to search for him, but without success. The draper's young man and Miss Sabina Dobkins found it necessary to keep arm-in-arm all the time; they seemed to be uniting in a perpetual search for mistletoe for the sake of illustrating its emblematical meaning. Streamy, Grimtop, and Badger had come out to sing, and sing they did, with all their heart and soul. Hoarseness did not venture near them, fog and sloppyness could not damp their ardour, and eating and drinking failed to produce either huskiness or the *tremolo* in their voices. They were male nightingales to whom song seemed life itself. As for Jimmy and his concertina, they hardly ever ceased making the night harmonious. He even insisted upon playing when everybody else was resting. "Can't you keep that 'rawter' quiet a minute?" Flipper would ask every now and then. "Quiet a minute!" Jimmy would exclaim, "I should rather think I can't." "Preshishely," said Grimtop, in his deepest bass, "if m'yushig ish ye foodvluv play on;

of doors. More swarms of boys continued to pour into the streets, and although some of the urchins sang that they were "not the daily beggars that go from door to door," they did not seem to proceed by selection. To them one door was as good as another, and they attacked them indiscriminately. "Pray dame a Kersmas box," was the salute these boxers gave to the happy morn. "I'll gi' thee a box o' t' ears, if ta artant off!" would be a frequent answer. Another would say, "Who arta? Whear duzta come throo?" "Aw, I'm Billy Splayfooit's lad." "Wah, bud I nawther knaw Billy Splayfooit nor thee nawther, so ger home wi' thee, ye young tyke, an' tell thy father thah's come'd." Some dames would be more charitable and perhaps say, "Well, come in wi' thee, tha'rt somebody's poor barn: here, tak this bit o' spicecake an' cheese, thah wants summat to blaw them cheeks aht a bit."

Amongst the other roamers of the night, or rather morning, the Bleatherhead Bands are entitled to particular mention. They seem to be an offshoot of the Ethiopian serenaders, and affect the manners and customs of the Gipsies. Their instruments are even more comical than themselves, being composed of all kinds of materials—soap boxes, tubs, and frying pans. Bladders, however, are their most favourite instruments, and with these they play a great many pranks, if not a few tunes. Wherever would appear at an upper window and a voice would say, "I'll be with ye in a minute." The head would then be withdrawn and the lads' eyes would glisten with expectancy. "He's a reight sort, is that," one of the boys would say, "I thowt we should get in somewhere afore long." Then the key would be heard turning in the door, and the lads would be putting their feet forward ready for rushing in. But when the door was opened it would be a fierce individual wielding a poker that would meet their gaze. The individual would rush at them and away they would fly pell-mell, some running this way and some that. At many houses where promises had been given that the carollers would be hospitably entertained, there was nothing but dead darkness in all the windows, and the inmates could not be induced to hear the knock, knock, knocking that was kept up so persistently at their doors. "I'll tell Mr. Smith what I think abaht him when I see him," one of the party would say as they turned away from the obstinate door, "askin' on us to be suar an' come an' let him Kersmas in, an' then weant oppen t' door." By three o'clock the lights had faded from the windows considerably, but the interval between going to rest and getting up again did not seem very long, for by four o'clock those who had gone to bed in something like proper time the night before began to turn out go home and dye. I had a suspicion from the first that that young man dyed his hair, and this appeal confirmed it. Instead of permitting him to go home, however, we left him in the hands of a relative of his in Bright Street, Lister Hills. At ten o'clock I, too, asked to be relieved from further duty. I am unable to say how many stones weight of Christmas cheer I had devoured between starting out to finally giving in, but, as Dominie Sampson would have said, it was "Prodigious!" I don't think I shall ever want to see, much less taste, a bit of Christmas cheer again. I was almost unaware that my stomach had got a coating until Christmas; I know now that it must have several coats, and that they are very much out of repair. There ought to be a hospital for Christmas dyspeptics, surely. Will none of our local philanthropists endow one? However, I have had my experience, and I am paying for it, but I do not regret having lost my hat on Christmas Eve for all that. Farewell, Flipper; farewell, Miss Dobkins; farewell, Miss Sabina and the rest—Jimmy and O'Moggarty, and the three Sunday-school teachers! May you have found rest! May your shadows never grow less!

IN A LIGHTNING MANUFACTORY.

T is not uncommon for a Yorkshireman, when wishing to show himself unusually active and agile, to boast that he will perform a given feat in " less than no time." Now, I have been accustomed to regard this figure of speech as of no greater value than the rash assertion of a man who is alive and hearty that he has recently been " killed with laughing," or the equally absurd statement that a certain individual has been "frightened out of his wits," when it is patent that he never had any wits to be frightened out of. But I have discovered that there actually is such a thing as " less than no time," and this is how I made the discovery. I was at the post office, waiting my turn at the counter, when in bounced a theatrical-looking gentleman, and asked the telegraph clerk what time a message despatched from Woolborough at one o'clock that morning would reach New York. " If it were sent at one o'clock this morning," said the clerk, " it

would get to New York between seven and e
o'clock last night." The theatrical loo
individual did *not* annihilate the clerk on the
nor did he attempt to wither him with a gla
he merely muttered his hasty thanks, and
his departure in peace. I appealed to the cler
an explanation, and I found that it was a mere
ter of longitude and not an attempt on his pa
exceed his latitude by chaffing the inqu
Having thus had my attention drawn to on
the wonders of telegraphy, it occurred to
that other important discoveries were to be i
in these electric regions, so I at once set a
arranging for an exploring expedition amo
the electric wires. But this was not a simple
ness of ask and have, as I had anticipated. T
was such an air of secrecy and mystery surroun
the telegraphic atmosphere that it was neces
to undergo almost as many forms and cerem
in getting thither as if I had been about to p
trate into the mystic recesses of freemas
By-and-by, however, the English Oberon
presides at Telegraph Street, London, and di
the movements of the great army of telegra
Pucks who never cease putting their gi
round the earth, gave me permission to e
into the magic arena; and thus it came to
that one day when I wanted to send a teleg

to my grandmother, informing her that I had quite recovered from an attack of toothache, I was allowed to follow the message through all the ramifications of the office, and see it finally despatched to my venerable relative on the wings of the lightning.

It was Thursday, and the time high 'Change. The Post Office steps showed a constant procession of comers and goers, and the in-door and the out-door tried zealously to outbang each other. Woe to the impatient lover who loitered on the steps to devour the clandestine letter she had just been to fetch; woe to the poor Irishwoman who hung about counting the few shillings she had just received in exchange for the post office order her "darlint of a bhoy" had sent her from Liverpool; woe to the couple of boy messengers who selected the steps as the scene for a wrestling match! They were all swept ruthlessly away by the human stream that poured in and out incessantly. Business first, if you please. The large room where all business done directly with the public is actually transacted, both in the postal and telegraphic departments, is an excellent place for the study of character. The left-hand side of the apartment as I enter, is devoted to the private box department, and juvenile messengers every now and then besiege this place for letters for the various business houses in the town. There, as everywhere

else, the most self-asserting are the soonest att
to, while the little timid fellow who waits pat
hopefully, but silently, sees himself passed
until at last, out of sheer despair, he summc
courage to make himself manifest. But wh
boys have gone and the coast is clear, a lad
perhaps steal in occasionally and ask, in a
accusing way, if there is a letter for Miss S
so, " to be called for," and on being answered
negative, she will heave a deep sigh and hurr
looking the very picture of fashionable misery
purchasers of postage stamps, too, present
variety of character and social status. There
poor old man who buys only one stamp, and
much licking, puts it on the wrong side c
letter; there is the sprightly young cashier
walks briskly up to the counter and buys
pounds' worth of stamps—penny's, twope
threepenny's, sixpenny's, and what-not, and do
whole business in less time than it takes t
man to lick and stick his single penny stamp.
stop, I am forgetting the telegram to my g
mother!

Well, I betake myself to the right-hand a
the large room, where telegraph forms and r
order forms jostle each other, and where appl
for both throng together this Thursday afte
with as much eagerness as if it were the ver

day on which such business could be transacted.
The white telegraph forms are filled up and handed
across to the receiving clerk with remarkable
rapidity, and the clerk counts the number of words
in each telegram with still greater rapidity, demands
the fees, seizes them, and then sends the telegrams
up a hoist to the instrument-room above. As the
messages are handed over to the clerk the senders
eye him earnestly, as if they expected him to show
violent emotion on having their important secrets
reposed in him; but, alas, such a feeble thing is
human curiosity when incessantly wrought upon
that I don't believe the clerk has the least knowledge of anything that a message contains, except
that it is composed of so many words, and that so
many words represent a certain fee that he is
expected to possess himself of. Some senders come
in with a rush and a bang, and scribble their
messages in great haste; some exhibit as much
patience, and move as slowly as if they were merely
despatching a letter; some ask all manner of questions—when their message will arrive at its destina-
tion, how soon an answer can be received in reply,
how much so many additional words will cost, and
whether the message will be *sure* to go. To all
inquiries the clerk returns the most placid answers;
he is willing to use all speed that he can on your
behalf, but he resolutely declines to be agitated by

т

you. Some messages are sent by boys under cov
some, for perfect secrecy, are sent in cypher; a
some are sent with a recklessness as to direct
which defies all the attempts of the officials to c
with. On that same Thursday afternoon a mess
had arrived from some race-course with no ot
address on it than "Woolborough Post Office;
be called for," but who was to call for it, whet
John Jones or William Smith, Sam Noakes or T
Stylus, it was impossible to say. The message l
come from the race-course, but had only got to
grand stand after all. Most of the blunders t
arise in telegraphy are due to the same cause—
carelessness of the sender, who either omits imp
tant words, or writes in such a slipshod style t
the clerks have to guess at the meaning.
examples of the mistakes that are made, I n
mention one that occurred in transmitting a t
gram to the *Times* from Woolborough last S
tember, when the Archbishop of York, who l
been preaching at our Parish Church, was rep
sented to have referred to the "Post Office T
graphs of the age" instead of "the *poet* of
age." The sender of the telegram had, no dou
written the word "poet" carelessly, leaving g
between each letter, and almost ignoring the *e*, a
the clerk had read it, in his mechanical fashi
p o t, and interpreted it "Post Office Telegraph

Akin to this mistake was the telegram that was meant to carry the information to a husband that his wife had presented him with a fine daughter, but which, as it reached him, gave him the startling intelligence that he had been presented with "five daughters." In announcing an event of similar importance, a telegram was once received which said, "Your wife had a fine box this morning," instead of "a fine boy;" and a gentleman who sent home for his gig to meet him at the station, had the word "gig" transformed into "pig," but it is not stated whether the former or the latter had the honour of being taken to meet the train. A thousand other stories of errors in telegraphy are floating about, but I will merely repeat one more at present, and that only because it is capable of special appreciation in Woolborough. A message was sent in the following terms:—"You can have the hundred pieces at sixteen and nine. Thousand more at same rate." When delivered in London the telegram read—"You can have the hundred pieces, at sixteen, and nine thousand more at same rate." The favourable terms indicated in the telegram as received were immediately accepted and immediately afterwards repudiated, and a law-suit was only narrowly escaped. So much for punctuation, but it is as well, in telegraphing, to write sentences so that the misplacing or omission of a comma cannot affect the meaning. As a rule, however, the mistakes which occur are traceable to the senders of the messages. At all events, I am convinced that the telegraph clerks are often blamed when in reality they are quite innocent.

But it is time to see that the message to my grandmother is properly despatched. I have paid for it at the counter, and the clerk has shot it up the hoist. I must now follow it. The hoist is too small and too fragile to admit of my ascending to the instrument room by its help, so I retrace my steps to Piccadilly, and making my way through a knot of smart, noisy telegraph messengers, soon find myself in the upper region of the Post Office premises, amongst the wires. A glance at the roof shows me a mighty crowd of wires threading their way into the building, looking like a gigantic Æolian Harp, specially constructed for that most powerful of all harpists—the wind, *alias* rude Boreas, the blustering railer, &c., &c. And sometimes, when the great harpist is moved thereto, there comes some strange, weird music from the electric strings—long wails of agony, wild shrieks of despair, tender lullabies, and strains of mirth and joy. I often listen to this wonderful music as it ebbs and flows in the night: and when the chimes happen to be going at the same time the concert is very effective. The way in which the wind dashes the beautiful Wedding March of Mendelssohn's about over the roofs, chimneys, and spires of the town at midnight, and at the same time blows its mighty breath among the telegraphic wires that cross and recross over the tops of the buildings, is something marvellous. There are sounds to be heard then which outdo anything that the skill of man can produce.

I am now on the threshold of the local lightning manufactory, and, though I am not altogether as ignorant of the why and the wherefore of things telegraphic as the two "niggers" were, I have, as will be seen, very much to learn by my visit. The two "niggers," it will be remembered, discoursed thus on the subject of the wires and posts. Quashee, pointing to the posts, demanded of Sambo, "What am dem postes for?" "To keep up de wiresses," said Sambo. "An' what am de wireses for?" further inquired Quashee. "To keep up de postes," replied Sambo. "'Zactly," said Quashee, "jist so; thought you'd rumderstand 'em." Passing along a long and somewhat gloomy corridor, I am at last ushered into the instrument-room. Nor is its title undeserved. Furthermore, it might not have been inappropriate to have styled it the *musical* instrument-room, for as I enter I observe a large number of instruments being played upon by nimble fingers and hear a variety of sounds, musical and unmusical,

proceeding from bells and what not. Indeed, one
might be excused for imagining on first entering
the room that it is some gigantic establishment for
teaching instrumental music, and that the clerks
are musical pupils. A closer examination of what
is going on, however, soon dispels the illusion. It
is a large well-lighted room. Broad tables extend
from top to bottom, as well as across each end; in
fact, all the space that is available seems to have
been carefully utilised. At these tables, which are
covered with instruments of all the different kinds
in use, there sits a little army of men and youths
busily engaged sending and receiving messages to
and from all parts of the globe. Over each instrument, in a very prominent position, there is a label
bearing the name of the town or series of towns, or
the name of the particular private firm, with which
that instrument is in communication. There is an
incessant stream of words flowing between Woolborough and such places as London, Leeds, Manchester, Liverpool, &c., and the clerks who receive
and transmit for those places scarcely seem to have
a minute's breathing time early or late. Ting, ting,
ting go the bells—Bright's merry bells—rap, tap,
tap go the perforators; while the needles · twist
about from left to right and from right to left, and
long coils of green and white paper in tape-like
strips pass in and out of such instruments as are

managed under the Morse system. But where is that telegram which I want sending to that dear old grandmother of mine? Ah, there's the hoist by the middle window. The whistle from below sounds every few seconds, and the boy at the mouth of the hoist is kept constantly taking out those white messages which the senders write and pay for in the lower office. The messages (including the one to my grandmother) are immediately distributed amongst the operators, and there is certainly no delay in despatching them. Now, although I had the power and peculiarities of the several instruments very lucidly explained to me by the district Superintendent of Telegraphs, it hardly comes within the scope of a merely descriptive paper to enter into scientific details. Suffice it, that almost all the instruments now used for telegraphic purposes are in use at Woolborough. There are the Morse, the Wheatsone automatic, and Bright's bell instruments. The process of sending and receiving is exceedingly simple, and the operators seem to have acquired a rare facility in translating the messages. A clerk will have his ear down at the instrument, and as it rings or punches he writes down the words as they come, nothing but the sound being necessary to make him understand the message. He listens very intently, and writes very expeditiously; it seems as if he really had the

words whispered to him in some mysterious way, so
steadily and quietly does he proceed with his work.
What a number of secrets are whispered in this way
through one operator's ears during the course of a
single day! As this thought passed through my
mind I mentioned it to my guide, Sir Courteous,
and he said, " Very well, let us see if it be so." We
went up to one of the operators, an intelligent-
looking youth, and Sir Courte us asked, " What is
that message about that you have just been
receiving?" The youth scratched his head, then
shook it slowly, and declared he was blessed if he
knew. " We'll try another," said Sir Courteous,
and we advanced upon another operator, a more
ancient carle than the other. " What is that message
about that you have just been sending?" Sir Courteous demanded, with a smile. Operator No. 2 was
staggered for a moment, but as he evidently thought
his reputation was at stake, after a brief plunge
about in the depths of his memory, he said, " It's
about buyin' summat, or sellin' summat, or summat
o' that sort." Sir Courteous looked at the telegraphic
form, and behold! it had nothing to do either with
buying or selling; it was " summat else." Here, I
had been imagining, these young men become
acquainted with the secret transactions of half the
town, and lo! they knew no more of the mystic
messages that were entrusted to them than the

crowd that passes up and down Kirkgate. Messrs. Broadcheck & Co., at Pudsey, Wibsey, Horton, or Shipley, might telegraph a reply to their Bradford warehouse that those ten thousand pieces which Mr. Graspall was at that moment trying to bargain for might be sold at a farthing lower rather than lose the chance of selling; Miss Kurblanc might telegraph to her devoted Roberto that she would meet him two hours hence in front of the Town Hall; Herr Creditheim might send word to his firm at Dresden that he had arranged that little loan all right; Mr. Johnson might telegraph that Mr. Wilton might lay two hundred more on The White Squall; Mrs. Jones might send to her husband in London to say that poor little Willie was dying, and he must return by the next train; all these things were nothing to the operators. To them they were simply letters and words, " sound and fury, signifying nothing "—

"A prone and speechless dialect."

But, understand the message or not, there was no cessation from labour. The operators both " wired in " and wired out, and boy messengers kept flitting to and fro, record being taken at each successive stage, of time, name, code, &c. Two overseers, one for the night and one for the day, are kept to watch over and superintend the operations of this depart-

ment; but on this Thursday afternoon, it being
market-day, and there being a pressure of work,
both the overseers are at their posts. Doubtless
they will sometimes be called upon to repress an
outbreak of youthful exuberance on the part of the
more juvenile of the operators, but as a rule there
is little time for fun-making I should fancy. The
work of the operators is not arduous, but it is such
as to demand close and steady attention. At the
upper end of the room there is an elevated desk,
which seems like an enlarged pulpit. This is the
sanctum of the chief of the bureau; the perch up
aloft from which Sir Courteous keeps watch o'er the
interests of the postal telegraphs. From this
height I am enabled to survey the entire operations
of the department. Close underneath me there is
the wonderful transmitter at work, gobbling up
messages at the rate of 140 words a minute. A
youth is punching holes in lengths of tape on the
right hand side of the instrument, and as he reels
the tape off, the transmitter takes it in and flashes
it away to London instanter. At another instrument they are receiving newspaper messages, the
said messages being uncoiled out of the instrument
like interminable tapeworms with printed dots and
dashes inscribed upon them. As the tape glides
steadily out, the translator reads the strange hiero-
glyphics, transcribes the message upon the news

forms, and gathers the tape into his left hand, crushing each successive inch up as he finishes with it. And the bells of the other instruments keep ring, ring, ringing; the punchers keep on rap, rap, rapping; the needles keep on oscillating; the hoist whistle keeps on sounding; the clerks never cease their listening to the whispers of the lightning; and rest is unattainable.

But while I am sitting up aloft with Sir Courteous I became aware of a presence at a window at the other end of the room which gave me some uneasiness. This window looks out of a small ante-room into the instrument-room. Every minute or two a stern, military-looking face peers through that window and disappears again like a flash. Could Mr. Scudamore have sent some one down to watch that I did not attempt to read any of the messages? Had I been pursued by a detective who was about to make me a victim of mistaken identity? Sir Courteous in vain sought to engage my attention by trying to teach me the telegraphic alphabet. When he told me to look at group 1, and to remember that "earwigs infest summer houses," I only saw the military-looking face at the window. When he bade me recollect that the sentence which would assist me to keep in mind the letters included in group 2 was "Turnips make oxen cheerful," I only thought that nothing in the world could make *me* cheerful, unless that mysterious face ceased to haunt the little window. By-and-by, however, I mustered up courage to inquire who the man was. "I'll introduce you to him," said Sir Courteous, and I was forthwith led to the little ante-room. My suspicions were immediately allayed. The military-looking individual was none other than the overseer of the telegraph lads. The medals that he bore upon his breast showed that he had formerly served his country in an active military capacity, and it is evident the taste for fire has not left him. There is not so very much difference, after all, between a flash of gunpowder and a flash of lightning; in his younger days this military overseer was the servant of the former; he is now the servant of the latter. In this little room there were about a dozen boys in their smart official uniform standing "all in a row like birds on a bough." The topmost boy stood with his elbow near a large sliding window, and as soon as a message was handed through ready for delivery off he started, boy No. 2 taking his place. As the boys returned from delivering messages they took their stand at the bottom of the row, and so *ad infinitum*. The boys being paid a penny for each message that they deliver, they take good care not to lose a turn

'ccasionally, when they have to go a long distance
ith a message, a penny will hardly recoup them
)r the loss of shoe leather on the journey, but,
iking the good with the bad, the lads realise very
ecent wages. There is a vast difference in the
ipabilities, intelligence, and appearance of the
)ys. Some of them frequently make as much as
3s. a week, while there are others who do not earn
1 an average more than half that sum. They are
rceedingly precocious, and exceedingly lively.
he denizens of Piccadilly are well acquainted with
ieir nightly frolics; they indulge in all known and
iany unknown outdoor games, and have evidently
irong theatrical tastes. Pantomine ditties are sung
y them nightly, and their Piccadilly concerts in-
lude occasional performances on the tin whistle
nd the English concertina. But in the little ante-
)om, while on duty and under the eye of the
'ergeant, who is a rigid disciplinarian, they are
ime and subdued. The Sergeant not only keeps
hem in order, but puts them through regular
iilitary drill, a bit of exercise for which the boys
'ill one of these days have reason to feel grateful to
ie Sergeant. I saw them go through their drill,
nd exceedingly well they managed it, but, drill or
ot, the topmost boy was always ready to fly as soon
s a message was put through the window. A post-
ian does not let the grass grow under his feet, a

lamplighter has some reputation for rapidity of movement, but the fleetest of all our Mercuries is, I imagine, the telegraph boy. He can jump, sing, dance, and tumble as he runs with his despatches, and still put on more speed than any other of our public messengers. In the room where I had the pleasure of seeing the Sergeant drill his juvenile army there is a range of cupboards for the boys to deposit their dinners in. There are two boys to a cupboard. We took the liberty of looking into one or two of these receptacles. In one there was a small square of looking-glass, in another a number of coloured figures of theatrical generals were pasted up, in a third there were several numbers of popular periodicals, the taste of the occupants of each cupboard being thus indicated in each cupboard. I was much interested in the proceedings of these messengers and their Sergeant. On paying a visit to the office at night I found the Sergeant drilling his little men in the long gallery, giving the word of command with the sternness and precision of a Wellington, his eye gleaming with pride, and his whole frame seeming to quiver with martial fervour. Ah! I shall long remember thee and thy glittering eye, my telegraphic Sergeant!

After seeing the military review I was introduced to two other sights. In one room I came upon the telegraphic doctor, a staid gentleman in a white "smock," whose business it is to attend to the instruments that happen to fall out of sorts. The diseases for which this doctor has to administer are mostly internal, and, doubtless, tax all his skill. It is in this room that I have explained to me the working of the resisting apparatus, and am made to understand how the electric current rushes about the country in circuits, and finally runs to earth. All this, however, has been so often explained and written about, I am glad to say, that there is no need that I should make the attempt to be an exponent of popular science on this occasion. I must deal with things in their outward seeming only. The doctor has a good many patients on his hands just now. Whether some epidemic has broken out amongst Bright's bells or not I was unable to make out, but there was clearly something serious the matter with some of them. Leaving the doctor to his work, we next mounted a flight of steps and came upon a room apparently full of butter-boxes placed on racks. But I soon discovered that there was something very different to butter in this boxes. It was here that the lightning was made and bottled up. In these boxes there were various electricity-producing chemicals in full operation, supplying the wires with the means of talking in that wonderful speech of theirs. The genii who presided over this mystic region

were, like the doctor, clad in white "smocks," and
their movements were silent and mysterious. I
regarded them with a good deal of quiet awe as
they dipped their fingers into the liquids in the
boxes, which glittered and sparkled with great
brilliance. To me the men appeared akin to the
alchemists of old, and the boxes were the crucibles
where they compounded their elixirs, philters and
charms. But they are even greater than the
alchemists, for they are masters of a grander
discovery than their ancient predecessors ever
dreamed of.

I next got a glance at the wire coils hanging in
festoons in the cupboards which lined one side of
the instrument-room. It was explained to me that
these coils were connected with the earth and conducted the current, when it had completed its
circuit, into the ground.

I paid a final visit to the instrument-room at
night, when the news wires were in full work.
Parliament was sitting, there was a debate on, and
special telegrams were being received direct from
the House of Commons. In a very short time after
the words of the Parliamentary speakers were
uttered in the House they were flowing through the
automatic instruments and being transcribed upon
"manifold" paper, and as each sheet was completed
it was despatched to the newspaper offices, and

there was an end of it. So the operators are kept at work in one way or another all the twenty-four hours of the day. They work on the shift system, however, no man working more than eight or nine hours a day, unless it is that there is some special call upon the department, in which case his over-work is rewarded with overpay. When I took my leave of Sir Courteous I was moved to acknowledge to him that his lightning conductors are a very efficient staff, and that their supervision is such that I am not able to find a loophole of neglect anywhere, from the pulpit desk to the battery. On arriving at home I find that my grandmother has tele-graphed an answer to my message. She says she is delighted to hear that my toothache is better, and invites me to run over and take a cup of tea with her the next day. The dear old lady might very well have said all this in a letter that would have reached me next morning, but the telegraph seems to her, as well as to me, such a marvellous inven-tion that she likes to patronise it.

IN THE FOOTSTEPS OF A GHOST.

THE appearance of Bradford in the olden times is difficult for the imagination to realise, so effectually has modern progress crushed out of existence nearly all local vestiges of antiquity; but there is still left to it on the scarred hill side, between Bowling and Bierley, a fine specimen of the ancient baronial hall; a building which has held so prominent a part in Bradford's past history, that by examining its archives and disclosing its forgotten associations, we are enabled to recall much that is curious and interesting concerning both the Hall and the town itself. Beyond a widely-accepted belief in the "pity poor Bradford" legend, and a vague notion that the Hall is not altogether a modern structure, very little appears to be generally known about this ancient seat of the Lords of Bolling; and not even the researches of the late Mr. John James have availed to unearth the date of its erection. Supposing that the Lancasterian Bollings, or whoever else may have been the founders of the hall, had laid a first stone with such formality of coin and document hiding as is now the custom at first-stone layings, inviting to the ceremony the jolly old abbot of Kirkstall and the heads of the half-dozen noble and distinguished families of tax-leviers who then lorded it over the surrounding twenty miles of waste, fields, and straggling hamlets, it may be expected that when the spirit of worsted manufacture comes to add another circle of houses to the town, and commands the old fabric to get out of the way, there may be found beneath its venerable walls some evidence which will assist us in establishing a date for its origin. As it is, we can only heap conjecture upon fact in regard to its primal days, and content our-selves with taking up the first bit of the broken link of its history which presents itself to us.

At the time of William the Conqueror's confisca-tion of this country, it would appear that a certain Sindi was the owner of Bolling, for in Doomsday Book it is mentioned that, " In Bollinc Sindi had four carucates of land," and that " Ilbert [de Lacy] has it and it is waste. Value in King Edward [the Confessor's] time 5s." It is hardly probable that a Bolling Hall existed at this period, but it is more than likely that when the manor got into the hands of the Bolling family (and there is evidence of a Robert de Bolling having held

it in the reign of Henry III.) they would keep
such a mansion as befitted their estate. The
Bollings were a prolific race, and a direct succession
of Lords bearing the Bolling patronymic was
kept unbroken, it is believed, for more than four
centuries. The importance of the Bolling family
in the county was manifested in divers ways. A
William de Bolling gave twelve acres of land in
Bolling to the Hospital of St. Peter at York; and
a subsequent William sought relief for his soul by a
gift of "common pasture in Bolling" to Kirkstall
Abbey. In Edward III.'s time the then Lord
of Bolling intermarried with the heiress of Roger
Thornton, of Thornton, and thereby became possessed of the manors of Thornton, Allerton, and
Denholme, in addition to the one he already held at
Bolling. Thenceforward, down to the reign of the
fourth Edward, nothing seems to have occurred to
mar the prosperity of the Bollings. The wars of
the Roses, however, brought misfortune upon the
ancient house, and at one time nearly effected its
complete overthrow.

Robert Bolling espoused the cause of the Red
Rose of Lancaster, and fought under the hot-
blooded Lord Clifford, of Skipton Castle, on the
battle-field of Towton. It seems that, on the final
victory of the Yorkists, this Robert Bolling was
attainted for high treason because of the part he

had taken in the Palm Sunday business at Towton,
and his estates were forfeited to the King; and so
reprehensible was his conduct deemed on that occasion, that, in the Act of Resumption of forfeited
estates, passed in the following year, it is specially
provided that the Act "should not be to the prejudice of Thomas Radclyff, Esquire, of the grant to
him made by letters patent of the Manor of Bolling."
During the period that Radclyff held sway at Bolling, the attainted Robert Bolling, with his wife and
ten children, must have passed but a sorry time;
for in 1472 he petitions the King, in the most
piteous terms, to restore him to his "lyvelode," and
tries, with much speciousness, to shift the entire
blame of his action at Towton upon the shoulders of
his leader, Lord Clifford, saying that he had been
"dryven, not of his own proper wille, ne of malice
towards your Grace, but oonly by compulsion, and
by the most drad proclamations of John, then Lord
Clifford, under whose daunger and distresse the
lyvelode of your suppliant lay."   It is evident, however, that soon afterwards this Lancasterian Bolling,
either by the death of Radclyff or by the special
clemency of the King, regained his ancestral posses-
sions; for, in 1477, he is represented to have made
his will at Bolling Hall, which may be regarded as
presumable proof that he not only then resided at
the hall, but that he had property to bequeath.

In 1477, therefore, it is absolutely certain that Bolling Hall existed, and it may be taken for granted that it had been in existence for a long time prior to that date. At that day, Bolling Hall would be looked upon as one of the chief residences of the county, and the scanty population of Bradford would be in a sort of vassalage to the manorial lords who resided there. An extensive, well-timbered park stretched round it for a great distance, and the grand spaces of green turf and oak glades would be thronged with antlered deer. Foresters clad in Lincoln green, with horns slung carelessly over their shoulders, and carrying trusty bows and well-seasoned arrow shafts, would be seen keeping watchful guard against adventurous poachers ; while down in the valley below, the few rudely thatched cottages which then constituted the whole town of Bradford, would be quietly reposing, their inhabitants—the "jolly shoemakers," whose exploits with the quarterstaff won them such renown ; and the fullers and clothiers, who were the forerunners of our present woolstaplers — little dreaming of the time when their peaceful vale and its surrounding slopes would be densely packed with mills, houses and warehouses, and when the price of a single yard of ground in the heart of the town would be of more value than in 1342 was the annual value of the entire manor.

Following the fortunes of Bolling Hall and its owners from the death of the attainted Robert Bolling, whose body was buried before the altar of the Parish Church, we find that in the reign of Henry VII. Tristram Bolling died, leaving an only daughter, Rosamund, his heiress; and that on her marriage with Sir Richard Tempest, of Bracewell, the name of Bolling ceased to be associated with the old Hall. Both Rosamund and her husband seem to have been persons of considerable note. On a recent visit (more particularly referred to hereafter) which I made to the Hall, I saw the portrait of this same Rosamund, which is still extant on an oaken panel in one of the upper rooms. The portrait gives the impression of a high-souled matron who would be well able to uphold the dignity of her knight-husband. On a companion panel is the portrait of another personage in the quaint costume of the period, whose name and sex are alike a mystery; it ought to be, and not improbably is, the likeness of Sir Richard, but the garb and *coiffure* represented will permit of almost any interpretation. Rosamund Tempest bore her husband no less than nine children, all of whom grew to maturity and married or were given in marriage to members of great families in the neighbourhood. The fifth son, Henry, espoused Ellinor, daughter of Christopher Mirfield, Esq., of Tong Hall, and became the founder of the present family of the Tempests of Tong. On Rosamund Tempest's decease, which occurred in the same year that witnessed the accession of "good Queen Bess," her second son, John, succeeded to Bolling Hall and Manor; after him came his brother Nicholas; then Nicholas's son, Richard; then another Sir Richard assumed the manorial title, he being a nephew of the last-named Richard. On Sir Richard's death, in 1639, there came into the inheritance still another Richard Tempest, who was the last of the long line of Tempests who held Bolling Hall. This last Richard Tempest proved himself an unworthy successor to his ancestors, for, like many a modern representative of ancient and noble houses, he seems to have sacrificed his patrimony and his honour at the shrine of dissipation. It was during his tenancy of Bolling Hall that the great civil war broke out, when, being a Roman Catholic and a Royalist, the scapegrace gave in his adherence to the cause of King Charles, and was honoured with the command of a troop of Cavalier horse. Probably his affairs had not then assumed such a desperate aspect as foredoom his ultimate ruin; and it is easy imagine the scene of the young cavalier setting forth from his ancestral hall, with a gay retinue loyal supporters. What a picture for fancy draw! The lofty oaks rustling their green branches

to the songs of the thrush and the linnet ; the
rooks wheeling high in air, and cawing defiantly at
the deer which are herding timidly together in the
distant glade, frightened at the presence of strange
forms about the hall.   A crowd of rustics, most of
whom are staunch Puritans, and strong haters of
the tyrannical upholders of feudal bondage, press
around the park gates, and sneer and jibe at the
proceedings of this Cavalier Tempest, while waiting in anxious expectation of his coming forth.
Retainers hurry to and fro near the Hall, and a
number of horses, ready saddled, stand pawing the
ground in the front avenue.   Presently, a trumpet
blast is sounded, and there spring from the southern
porch the gay young Tempest and his gallant
followers, clanking their swords, and looking the
very incarnation of bravery.   Mounting their
steeds, they partake of the stirrup cup from the
hands of some fair member of the Tempest family,
and then "To horse and away ! "   So, with a
hearty shout and many a murmured blessing, the
little band sallies forth, heedless of the frowning
looks of the townspeople it has to encounter on
emerging from the park.   But before Richard
Tempest could return to the hall of his fathers,
scenes more strange than ere had been witnessed
within its grim old walls in days gone by were to
be experienced.

It is needless here to recount the facts connected
with the siege of Bradford by the Royalists, except
so far as they immediately affect the old Hall of
which I now write. While the King's troops were
quartered in the town there is no doubt their communication with Bolling Hall would be frequent;
and when at length they were recalled, such of the
Tempest family and adherents as remained at the
Hall would probably fly to some safer refuge. At
all events, the Hall appears during the sieges to
have been fixed upon as the head-quarters of the
besiegers. After the first repulse of the Royalists
they augmented their strength, bringing Sir
William Saville and a large force against the town.
Then came the Earl of Newcastle, full of vindictive-
ness, and took up his quarters at the Hall. Our
valiant Puritan forefathers, with their scanty
ammunition but plentiful supply of woolpacks, which
they turned to such effective purpose, strove manfully to protect the old town, but the Earl was too
powerful for them. Bolling Hall would then be
thronged with armed men, and its beautiful park
converted into camping ground. At night the
camp fires would throw their lurid flames into the
wide sky, and sounds of gay carousal would fill the
air; while down in the trembling town the besieged
would be singing their holy psalms, and seeking
solace in prayer. Imagine what would be taking

place the night previous to the day on which the
Earl proposed storming the town! How heartrend-
ing it would be to watch those brave defenders of
their homes, who, amidst the tears and supplications
of their wives and children, were toiling for a hope-
less defence! How strange a contrast there would
be to this in the scenes being enacted around
Bolling Hall. Soldiers flushed with victory, eagerly
anxious to swoop down upon the town in the
morning and make an easy conquest. Telling
their Atherton Moor exploits to each other, exulting
over the defeated Fairfax, and gaily drinking to the
morrow's success, they laugh and make merry under
the shadow of the old Hall, as if death and blood
had no share in their designs. "O! what a
dreadful night was that on which Bradford was
taken!" says Joseph Lister. "What weeping and
wringing of hands!" The Earl's soldiers entered
the town and pillaged it. And now from the
historical we must dip into the legendary, for is
there not a ghost connected with the Hall? Legend
says, and I would fain believe there is a substratum
of fact underlying it, that on the night when
Bradford was taken the stern Earl who had wrought
all the mischief upon the poor town was subjected to
a ghostly visitation while lying in bed at Bolling
Hall. The room where the Earl is supposed to
have been resting on this momentous night is the

one where the portraits of Rosamund Tempest and companion are still to be seen. It is only a small room, with one window looking out towards Dudley Hill. The ceiling is a great curiosity, being of carved oak (now painted over, unfortunately), and crowded with grotesque figures of birds, reptiles, and leaves, out of which it would be very easy for a man of imaginative temperament who had been tasting the "flowing bowl" pretty freely—as it is not unreasonable to suppose the Earl would have done before seeking repose on such a night of triumph—to conjure up a good many ghosts. It is quite possible, too, that the face of the matronly Rosamund may have assumed a weird, unearthly aspect in the dim light of a flickering lamp, and that the Earl imagined he heard it speak those solemn words which, the supporters of the legend maintain, saved Bradford from total destruction :—
"*Pity poor Bradford! pity poor Bradford!*" It has been suggested, also, that the ghost might have been but the fleshy impersonation of some stout-hearted and stout-limbed serving-wench, whose compassion had been too much for her zeal in the Royal cause. Be this as it may, the Earl relented somewhat, and speedily withdrew his troops from the town; but not before he had allowed them to hold a fair in Bolling Hall park, in order to sell back to the inhabitants the things which they had stolen from them.

History deigns not to chronicle the exploits of the Cavalier, Richard Tempest, as a commander of horse, but it does condescend to mention that, on the overthrow of Charles I., he was first called upon to compound for his estate by paying £1745, and then had his manor sequestrated. Before this event, however, he seems to have taken to gambling, amongst other vices; and so desperate did he become, that it is said—though no one makes himself responsible for the statement—he staked the Hall and estate at a game of "put," exclaiming while the cards were being dealt—

> "Now ace, deuce, and tray,
> Or farewell Bolling Hall for ever and aye."

And so, irresponsible history proclaims, Bolling Hall was lost to the Tempests; and in 1657, three years before the restoration of Charles II., Richard Tempest died in King's Bench prison, where he was confined for debt.

History also speaks of a certain Mary Sykes being charged, in 1649 or 50, before Henry Tempest, Esq., of Bolling Hall, with being a witch, but I am unable to make out what relation this Henry Tempest bore to Richard Tempest. This charge would no doubt be heard in the great hall, and we may imagine the horror of the justice at being confronted with a reputed witch, against whom such terrible evidence was adduced that he committed

her to York Assizes. "She appeared to me," said
one witness, "the foulest feinde that ever I saw,
with a pair of eyes like sawcers;" and six women
who searched the body of Mary Sykes, gave testimony as to the finding upon her left side, "neare
her arm, a little lump like a wart, and being puld
out, it strecht about halfe an inch." It is comfort-
ing to know, however, that the Judge of Assize was
less credulous than the justice, and acquitted Mary.

After the Tempests, Bolling Hall passed through
the hands of several good families, being held by
the Savilles of Thornhill, and then by the Lindley
family. In 1816 Messrs. Sturges, Mason & Paley
bought the Manor and estates, and in 1834 they
became the sole property of Mr. Paley, whose representatives are the present owners.

And now, thanks to the previous labours in this
field of Dr. Whitaker, John James, and Abraham
Holroyd, I have been able, by throwing in a slender
thread of my own fancy, to give a more or less
faithful picture of the Bolling Hall of the past;
and, by the courtesy and kindness of the present
occupier of the hall, to see for myself the Bolling
Hall of the present.

The approach to Bolling Hall at the present day
is not prepossessing, whatever it may have been in
the days of the Tempests; the smoke-clouds seem
not only to have dimmed the lustre of the building

itself, but to have rendered sterile the fields and woods around it. The park where the deer once found a home, and where many a joyous hawking party sported in mediæval days, is now parcelled into fields, where a stray horse or donkey may be found browsing occasionally, or a little flock of sheep bleating. The " branched-charmed " oaks are no longer visible ; nor is there anything to be seen of the Spring Wood so well known to our fathers, which used to be one of the chief features of the Bolling landscape. The locomotive now rushes screaming through the fields below, and the noise and steam of the Bowling Dyeworks, which lie close by, remind the visitor that commerce, and not " storeyed walls " have built up our prosperity. Down in the hollow, about a mile distant, the crowded town lies panting and struggling amidst its smoke, and the merciless wind beats it Bowling-wards, as if it had some vengeance to wreak upon the old baronial building. Above the hall, on the Bierley Hill Top, rise two sturdy mansions which seem to carry relationship into every inch of their stone walls. A sparsely timbered plantation straggles down from these modern residences in the direction of Bolling Hall ; and a footpath or two,— one threading through the edge of this plantation, and others running close by the walls of the old hall—make pleasant whispering ground for Bowling

lovers, while the adjacent fields afford the Broom-
fields roughs an opportunity for the pleasant
pastimes of Sunday dog-racing and arrow-throw-
ing. But the nearer one gets to the hall the more
attractive it appears. Standing at the gates, with
your back to the smoky town, and looking at the
mansion through the tall trees which overshadow it,
a feeling of veneration for the "good old times"
naturally arises in one's breast. The dusky rooks
chattering on the topmost boughs sound like echoing voices from the distant ages. Passing through
the gateway and over the gravelled path which
winds up to the northern porch, and glancing
lovingly at the crumbling walls and small-paned
windows, and up at the two square towers which
flank the building on the east and west sides, we
come to the hall door. On being admitted to the
interior, we at once proceed to the large hall, which
is the chief apartment of the building, and the one
best calculated to recall its ancient associations.
Here would the Christmas revels of the manorial
lords of Bolling be held ; here would Mary Sykes
the alleged witch, and her accusers appear before
the superstitious Tempest who committed her to
prison ; and here would the cavalier officers carouse
the night before the siege of Bradford. The good
taste of the present occupier has, while adapting
the hall to modern notions of comfort and elegance,

preserved its antiquarian aspect as far as was possible. Different portions of the walls are adorned
with battle-axes, spears, cross-bows and other
instruments of ancient warfare ; and the remaining spaces are fittingly occupied with portraits of
historical personages, and other suitable paintings,
by good artists. An immense window, consisting
of three rows of ten compartments each, looks out
upon the south garden terrace, which, we can per-
ceive, is laid out into prim parterres, and dotted
here and there with flower urns and sculptured
figures, after the modern style of garden ornamentation. A good-sized kitchen garden, separated
from the terrace by brick walls, runs up each side.
A number of heraldic devices seem to have been
painted on this great window, but the only
coat of arms which can now be easily de-
ciphered is one of recent date—that of the
Sturges family. Above the window is a fine
stag's head, and about the room are some
really splendid specimens of carved oak furniture.
To describe the appearance of the room more fully
would be, I fear, to overstep the bounds of propriety, so I will content myself by saying that a
long wooden gallery (over which one member of the
ancient house is said to have been hurled by an
enemy) runs across the hall, connecting the upper
portions of the eastern and western wings or

v

towers. It takes a long time to satisfy one's
curiosity in a place so sacred to past memories as
this is; there is so much to think and wonder
about. From the large hall I was led through the
gloomy corridors, with massive walls more than
three feet in thickness, up staircases wide and staircases narrow; seeing here an unintelligible inscription, and there a piece of quaint oak panelling.
The dining and drawing rooms constitute the most
modern wing of the building. On our way to these
rooms from the hall, I am shown a narrow diamond-
paned window of stained glass, which is said to
have been the handiwork of Mr. Paley while resid-
ing at the hall. Arriving at the upper series of
rooms, we tread upon memorable ground at every
step, but the most interesting room by far is that
containing the portraits before referred to, and in
which the Earl of Newcastle is said to have slept.
Threading in and out through corridor after
corridor, out of one room into another, we at
length come upon what is to-day the nursery, but
which in bygone days must have been an apartment
of some importance. Over the mantlepiece is a
rude view painted on the oak, which, although it
cannot be said to be a representation of the hall as
we now know it, may probably have been meant as
a picture of it as it once was. The figures in the
foreground of the painting are shown as wearing

the costume of Queen Anne's period. From here we ascend a narrow flight of stairs leading to the top of the western tower. Reaching the roof through a mysterious trap-door, we at last stand on the tower, where we have an extensive view of the surrounding country. After a short stay on this place of outlook, we descend and continue our quest in another series of rooms on the ground floor. To describe the different rooms as they now appear would be to trespass on forbidden ground. I may say, however, that in addition to containing all the elements of modern luxury, they are permitted, so far as is consistent with comfort, to retain their ancient character. The hall is, altogether, one of the most interesting mansions which the West Riding can boast, and I cannot but express my gratitude to its present occupier, who reverences it for its time-honoured associations, for having allowed me an opportunity of storing my memory with pleasant recollections.

BARNACLES AT BARKEREND.

 DO not suppose that *Bell's Life* or the *Sporting News* could, in answer to any inquiring correspondent, give you the name of the winner of the last Barkerend Handicap; nor do I imagine that any of the turfite Zadkiels— those mysterious Arguses, Hotspurs, Meteors, and others who dispense prophecy through the medium of the London and provincial press—could bring their prophetic vision to bear, with any degree of success, upon the "turf events" of Woolborough Moor. I do not even believe that the gentleman who indignantly asks day after day, through the advertising columns of the *Northern Squealer*, if it was not he who sent you "Staggers" for the "Knock-kneed Sweepstakes," could, in return for the most fabulous amount in postage stamps, give you an equally reliable "tip" for the "Laisterdyke Cup," or "The Woolborough Moor Twenty-year-old Plate." No; these are racing events beyond the ken of aspiring wizards; they know them not; of their lives they are "things apart." Thrice happy are we, then, to whom these events are familiar, to whom once in a year there comes the double enjoyment of feeling the fresh moorland breeze and witnessing an exciting horse race.

In this exulting frame of mind it was that I, accompanied by the estimable companion of my saunterings, Barnacles, set out one Monday in October last for the Woolborough Moor races. I had long been looking forward to the day, and preparing to spend it in proper style. When first I mentioned attending the races my friend had treated my proposal with scorn and contempt, but in the end I overcame his prejudice by reminding him that it was there that duty called us. "Is it not right," said I, "that such an important town as Woolborough, with more population and more wealth than a score of places I could name where great races are annually run, should be able to compete with them in this national pastime; and can it ever do so unless we, the inhabitants, are willing to extend our patronage?" This, and more in the same strain, had the desired effect. Barnacles succumbed.

Monday morning's sun rose bright and joyous; its beams struck direct to the heart, for the atmosphere had been purged by long rains of those materials for the spontaneous generation of "midges" and other ephemeral annoyances to which the "mists and mellow fruitfulness" of autumn are so peculiarly favourable. It felt like a holiday. No wonder, then, that Barnacles and I, as we stood at the bottom of Church Bank waiting for our "trap" to arrive, gave ourselves up to the day's natural influences. Laughter simmered on our lips, and played at hide and seek in our eyes; the pride which springs from a devoted attachment to local institutions distended our chests; the confident anticipation of pleasure gave elasticity and sprightliness to our limbs; and, altogether, we looked and felt as happy as if we had been waiting to bear off a couple of well-fortuned damsels to the Parish Church, the venerable gateway of connubial felicity. The "trap" we were watching for belonged to our mutual friend, Buffkins, the wholesale tea dealer. He had promised to send his man round with it at two o'clock prompt, and exactly at five minutes past it came. The moment we saw it approaching we cross-questioned each other upon our horse knowledge, in order to see who was best entitled to take the reins. It turned out, however, that our claims to the leadership were about equally balanced; we both possessed near relations who understood horses to perfection, but neither of us had ever had the least experience of horsemanship personally.

"Woa, my lass!" said the man, soothingly, as he drew up at our feet and jumped out of the gig.

"Woa!" cried Barnacles, with the air of a man who has made up his mind for generalship.

"You mustn't snap her, sir," said the man; "coax her a bit, and you'll find her as quiet as a lamb."

We got in. Barnacles was now put upon his mettle, so he seized the reins with one hand and flourished the whip in the other. We began to move, but the movement was a retrograde one; one right flank making an attack upon an adjoining warehouse, and had not the groom been at hand to aid us we might have come to sudden grief. However, after the man had administered a few pats and "Woa my lass-es!" to the animal, we started off in a mild canter in the direction of the Junction Hotel. And now my friend began to gain increased confidence at every stride, and by the time we had got fairly into Leeds Road I, too, began to have faith in him, and to regard him as one possessed of horse-y instincts to which I could lay no claim whatever. I wish I knew enough of horse language to enable me to give you a description of our quadruped, but I do not; my vocabulary fails me in technicalities. It was not a chestnut, it was not a black, it was not a grey, it was not a piebald; it was simply a nondescript. Its hue was a mys-

tery. I should think it must have been at some
time or other employed at a dyer's establishment,
where it had contracted dye upon dye until its hide
had become as muddled in colour as an artist's
palette. Although its trot seemed a series of electrical jerks, and its shoes sometimes knocked together in a rather stumbling style, we got along
tolerably well until we came to the "Royal Oak "
Inn at New Leeds; but there our Rosinante came
to a full stop. Whether it was that the crowd of
people moving towards the race-course was too
much for its modesty, or whether it was that in one
of the horses standing by the door of the " Royal
Oak " she recognised an old acquaintance and
longed to exchange greetings, I know not; but results draw our attention from causes, and the result
in this instance was the obstinate refusal of our
mare to go another inch. Barnacles' first im-
pulse was to flog her, but I restrained him by
reminding him of the groom's warning. This
caused him to descend and try to wheedle the mare
into going forward, but she merely turned her head
away from him, sulkily, and planted her feet all the
more firmly in a standing position. A knot of idlers
soon gathered round us, and made us the butt of
their vulgar "chaff." We were asked if that
was not the winner, if we were not intending to
enter her for the next Derby, and so on, until

our situation became almost unbearable. Barnacles waxed " exceeding wroth" at the animal's continued obstinacy, and brandished the whip threateningly over its head. All was in vain ; she only reared or staggered back a few yards each time, and then settled into her old position. After about ten minutes had been spent in this profitable manner, a coal cart laden with rollicking holiday makers came up. The driver of the cart carried a stout cudgel in place of a whip, and observing our dilemma, it occurred to him that an application of this cudgel to the back of our quadruped might be attended with beneficial results. Nor did he think wrongly, as the sequel will prove. Without asking our permission, or giving us a single word of warning, he bestowed upon the mare a most tremendous blow ; and no sooner had he done so than off she started "upon the pinions of the wind" towards Woolborough Moor. Barnacles was standing by the side of the mare, holding the reins, when this turn in the tide came, and away we went, like John Gilpin, "neck or nought." Barnacles stuck fast to the reins and was borne rapidly on at the animal's side. Considerations for my safety alone prevented him letting go. All this time I sat clutching the seat in a terror-stricken attitude. The stream of people divided to let us proceed on our wild career. Some cried "Heigh up! shoo's ta'en t'boggard!"

some cried "Stop it! stop it!" and ran away as fast as possible; others shouted "Stick fast, lad!" but succour there was none, at least, not from the people. Fortunately (as our pastors tell us) at times when we seem to be utterly forsaken, when Hope dies, and Fate seems to be on the point of dealing a death stroke, there comes a providential interposition in our favour, and we are saved. It happened so with us. An apple cart came to our rescue. Giles Scroggins, its owner, was standing beside it, and calling the attention of the passers to the fact that the fruit thereupon was only a "penny a pewnd," when our mare ran at the apples, and came to a dead halt, appearing to regain her sanity as suddenly as she had lost it. I cannot attempt to explain this strange freak of the mare's, nor could Barnacles, for he was as exhausted as Mazeppa was after his wild horse experience. Suffice it to say that we were enabled by this fortunate intervention to put the mare into complete subjection, and to go on our way like ordinary mortals. We now walked at a hearse-like pace towards the race-course, and became less conspicuous objects of the crowd than before; but, strange to relate, as we came up to the barracks our panting steed stopped once more. A red-coated sentinel stood at the gateway amidst a knot of admiring gazers, and it is my belief that our equine oddity was simply stopping to laugh at them; but be that as it may, we had received ample proof that there was an incompatability between the mare and ourselves, so we speedily resolved to effect a divorce. We both got out of the trap, and, securing the services of a neighbouring hostler, had the animal marched off into the seclusion of an outlying stable, until such time as we could effect her deliverance through the aid of her master, our friend Buffkins.

And now we were free to roam at pleasure, without endangering our lives. What a sense of relief I felt to be once more an ordinary pedestrian! "Horses are fickle creatures, Barnacles," I said to my friend. "Yes, perhaps they are," he responded, "but I'd have managed the beast if it hadn't been for your dreadful timidity." Unfair as this remark was, I alluded to the matter no more, and we pressed on in silence to the heart of the immense crowd of sightseers. Thousands upon thousands of persons came thronging in from every available approach; up the steep brow of Bunker's Hill, across the fields by Swaine Green, and along the Leeds Road and its various tributaries. Omnibuses, cabs, carriers' waggons, greengrocers' donkey-carts, gigs, and spirit merchants' elaborately-painted vehicles were amongst the conveyances that came pouring in; and as for the people, they represented life in almost every aspect, the only element of society which I found

to be absent being the clerical element. Mill
operatives were there in immense numbers, some of
them in holiday garb, and others with the evidences
of their work apparent both on their clothes and
in their faces. This latter fact will account for
the deserted looms and spinning frames of that
Monday afternoon. Foundrymen and colliers also
mustered in strong force, many of them being
burly and clean, and many of them burly and
drunk. Prosperous publicans might be seen riding
hob-a-nob with young sprigs of manufacturers;
thick-necked, short-haired youths of pugilistic
contour, holding mysterious converse with over-
dressed damsels of "fast" appearance; connois-
seurs in horseflesh speaking in unintelligible jargon
to such horsemen as they could find weak enough
to listen to them; and fathers, mothers, sweethearts,
and children mingling together in happy innocence,
almost unconscious of everything around them in
their eagerness to gain some place from whence
they could obtain a full view of the race. I hear an
irate matron exclaim, on turning round to her husband, who is struggling with one of their offspring
in his arms, "Come on wi' thah, what's ta shillokin
i' t' loin like that for?" On the edge of the course,
a long line of vehicles is visible, and their owners
are very demonstrative in their shoutings of "All t'
way rahnd for a penny!" The ladies are the best

patrons of these extemporised grand stands, and whenever they recognise an acquaintance in the crowd they call lustily for him or her to come and join them. Walking in the direction of the starting post, from which a little streamer was waving, with the words "Long live the Prince and Princess," upon it, we get amongst the sporting characters. Here we obtain some information as to the state of the betting, and as the horses and jockeys are just coming up to be weighed, I may as well adopt the course of other sporting correspondents, and give you the latest quotations.

BETTING.—3.10 P.M.

Bottle of gingerbeer to a "pennorth o' nuts," against Blue Sash (off).

Quart of ale to another quart against Red Jacket (t and off).

3d to 1d. (money staked) against Green Sleeves (t).

St. George's Hall to the Parish Church against T' Little un' (t. and off. freely).

I tried hard to get to know which horse was the favourite, but the excitement was so great that I was prevented. Barnacles now proposed that we should cross over to the inner inclosure, or the middle of the moor, and endeavour to get ourselves temporarily fixed upon one of the coal-pit mounds which constitute such a picturesque feature of the moorland. We went, and succeeded in obtaining such a position as he desired. Standing on this

mound we had a full view of the imposing array of
conveyances before alluded to, and as they were all
filled with people, and many of them bore some
gorgeous lettering upon their sides, we were enabled
to extract a considerable amount of amusement from
them.   One vehicle, crowded with ladies of mature
years, was lettered "London and Dublin Stout;"
another, laden with a mixed company of men,
women and children, bore the inscription, "Goods
carefully removed to all parts of the country;" and
a third, similarly occupied, announced somebody's
"Celebrated Gingerbeer."   Itinerant vendors of
beef and ham sandwiches, nuts, ginger-bread, pears,
apples, hot pies, roast potatoes, sheep's trotters, and every conceivable article of food which
was capable of being dragged about, clamoured
noisily round these vehicles, and seemed to meet
with ready purchasers, for holiday-making Britons
have generally good appetites.   Behind us, in the
enclosure, a number of hardy youths and soldiers
were indulging in gymnastic sports; leaping
against each other for small wagers, and straining
their muscles for the amusement of the bystanders.
Here and there we could see a group of men
gathered round a piece of ground desecrated to the
worship of Aunt Sally.   All the worst elements of a
fair were to be met with, and the occasional presence of a disguised detective proved to us that the

police authorities were quite aware of the fact. As four o'clock approached the vast surging multitude became more concentrated, and seemed eagerly anxious for the race to come off. At length the horses were actually seen to be getting themselves into position for starting, and one or two officious horsemen galloped round, flourishing their whips to clear the course. Then follows a solitary rider, who comes in for the jeers of the crowd, for he is fat, and rides clumsily. "Hooigh, lad! thah hez it!" "Ten to one on t' fat un!" and similar wit sallies are levelled at him, but he canters on with a smile, which shows him to be invulnerable to their raillery. The criticisms passed upon the animals, which have to enter upon the contest, are of small moment compared with those which are passed upon the jockeys, but as these relate merely to their personal appearance it is not worth while repeating them. The race was called "The Woolborough Moor Stakes," and, seeing that it originated with the publicans, the said stakes may not improbably have some connection with Ale. Eight horses came to the scratch (I think that is the proper sporting phrase), and got off in a very uneven style. "Blue cap's t' first" is the cry as the horses gallop down the far side of the course; but the cry changes almost every moment; now it is "Red jacket hez it;" now it is "Green sleeves is bahn to win;" and so the excitement continues through the heat, culminating when the horses scamper up "the straight" for the last time. "Here they come!" shouts the crowd, every member of which is stretching his neck to the utmost to get a final glimpse of the panting animals. They come with a rush, and in a moment they have flown past the winning post, and the victor of first heat has been greeted with immense cheering. Now the male portion of the spectators jump from their stands and cluster eagerly round the poor horses, which present a melancholy appearance. Bespattered with mud and steaming with perspiration, they are led from the course by their respective jockeys, and the crowd presses after them through the dirt in a most enthusiastic style. It turns out, however, that there has been a false start, and that all the fierce contention and excitement have resulted in nothing. Up by the winning post a number of backers and proprietors of horses are quarrelling with each other on the subject; but it is all to no use, the race is declared void by the judge, and there is no appealing from his dictum. "What do you think of it?" I ask of Barnacles, as soon as we have freed ourselves from the jostling crowd. "Oh, I think there's quite as much excitement about a race between cab horses as there is in a race between the cracks of the St. Leger, so long as the animals are pretty evenly matched," replied Barnacles. "They're noan cab horses, yond," exclaimed a bystander who had overheard my friend's observation, "there's a bit o' blooïd abaht yond first 'un. It comes through Harrogate, an' belongs to Fiddle-up-Jerry." "Ger aht wi' tha," interposes another man who has been listening; "it's nowt bud a horse 'at goes wi' a milk cart. I'm like to knaw when it 'livers milk at ahr hahse." We leave the two to end the dispute as best they can, and escape to the lower end of the course. Disorder reigns everywhere. Youths pelt each other with ham sandwiches; women without morals shout and bawl in intoxicated fashion; gangs of cursing roughs push about in the anxious endeavour to force a quarrel; horsemen canter excitedly up and down; keepers of stalls and vociferous hawkers call upon the public to "Come on an' buy another pennorth;" and the more respectable portion of the crowd is thrown into a state of dire confusion. Such a saturnalia of irrepressible humanity is, happily, seldom to be witnessed. Each public-house is the scene of general turbulence. Every inch of room, even to the backyards and passages, is made available for the accommodation of their thirsty customers, and there is such crushing for admittance that it is impossible for any one who has once reached the inside to get out by the way he entered.

w

Further down, in the open space in front of the barracks, we come upon the usual characteristics of a "tide"—swinging boats, merry-go-rounds, height, weight, and strength gaugers, stereoscopic exhibitions, and numerous booths where fat ladies, learned pigs, and ghost illusions are being shown. The race, however, is the all-engrossing event, and the visitors bestow but small attention upon these more ordinary features of holiday festivity. By the time we have emerged from the tide proper we find the people scrambling back to the course for a view of the next heat. For the sake of change, we now mount the outside of an omnibus, where we are able to see the entire course with comfort. Our companions are—a ruddy-visaged manufacturer, whose betting propensities are so strong that he offers to stake three half-crowns to one that the winner of the false heat proves the final victor of the race; a couple of jovial publicans and their equally jovial wives; a music-hall singer; a questionable female; three or four pomaded young swells; and a number of miscellaneous characters who possess no special distinguishing trait. Letting our eyes wander over the variegated sea of human heads which undulated before us, we were able to see that not a nook or corner of the barren moorland was unoccupied. Far away to the pleasant country lanes of Fagley, to the distant bleakness of Thornbury, to the sombre seclusion of the Undercliffe Crow Trees, to the gray slopes of Barkerend, and the stony dinginess of Laisterdyke, the dense multitude of local sportsmen, pleasure seekers, and idlers crushed and fought and scrambled as if for very life. I trust the gratification they derived from the race was such as to compensate them for all the trouble and discomfort they endured in obtaining a sight of it. When the horses reappeared the spectators went through the same course of excitement as before— craning their necks, shouting words of encouragement or derision to the jockeys, and ending with a shout of triumph when the victor of the previous heat came in in advance of the rest. Another interval of confusion and disorder followed upon the second heat, which interval we spent in seeking new experiences; but beyond a scene wherein a gaily-attired black woman figured as a subject for the scoffs of the roughs (until a champion arose on her behalf and silenced them) we met with little change of incident. We awaited the third heat with a feeling of weariness, not being able to screw up any particular interest in the fortunes of the runners, and when, at last, we saw the hero of the two previous heats scamper on in front of his opponents, we gave a sigh of satisfaction, and, in company with the great majority of the crowd, turned upon our heels and "made tracks" for home.

On the following day I went up to the Moor again with my friend Buffkins, for the purpose of recovering the eccentric quadruped whose gambols had brought Barnacles and myself into such peril the day before. After we had got the mare once more into the shafts, her owner took upon himself the responsibility of guiding her, and she seemed as mild and amiable an animal as on the Monday she had appeared wayward and perverse. Buffkins laughed immensely when he first heard of our Leeds Road adventure, and endeavoured to explain to Barnacles the manner in which he had probably offended the mare. Being on the spot, Buffkins and I made up our minds to ride up to the racecourse for half an hour, in order to see if Tuesday's gathering was any improvement upon that of Monday, but we found that, except as to diminished numbers, the "life" was much the same. Four horses, including the two which won first and second places the day before, came to the starting post, and hurried away in close company for about a quarter of a mile. Then a series of misfortunes befel three of the competitors. A dark animal, ridden by a lad wearing a blue sash, got away from the course altogether, and was out of the race. Another rider was thrown to the ground, and his horse galloped on by itself amidst the laughter and cheers of the spectators. Two horses were then all that were left to finish the race, and just as the animals were turning the last corner, close together, their jockeys whipping and spurring them on to the uttermost limit of their speed, a too eager bystander pressed too far into the course, and the winner of Monday tumbled over him, pitching the jockey violently over his head. The three were then led away wounded and bleeding, the only remaining horse being left to canter in at his ease. Such a series of disasters was enough to sicken the most enthusiastic patrons of this amateur St. Leger business, so we were not surprised to see the main portion of the crowd turn away towards home, with sadder faces than they came with.

A NIGHT WITH THE WAITS.

THE Christmas Waits are among the profoundest mysteries of creation. · Like owls and bats, they belong to the night, and, like them, they are more frequently heard of than seen. I never knew a real live Wait in my life, but I have a friend who once conversed for ten minutes with the Clarionet over a pint of Yorkshire stingo ; and to that fact, perhaps, I owe my appreciation of their talents. I am not one of those persons who regard these nocturnal wanderers as intolerable nuisances, and I have little sympathy with those newspaper correspondents who whine about them annually in public print. To me there is a more touching melody in the weird tootle of the clarionet, the steady see-sawing of the violoncello, and the gentle squeak of the fiddle, when heard "in the silent watches of the night," than in the more artistic strains of a concert band or a Christy Minstrel troupe. The Waits stir up old recollections, and cause past associations to crowd

upon the mind in such a delicious dreaminess that
criticism is forgotten. Judged, therefore, by the
impression produced, it is safe to aver that, despite
the petty objections advanced by their detractors,
the Christmas Waits are not generally despised.
To sour old maids, writhing under a sense of forced
celibacy; to mean old bachelors, whose humanity
has been drowned in grumpiness, they are, I dare
say, most annoying; but, then, most things are
annoying to people of that description. When, a
few weeks prior to Christmas, I was awoke from
my night's slumber by the Waits for the first time
during the season, I listened to them with even
greater delight than usual; and as their music died
off in the distance of remote streets, I conceived
the idea of making their acquaintance. Opportunity did not favour me, however, for some time.
Although my inquiries respecting them had been
numerous, I was frustrated in my attempts to discover their names and locations.

On the Monday night I had received information, from what I considered to be a reliable
source, that the Waits would be taking the Manchester Road turn on the Tuesday morning. I
conveyed this information to Barnacles with all
speed, and requested the honour of his company.
He at first declined, and seemed disposed to side
with the opposition. By what means I overcame

his scruples it is needless to mention; suffice it that he at last gave his hearty consent to the expedition.

On the Monday night, then, as the clocks were chiming the hour of midnight, we two crossed the town and directed our steps towards Manchester Road. There was a strong wind blowing, and the streets wore a frightened appearance. Doors banged mysteriously, dogs barked furiously, and occasional pieces of house-tops plumped down into the streets from time to time. Policemen walked cautiously in the middle of the road, and to our passing greeting of "good night" gave but gruff response, evidently suspecting us of burglarious intentions. I was muffled to the chin; Barnacles was muffled to the eyes. Every vestige of cloud had been blown from the sky, and the stars shone tremulously bright. We had not much time for star gazing, however, so we passed on our way. Except a party of noisy young addle-pates singing the chorus of a meaningless music-hall ditty, and the idiotic ravings of a drunken woman, who was afterwards borne off to the police station, we could hear nothing disturbing. Presently, even these uncouth noises subsided, and in the pauses of the wind we listened for the music of the Waits. We stood still and bent our heads in hearkening attitude, but were not rewarded by a single welcome note. A stalwart policeman waddled up with his lamp and stick, and looked at us with the steadfastness of conscious authority. We advanced towards him with some effrontery, and asked him if he had heard the Waits, or if he knew where they would be that night. With that instinctive acumen for which policemen, as well as the more distinguished representatives of the law are remarkable, he declined to commit himself to anything, although he looked very much as if he would have enjoyed committing *us*. He frowned ominously, and said he did not know anything about the Waits. We were turning away discomfited, when he remarked with cool indifference that "one on 'em" had just gone up the road, and pointed to a male figure some distance away. We ran with greyhound fleetness and stealth after the figure, and soon came within a few yards of it. It carried something in its hand, which had the appearance of an instrument encased in a bag. "All right; that's the man," said Barnacles; "we must not lose sight of him whatever we do." The figure walked rapidly onward, and in a while took a turn up one of the streets to the right. We kept on his track, like a couple of bloodhounds. Then the pursuit became most exciting. He dodged across waste patches of building ground, through gloomy short cuts and passages, and led us a zig-zag chase for about a quarter of a mile, until Barnacles and I were as completely lost as if we had been traversing the streets of Constantinople. "Suppose, after all, that he is not a Wait," I said. "He must be," answered Barnacles, "he's got his instrument with him, hasn't he?" We persisted. Fortunately for us we encountered no policeman during this chase, or we might have had our game stopped. At last the figure emerged into a quiet street of cottage houses and knocked at the door of one where there was a light. "He's going in there; we have been misled," I whispered to my friend! "Nothing of the kind," he replied, and ran up to the door. "Do you know anything about the Waits!" asked Barnacles of the man. He looked round in terror, evidently much excited by our having dogged his footsteps so persistently, and was only able to ejaculate, "Whor?" A woman from the interior then came to the rescue, and said, "What is't ye want?" "We only wish to ask if you can tell us where the Waits are going to play?" I said. "Wakes!" she said, with an air of supreme astonishment. "Wakes? They're playing somewhere every neet. Come in Tom." No sooner had she said this than she pulled Tom into the house and shut and locked the door. It was clear we had not made a favourable impression. We stood still and stared at each other like a pair of foiled conspirators. Then we adjourned to a shielded gable corner and went into committee. Recrimination would not settle the matter, so we decided to wait there for a few minutes with open ears, in the hope of hearing the Waits strike up. The view from our reconnoitring ground was a sombre one. Four dark mill chimneys were the most conspicuous objects of the scene; its minor objects being a row of cottages, a piece of vacant land, and, in the remote distance, the Bowling foundry cinder heaps. But the voices of the night were most unearthly. An unfastened factory gate creaked and groaned and banged, under the wind's imperious treatment; a watch-dog barked and howled; a cabman in an adjoining stable cursed at his tired horse; two Irishmen in a distant street called each other liars in the most superlative terms; coquetting cats caterwauled in back yards and upon the roofs of outbuildings; an infuriated cottager threw a few items of crockery at his wife's head, while the children added harmony to the crash by screaming violently; and panting railway engines, dragging the town's merchandise away upon their iron roads, shrieked and screamed to the wind as if on the verge of explosion. Any sound was to be heard except the one sound of the Waits. Barnacles began to look gloomy, and despair was settling upon the souls of both of us. Just as we had made up our minds to forsake our wild quest, a shrill

tootle broke upon our ears, which proclaimed that
the minstrels were going their merry round. A
minute of intent listening, and then we galloped off
in the direction from whence we fancied the music
came. Several streets were passed in joyous expectation, but, alas! when we came to a standstill the
music seemed just as far off as at first. Twenty
minutes were passed in this kind of pursuit, when
the music suddenly ceased, and we heard it no more.
This was as wonderful as the magic flute! In the
end, my friend and I gave the night up to its own
waywardness, and returned to our respective domi-
ciles, disappointed and disgusted.

Tuesday and Wednesday were devoted to fresh
inquiries. In a reply to a query put at the police
station, the Pickwickian inspector on duty said,
"Waits, bless you; we nivver bother with 'em."
Another person told us they met at the "Old Hat
Crown," but on asking for information at the house
in question, the offended landlady observed "They
don't meet here, an' what's more, they never have
done." Success crowned my efforts at last, however, and I was told of the place of residence of the
Clarionet. To him I despatched a trusty messenger,
and the T.M. brought me word of the Thursday
morning's rendezvous.

Between the hours of twelve and one on the
Thursday morning, three men loitered within the

shade of the Old Brewery buildings, sniffing the odour of malt liquor and looking patiently sad. These three men were Waits. The oldest of the trio was a tall, gaunt man, with a face of silent melancholy. This was the Clarionet. The other two were players on stringed instruments—the second violin and the violoncello. He of the second fiddle wore a picturesque " billycock," and evinced a gaiety of demeanour which was lacking in the others; the manipulator upon the violoncello seemed deeply impressed with the gravity of his occupation, and uttered not a word. When we made ourselves known, the musicians became communicative, and we were permitted to discuss their grievances with them. In reference to the letters which had appeared in a local paper, complaining of their nightly patrol, the Clarionet remarked, with dignified contempt, " We gat to knaw who one o' t'chaps wor 'at wrate them letters. An' what wor he, .think ye, when he cam' to be reight reckoned up ? He were nowt but a lodger i' t'topmost hahse i' Blemham Road ? " In the Clarionet's mind, the fact of this grumbling correspondent being merely a lodger in Blenheim Road, and in the topmost house too, was sufficient to dispose of that person's claim to notice. " How long have you been on at this game, then ? " asked Barnacles. " This 'll be my nine an' twenty't year," said the Clarionet; whereupon we congratulated the weather-beaten minstrel, and expressed a hope that he might long continue at his post. "You are rather late in starting, this morning, are you not?" I asked. "Rather," exclaimed the Second Fiddle, "we're waiting o' Dick coming; he's some engagements 'at keeps him late." By and by, the sound of clogs came from the bottom of Horton Lane, they all cried, "That's him!" and a little man, with muffled face and fiddle bag, came jauntily towards us. After some little conservation, the tuning of the instruments began. "Nah, Jim," says the newly arrived Violin to the Clarionet, "let's hear thy C." Jim blows his C, then the violins scrape themselves partly into tune. "Let's hear thy D nah," goes on the fiddler, and so on until the violins are properly strung. The violoncello now becomes the object of their united attentions. First, the instrument is carefully tied in front of the operator, and then No. 1 asks Jim for another of his notes, and proceeds to tune the instrument. "Nay, for suar," he says, "it's a foot ta heigh! What's ta been doin'?" The violoncello makes no response, so No. 1 lets it down "a foot." Before the tuning process is fully completed, a policeman ventures up, and, on seeing us, asks if they have "gotten two more!" At this moment a dog rushes out of Rand's mill yard, barking furiously, and it is with some difficulty that the animal is prevailed upon to return to his quarters. All being ready now, the four musicians get into marching order, and at a given signal from the chief violin they begin their music and their tramping, with Barnacles and me walking behind them in solemn state. Barnacles laughs heartily at the first few squeaks, and suggests the propriety of dropping a little further into the rear. I object, and as the music grows more familiar to us, we acknowledge that it is "not so bad, after all." The veteran Clarionet boldly leads the way up Great Horton Road, and expends a considerable amount of wind upon his instrument. The tune is a mixture of the music-hall air of "U-pi-dee" and something else of equal liveliness. There is a pleasant lilt about it, and it has the advantage of being softened and mellowed by the reed of the clarionet. Heads appear at bed-room windows, some people come to their doors to look at us, but being well accustomed to worship of this kind, the Waits go on their way regardless of it all. Attaining the summit of the first hill, the leader calls out "Off!" and there is a sudden cessation of harmony. But it is only for a moment. The Clarionet begins a passage in another key, and the other three join in with him, and sing the following words :—" Good morning, ladies and gentlemen all; past one o'clock, and a fine mawr-ninn'." At this point we have a minute's discussion about the weather, the Leading Violin remarking that "There's a gooid lot o' nail heeads aht to neet." We represent our ignorance, and he adds a further explanation by pointing to the sky and saying "Revvits;" from which we gather that he means to say there are a good many stars visible. We now plod along up the road, and over cross streets, until, in the course of time, we arrive at the gates of the Vicarage. The gates are open, and the Waits walk in and up to the door, and give a few extra bars of their lively air. Having done this, they wish the inmates a musical good morning, and return into the road, and give us some reminiscences of the late vicar. Another tuning bont takes place here, the violoncello appearing to resent being let down as it had been. As we stop here a gentleman amateur of the double bass, probably returning from the Christmas performance of the *Messiah*, comes up the road, with his servant carrying his instrument. Barnacles sees him, and just as the gentleman gets within earshot asks in the most perfect simplicity if this is not "another of the Waits." The look of contempt which flashed across the gentleman amateur's face is with me yet. He spoke not, but passed on with a look of offended superiority. Our tramping from this point proceeds very calmly. From one house the female servants scamper down to the garden gate for a friendly word; from another house a cheerful-tongued lady calls out, "Now, you must be sure and come at Christmas." We take this occasion to remark that if some persons are against them, they at all events find others who are in favour of them. "Ay," says the Clarionet, "whear there's one agean us there's a thahsand for us." There was no denying, however, that the aspersions of the "lodger" in the "topmost hahse i' Blemham Road" had annoyed them to some extent, and I have no doubt the top of Blenheim Road will, in consequence, be treated to a larger share of harmony than most other parts of the town. When entering Claremont the Clarionet proposes a fresh tune for a change. Thereupon they strike up "Peter Grey," but by the time they have got into the road again the first violin desires to return to the original tune, and his wishes are complied with. In playing they seem to take turns in the leading, although, generally speaking, the Clarionet is the leader. But every now and then the poor Clarionet gets out of breath, whereupon the first violin is left in sole lead, and, as a relief to him, the second fiddle sometimes takes up the strain and the other contents himself with vamping. In Claremont a drunken man came up and insisted upon shaking hands with the second violin, with which request the instrumentalist at once complied. Then

x

another straggler joined us, which increased the
number of our party to eight. We were not a
merry party, however; the wit-sallies of Barnacles
being about the only incitement to anything like
mirth that we had. For one thing, the musicians
had enough to do with their playing, and after an
hour's steady march to the disconsolate music of
the clarionet, one's feelings naturally become a little
saddened. The scarcity of incident, too, is depressing; for, after a while, the presence of a night-cap
at a bed-room window ceases to be a matter of
interest, and the forlorn petitions of the serenading
cat, and the savage barkings of the wakeful yard-
dog, fail to inspire either sympathy or terror. The
streets look awfully stony and cold, and the lamps
burn with such sickliness that we should almost
prefer being left to the starlight alone. In Ashfield
we lost the tipsy gentleman, but whether he
intended honouring the gutter of Horton Road, or
the more soft gutter of Manchester Road, with his
body, was more than our discernment could tell us.
Our Dead March procession went on and took us
out of his sight. The policemen seem to be the
only night-prowlers who openly fraternise with our
friends, but, as the force is not remarkable for
originality of observation, I need not trouble my
readers with any of the dialogue which passed. At
two o'clock the ground began to freeze slightly, and

from that time our adventure became somewhat perilous. Pointing to a light which was burning in a bed-room a little distance away, I hinted to my friend the probability of the room being tenanted by one in sickness, over whom loving eyes might then be watching. "I pity the poor invalid, then, that is all," said Barnacles. "What an annoyance it must be to hear—." The remainder of the sentence is yet unuttered, for at that moment he planted his heel upon an inch of slippery asphalte, and fell prone upon the ground. His head must have been damaged by its concussion with mother earth, for he appeared quite oblivious of any previous conversation when he rose to his feet. There was a laugh, of course, at my friend's mishap, as there always is on such occasions. The first violin said that he thought Barnacles must have injured his "canister," and recommended him to take to the middle of the road with them. This advice was followed, but all my efforts were fruitless to restore my friend to his wonted equanimity. He began to whisper of home, to talk of the duties that awaited him on the coming day, and to depreciate the "concerted movements" of the four minstrels. He also began to evince a strong desire to know where they were going next, and what time their wanderings would be over. The Clarionet's twenty-nine years' experience was hurt, no doubt, by the questionings of Barnacles, and the instrumentalist's answers were consequently shrouded in vagueness, "Can't you call and see our melancholy Clarionet to-morrow, and get his 'full, true, and particular account' of all these things?" asked Barnacles of me, when we had gone a little further. "It seems to me that you can study the genus to better advantage in its native lair." I refused to argue on this head, but at the next singing point, I requested the four to give me some particulars as to their habits and experiences. "Why, you see," said one of the Violins, "there isn't much to be seen any night different to what you've seen to night. Of course, when there's snaw on t'grahnd it maks it rayther wahr, and wer fingers get awfully cowd after a while. Bud it's been a varry fair season hez this; nice an' mild. It's rayther awk'ard, too, when it's wet, for we're forced to shelter, an' it izzant allus sich a nice job." In answer to our inquiry as to the length of time they continued their rounds, he said, "We begin five weeks afore Kirsmas an' give over at Kirsmas Day. We meet ivvery neet—ah mean mornin'—between twelve an' one, an' tak up whear we left off t'mornin' afore. This mornin' we'se hev to go throo this quarter up into Silsbridge Loin, an' finish a toathre streets ower t'other side o' t'tahn." "There's another set going about, isn't there?" I asked. "Ay," he

replied, "an' it happens rayther awk'ard sometimes."
"Do you join with them?" Barnacles said. "Nay,"
the dignified Clarionet broke in, "we've no connection wi' 'em, we're t'owd original set, we are, an'
we're bahn to appear at Pullan's o' Friday neet for
t'benefit o' Macdowell." Barnacles at once admitted
that this statement was proof conclusive of their
being "the real genuine article." "How does it
affect you when you go round collecting?" I ask.
"Aw, it affects us a girt deeal," responded the
veteran Clarionet, "'cos we sometimes finnd they've
been at places afore us. Some fowk divide what
they hev to give between us, an' other fowk 'll
nobbut give to one, so them 'at goes t'first hez
t'best chonce, don't you see?" We confessed that
we saw. Barnacles then asked, "Do the other set
call themselves 'the old originals' also?" "They
may call thersens what they like," said the second
fiddle, "but callin' it so weant mak it so for all that.
Lewk at Jim thear, he's hed nine an' twenty year
on't." "Nay," Jim said, with an air of proud
responsibility, "*this* is t'twenty-nine't year." After
this careful correction, the four got into procession
once more, and "U-pi-dee" was resounding upon
the air with increased liveliness. On we went down
one street and up another, singing every now and
then the hour of the morning and the state of the
weather. The denizens of Great Horton Road

must have been aware that morning of an increase of power and harmony in the singing of the Waits, and to those whose curiosity on the subject may have been aroused, I may explain that this added force was due to the fine voice of Barnacles, who, besides being— But stay, I must not reveal further.

When the Waits had completed their Horton Road round, we decided to bid them adieu. Perambulation of this description is not by any means invigorating, and, as my friend and I had duties of a more onerous nature to perform on the ensuing day, we deemed it best to betake ourselves to our respective homes, in order to obtain a refreshing sleep in the meantime. The hallowed spot where we took leave of the musicians must ever be remembered by both of us. The lanky clarionet, with his face of chronic melancholy; the muffled-up conductor, with his clogs and close-fitting cap; the second fiddle, with his jaunty air and pliable "billycock;" and the ever-silent violoncelloist, with his instrument tied tightly to him. They were courteous and warm in the expression of good wishes to us, and we left them with their music echoing in our ears. Barnacles acknowledged that they earned any money they might be able to collect, and was less disposed to regard them as obnoxious characters than he previously had been; but for all that he gave a very decided refusal to a proposition I made to him with regard to spending an hour with " the other set " sometime.

A single night's perambulation of this kind may be indulged in without any serious detriment to one's health, but I had rather be a policeman, and go about trying doors and picking up drunken men out of the gutter than one of these same wandering minstrels.

THE FOUR OLIVERS.

ITERARY Clubs are looked upon as one of the special features of Metropolitan life, and those great and wise people to whom London is the world would never imagine that any nearer approach to such a club than might be found in a Mutual Improvement Class could exist in a manufacturing town like Woolborough. Permit me, then, to produce some evidence on the subject that, it is to be hoped, will enlarge these people's ideas. My evidence consists of a letter which was addressed some time ago by an aspiring local author named Sempronius Jubb to his friend, Muley Tomkins. It ran thus :—

My dear Muley,—I am beginning to fulfil my destiny. The early rays of the Sun of Greatness are already upon me. I am warming into a glorious existence. Hitherto my genius has been hybernating in the cold winter of opposing circumstances, but now, thanks to the " Woolborough Conglomerated Literary Smatterers," I have been thawed into my natural splendour. My genius puts forth its buds; nay more, it blooms — blooms in all its strength and pristine freshness, and claims the admiration of all the widespread English-speaking public. You remember, dear Muley, at what an early age my literary talent began to display itself; what varied compositions proceeded from my pen even during our schoolboy days; the valentines I compiled at the early age of nine and three-quarters; the " Peace Egg " I re-modelled so as to be capable of entire representation by only two performers; the sequel I wrote to Jack and the Bean-stalk, called " John and the Peas-talk; " and the verses I effused on Polly Jones being caught receiving a lollipop from Jack Turton. I loved Polly, you know, and up to that time had reason to believe my passion was reciprocated. Didn't I give it to Polly in those verses? Didn't I enlarge upon the baseness of woman? Next to the lines I composed on seeing my father take a box of Holloway's pills, I regard them as the most touching of all my juvenile efforts. What a fine couplet that was in which I said,

> "Oh! Polly, pop the lollipop into Jack's mouth again,
> Or I'll away and roar this day upon the roaring main."

Tempus fugit, Muley. Those days have died into the never-to-be-resuscitated past; yet have I ever continued true to my mission, confident that the world would espy me in due time, bring me from my modest retirement, and crown me with the laurel of recognition. I was not born to blush unseen, neither to blush on being seen; Fate guards me against the one misfortune, Nature against the other. In fact, as I said at the commencement, I am beginning to fulfil my destiny. The last time I wrote to you I sent you the MS. of a story upon which I had been some time engaged, called "The Maimed Mechanic; or, The Broken Fly Wheel," and you were pleased to remark that it reminded you of Dickens in his ante-Mutual-Friend days. Perhaps it might. It is not for me to gainsay the opinion of the friend of my youth.

Well, one evening, after having received the MS. of the "Maimed Mechanic" back from you, I was sitting poring over the last chapter, considering whether or not it would be prudent to alter the *denouément*, and let the Mechanic kill Sir Storman Tempest in a duel instead of stifling him in the mill chimney, when my attention was arrested by a double knock at the street door. It was the postman with a letter addressed to "Sempronius Jubb, Esq." The "Jubb, *Esquire*," certainly seemed to add an inch to my boot heels! I opened the letter in some little agitation. I here transcribe it.

39, Browning Place, Tennyson Street,
3rd November, 187—.

SIR,—A few gentlemen of literary tastes have
recently formed themselves into a club for the
encouragement of English literature, under the
name of 'The Woolborough Conglomerated
Literary Smatterers.' Your name has been mentioned as the author of those very celebrated lines
on 'A Squashed Caterpillar,' and the still more
celebrated five-shilling prize essay on 'The Impe-
cuniosity of Paupers ;' therefore, as secretary of
the club, I am requested to urge you to join us.
Dickens, Lytton, George Eliot, and Tennyson have
had their day. The time demands new blood. We
see a rich vein of it in you, and are anxious to show
it to the thirsting public. Half-past seven on
Saturday night, at the above address. Don't fail.
—Yours admiringly, SAMUEL CRUSOE.

Sempronius Jubb, Esq.

The pen of a Shakspeare would fail in attempting
to pourtray my feelings on perusing the foregoing
letter. The heavens seemed to open above my head,
showing angels, silver clouds, and laurel wreaths ;
while beneath me the earth appeared to divide and
disclose to me the upturned faces of a worshipping
multitude. I beckoned old Morpheus away that
night, and turned the full force of my powerful
imagination upon the next Saturday evening.

However, I will avoid needless detail. Suffice it
to say that *the night* did come, that I went to 39,
Browning Place, was received with rapturous
warmth, and duly installed a member of the
Woolborough Conglomerated Literary Smatterers.
Henceforth I was a man of letters. To give you
some faint idea of the importance of our club, and
of the immense influence it exerts, I will describe
one of our club nights, after which, I think, you
will congratulate me upon my new associations.

To begin, then, I will take our last meeting night
as an example. The hour is eight o'clock, the
place, a snug room in " The Laurel Wreath Inn,"
to which establishment the club has recently removed its head-quarters. The members of the club
are assembled. I will give names and descriptions
as I proceed—glasses on table, pipes in mouths,
cheerful fire, smiling faces.

The Chairman, Mr. Botton, rises, rests his hands
on the table, and opens the proceedings. He is dark
haired, dark eyed, and impetuous looking, the author
of "Born a Clod," "Gay Stories from the Cloak
Room," &c., &c. "Gentlemen," he says, "this
evening, our friend, Mr. Lemonty, will give us an
essay on 'The Olivers.' I trust you will give him
due attention ; get your supplies of drinkables before
he begins, and when he has begun, let him proceed
without interruption " ("hear, hear," from all sides).

The potboy runs up and down stairs for the next five minutes.

Then Mr. Lemonty—a tall, thin gentleman,—stands up, pulls his whiskers nervously, and smiles benignantly on the company. He is known to the world as the editor of "The Small Beer Denouncer," and author of "The Parish Pump Guide," &c.

Mr. Chairman and gentlemen,—(proceeds Mr. L.) John, shut the door. The subject of the following remarks is—it's no use going on unless you are quiet. The subject of the following remarks is— now, Mr. Ventnor, do keep your pleasantries until I have finished. ("Silence for the Olivers," from Mr. Ventnor.) Oliver Cromwell, Oliver Goldsmith, Oliver Wendell Holmes, and Oliver Twist. These, or rather those, are the Olivers upon which I am about to speak. In the days of Charles the First lived Oliver Cromwell. He was a descendant of the Cromwell mentioned in Shakspeare's Henry the Eighth. The name is derived from "Cram well," the original ancestor having had that epithet applied to him in consequence of his being such a great eater. And this, gentlemen, affords an opportunity for serious reflection ("He's going to try the 'local' dodge now," whispers Mr. Ventnor to the one next him) on the infamous practice of gluttony. How detrimental it is to the well being of man. Does it not degrade him to the lowest of the low, I

mean the beast portion of the inhabitable creation?
Yes, my friends, the sin of gluttony—("Subject!
subject!" shouts a voice). If you object to my
essay being read—("Go on, Lemonty," from the
Chairman). Oliver Goldsmith was simple and
generous; in short, to use the language of the poet,
he may be said to have

> " Loved his neighbour as himself,
> And paddled his own canoe."

He was the associate of Dr. Johnson, Burke, and
others too numerous to mention. One of his friends
had a parrot which Oliver seems to have been able
to imitate to perfection, for it was said of him that
" he wrote like an angel and talked like poor poll."
He was fond of venison, when he could get any,
and sometimes got into difficulties with his landlady. At one time of his life he appears to have
been a piper, in which capacity he wrote his poem
of "The Traveller." He was partial to auburn
hair. His poem of "The Deserted Village" com-
mences with the words, "Sweet Auburn." In
addition to a number of poetic pieces, he wrote a
novel entitled "The Vicar of Wakefield," and
although there is no record of his ever having been
sent to Wakefield ("Oh! oh!"), he must have had
some experience of it to have enabled him to pen
such glowing descriptions of the place, and notably
of the prison cell. I need only add that he died a

natural death, and was buried in Westminster Abbey. That reminds me that the much abused Lord Byron was refused burial (cries of "Shame, shame! down with Mrs. Stowe!") within the solemn precincts of that venerable pile. Then occurs the serious reflection—("Cast no reflections" from Ventnor)—death comes to all, to old and young, rich and poor, innocent and guilty, male and female, infirm and healthy, Christian and pagan, and every other kind of individual, no matter what; yes, my friends—("Subject,") &c., &c.

Mr. Lemonty then goes into a lengthened disquisition on the two other Olivers, but as his remarks would cover such a large extent of paper, I refrain from giving them further.

I have now to describe the criticisms passed upon Mr. Lemonty's essay. They seem, like the postscript to a letter, the most important of all.

Mr. Botton turns round and says, "Will Mr. Ventnor favour the company with his observations upon the essay."

Mr. Ventnor stands erect, shakes his locks, wipes a few hundred drops of perspiration from his expressive countenance, extends his right arm and smiles knowingly. He is the author of various works of fiction, amongst which I may enumerate "Out of Work," "Over our Porridge," and "Who can I Fleece?"

He proceeds: "I have listened, I won't say with pleasure, nor I won't say with pain—for I scarcely know which feeling is most predominant—to Mr. Lemonty's essay. I think we have had too much Oliver and too little Lemonty. There is one remark,—well, I don't wish to hurt the reader's feelings, so I'll say no more about it (wipes another pool of perspiration from his face). Mr. Lemonty speaks of Wakefield. Now, I mean to say, I suspect—"

CHAIRMAN: You've no business to suspect any-body. Keep to the point.

Mr. VENTNOR: I will when I get there, Mr. Chairman. Allow me to proceed. 'I say, I sus-pect—'

A VOICE: Sit down.

Mr. VENTNOR: To suspect that Mr. Lemonty has never read the "Vicar of Wakefield" at all.

Mr. LEMONTY (Blushing and giving a few tre-mendous tugs to his whiskers): Prove it. You're always on with your blarney.

CHAIRMAN: Order.

Mr. VENTNOR: I have visited at his house, shared his purse, partaken of his victuals and beer, and been his bosom friend for the last thirteen years, and I never saw him read a line of Goldsmith in my life.

Mr. LEMONTY: I consider it beneath my dignity to notice such a fool's remarks.

Mr. VENTNOR: *Your* dignity, indeed? I like that.

The other members are now violent in their demands for order, so Ventnor is obliged to sit down. He spends the next five minutes in mopping his head and face.

CHAIRMAN: Mr. Crusoe, it is your turn now.

Mr. Crusoe, a young gentleman who has not distinguished himself in the literary arena, but hopes to do so, which is the next best thing, stands up, barrister fashion, with one foot on a chair and pointed forefinger, and speechifies.

Mr. CRUSOE: Mr. Chairman and gentlemen, the essay we have listened to to-night is one which, speaking for myself, I may say has given me excessive entertainment. I have not much to say, I mean to observe, upon it, except that it has been very instructive to me. I confess that until to-night I never knew of the existence of Oliver Goldsmith. One thing struck me during the delivery of the essay, which was the remark that Goldsmith had once been a piper, as if that was any disparagement to a man. A piper may be an honest man, may he not? There are lawyers, there are doctors, there are merchants, there are shopkeepers, and there are writers. But can any one say a piper is not as good as any of them?

Mr. VENTNOR (who has just finished mopping): He's a good deal better than some essayists.

x

CHAIRMAN: I think Mr. Crusoe is treading on delicate ground, and had better finish.

Mr. CRUSOE: Very well. [Sits down with a look of disappointment.]

CHAIRMAN: Mr. Frost, will *you* oblige us now ?

Mr. Frost, an elderly gentleman, whose heart seems too full for his personal comfort, here rises, takes a pocket handkerchief from one pocket, spectacles from another, wipes the latter, looks magnanimously round the company, and clears his throat. While he is doing this, I may inform you that he is a poet—the author of "A voice that amuses."

Mr. FROST : Gentlemen!—[long pause and thump of fist on table]—Gentlemen!—[second long pause and thump]—Gentlemen, I say—[third long pause and thump]—I am an old man (loud cheers), and I am proud—proud, I say—to be here before you, on this most noble, most auspicious occasion—[fourth long pause and thump]. Gentlemen, Mr. Lemonty is one of the shining lights (loud applause). If an angel from heaven had penned that sublime, that exquisite, that beautiful, that profound, that learned composition which has just been read to us, it could not have been more—well—good—I mean elegant. [Rolls his eyes poetically, looks heavenward, and seats himself amidst deafening applause.]

The CHAIRMAN: Now, Mr. Tubgarth.

Mr. Tubgarth, a florid-faced individual of desperate earnestness, now stands before us. He is no author, but an immense critic; if one's writings pass Tubgarth they are safe to pass anywhere else. He spreads an enormous white pocket handkerchief before him, and fires away rapidly. He has a sniffing manner, which seems to say, "Beware, ye self-conscious mortals! Tubgarth is on your track; he has already scented out your minutest errors, and means to impale them on the spot!"

Mr. TUBGARTH: Mr. Chairman and gentlemen,— For Mr. Lemonty's sake I should like to be able to call what he has just spluttered over an essay, but I can't. It's neither an essay nor anything else intelligible. If he cannot do better than that, I would recommend him to keep his papers at home for the future, or, at least, to give them to his children to correct before he brings them here. What does he mean by saying that in the days of Charles the First lived Oliver Cromwell? Did nobody else live but those two? Doesn't he think there might have been a John Smith, a James Jones, a William Brown, or a Samuel Robinson? Pooh! absurd! Then, what a style the essay is written in. It reminds me, in one place, of a steamboat collision; in another, of a fox-hunt; in another, of going to sleep; in another, of—why, himself. The reading, too! I don't like to be severe, but really I'd never stand up again unless I could improve that mumbling. A coffee-mill would be music in comparison. He seems to have forgotten, likewise, that the English language contains an h. It is simply hawful. Altogether, then, the matter has been bad, and the manner has been bad—if possible, worse; and if he will give me due notice of his next reading, I'll take good care to be found missing.

CHAIRMAN: Will Mr. Highdonyer favour us?

Mr. Highdonyer, a young fellow with poetic hair and pale face, gets up, with some show of nervousness, holds in his hand a slip of paper, on which he has made a few notes, and speaks. He, too, is a poet, one of the intense school, author of "Out on ye!" and other poems.

Mr. HIGHDONYER: There is a great deal to be said on both sides. Mr. Tubgarth is too severe, Mr. Frost too laudatory, although I partly agree with both parties; in fact I never disagreed with anybody in my life. I am inclined to think, however, that Mr. Lemonty has scarcely enlarged sufficiently upon the genius of the Olivers. I intended saying something more, but really I think there has been enough said already. I hope I haven't offended any one. I beg to sit down.

CHAIRMAN: Mr. Frenchicur, what have you to say?

Mr. Frenchicur, a large-browed, beardless man, verging upon thirty, an adept in foreign languages, and author of innumerable letters to the newspapers, stands disclosed.

Mr. FRENCHICUR: I think, Mr. Chairman, if Mr. Tubgarth had not been so severe upon our friend I might have been led to observe—

Mr. LEMONTY: Oh, you needn't spare me.

Mr. FRENCHICUR: Don't be alarmed, I don't mean to. I was going to say, if Mr. Lemonty had not been so kind as to interrupt me, that but for Mr. Tubgarth I should have said that the essay was a disjointed, fragmentary, hodge-podge of nothing in particular. At times during the reading I have said to myself, "that's like Hazlitt," "that's like Professor Wilson," "that's like Lemonty himself again," and so on. The fact is, I am so confused amidst the super-excellent and the bad, that I don't know what to say, and in this state of muddle I beg to resume my seat.

CHAIRMAN: Now, Mr. Hardbaker.

Mr. Hardbaker is a renowned poet and punster, so when he gets up there is a general titter, and an evident expectation of a little comic business.

Mr. HARDBAKER: It's all over with Oliver (laughter). That reminds me of a conundrum I once made at an evening party. " At what period of Charles Dickens' life was his penmanship the most discreditable? " I asked. No one could tell, so I replied, " when he wrote *all of a twist* [Oliver

Twist] (immense laughter). I've read *Goldsmith*, and I'm acquainted with a *Silversmith*. I've also read Oliver Wendell Holmes, and am inclined to think highly of "Holmes, sweet Holmes." As for Cromwell, there is some affinity between him and myself, he was a *Roundhead*, and my *head* is not altogether *square*. I won't criticise, it's a thing I don't *believe in*, so I'll *be leaving* you in the hands of some other member (loud laughter).

CHAIRMAN: Mr. Schoolman will oblige us now.

Mr. Schoolman, a light-complexioned gentleman, with no parting in his hair, lecturer on education, takes his turn now. He is good humoured, talks small, with a slight hiss, and keeps unruffled.

Mr. SCHOOLMAN: Well, gentlemen, if the essay has been wanting in itself we may be thankful that it has opened out, or, I may say, divulged a new light. I allude to the question of education. If Goldsmith hadn't been educated, we should not have had a Vicar of Wakefield. If Oliver Twist hadn't been educated, he'd never have had sense to have asked for more. If Cromwell hadn't been educated, he'd never have succeeded to the throne of England.

Mr. TUBGARTH: He didn't succeed to the throne.

Mr. SCHOOLMAN: I say he did.

Mr. TUBGARTH: Then you don't know anything about the throne.

Mr. HARDBAKER: Let the question be *thrown* over (laughter).

Mr. SCHOOLMAN: At all events he was created Lord Protector. So you see, education is important. I will show you in what way it is important.

Mr. TUBGARTH: I wish to remind Mr. Schoolman that education, though it may be the question of the day, it is not the question of the night.

Mr. SCHOOLMAN: Oh, very good, very good. Thank you. Upon the whole, then, I think Oliver Goldsmith was a sort of a kind of simple—why, not exactly simple, you know what I mean, a sort of—how shall I express it?—a chicken-hearted fellow, in short, what, in this day, we call a duffer. I mean practically, of course. He may have been generous—I believe he was, but it was a mawkish, and what I may call sentimental sort of generosity, &c., &c., for ten minutes [a good fellow, but long winded].

CHAIRMAN: Now, Mr. Civil, if you will favour us with a few words, Mr. Lemonty will reply, and the business of the essay will be concluded.

Mr. Civil is the Dundreary of the Club, a thorough cockney—need I say more? His chief displays of literary ability consist of letters of excuse for non-attendance.

Mr. ·CIVIL: Mr. Chairman, I waws vewy much intewested with Mr. Lemonty's description of—aw

—Oliver Cwomwell, as indeed, considewing my—aw—femily connections—aw—I have good wight to be. Cwomwell was a militawy indiwidual, and—aw—so was my fawther, so was my gwendfawther, and—aw—so is my bwother Bill. My bwother Bill, gentlemen, is a wawior, a perfect Twojan. I am pwoud of my bwother Bill. He is a man of the wawld.

Mr. TUBGARTH: I wish to say that I should very much like to see Mr. Civil's bwother Bill. I have heard much, exceedingly much, about that gentleman, in a fraternal way, and I intend taking an early opportunity of moving that "Bwother Bill" be produced.

Mr. CIVIL: Sir, my bwother Bill is not a subject to be jested about; the man who insults my bwother Bill insults me.

Mr. HARDBAKER: Mr. Tubgarth evidently thought "Bwother Bill" was a *Myth;* he was *myth*-taken (roars of laughter).

Mr. CIVIL: I pwotest, gentlemen, this is unfair to my femily.

Mr. VENTNOR: Blow your family.

Mr. HARDBAKER: Yes, instead of the family trumpet.

Mr. FRENCHICUR: Couldn't Mr. Civil make "Bwother Bill" the subject of his next essay?

Mr. CIVIL: You're a set of confounded donkeys [sits down in disgust].

CHAIRMAN: Order, gentlemen! Come, Mr. Lemonty, make haste with your reply.

Mr. LEMONTY: I am a gentleman (laughter), and
expect gentlemanly treatment. I don't come here
to be badgered, and, what's more, I won't be
badgered. I don't come here to be found fault
with; it is no part of the club's duty to find fault;
we are gathered together for the encouragement
of rising talent, and I can't see any encouragement
in fault-finding. With the exception of Mr.
Frost's remarks, there has not been a sensible
word expressed this evening, therefore, I shall not
trouble myself to reply. I am disgusted!

CHAIRMAN: The business is concluded.

Dear Muley, am I not fortunate beyond all pre-
cedent in being connected with so distinguished a
society? You see how cleverly the most abstruse
questions are discussed, turned inside out, scarified,
and re-modelled; what power of mind is brought to
bear upon the subject under consideration. Truly,
this is a day of great things! There is very little
doubt, that by this time next year, I shall have to
report to you something far more important. Our
club will ere long be corresponding with Metropolitan Clubs, by which means we shall launch ourselves upon the London literary sea, get introduced
to all the celebrated living authors, and force ourselves into public recognition. Yes, Muley, the

"Maimed Mechanic" will then be ushered before the world, and your friend will be made for life, ay, for eternity. Jubb will be immortalised !—I remain, your affectionate friend,

SEMPRONIUS JUBB.

P.S.—I would advise you to keep my letters. They may be worth something hereafter.

Further P.S.—Could you lend me £1 till next month ? Please do ; then I can repay it and former sums at the same time. I am rather hard up, but when my better days arrive, you will find me still true to the friend of my poverty. S. J.

TWO YORKSHIRE FEASTS.

EASTING in Yorkshire is the very antithesis of fasting. The Yorkshireman is not a *gourmand*, nor an epicure, yet he has no relish for Barmecide feasts or Lenten entertainments. He believes in substantial fare and plenty of it, and would as soon think of feeding off the grass in the fields as of meddling with any of your French dishes. He has more faith in the virtue of roast beef than in all else that the world can offer in the shape of food. Like Queen Elizabeth in the ancient ballad, he would

> " Swear it was his belief
> That the devil himself couldn't conquer this isle
> While Britons were fed upon beef."

Beef is always the centre of the Yorkshireman's feast—its foundation, its backbone, its main column; where beef comes not, the Yorkshireman will fare but poorly. His tastes in the way of eating and drinking are thoroughly English; except in the large towns he has not had his palate vitiated by the artistic devices of the fancy cook. He believes in what is plain and homely, and when the cheer is after his own heart he will not fail to give his digestive apparatus plenty of work to do. His opportunities of feasting, too, are most numerous, for his forefathers were excellent trenchermen, and appointed for themselves and their posterity no end of special days for administering special nourishment to their capacious appetites. All through the summer and autumn the local calendar is thickly strewn with feasts, "tides," "rush-bearings," "thumps," "rants," and what not, which are the means of keeping up a continual interchange of sociability. Friends and kindred rally round "the festive board" on these occasions, and they "eat, drink, and make merry" as only Yorkshiremen can. In winter there are numerous "fairs" that contrive to carry on the game in the intervals before and after Christmas, and even when all else fails the people can easily fall back upon such common events as weddings, christenings, and house-warmings, for the indulgence of their stomachic desires. It is not of the ordinary "feast," however, that I purpose writing at present; my intention is to draw a picture—first, of a Yorkshire rejoicing of the last century, and then, by way of contrast, of a Yorkshire feast of our own time.

More than a hundred years ago,—on the 13th May, 1751,—there was assembled at Wentworth

Woodhouse a goodly company of ladies and
gentlemen, yeomen and peasants, to celebrate the
coming of age of the last Marquess of Rockingham; and there was provided for this company
such a magnificent entertainment as had hardly
ever before been heard of even in Yorkshire. All
the country side had been invited to take part in
the festivities,—servants, tenants, neighbours, lords
and ladies, peer and peasant, gentle and simple,
were all welcomed to this right royal feast, and the
rejoicings were kept up with a will and a spirit that
did honour to the county. And the Marquess not
only threw his gates open to thousands of guests,
but he spread before them a banquet which showed
that he was fully acquainted with the sturdy Yorkshire appetites that he had to deal with, and that he
catered most substantially for their satisfaction.

The following is a list of the good things provided on this great occasion, as given in the
Gentleman's Magazine for July, 1751 :—

One Ox, weighing 120 stones 11 lb., and the Tallow 26
stones 6 lb.

Another Ox, weighing 103 stones 3 lb. The Tallow 18
stones 11 lb.

A lesser pair, weighing 142 stones.

Fifteen Sheep, weighing 95 stones 6 lb.

Nine Calves, weighing 67 stones 6 lb.

Fifteen Lambs, unweighed.

Pigeons, one hundred dozen.

Fowls and Chickens, 177.

Hams, 48.

For Bread and Pyes, 3 hundred and 50 bushels.

Salmon to pickle, 60 lbs.

Cod and Salmon, dressed fresh, 32 stones.

Crabs and Lobsters, a horse load.

A chest of China Oranges.

A Bill of Fare.

110 dishes of Roast Beef.

10 Pyes.

48 Hams.

40 dishes of Fowl and Chicken.

50 dishes of Mutton.

55 dishes of Lamb.

75 dishes of Veal.

104 dishes of Fish.

100 Tarts and Cheesecakes.

60 dishes of Crafish, Crabs, and Lobsters.

Upwards of 24 Tables was intermixt with each two
dishes of China Oranges.

Tables, 55.

In the Grand Hall was 383 seats.

In the Drawing Room one hundred and ten.

In the Anty Room ninety and five.

In the Corner Room fifty and two.

In the Far Room one hundred forty and six.

In the New Servants' Hall one hundred and three.

In the Steward's Hall thirty and two.

In the Old Servants' Hall thirty and six.

In Bedlam and Tower four hundred and twelve

In the Dining Room sixty and six.

In the Supping Room thirty and eight.

In the Pillar'd Hall three hundred and four.

In the Lobby thirty and six.

In the Powder Room thirty and two.

Liquors.

Small Beer at dinner, three hogsheads.

Strong at dinner, seventeen hogsheads.

Punch, six hogsheads.

Port Wine, seventy dozen of bottles.

Claret, not counted.

24 hogsheads of Strong Beer and Ale were distributed
to the people without the doors.

Seats and Tents were prepared for 5,500 without the
doors.

Between seven and eight thousand persons would
be present at this monster "feed," and for years
after it would serve as a fireside tale for the stalwart farmers and yeomen whose happy lot it had
been to be present at the Marquess's banquet.
This feast was not an unbecoming prelude to a
distinguished and honourable life, and the Marquess
would be as likely to live in the memories of his
Yorkshire friends and neighbours almost as much
by reason of the liberal way in which he honoured
his majority as by reason of his services to the
nation in the capacity of Prime Minister.

In the year 1751 it would have been thought a
sheer impossibility that a man who engaged himself
in commercial pursuits—but especially one who was
merely the owner of a number of looms—should ever
be able to vie in festive generosity with such a feast
as that given by the Marquess of Rockingham.
But, since George the Third was King, many strange

changes have come over the aspect of English
affairs, and the most striking of these changes is
the wonderful development that has taken place in
the trade of the country.   Such a factory as that at
Saltaire was beyond the bounds of the wildest
dreamland of the last century ; and such a feast as
"The Lord of Saltaire" has on more than one
occasion given to his workpeople will match with
the greatest aristocratic efforts in this direction,
either in our own or our ancestors' days.

It was my good fortune, during the time of the
meeting of the British Association at Bradford in
1873, to be present one Saturday at one of these
modern feasts, and it may not be uninteresting to
give some account of that celebration as a contrast
to the previous picture.

Red-letter days have been thickly scattered over
the twenty years' calendar which marks the rise
and development of the great industrial community
of Saltaire.   But it may be questioned whether any
one event in the history of that model colony will
be borne longer in remembrance than the festival
which was held on the Saturday I refer to, to celebrate the completion of the twentieth year of the
existence of the flourishing little town.   A retro-
spect of twenty years is something worth surveying
when it is studded with such remarkable landmarks
as have distinguished the progress of Saltaire.

During that period not only has Saltaire extended and improved itself industrially and socially, but the manufacture of the entire district has expanded wonderfully. Saltaire, as it now stands, represents the completion of a grand idea, the combining of the interests of employer and employed and the acquirement of as great an amount of health and comfort as is compatible with factory life. That Sir Titus Salt has succeeded in carrying out the idea that took him to the banks of the Aire upwards of twenty years ago has been abundantly testified, and the celebration served to mark this fact as well as to honour the two events which the festival was intended more particularly to commemorate. Festivities have frequently been held in connection with the Saltaire Works since the memorable opening in 1853. In 1856 all the Saltaire workpeople had been entertained at Crow Nest, Sir Titus's residence, in the same bounteous manner. Besides this, they had had numerous gala days and trips. During the time of the Manchester Art Treasures Exhibition they were treated to an excursion to that interesting place, and altogether, numerous as the workers are at this giant manufacturing establishment, they have fallen in for far more generous treatment than is usually accorded to workpeople.

Early on this Saturday morning, then, Saltaire was deserted. The mill, sheds, warehouses, and dwellings were left tenantless, the deep rumble of machinery was not to be heard, and all the people were at the railway station dressed in holiday garb. Three special trains had been chartered to convey the workpeople to Bradford, and so excellent were the arrangements that there was not the slightest confusion; each person had been furnished with a ticket for one of the three trains, and had no more difficulty in getting conveyed to Bradford than if it had been an ordinary day. The Saltaire Brass Band and Rifle Corps accompanied the party, and when the three trains had been fully emptied of their living freight at the Bradford Midland Station, a procession was formed four deep, and the excursionists made their way along Market Street and Bridge Street to the Lancashire and Yorkshire Railway Station, preceded by the band playing a lively air. Arriving at the last-named station, they found four trains waiting to convey them forward to Lightcliffe, and there in due time they were safely landed. Here the party were met by the Meltham Mills Brass Band, and proceeded towards Crow Nest, where everything was well arranged for passing a pleasant day. The weather, certainly, did not smile, but the smiles and cheerful looks of the holiday-makers were quite sufficient to counterbalance the dreariness of autumnal mists and threatening rain clouds.

Crow Nest Park is excellently adapted for a festive gathering, being situated in a picturesque spot, and presenting gentle undulations of ground which are alike agreeable to tread and pleasant to look upon. The processionists filed good-humouredly down the carriage drive, passed the front of the mansion, and ascended the higher ground, whereon spacious marquees had been erected for their accommodation. The three bands—Saltaire, Black Dyke, and Meltham Mills—betook themselves to the stands prepared for them, and were not long before they began to send forth a flow of sweet sounds across the Lightcliffe valley such as had not been heard there for many a long day. But there were other attractions provided in addition to the important one of music. In one part of the park might be heard the well-known squeak of Punch, as he went through his desperate encounter with Toby, and the audience that gathered round this primitive theatrical exhibition included as many upgrown people as children, and it would be hard to say which enjoyed the performance the most. An enclosure was fenced round in another part of the park for the exhibition of athletic sports, and the entries to these sports were very numerous. There were no fewer than ten events included in the programme, and the prizes were of a very substantial character. These sports commenced about half-past twelve, by which time the large concourse of people had got thoroughly warmed to the work of playing. There were high jumps, hurdle races, flat races, long jumps, and to end with, later on in the day, a most amusing sack race. The prizes varied from 20s. to 2s. 6d. The events were remarkably well contested, and the spectators entered into the spirit of them almost as heartily as the competitors themselves. There was no lack of healthy amusement. All kinds of gala games were indulged in, and now and then a little dancing party would be got up, so provokingly merry was the music. Seldom have I noticed a gathering of people to compare with the well-dressed, cheerful assembly which that day gathered in Crow Nest Park. There were managers, book-keepers, overlookers, weavers, woolsorters, spinners, engine-tenters, and messengers, but they all wore such an aspect of health and respectablity about them that it was impossible to say to what particular occupation any one of them was allied.

The games and sports went merrily on until two o'clock approached, and then large parties began to make towards the immense tent which had been erected on the upper ground. And here in due time the whole 4,200 workpeople-visitors were assembled, presenting a sight which I should like to have seen reproduced in a photograph. This great tent was formed in the shape of the letter T.

The portion of the tent corresponding with the top
of the T was 112 yards long and sixteen yards
wide, and the portion corresponding to the perpen-
dicular stroke of the letter was also the same length
and width. More than 4,200 superficial yards of
ground were covered by this gigantic tent. Five
rows of tables were arranged down the entire
length of the tent. The tables comprised 1,188
yards in length, and the seating was double
that length, viz., 2,376 yards, or nearly a mile
and a half. White glazed calico served for
table-cloths over the whole extent, and if ever
tables did really groan with the weight of a
feast those at Crow Nest must have done. Old
English roast beef was spread over the tables in
large joints at distances of every few yards, the
intervening spaces being filled in with tarts, cakes,
buns, and fruit, in rich profusion. Such a feast, I
should imagine, has rarely been spread under one
covering. Tea urns and crockery were there in
quantities sufficient to have stocked a dozen ordinary
shops. Some idea of the extent of the providing in
this direction may be gathered from the following
particulars. The glass, china, and earthenware, comprised : — 10,500 plates, 4,430 china cups and
saucers, 1,050 glass " salts and mustards," 400 large
meat dishes, 200 large jugs, 360 pint milk jugs,
360 slop basins, 360 sugar basins, and 500 pickle

dishes. The weight of all this glass and crockery was about eleven tons. What the total weight of the viands was I could not ascertain. I was informed, however, that there were 2,400 lbs. of beef, in addition to one magnificent baron of beef weighing 195 lbs., which alone took two or three carvers to operate upon. There were 2,146 lbs. of ham, 500 lbs. of tongues, 896 lbs. of sugar, 60 gallons of milk, 125 stones of plain bread, 700 lbs. of currant bread, 500 lbs. of seed bread, 4,500 tarts, 4,500 plain buns, 140 pork pies, 80 lbs. of sponge loaves, about 200 lbs. of biscuits, 4,000 currant buns, 3,000 seed buns, 100 stones of apples. To help off all this it took 140 lbs. of tea, and 300 lbs. of butter.

It is customary at Christmas time for us to read of the splendid provision made for Christmas at Windsor Castle, but not even Royalty can compete in extent with the Crow Nest feast. Flags were flying in all parts of the tent, and everything looked as bright and as joyous as it possibly could when Sir Titus and Lady Salt and their more distinguished visitors made their appearance at two o'clock. The sight was wonderfully impressive. Sir Titus took his seat at the centre of the table, where he commanded a full view of all his guests.

When all were properly arranged the signal was given, and the bands struck up the fine old tune of "Windle." Then the whole assembly rose to their feet and sang the grace with a fervour which was very thrilling. After grace had been sung all fell to with a will and an appetite encouraged by the fresh air and the healthful recreations they had been enjoying. Joints of beef, tarts, buns, and what not, soon disappeared, or at least a great portion of them, and as the people ate and drank and made merry the bands played appropriate selections of music. The dinner, of course, occupied a considerable time, but the attendance was very efficient, and every want seemed to be capable of being speedily supplied. When the meal was finally concluded, and the 4,200 guests had eaten as much as they could, all eyes were directed towards the host, and it was evident that this was the time for the people to express the gratitude they felt for the generosity and kindliness which had provided so excellent a feast for them. The music stopped and a whispered "hush" passed through the entire length of the immense tent. Not so much as the rattle of a single fork was heard in any part of the temporary banqueting hall, and all faces turned to the spot where the founder of the feast sat enthroned, as it were, amidst the lesser luminaries of the gigantic factory of which Sir Titus is the ruling power. There was no stiff formality to be observed, neither the masters of Saltaire nor the workpeople had

been at the trouble to collect any oratorical strength
to give word-gilding to the feast; everything was
spontaneous, unaffected, genuine. One of the workmen, a designer, stood up on one of the seats and
delivered a little speech, which was far more effective than a stilted oratorical flight would have been.
He alluded in simple, enthusiastic words which
touched the hearts of the whole assembly to the two
events which they were met to celebrate—the
twentieth anniversary of the opening of Saltaire
and the seventieth anniversary of the birthday of
Sir Titus Salt, and concluded by wishing, in the
name of the whole of his workpeople, that Sir Titus
might long be spared to live amongst them, and
that he might see the return of his birthday many
and many times. A foreman woolsorter, rude in
speech and little blessed with the soft phrase of the
platform, but who bore with him much higher
credentials in the mere fact that he had been
associated with Sir Titus since the first introduction
of the alpaca manufacture, now rose to second the
vote of thanks which the previous speaker had
proposed. His heart was too full to permit him to
say much more than that he had great pleasure in
seconding the proposal that had been made; but
there was little need for further words, his face
glowed with the emotion that his tongue had not
the skill to express.

The vote was then put and carried amidst the greatest enthusiasm. Three cheers for Sir Titus, three for Lady Salt, and three for the rest of the family were given in rapid succession, the immense gathering taking up each cheer with a heartiness that demonstrated, more effectually than any words could do, the affectionate feeling that existed between the head of the firm and his family on the one hand and the four thousand workers who give life and earnestness to Saltaire on the other. Such applauding, such waving of handkerchiefs and hats, such fervent unanimity, could not fail to touch many a heart besides that of the honoured baronet who had called it all forth. Sweet as much of the music was that the three bands played during the day, there was no sweeter or grander music heard in Crow Nest Park than those spontaneous outbursts of cheering which rang from end to end of the crowded tents. When Royalty and Loyalty occasionally get together in the streets of large cities there may be something heard in the way of cheering that will correspond in loudness with the cheering of these workpeople, but for downright heartiness commend me before all to such manifestations as those which startled the birds at Crow Nest that Saturday afternoon. Well might the united bands at this moment chime in with the feeling of the people and play, " The Fine Old

English Gentleman,'' only instead of thinking of the founder of the feast as "of the olden time," as the song has it, they were enabled to claim him as essentially of the *present* time. Struggling to control the emotion so natural to be felt by him at the moment, Sir Titus rose to respond, and was again vociferously cheered. He said : " I am exceedingly glad to see all my workpeople here to-day. I like to see you about me, and to look upon your pleasant, cheerful faces. I hope you will all enjoy yourselves this day, and all get safe home again, without accident or mishap, after your day's pleasure. I hope to see you many times yet, if I am spared ; and I wish health, happiness and prosperity to you all."

Sir Titus and Lady Salt now left the tent, and the people followed them into the grounds, and the sports and games and dancing began afresh. At intervals balloons were sent up. The weather looked more threatening than in the morning, but so long as it did not actually rain the workers did not care. All seemed to give themselves up to the pleasure of the hour, and the very most was made of the various amusements provided. Some of the more sedate visitors strayed about the grounds, admiring the scenery and indulging in pleasant gossip. The alpaca which was penned up with a couple of sheep at the bottom end of the park attracted a good deal of attention. Shortly after five o'clock the people got together preparatory to returning home, and in the presence of the host and hostess and their private guests, sang the National Anthem with an effect that was truly grand. Then there were more rounds of cheering, and the work-people formed into procession back to Lightcliffe Station, the bands accompanying them as before. The several trains were ready to convey them back, as they had come, and the day ended for the party, as it had begun, pleasantly.

A SATURDAY NIGHT DRAMA.

T is when the autumn mists come creeping around us, and dead leaves lie shivering on the country footpaths; when "our changeful equinoxes" begin to play havoc with our bronchial tubes, and to blow heavy rain clouds over our heads about every other day; when the railway companies conspire with the Weather Office to deprive us of our Saturday afternoon excursions in search of "health and quiet breathing;" when the tuneful strains of the band are no longer to be heard amongst the stately sycamores of the Park, that we are thrown back upon our native resources for our Saturday night pleasures; but, fortunately, of these there is no lack in Woolborough so long as enterprising caterers, well-lit streets, and jocund faces are to be met with wherever we turn in the heart of the town. When Woolborough has been hard at work in factory, warehouse, shop, and office from Monday morning to Saturday noon, it is but natural that it should turn its mind to relaxation, and be determined to have it as best it can, not being over particular as to the kind.

If it were not for the Saturday night, it has been said, there would be an end of the local drama. In spite of manifold counter-attractions — and not mere shop counter-attractions either — the theatre holds up its languishing head on a Saturday night, and looks the very embodiment of vigorous life. It is found necessary on a Saturday night to open the doors three-quarters of an hour before the accustomed time, and not only that, but, to please the refined taste of the audience which reserves its patronage for that " one night only," the pieces which have been performed during the week are shunted, and dramas are put on specially to accommodate the Saturday night taste.

On a recent Saturday night I dropped in with the rest for an hour's enjoyment, and I am willing to acknowledge at the outset that I found it. The " gods " were packed on the Olympian heights of the gallery as thickly as they could possibly be, and they conducted themselves as noisily as if they had been celebrating their bacchanals. The pit was crowded with a jovial throng, although less demonstrative than the whistling and shouting denizens of the heights above. The side boxes were also full, and in the front boxes, a goodly number of young sprigs of swelldom posed themselves in graceful attitudes, and tried to look "very much above that sort of thing." But from gallery to boxes, I believe, there was not a person present who did not enter into the enjoyment of the entertainment. From first to last the applause was continuous. I entered the house determined to accept everything just as I saw it, listening to no detracting remarks of would-be critics upon the piece, and refusing even to look at a bill of the play. The innocent reader who confines his study of the drama to quiet perusals of dramatic poetry by the warm fireside, will, doubtless, imagine from what I have said as to the enthusiasm displayed by the audience, that they had come to witness the representation of some of Shakespeare's sublime imaginings, or that, at all events, the performance would be of a very superior character, —if not "Hamlet" or "Othello," perhaps "Venice Preserved" or "The Lady of Lyons." Alas, no! A successful London manager told us, not long ago, that Shakespeare meant bankruptcy, and so it would seem even with our Saturday night audiences. They want to listen to no philosophical soliloquisings, no lofty flights of poetic fancy; to them there is far more meaning in a rattling good broadsword combat or a bit of assassination, to the accompaniments of hurried music and thunder and lightning, than in the measured phraseology and lofty sentiments of blank verse. With Dowton they would say, "Hang your dialogue! give me the situations;" or with Ducrow, the equestrian, "Cut out the *dialect*, and come to the 'osses!" The piece of that Saturday night was "Cartouche." Its *dramatis personæ* were :—Cartouche, the leader of a gang of French thieves; Gamboge (or some such name), the second in command, and chief comic character; Red Judas, a rebellious member of the gang, who is always plotting the downfall of Cartouche; Louise, an angelic being with whom Cartouche is in love; ——, a servant girl, whose savings attach Gamboge to her; a marquis; a count; an innocent young man, who dresses in the garb of a superior woolsorter; and a cowardly leader of musketeers, and his buxom wife. When I dropped in, a scene representing a market-place was the dramatic background, and Cartouche and his associates were in mysterious parley. Cartouche was dressed like the typical highwayman, with cocked hat, top boots, embroidered coat, and lace cuffs; and he swaggered about in a fashion· which might have passed unnoticed in a market-place *once*, but now, alas, they would lock a fellow up for five minutes' duration of such conduct. Cartouche is supposed to be *nonchalance* personified, and he therefore flings his legs about, and shouts and bullies like a tipsy navvy. The rest of the gang were marked with sword-cuts

about the face, and were as hang-dog a crew as ever
swung on the gallows tree; still, they looked much
more like pirates than landsharks. Their special
business seemed to be to frown and growl and strike
murderous attitudes in the streets with daggers and
broadswords, regardless of consequences, and it
must be admitted that they won the approbation of
the spectators. Red Judas and Cartouche quar-
relled in this scene, and the former sneaked off,
shaking his fist at the "gods," and vowing eternal
vengeance. After this split in the robber band, and
a supplementary display of dagger brandishing, the
comic characters have a brief encounter in a cottage,
and then the scene changes to the saloon of the
Count de Something or Other, and we find Cartouche passing off as a Marquis, and displaying his
capabilities of pocket-picking in a manner which
the audience seemed thoroughly to appreciate. He
robs the Count of his purse, watch, and other personal valuables, while staring him in the face and
engaging him in conversation about the depreda-
tions of "that rascal Cartouche, who had sworn to
rob you of your watch, Count, before two o'clock."
As each article is stolen the "gods" applaud in
frantic approval, but subsequently, when Cartouche
has entrusted to him a large sum of money to convey to the bank on behalf of a charity, he casts his
eyes up to heaven and exclaims hoarsely, "Scoundrel

and villain though I yam, I—yah—will not rob the
yelpless and the yinnocent,"—for which noble sentiment he is rapturously cheered. By and bye, however, the real Marquis comes, and, after Cartouche
has caused some amusement by denouncing the
visitor as the veritable robber chief, he acknowledges
himself the thief, and with a pistol in each hand
laughingly holds the party at bay. Another cottage
interior is drawn across this impressive tableau, and
Cartouche, not caring to avail himself of the door,
enters through the window, jauntingly intimating
that "they" are hunting him down. After spying
about for a hiding-place for some time, he at last
takes refuge in the chimney. Red Judas then
sneaks in, and after looking for Cartouche in the
pit and side boxes for a while, he at last turns his
vision upon the right place, and exclaims, "Ah!
the chimney! I shall have him now!" Then
follows a terrible scene on the house-tops. Cartouche in the course of his ascent has divested himself of his laced coat, cocked hat, &c., and appears
in his shirt sleeves, spotlessly clean, from which fact
it is to be inferred that there had not been a fire in
the chimney for some time previously. First one
and then another "super" struggles on the house
tops with Cartouche; but he bravely hurls them all
down into the street below. Then Red Judas and
he have a fierce wrestling match on the tiles, to the

2A

enthusiastic cheers of the audience.   Cartouche
masters Judas; but is eventually overpowered by a
number of musketeers, who previously fire several
shots at and miss him.   Red Judas now gives a
shout of triumph at the capture of his old leader;
but Cartouche roars out, "Fool, fool, the prison is
not built that can hold Cartouche!"   The cheers
which this outburst evokes prove that the audience
is in entire sympathy with the thief and murderer,
and he is called panting before the curtain to
receive the guerdon of approval.   In the second
act the unhappy Cartouche is in prison, having
changed his shirt of spotless white for another
of black and white stripes.   A wigged func-
tionary attends to read Cartouche's death sentence (the trial having obviously been omitted) and
asks if he is prepared.   "Ay, I'm prepared for a
good dinner and a song," returns Cartouche with a
toss of his head and a clink of his fetters.   Red
Judas happens somehow to be present in the cell to
gloat over the imprisoned thief, but Cartouche
laughs in his face and says, "I have sworn to kill
you, and I never berreyk my word" (cheers).   Red
Judas: "If you escape I will give you my life."
Cartouche: "It is a bargain.   Either I die in an
hour or you die in twenty-four.   Now go and order
your grave and prepare for your funeral" (cheers).
When Red Judas has departed, Cartouche's comic

officer comes to see him, disguised as an Eastern lady, and the young woolsorter also gets admittance into the cell. The latter gets a silencing dose of laudanum, and Cartouche (the gaoler and Red Judas obligingly remaining out of sight) frees himself from his manacles, climbs up to the barred window, breaks the bars, passes to the outside, and remains clinging to the bars until the gaoler, Red Judas, and a number of musketeers come in. They rush madly about, and finally discharge their pieces at him, but he is unhurt and laughs in their faces, puts his hand to his nose, and shouts, "I told you the prison was not built that could hold me!" (frantic applause). In the third act we find Cartouche soliloquising in the open country in this style: "The child of the streets, spurned and abandoned, kicked about, the very football of chance, I descended the ladder of crime. Whipped as a boy, imprisoned as a man, my heart became stone, and now I am the dread of Paris." Red Judas interrupts this soliloquy, however, and Cartouche is reminded of his threat to kill him. They fight with cutlasses in the street, and Cartouche succeeds at length in giving his opponent his quietus, after which he robs the body. The audience applauds again in approbation, and Judas is left lying on the stage. Presently, though, he rises to his feet, notwithstanding having been several times run through beneath both arms, and hobbles off, still vowing deadly vengeance against Cartouche. Amongst the papers stolen from the pouch of Judas, Cartouche finds some documents which tell him that he is heir to a marquisate and large estates. In the next scene we find the robber chief is about to be married to a beautiful young damsel, who, to say the least, is not over scrupulous as to the character of her bridegroom. Just before the wedding party sets out for the church, the inevitable musketeers appear and interrupt the progress of affairs, and the identity of Cartouche is fully established. But even then his Louise will not desert him. She says, " Cartouche, robber, villain, take me, I am yours !" Thus encouraged, the "robber, villain," cries to the officers, "Bal-hood hounds, I def-a-hi ye ! Cartouche will die as he yas a-lived !" The lady further adds, " We will never part. In life, in death, thou art mine ; my own, my beautiful !" (cheers). Red Judas staggers on at this juncture and fires at Cartouche, missing him but killing his bride. Then the robber seizes his dead Louise, and although surrounded by a crowd of musketeers and country people, carries her away to the Catacombs, where he is eventually despatched, dying bravely amidst a stage full of fierce up-and-down fighters, and receiving the sympathetic applause of the audience. Talk about

"Jack Sheppard" being a fine play! Is not this a superior thing altogether? Crime was never more sympathetically treated. Jack Sheppard had some occasional gleams of stupid propriety, but not so Cartouche. When Blueskin used to say to Jonathan Wild, "We despises ye and we defises ye!" we used to laugh and forget the burglars; and his song of "Jolly Nose," too, was a thing to draw off the attention from the main villainy of the piece; but in "Cartouche," pocket-picking, burglary, and murder, so long as "the yelpless and the yinnocent do not suffer," are all along set up as a standard of fine morality, and I do not think the audience are at all satisfied with the tragic *denouement*. At one point, when Cartouche had made his clever escape, the audience shouted and cheered as if they had been assisting at a political demonstration, and when the "hounds of justice" came on they got severely hooted, and Cartouche had to come forward and bow his acknowledgments in the middle of an act before their enthusiasm could be toned down to the level of listening to any other actor.

To anyone who desires to study the tastes of the people, anyone who likes his mental food highly-spiced, or anyone who delights in "blood and thunder" pure and simple, I say, "Go to the Theatre on Saturday night, and one of the desires of your heart will be fulfilled."

A DESERTED PROMENADE.

OM MOORE has told us that "the best of all ways to lengthen our days is to steal a few hours from the night;" and if this be true I ought to be able to look the future in the face with some confidence, for I have been a very owl for many months back. Of the night side of local life I have had a somewhat wide experience, and I must confess that in some respects the night is far more interesting than the day. The familiar presences which flit across your path by day do not obtrude themselves upon you in the "wee sma' hours;" you are neither in danger of meeting the too demonstrative friend, nor of being withered up by the scorn of your enemy; you can tread the streets unannoyed by the sight of degraded humanity or the stilted pompousness of the "brother man" who has been lifted over your head by a few lucky bargains; indeed, like the William Tell whom the wiseacres have lately been assuring us is a mere myth, you can walk erect and thank God

you are free. There are many other advantages,
too, which the night possesses over the day, much as
it may be shrunk from by those comfortable citizens
who " sleep o' nights " and live in horror of chills
and dews and darkness. If you have anything
weighing on your mind (providing it is not a small
debt), the way to get it off is to take a quiet walk
an hour before sunrise, when you can think your
little difficulties out far more completely than while
struggling with sleep in a pent-up bed-room. If
you want to do a bit of star gazing, come out boldly
into the night, and don't stand shivering on the
inner side of your chamber window while Mrs.
Caudle rates you for a donkey. If natural history
be your hobby, then out with you by 3.30 a.m. and
see the sunrise, when you will have " objects "
innumerable revealed to you. Anyone who has an
ambition to write a work on " The Habits and
Customs of the Domestic Cat," for instance, could
not possibly do justice to the subject unless he had
the opportunity, as I have, of studying the animal's
nocturnal movements and hearing its melodious
caterwaulings. However, just to show that the
hours between midnight and cockcrow are not altogether so dead and unutterably dull as is generally
supposed, I will recount a few of my experiences
during those hours, and take Manningham Lane as
the scene. " Manningham Lane, forsooth ! " I

think I can hear my friend Somnolus say, as he reads these lines, "What can there be to be seen *there* at such a time? If he had said Bolton Road or Silsbridge Lane, I might not have been surprised; but to take Manningham Lane, where nobody but respectable people live and proper hours are kept; it is absurd!" But have patience a moment, my revered Somnolus; you are evidently speaking in blind ignorance. I think I can prove that there is both plenty to be seen and plenty to be heard in the first hours of the morning in Manningham Lane. True, the gay throng of promenaders have gone home to dream of love and honour and riches, or to be racked with nightmares and hideous forebodings; the manufacturer's smart "trap" no longer glides along the limestone road; the omnibus, as well as its passengers, has retired to rest; the servant girls have left the area gates "to darkness and to me" and the policeman; the lights have vanished from the windows, and all the familiar associations of the day have disappeared.

By this time the virtuous reader will doubtless have begun to regard me with suspicion. He will have said to himself. It is during the night time that robberies, burglaries, and murders are committed; it is during the night time that disreputable characters wander abroad; it is during the night time that decent, honest people take their rest; what, then, can a "Saunterer" be doing in the streets so frequently at unearthly hours? Ah, there's the rub! Let me assure my suspector, however, that my early morning walks are not prompted by any evil designs, and that, although I am neither a policeman, a lamp-putter-out, nor a scavenger, I am often going about my legitimate business in walking through the streets of Woolborough between the hours of 12 and 5 o'clock a.m. Perhaps I have a secret mission in hand; perhaps I am a poet, anxious to take a few sketches of nature while she is asleep; or perhaps I —— but that will do, more particular confessions are really unnecessary.

First, then, I will say something of the appearance of our favourite promenade during the opening hour of the morning. We will suppose ourselves in Cheapside just as night and morning meet, our purpose being to accompany the latter as far as the park gates. A policeman stands at the top of Salem Street striking his iron-tipped stick upon the stone pavement, much in the same manner as a musician strikes his tune-fork, and the sound is taken up by another stick in the distance, after which signal of "all's well," the policeman adjusts his bull's-eye and lets its white light play upon the door handles and fastenings on the right-hand side of the street, as he walks down with the easiful tramp which distinguishes the footstep of the night policeman from that of any other individual who walks the earth. It is a Brobdingnagian tramp, slow, ponderous, and awe-inspiring.

At the bottom of Hanover Square there is a certain attic window which seems to be the abode of eternal light. There are several beacons of this description which I never fail to take note of in the darkness. For each of these lights I have conjured up interior visions, and I seem to have by this means set up a real acquaintance with the inmates of those lighted rooms. It would be in vain for you to tell me that old Mr. Heavynop is lying sick in one of those rooms, that Mrs. Shiver-limb keeps the gas burning in that other room merely to keep the atmosphere warm, or that Mr. Dobler's servant, Mary Jane, by a third light is reading the *London Journal* in bed. Even if I saw these things I would refuse to believe. Would you rob me of the picture of that young and beautiful damsel who reclines on a bed of down reading the love epistles of the handsome young gallant whose portrait hangs by her side? Would you have me believe that there is no reality in the picture of the three dark-visaged conspirators who, by the flickering light of a farthing candle, are frowning at each other, signing manifestoes, and making mysterious vows to upset thrones, and kill, rob, and plunder in the interests of Freedom, with a capital F ? Would you prevent me sorrowing for the boy-angel who is making a Jacob's Ladder for himself out of his own rich fancies, and carrying thoughts to heaven with him which, had he been destined to live, would have made him great upon earth ? No; you will not attempt to do anything so cruel.

At the bottom of Belle Vue I see standing against the wall a drunken man. " Yeh-young man," he says, looking lovingly at my boots, " wa-what's o'clock ? " I inform him, and he then proceeds to divulge the inmost secrets of his soul. " Look here," he goes on, " I'm worth twothousanpouns; an' I'm goin' t' marry twothousanmore. What d'ye think o' that, young man ? " I hint that it is, no doubt, a state of things to be proud of. " Per-oud ! " I hear him exclaim as the distance increases between us ; " Per-oud ! I'm the per-oudesmaninWoolborough ! "

The next time I walk on the Lane it is perhaps between the hours of one and two in the morning. It is rather windy, and I have a companion with me. This companion, whom I will call Aspenleaf, is as gentle as a dove, as timid as a fawn, and as sentimental as a newly fledged poet. He has the habit of heaping horrors upon horror's head ; he fancies himself incessantly pursued by some mistaken Nemesis, and sees a ghost in every shadow. But

he is a fine, imaginative, tender, loveable creature,
for all that. "I wonder you are not afraid of
walking on the Lane at such dreadful hours," says
Aspenleaf as we pass the substantial-looking Savings Bank. "There was a man murdered on just
such a highway as this at Bricktown, and about
this hour too, only the other week." As we pass
the new Grammar School building a board tumbles
down. Aspenleaf's heart nearly jumps out of his
mouth, and at the same time he jumps about a foot
high, as if he were trying to prevent the said heart
jumping out altogether. "What's that!" he cries,
clutching me by the arm. I assure him that it is
only the work of the wind, but he maintains that it
is in such places as these that robbers and assassins
lurk in ambush ; and, as if in sportive substantia-
tion of his fears, at that moment a gust of wind
blows a sheet of paper across the road towards him,
with a rush and a rustle that are certainly startling,
and he gasps out a feeble "Oh lor !" and looks as if
ready to relinquish both his money and his life on
the spot. Shortly after recovering from the effects
of this fright he sees a dusky policeman standing
like an enlarged pillar-post at the top of Trafalgar
Street. Aspenleaf whispers, "I'm in for it now !"
"In for what?" I ask. "Why, there's a policeman standing there, and I've this bundle under
my arm," pointing to a rather large parcel of books

and papers that he happened to be carrying. "He's sure to think I've stolen them, and I shall be locked up." To pacify his mind I took the parcel from him and assumed all the risk myself, passing the policeman with a valiant "Good morning."

A little further on we heard a man running towards us at the top of his speed. Aspenleaf, of course, imagined that some dreadful crime had been committed, and that this was the criminal making his escape. "Let us get out of the way," he cried, "let us hide ourselves; he is sure to have a knife in his hand, and will think nothing of despatching us in addition to his other work." I refused to follow Aspenleaf's advice, however, and we had the satisfaction of seeing the man run by us and stop at Dr. Macnab's door, and shortly heard him asking for the doctor to go at once to Mrs. So-and-so's. The little domestic incident of which this was the prelude we could easily fill in from our own imaginations. We did so, and pursued our course. Luckily for Aspenleaf, there were only two other incidents to which our attention was drawn that morning. Near Clifton Villas a policeman was standing debating with a thick-set man, who was coat-less and hat-less, but otherwise bore the appearance of a man of respectability. He might have been a Corsican brother or a gladiator, but was probably either a lunatic or a drunkard. Whence he had come or

whither he was going could not be ascertained
either by the policeman or ourselves. All the personal information that he vouchsafed was that he
was an Englishman, and he disputed the right of
any man living to question his motives or intentions. Where had he left his coat and hat? That
was *his* business. Where was he coming from?
That was *his* business, too. Had his missing
garments been stolen, or had he lost them? He
had done what he liked with them. Was he going
to Shipley or to Woolborough? To either, neither,
or both, just as he pleased. What was done with
him eventually I do not know; we left the policeman to deal with him as he thought best. Not far
from this point of the lane Aspenleaf and I took a
turn further into Manningham proper, and when we
got into the neighbourhood of some new shops we
heard such a knocking of doors as would almost
have awakened King Duncan. "Whatever is the
matter now?" asked my friend. "A fire,
perhaps," I suggested. Arriving at the spot, however, we found that it was no fire, nor anything else
alarming. Two more policemen were upon the
scene. They were knocking with all their might
with their sticks at a door behind one of the shops.
Presently a ferocious head, crowned with a hideous
white night-cap—for this is none of your red-cotton
night-cap countries like the one of which Mr.

Browning sings—leaned out of the bed-room window and wanted to know what the blank was the matter. "The shop door's oppen," shouted the two policemen. "It's next door," cried the owner of the white night-cap, and down went the window. "Nah, what's to be done with a man like yond, 'at shuts t'window i' your face an' tells you to go to t'next door when you let him knaw 'at he's left his shop door oppen?" demanded one policeman of the other. "Knock agean, that's all," was the response; and they *did* knock again and with increased vigour. It was not until a great many heads had appeared at adjoining windows that the white night-cap presented itself again. "It's t'next door, I tell ye," bawled the disturbed sleeper, "an' if you don't stop your row I'll just throw a bottle at your heads," and down went the window once more. The policemen were now terribly puzzled. They knew for certain that the shop-door was open, and here was the sleepy owner refusing to be knocked up, and, what is still worse, trying to throw the entire blame and trouble upon his next door neighbour. "Let's go tak' possession," said one of the police-men. "Not we," rejoined the other, "we'll hev the beggar up, or else we'll get a ladder an' go rive him aht o' bed wersens." We could not wait for the issue of this fierce struggle between wakeful authority and the sleepy tradesman, but when we had got about three hundred yards away from the scene we could distinctly hear the sticks battering at the door again. Aspenleaf and I then went our several ways, and I have not had a morning's walk on the Lane with him from that time to this.

WM. BYLES AND SON, PRINTERS, BRADFORD.

9 783382 828691